
★

QUINTANA KINGSLEY COULD NEVER HAVE BEEN MISTAKEN FOR BEING ASLEEP.

Her head was cocked at an angle no living, breathing person could sustain. A thin thread of blood had dried in a jagged line from the corner of her mouth to her chin. Her hand still clutched the chopsticks. A stain of blood bloomed on her chest like a voracious blossom and right at its center, standing straight up, were the handles of "Old Reliable," the bud shears. The blades were buried to their hilt in Quintana Kingsley's chest. Calista felt an overwhelming coldness, as if her body were turning to ice on this warm summer morning.

★

KATHRYN
LASKY KNIGHT
DARK SWAN

WORLDWIDE.

TORONTO • NEW YORK • LONDON
AMSTERDAM • PARIS • SYDNEY • HAMBURG
STOCKHOLM • ATHENS • TOKYO • MILAN
MADRID • WARSAW • BUDAPEST • AUCKLAND

DARK SWAN

A Worldwide Mystery/June 1996

First published by St. Martin's Press, Incorporated.

ISBN 0-373-26203-5

DARK SWAN

ONE

THE VIOLENCE OF the gesture seemed entirely out of scale with the tools or the object. But Mrs. Elliot Kingsley obviously knew what she was doing as she stabbed the chopsticks into the tiny, tenacious roots. For this needle juniper, barely two feet high, was eighty years old.

"Mrs. Kingsley Senior gave it to me when I became engaged to Kingie. That was almost sixty years ago. The juniper and I are the same age." This Mrs. Kingsley, Quintana, looked up and smiled at Calista Jacobs, who was perched on a stool in the greenhouse and sketching madly, quick little smudgy drawings with graphite pencils or in some cases, when she wanted something more precise yet loose, she'd pull out her Rapidograph pen. She smiled quietly to herself. What was it about these old Brahmins that compelled them to call their own mothers-in-law Mrs.? Thank God that Archie's parents weren't that way. She couldn't imagine calling Nan and Will Mr. and Mrs. Baldwin. Of course, they were not her in-laws. In fact, they cheerfully referred to themselves as Calista's outlaws. Still, despite the Baldwins' impeccable pedigree, they had none of the oppressive formality that one could encounter on the North Shore, Dedham, or up here on Beacon Hill—where only a few of the truly old guard remained.

"Now I take my little scissors here. They tell me these are very similar to what cardiovascular surgeons use in open-heart surgery...." Quintana was bending over the plant with her reading glasses sliding down her nose and making expert little cuts. Calista could hear the sound of the needles being snipped. "Oh! Got to nip that bud. Hand me those shears over there, dear." She pointed to scaled-down needlenose shears with gleaming edges. Calista handed them over. "I call these 'Old Reliable.' You get a nice clean angled cut with them, and these buds tend to be quite fibrous. This old dear would just shoot completely out of bounds if that was allowed." There was a small crunching sound. Calista winced. This was an art form definitely not to her inclination.

"You will note, Calista, that the emphasis in the word *bonsai* is on the second syllable, *sai.* It is the verb meaning 'to grow.'" Calista blinked, the blink of irony mingled with disbelief, as she looked at the scores of dwarfed plants surrounding her in the greenhouse. "The *bon,*" Quintana Kingsley continued, "refers to the salver or tray in which they are grown. And now for the mighty little shears!"

The old woman picked up a set of shears that came as close to looking like a piranha's jaws as anything else and began paring away at some of the exposed roots near the trunk of the juniper. Calista bit her lip and turned to observe another tree, a Japanese zelkova with faint pink leaves the size of babies' fingernails. It was the tree, after all, in which the emperor's nightingale first sings.

Calista, a distinguished children's book illustrator, had been working for months now on the illustrations for her next book—a retelling of the classic fairy tale *The Emperor and the Nightingale.* She had pored over books of Oriental landscape design at Boston's

Horticultural Hall and spent hours at Harvard's Fogg Museum studying the exquisite seventeenth-century painted scrolls, but what had helped her the most was purely serendipitous. She had had to move temporarily into Nan and Will Baldwin's Louisburg Square house while her own was undergoing extensive work. It was impossible to concentrate with the pounding of five guys crawling on her roof to reshingle, not to mention the addition of a sunroom, which in her more high-blown moments she thought of as a conservatory. But Calista was neither a musician nor a particularly good indoor gardener. The whole notion of the sunroom had started when her mother had given her a camellia. It had survived admirably until the very day they began work on the new room. Was it the plaster dust, the trauma of the sledgehammers knocking out a wall where the new room would be added? Or had she mortally offended the plant's soul in some way? Was that plant saying to her, I'm a good old Yankee camellia. I don't need special treatment, a room of my own—what an extravagance!

Calista spent money—freely, if one didn't count the price of the guilt. She had most likely transferred some of that guilt to the plant, so that it began to shrivel on the day the workmen came and five days later was dead.

Calista and her son, Charley, soon had had it with the chaos of construction and sought refuge at the Baldwins' on Louisburg Square. Nan and Will were the parents of Calista's lover, Archie. Archie, an archaeologist who held a joint appointment at Harvard and the Smithsonian, was away on a dig. Calista would have liked to have been with him, but she was late on this book, which in turn was making her late on the next. So this was her summer to get things done. It had worked out quite well actually, as the Baldwins were at their summer place on Mount Desert Island in Maine, and Heckie, their faithful man-servant, who usually took care of things in Boston, had suffered a stroke.

Therefore, when Calista asked whether she might retreat to 16 Louisburg Square, Nan and Will were only too happy to have her there watering plants, taking care of the cats, and generally looking out for things. Charley, Calista's son, had a summer job working on the swan boats in the Public Garden, a mere seven-minute walk from the front door of number 16. And then when Calista discovered that her next-door neighbor Quintana Kingsley had a black belt in bonsai and she saw the extraordinary collection of plants—said to be worth hundreds of thousands of dollars—she realized the landscape for *The Emperor and the Nightingale* was all right there, next door at number 18! She would never have to go to the libraries again for research on this book.

Mrs. Kingsley, or Queenie, as she was called, although the other part of her matched name set, her husband, Kingie, had died some years before, was thrilled that her dear little trees were being immortalized in a fairy tale by the famous illustrator. "A consummation, indeed, devoutly to be wished," she had exclaimed.

Consummation all around, Calista thought, if one did not include the absence of sex, what with Archie being so far afield. But it was all so convenient—the proximity of Charley's job, the ready-made Oriental landscape, the escape from the noise and dust of construction. Calista did hope to get up to her vacation home in Vermont. So far, however, she had been working too hard. On occasion, she did miss Cambridge—but it was just across the river and she and Charley were always popping over for dinner and books. She was used to the Cambridge bookshops. In certain areas, Calista did not tolerate change well.

She now began to pack up her drawing equipment. "I better be going, Quintana." She could not bring herself to call her Queenie. At first, she had called her Mrs. Kingsley, but this apparently was not necessary unless one was a daughter-in-law or a servant.

"Oh, my dear, I enjoy your visits so much." Quintana straightened up now, with another, even smaller pair of shears in hand, and took off her glasses. Amazing what glasses could do for a certain kind of face. Without them, Quintana Kingsley looked remarkably bland and...well, yes, no mental giant. But that was not it, really. Without her glasses, she looked like a very old baby. There was a kind of innocence in her eyes that did not match the stringy neck and the mouth pleated with little vertical lines that made it seem as if her lips were on drawstrings.

"Well, Charley will be home soon from the swan boats."

"Oh!" The older woman touched her thin gray hair as if to jump-start a few neurons under the skull. "That reminds me! I think this job of his sounds marvelous—the swan boats. How lovely. You know my grandson, Jamie, he needs something like that. He's been down in the dumps for weeks now—refuses to go out to the country club for tennis. Refused to go to summer school to make up a poor grade in math.... So I don't know what'll happen there...I mean, I suppose Harvard will take him.... They always have...." She looked vaguely over at a small pine bent nearly double in a strange arthritic posture.

It took Calista a minute to fathom what Quintana had meant when she'd said "They always have." But, of course, this was the way it was with so many of these old families—a steady stream of males, and now females, passing through Harvard, generation after generation. Their children could have abysmal SAT scores and lousy grades, but they would still get in. With an intensive-care unit of round-the-clock tutors and sympathetic housemasters, they limped through. Getting in was the hard part, anyhow, at Harvard. Staying in was no great trick. And Harvard needed these families' money. The blood often thinned before the money. The brain tissue might be a bit frayed around the edges, but they were still good for a few more generations of giving. Calista was sure that many Kingsleys over the years with less than shimmering intellects had passed through with the requisite gentlemen C's. The idea was to pick and choose carefully in terms of curriculum and to avoid at all costs particle-physics courses like the ones that Calista's late husband had taught.

"Well, how old is Jamie?"

"Oh, he'll just be a junior in high school. But I think he needs to do something—you know it will look poorly on his application if he has no extracurricular or summer activities to list. So I was wondering whether perhaps your son, Charley, might take him round, show him the swan boats. Perhaps there's an opening."

"Well, I doubt it. Those jobs are very coveted. Charley, I think, went in last November. But you never know. I'll ask him about it."

"Oh thank you, dear. That's so sweet of you. Now can you find your way out?"

"Of course."

Calista walked out of the greenhouse, through a potting-shed area, and then into a back-hall region that was a nineteenth-century maze of old storage rooms—sculleries, butler's pantries, immense china closets, and silver vaults. She made her way down a putty-colored hallway that led directly into the kitchen. Funny, she had not really noticed the framed pictures on the wall before. They were children's drawings. She stopped now to look. They were nice. She could tell by the paper that they had been done many years ago by some Kingsley child—now grown up, most likely. There were the familiar stick figures standing in front of tall peaked-roof houses and often stiff little rows of flowers perched atop a line to represent earth. They were very typical of a child's early drawings—similar certainly to the ones Charley had done around the age of four or five. After he got the basic family figures down pat, he had moved on to dinosaurs and fast cars in his artwork. But there was something odd here. Did this child—or children, for there seemed to be more than one artist—have the family members down pat? What was strange? Calista stepped closer. None of them had hands! That was it. How very curious. Just then she heard a "Yoo-hoo" coming from the kitchen. A tall figure of a woman suddenly lunged through the pantry and into the hall.

"Oh!" She looked slightly appalled and covered her mouth as she saw Calista standing in front of the drawings.

"Oh, I'm sorry. I didn't mean to startle you. I'm Calista Jacobs and I was just over here..."

"Oh, I know. Yes, Mother told me all about you. You're Archie Baldwin's friend. I'm Bootsie Mc-Phee." She had wonderful celadon green eyes. They were slightly elongated and tipped down a bit at the far corners, which gave them a natural gravity that was distancing but not forbidding. These were the eyes of a very private person, Calista thought.

"How nice to meet you," Calista said. And both women shot out their hands, which collided awkwardly in a kind of glancing blow rather than a handshake. They laughed and tried again. "This is your artwork here?"

"Yes, and my sister's, as well. At one time, I actually had aspirations of being an artist, but it kind of petered out, I guess."

Petered out along with the hands, Calista thought. The more she looked at these drawings, the more interesting they became. They blended a kind of stasis and movement that was very puzzling. "I think they're rather good," Calista said suddenly. "I think maybe you should have stuck with it."

"Well, I take that as a compliment. I am familiar with your books. I read many of them to my son, Jamie."

"But didn't your mother tell me that you do something with art? Isn't that right? Art history?"

"Oh, not very seriously—museum stuff within the area of Japanese art and the China Trade." She paused and inhaled sharply. "I love your name—Calista, lovely name." This was a non sequitur that Calista couldn't quite follow. "What does it mean? Is it Italian?"

"No, Greek, actually. It means happiness."

"Are you part Greek?"

"Oh no. My mother just liked the name."

"Just liked the name," Bootsie said musingly. "How nice. Bootsie's such a silly name, isn't it?"

"Oh..." Calista was at a loss for words. Was it a silly name? She guessed maybe so, and then Bootsie articulated the very thought lurking around her brain. "It's just not really a name, is it? I mean, for a human. You have a real name." Bootsie paused, then continued in a more reflexive voice. "It's a bad habit, isn't it, in families like ours?"

"You mean the name?"

"Names," Bootsie replied with a sardonic grin. "My sister, Muffy, was really Margaret. Mine is Barbara. I have a cousin Elizabeth, who's called Bambi, and then there's her sister Frances, or Fluff."

"Is it something they do only to girls?" Calista asked.

"Yes, boys manage to stay intact for the most part. Their names, that is." She smiled briefly, running her fingers through her hair. "Well, I'd better get out to Mummy." She continued down the hall.

Mummy, thought Calista. That was the other peculiarity of impeccably pedigreed upper-crust girls and women. Now why in heaven's name would a handsome woman like Bootsie with all that commanding bone structure and honey-colored hair—good grief, she looked an awful lot like Lauren Bacall—why would she call her mother Mummy? Whom was she trying to convince of her affection? In Calista's mind, it was an affectation of affection, a confection, if you will, of affection. She tried to imagine Charley calling her Mummy. It was ridiculous. He usually called her Mom. Sometimes he called her "Peahead" when she had her hair pulled back tightly, which wasn't often. And in damp weather, when her masses of silvery chestnut hair frizzed up, he called her "Tiggy," short for Mrs. Tiggy-Winkle, the hedgehog immortalized by Beatrix Potter.

Calista paused for another half minute in front of the drawings. It wasn't just that the hands were unfinished, nor did the arms simply dissolve into nothingness. No. There were straight lines across the wrists. There was no doubt about it: These hands had been chopped off intentionally.

TWO

THE CORN BREAD WAS warm and the beer came in long-necked bottles just the way Calista liked it, but a sudden and decided crinkling of the brow on his mother's face indicated to Charley something less than savory as she sat across from him. They were in their favorite barbecue joint, Red Bones in Davis Square in Somerville. Although it was next door to Cambridge, Somerville was definitely more town than gown. The noise and heat of the restaurant swirled around them as Calista read Charley's better-late-than-never term paper that would solve his "incomplete" situation in English.

"You don't like it?" Charley asked.

"Is this one of these male-bonding things? You know what I think of Robert Bly and all that beating your primal tom-tom crap."

"No, Mom. I got the idea from Archie. It's just what the title says, 'Dawn's Early Eats: An Analysis of the Upper Paleolithic Palate.' "

"Sounds like guys in groups eating red meat to me." Just then the waitress arrived and slid a plate of pulled pork topped with coleslaw, onions, and pickles in front of Calista.

"Irony!" Charley said slyly.

"What . . . huh?" Calista looked up from the term paper over the top of her reading glasses.

"I said that's irony." Charley nodded toward the meat in front of Calista. The waitress then put down an immense platter of Arkansas ribs in front of Charley. "Double irony," he said, smiling like the cat who had just eaten the canary rather than the adolescent about to tuck into a mound of pig ribs.

"Oh, the meat!" Calista said, finally getting it.

"See, you think I'm just a tech weenie and don't know about these arcane things like figures of speech and devices of literary style. I know what they are and I can use them in context. You say guys eating red meat and I say—"

"Okay, okay." Calista cut him off. "I get it—very clever, very appropriate. And it's not that I think you're a tech weenie. It was just that when that cousin of Archie's who teaches Shakespeare came over and you said, 'A whole semester for Shakespeare!' as if you thought it could be done in a weekend workshop or something. Well, it was kind of embarrassing, and then when I found out about this incomplete, I really did begin to worry about the humanities side of your education."

"I didn't take one computer course the entire year, Mom."

"There's none left for you to take at the high school, or math courses, either, for that matter."

Charley Jacobs took after his late father, Tom Jacobs, who had been a preeminent theoretical physicist at Harvard. Gifted in mathematics, a computer whiz by the end of his freshman year, Charley had exhausted what the public high school had to offer in terms of math and computers. Now just finishing tenth grade, he had taken a fractals and chaos theory course at MIT, but at his mother's request, he had also signed up for extra art courses at the high school—and had enjoyed them immensely, especially printmaking. Some way or other, however, Charley had neglected to hand in a final term paper for his English composition course. He claimed it was an oversight. Calista was not sure how a term paper that counted a quarter of the grade became an oversight, but she had been ticked. Now she had to admit that despite the facetious tone of this paper—"In days of yore, when cholesterol was not a dirty word and jogging was for real"—Charley's effort was substantial and the paper was coherent—so far, no run-on sentences or comma splices. There was an automatic ten points off for that.

"This isn't bad...not bad, Charley." Calista put the paper into her bag so as not to stain it with the barbecue.

Charley was gnawing on a bone. On his upper lip, there was barbecue sauce that was the same color as his hair—red—and in the same place where his mustache had begun to show a shadow. She wasn't ready for this. A son who could shave. No more chortly baby face, triple chins, and all that. No more scrappy little boy. There was this rather lanky young man across the table from her with interesting angles in his face and a smart but hardly wise look in his eye. Babies' eyes were full of innocence, flecked sometimes with wisdom; yes, babies could on occasion look almost like sages. Adolescent eyes seemed masked by comparison. They were not innocent; yet they were far from knowing. Calista had looked hard into the eyes of Charley and those of his friends. When the masks lifted, there was an unsettling mixture of distrust and hope. It was of paramount importance for kids of this age never to let the hope show through, not even a glimmer. It was bad form to be caught out with hope in your eyes. It was really a balancing act. Of course,

that was what all of adolescence added up to—an incredible, nerve-racking balancing act. Thank heavens
Charley had a sense of humor. For both parent and
child, negotiating the shoals and drafts of adolescence without humor would be the absolute pits.

THEY FINISHED DINNER and headed back to Boston
and Beacon Hill. As she let herself and Charley into
the quiet darkness of the Baldwins' home and stepped
into the front room, as they called it, Calista always
thought of a description she had read in *George San-
tayana's America* of a Beacon Hill home, in which he
described so eloquently the "solemnity and hush," a
world of thick carpets and monumental furniture
"heavy and fixed like sepulchers," and armchairs that
"grew in their places like separate oaks."

AND, OF COURSE, recumbent in that armchair was not
Will Baldwin but Nestor, the goddamn cat. And on a
Duncan Phyfe couch in a pose worthy of Madame
Récamier herself was Ophelia, the other cat. Together, they constituted the only fly in the ointment of
16 Louisburg Square. Now, it was not that Calista had
anything against cats. She didn't. Calista was simply
not a cat person. She knew that the world was divided
into those who were and those who were not. And she
understood intimately the world of the cat person,
because it just so happened that a lot of people in
children's book publishing were cat people. Her editor, Janet Weiss, for one and her art director. But even
Nestor and Ophelia might try the patience of Janet
and Michael.

"Did you give them their sherry yet, Mom?"

"Yes, and Ophelia left a lot of hers, I see. She must be onto the fact that I'm watering it down." Ophelia slowly turned her head. Her luminous jade eyes bore into Calista: Fool who would water down Hawker's amontillado? It was all there in her eyes. No doubt about it.

Nan and Will had left a full page of notes concerning the cats. Sherry was one of their requisite snacks— although the vet had suggested watering down Ophelia's because of a chronic bladder problem. And Ophelia, in all her feline arrogance, seemed to be letting Calista know what she thought of this.

Nestor, not so arrogant, was just plain old mean and arthritic. So if she could get him fairly tight each night, he did seem a tad more pleasant in the morning. Nestor now rose from the mighty chair that grew like an oak, smirked at Calista, then languidly made his way toward the hearth, where he had the audacity to sniff at the chipped Royal Doulton saucer of adulterated sherry and walk away. This would all be quite touching if Nestor wasn't such a wanton son of a bitch in his behavior toward Ophelia—despite the fact that Nan and Will were convinced that the cats never really fought and indeed loved each other dearly, devotedly. Hah! Calista had seen old Nestor tomcatting around in the connected gardens, trying out uppercrust pussy, as it were. And once when Ophelia had a nice fish head that she had gotten from the alley out back, Nestor, the lout, pounced right on her. Some love match!

Nan and Will had a blind spot with cats. They also, to Calista's mind, tended to overname them. The predecessors to this couple had been Eleanor and Franklin. But Calista just called these two Piss and

Moan, because that was basically what they did all day long.

"You shouldn't have said that thing about the sherry out loud, Mom," Charley said, studying Nestor. "They both understood, and look at poor Piss limping over there to console her."

"So you think they're in love, too?"

"Piss and Moan?"

"Yeah."

"I don't know."

"Well, let's go to bed. You have an early date with the swans and I might have a nightcap on the back balcony while contemplating the mysteries of feline love."

THREE

ANOTHER PERK OF the house was the little balcony off Nan and Will's dressing room. It reminded Calista of a small afterdeck on a ship with a wrought-iron taffrail. There was a fairly decrepit but comfortable lounge chair and from this vantage a view of the Charles was afforded, if one was to look straight out; and if straight down, the Connecting Gardens were visible. These six contiguous gardens behind Louisburg Square had been formed in 1929, when the owners of the homes on the square and the two side streets decided to tear down the walls separating their small yards in order to create a larger space. The various gardens still emerged as separate entities through the construction of low walls and hedges. But the overall effect was one of unity and harmony.

The moon was full tonight and the plots thick with shade plantings. Ivy, hosta, and varieties of mosses were punctuated in the moonlight by occasional splashes of woodland flowers. There was a luxury of growth balanced with simplicity and perfect scale. Calista loved her perch above it all. She had poured herself a tumbler of seltzer and put in a splash of Grand Marnier. The moon was so bright, she barely needed her reading light. She was rereading *Barchester Towers*. She settled back and extended her legs delicately in a pose perhaps reminiscent of Signora Neroni, a character in the Trollope novel. La Signora Madeline Vesey Neroni was one of Calista's all-time literary favorites. With her mutilated legs that required her to be carried everywhere and then deposited on various chaises, the beautiful but crippled Madeline in her Grecian head bandeau and Empire gowns was a source of endless charm. So Calista skipped back a few pages to her favorite part—La Signora's entrance to a reception at the bishop's house. The fair lady was carried in from her carriage by shoals of attendants—an Italian manservant, a lady's maid, a page. It was a "perfect commotion" and "in this way they climbed easily into the drawing room....the signora rested safely on her couch."

Calista delighted in this prose. Trollope was to writing what Randolph Caldecott was to drawing. Her favorite line perhaps in the whole book was when La Signora referred to her small daughter as having the blood of Tiberius flowing in her veins. "She is the last of the Neros." And then Trollope's wonderful disquisition on the peculiar phrase through the eyes of the bishop, who thinks that indeed he had heard "of the last of the Visigoths and the last of the Mohicans, but to have the last of the Neros thus brought before him for a blessing was very staggering." This was a shining moment in nineteenth-century wit and irony. Now this truly was irony, Calista thought, recalling Charley's reference to the pulled pork and Arkansas ribs. She wondered whether Charley was ready for Trollope. Fat chance!

She read for half an hour, enjoying every moment as the porcelain wit and charm of Trollope's words washed over her. She should really get to bed. She wanted to make one last drawing at Quintana's and had promised to be there as soon as she got Charley off to the swan boats. There was still a light on in the

Kingsleys' greenhouse. She had hoped Archie would call tonight. But it was very hard for him to get to a phone down there in Guatemala. He had written her one fabulously sexy letter in which he had told a story about a strangely beautiful flower that grew in the rain forest where he was working. He described the anatomical charms it possessed to lure a particular hummingbird to its nectar, its nectar being particularly sweet and held in a cup within a cluster. Oh Lord, it made her horny just to think about it. Well, he'd be back in a few more weeks.

Calista went to bed. She thought about her conservatory. She would try some more camellias, and maybe some strange small orchids with parts like females. They were so exotic. A mini rain forest in the dead of winter in Cambridge was appealing. She tried to imagine bromeliads, pink and spiky, in the drab New England January. She had read about tank bromeliads in the rain forest that held gallons of water and became small aquatic worlds, containing a life of their own with frogs and salamanders. Worlds within worlds, rather like multiple-universe theories. That was what Tom had just started to toy with at the time of his death—black holes and multiple universes, and strings and wormholes as corridors to simultaneous universes. He and Hawking had just begun to correspond and then . . .

Calista fell asleep thinking about gravity and black holes, bromeliads and orchids—orchids with spilling cups of nectar.

It must have been around three in the morning. The screeching tore like claws on the silk of the night. Calista opened her eyes wide. A terrible screaming seared the air. "Fucking cats!" she muttered. She rolled over

and tried to go back to sleep. They kept the screeching up. She got out of bed and walked through the
dressing room and looked down on the Connecting
Gardens. There they were, the two of them standing
on a low stone wall, wailing to beat the band. This was
more than just the sherry. Nestor was absolutely
prancing around, looking quite unarthritic.

Calista went downstairs muttering. She poured two
saucers of milk laced with sherry. She stepped out the
back door. "Come on, kitty, kitty." The cats came
running. This sudden obedience startled her. Neither
cats, children, nor lovers had ever responded with so
much alacrity. She went back upstairs, amazed to see
them following her.

"Oh no, guys. You're not sleeping with me." She
scooped them up and took them into the breakfast
room, where their cat beds were, and deposited them.
They looked up at her with an alarming mixture of
contrition and respect.

Calista went back to bed and fell asleep with the
disturbing thought that the cats might begin to like
her, become attached in some way.

FOUR

"LISTEN TO THIS, Piss." Calista was in the breakfast room with her first cup of coffee.

"You talking to the cats, Tiggy?" Charley said as he came in, his hair still wet from the shower. Calista's had frizzed in the heavy humidity of the morning.

"Yeah, last night they had bad dreams or something and I had to get them in from the gardens. They were actually very nice to me. But this morning, Piss is as ornery as ever. I'm just reading this rather interesting little piece buried on page seven of the *Globe*."

"Which is?" Charley popped a bagel in the toaster.

"Okay, listen up, Piss. Dateline Edwards, Tennessee. 'A devoted couple who died within seconds of each other in a nursing home were buried on the day that would have been their seventy-fifth wedding anniversary. Luke and Dot Peters died while side by side in single beds in the Pleasant Meadow nursing home. Both were ninety-five years old. "It was almost simultaneous," said Dr. Louis Matchen. A nurse reported that Dot stopped breathing and then she heard Luke give a short gasp. Luke Peters had been comatose for a week and would not have known of his wife's death, but the couple had repeatedly said that they wanted to die together.'" Calista looked over the top of the newspaper at Piss, who was trying to stretch his creaking back. Moan was whimpering in her basket. "Isn't that sweet, Piss?" Calista asked. The cat didn't even look at her. "I'm worried about Moan.

She really hasn't eaten anything for two days. The doctor said it wasn't really worth it to do that laser stuff with her bladder.''

"So you think she might kick—buy the farm—and you're hoping that Piss will go with her?" Charley asked.

"Well, I just thought it was a touching story."

"Piss doesn't."

"Guess not." She watched him waddle off toward the cat-treat bag on a corner shelf, then look directly at Charley.

"Okay, okay, I'm a-coming." Charley got up and poured some into a bowl. "Ooh, I'm late. I got to be going.''

"Well, take that bagel with you. You don't eat enough. I don't see how you pedal halfway round the pond on what you eat."

Calista cleared up the breakfast dishes and went upstairs to shower. There was no hope for her hair on a day like this. It was already kinking madly as she piled it wet on top of her head. She looked out the window. The skies looked just like gefilte fish—lumpy and gray. And there was a heavy low-tide smell in the air, the way Boston always smelled when the wind came in from the southeast on a warm summer day. She put on a pair of shorts, a T-shirt, flip-flops and grabbed her bag with her pencils, pens, and drawing pad. She went back downstairs and out the Baldwins' back door, for she knew Quintana would already be at work and not hear the front doorbell ring. She crossed their terrace, went down two steps into another garden, across it, then up into the Kingsleys'. There was a small stone squirrel perched under a seedling oak surrounded by carpets of ivy and edged with red-and-white trillium that backed up to the greenhouse. The door was on the other side. Calista walked around and went in.

"Quin..." The sound died on her lips. At first, she saw the juniper, its salver broken on the floor. But Quintana Kingsley could never have been mistaken for being asleep. Her head was cocked at an angle no living, breathing person could sustain. A thin thread of blood had dried in a jagged line from the corner of her mouth to her chin. Her hand still clutched the chopsticks. A stain of blood bloomed on her chest like a voracious blossom and right at its center, standing straight up, were the handles of "Old Reliable," the bud shears. The blades were buried to their hilt in Quintana Kingsley's chest. Calista felt an overwhelming coldness, as if her body were turning to ice on this warm summer morning. But she felt her heart swell in a tumultuous thudding. Her rib cage seemed too narrow for her heart. It would burst, burst like that dark red blossom on Quintana's chest. Calista screamed and ran from the greenhouse.

FIVE

THERE WAS A blank period, lost minutes, between the time she fled from the greenhouse and ran back into the Baldwins' to call the police. She could not remember exactly what she had said or done. She could not even be sure of what she had seen, the reality of it. It was as if all images and words had been erased; that sentient life had suddenly stopped; that she had entered a state of suspended animation. Had she told the police to come to the Baldwins' or the Kingsleys'? Where was she standing when they arrived in their screaming cars, the sirens splitting the shady green calm of the square. The double-parked cars with the flashing lights looked odd on the street with the handsome redbrick Greek Revival row houses facing the meticulously kept enclosed rectangular green.

"You mean I have to go back in there?" she heard herself saying to a policeman.

"Yes, deah." It was the Irish *dear* of an old rheumy-eyed Irish cop. "Don't worry, there are lots of people in there now. You won't be alone, deah. We'll all be there to help you."

"Help me do what?" Calista said. Just what was expected of her? The radios from the patrol cars were blaring. The cop walked over a few feet to it and reached inside. "Five-three here, Jimmy, confirmed homicide. Go ahead."

"Eight-two, detectives have responded," a voice crackled back.

An officer came out the front door of the house. He wiped his brow. "Day like this, we're going to need some floaters.

"Ma'am, will you just follow me in. And please remember when we get inside, it's very important not to touch anything."

Two more cars pulled up. A woman in a beige pleated skirt got out from the driver's side. From the other side, a man stepped out into the street. Neither one was in uniform. The woman carried a large black satchel.

"Hi, Donna."

She ran her fingers through her dark hair and pulled off her sunglasses. "We need masks yet?"

"Not yet, but soon on a day like this."

"Don't tell me about it. I'm supposed to be at the beach with my two kids."

"Al sick?" the first, older cop asked.

"Well, he better not be at the beach!" They all laughed. "Let's go." She nodded at the two officers and Calista. Calista's feet moved, although her mind seemed to remain somewhere out on the sidewalk. But she flowed along with the others on a current of small talk.

"Nice house."

"Most of these are condos now... just a few single owners, I'd imagine."

"Taxes'll kill you on something like this."

"Apparently, it wasn't taxes, however." Donna tossed a laugh over her shoulder, then looked up at a rather severe portrait on the wall. "Who's that?"

"Cotton Mather," Calista offered. Oh man, she thought, count on me. A veritable fount of useless information. Anyone want to play Trivial Pursuit at the scene of the crime? Calista Jacobs can be your genial host. But it was a rather good portrait of a rather bad man. Calista had been curious about the picture the first time she saw it and Quintana had said that indeed both the Kingsleys and her family, the Parkingtons, were descendants of the grim Puritan preacher.

They were making their way through the maze of pantries and back halls off the kitchen. Suddenly, Calista stopped. She could not move. She turned her head. A drawing on the wall stared at her with its saucer eyes and lopped-off hands. She thought of those shears plunged into Quintana's chest, the blossom of red blood swelling on her breast.

"Something the matter?" someone said to her. Everything! What a stupid question. She swallowed and looked at them. They were all looking at her with great expectation. She licked her lips and scratched her head. "Look." She inhaled sharply. "I don't know whether I can do this. I don't know what you want me to do." Donna had walked on. All business, that woman. "I know this is old hat to you. I read the papers. I know this is the—what?—the one hundred and twentieth murder in Boston this year, but for me..." Calista's voice trailed off.

"It's okay," said Jack, the older cop. Then the other officer and the man who had accompanied Donna plunged in with all the robust charm of cheerleaders at a pep rally.

"Don't worry."

"You'll do fine. Just don't touch anything."

"Yeah, don't touch. That's important until the Crime Scene Unit gets here."

"It won't take long. You'll be terrific."

They were better than cheerleaders; they were like your best buddies at camp telling you that yes, you could dive off the high board. There was nothing to it. Then someone said something about a witness.

"Me? Why?" Calista asked.

"Well, you discovered the body."

AND BEFORE SHE KNEW IT, she was moving along, out the scullery, through the potting shed, and into the greenhouse. Quintana was still there. Kneeling beside her, Donna had one hand jammed in her skirt pocket and with the other she held a small rectangular box into which she was mumbling. The man who had come with her was moving around the greenhouse, also mumbling into a small box. Another squad car had evidently arrived with one uniformed cop and two plainclothesmen. The greenhouse seemed ready to burst.

"So what have we got?"

"One white female, late seventies." So this is what it all comes down to, Calista thought.

"Donna," one of them said, "do me a favor. Let's not move her yet."

"Okay by me. Did you bring your mask? It's hot today."

"Any witnesses?"

"One."

The man turned immediately to Calista. "I'm Detective Brant. Can you tell me what you know?"

"I came here...well, I don't know what time it was, maybe nine o'clock, to sketch here in Mrs. Kingsley's greenhouse. I...I was drawing pictures, making studies of her plants...these bonsai plants. She was an expert in their cultivation."

"Hurh." The detective made a low grunting sound
that Calista supposed was to indicate some mild curi-
osity. Although it was hard to imagine bonsai was a
consuming interest of this man. Flashbulbs started to
pop; another man was laying out a tape measure and
another chalking the brick floor. Calista watched as he
drew a chalk circle around the smashed juniper, the
needles of which rested in a pool of blood.

A lover's pinch was death. The words seemed to pop
from nowhere into her head. Who said that? Calista
wondered. What dumb fool had written that nonsense? "The stroke of death is as a lover's pinch,
which hurts, and is desired." Calista could not take her
eyes off the shears sticking straight out of the chest.
Some lover's pinch! Shakespeare...that was the fool.
Antony and Cleopatra. Something about "thou and
nature can so gently part." Calista looked at the
smashed juniper. Eighty years, it had lasted—the two
of them had lasted—and now this.

"Ms. Jacobs?"

"Oh, I'm sorry. I was distracted."

"It's understandable."

"By the way, she is not late seventies. She's eighty.
Same age as the plant on the floor." At that moment,
everyone paused in their little ministrations and
looked at Calista, then resumed their work.

"Did you use the phone from here when you reported the body?" the detective asked.

"No, no, I ran back to the house where I'm staying."

"Good."

Why would that be good? Calista wondered. Her
question was soon answered. "Would there be any
prints of yours around here?"

"Why yes. On those." She pointed toward the shears protruding from Quintana's chest.

"The scissors?" Nobody missed a beat, but Calista was rather overwhelmed by what she had just said. "Well, yes. I was here yesterday and Quintana—Mrs. Kingsley asked me to hand them to her.

Donna was now lifting the hand and putting each finger over a small bowl, then scraping underneath the nails. Calista watched. At some imperceptible moment, the body had ceased to be a person. It was now an object. A name seemed superfluous, almost ridiculous. She had to stifle a giggle. She remembered suddenly that when Charley was seven or eight, he'd had a wart removed. The doctor had let him keep it in a little bottle of preservative and Charley had named it Freddy. She was trying to stifle the giggle, but then suddenly there was a tincture in the air. Someone slammed a mask under her chin, but it couldn't catch it all. She was throwing up. The sour-sweet stink in the air was roiling in her sinuses.

"It's okay. Happens all the time." They were all busy getting their masks on.

"I don't think we need her here anymore."

"Okay, I'll take her home," the old cop said with that wonderful lilt in his voice.

As she began to walk from the greenhouse, she saw them affixing a tag to the left big toe. Tag 'em and bag 'em. Or, as Henry James was reputed to have said of his impending death, "So here it is at last, the distinguished thing!" No slouch when it came to irony, that man.

SIX

CALISTA HAD A tremendous urge to go home and get clean, or get clean and then go home, home to Cambridge. For if she recalled correctly, this week all the water was turned off in her house while they were redoing the piping—five thousand dollars' worth of copper piping. All the perks of the Louisburg Square house that she had so frequently calculated had suddenly evaporated. She was left with fear and this dreadful stench still hovering deep in her sinuses. She stood in the shower and scrubbed furiously. She wished she had brought the Dr. Bonner's peppermint soap, or was it eucalyptus? Whatever it was, it was strong. If anything could chase away that horrific sweet-sour stench, it would be Dr. Bonner's. She felt the bile rising in the back of her throat again. She squeezed her eyes shut and bit her lip while the hot water beat down on her head. She rode it out. The wave of nausea passed. She got out of the shower and toweled off.

She put on her robe, sat in a chair by the window, and propped her feet up. A crowd had begun to gather. Neighbors from the other houses around the square were milling on the sidewalk. Some of the police were leaving. The body had evidently been removed. Oh dear! She saw a young cop bending over an open hydrant. He was washing out something. She knew what. It was his mask, which she had thrown up into. Her vomit flowing down the gutters of the elegant streets of Louisburg Square. There goes the neighborhood!

She had to get her wits together. First things first. She must go over to the Public Garden and tell Charley. Then she had to go over to Cambridge and see just how livable their house was. Certainly they should be able to camp out in some fashion. But what about the cats? The fucking cats. Did she have to take them to Cambridge, too? No, that's why they weren't in Maine. Traveling, changes exacerbated their conditions. Too unsettling, that's what Nan had said. Cambridge seemed as far away as Maine at this moment; the Charles River as definitive as the Rubicon. So that meant no for Nestor and Ophelia. Calista would come back to feed them and let them out for romps in the garden, but she'd be damned if she were going to schlepp Piss and Moan to Cambridge. She was sure her house would be very upsetting to them. It would deliver the coup de grâce to Ophelia's bladder and Nestor's psyche. Not that she cared, but it would not endear her to Nan and Will, for whom she did care a great deal.

AS SHE WALKED DOWN Charles Street toward the gardens, she wondered exactly how she would tell Charley this. Not that he even knew Quintana Kingsley. Maybe he had met her once. This was the height of the tourist season in Boston. The swan boats were loaded with good folks from Iowa or Washington State or wherever, drinking in American history and doing quaint things like riding the swan boats. Calista tried to picture herself telling Charley. Most likely at this very moment, he was sitting between the immense wings of the boat and pedaling benchloads of passengers. Didn't seem quite kosher to break the news in such idyllic surroundings.

When she arrived at the duck pond, the line for the swan boats seemed half a mile long. Charley was not on line patrol, nor was he at the ticket booth. As far as she could tell, he was not on the float, either, guiding people onto the boats. This meant he was on the high "mimic sea," a poetic name sometimes given the kidney-shaped pond. Matthew, Charley's friend from Cambridge, spotted her as she approached the ticket booth. He, too, was working on the swan boats this summer.

"Hi, Cal. Charley's out. He's coming under the bridge now."

"Do you think he can take a break? I gotta talk to him."

"Nope. We're really shorthanded this week. Can you talk to him on the boat?"

She hesitated. Beside her, she could hear a family having an argument about whether to finish the Freedom Trail before or after lunch. They all looked hot and tired and very aggravated with one another. Typical family vacation. What would she be ruining with a little talk of murder? She'd keep her voice low. "Sure," she said quickly to Matthew. "Can you get me on?"

"Yep."

"Let her through," he said to the man at the turnstile. "This is Charley's mom. She needs to talk to him."

FIVE MINUTES LATER, Calista, her hand gripping the scalloped edge of the swan's fiberglass wing, stood

next to Charley. He pedaled steadily toward the
northwest corner of the pond.

"You actually threw up?"

"Charley, I don't even want to talk about it. The
very thought of that smell." She began to taste it again
in the back of her throat. And she could hardly claim
seasickness on a swan boat.

"Well, who'd want to kill that old lady?" A man
with a baby on his lap on the bench directly in front of
Charley turned around. He wore a Miami Dolphins
T-shirt and had a very sunburned nose.

"Not so loud, Charley?" She bent over and whispered the words in his ear. "So listen, can you get off
early?"

"No way, José. They need all the help they can get
here. They've got two people out this week. And the
crowds are brutal."

"Oh gosh, that reminds me. Mrs. Kingsley asked
me if I could ask you about a job for her grandson. I
didn't give her much hope." It sounded strange to talk
about hope now.

"They'd hire him in a minute this week."

"Well, I doubt if he'd be in much shape after all this
to pedal a swan boat."

"They'd hire a quadriplegic with a strong tongue
today."

"Oh, Charley!" Calista couldn't help but laugh.
She might as well settle back and enjoy the rest of the
ride. They were just going under the bridge now and
would round the rock island at the east end of the
pool, where the baby ducks floated like little fluff balls
behind their mother. Boy oh boy! she thought. Robert McCloskey had really hit it when he came up with
the idea of *Make Way for Ducklings*. People from all

corners of the earth came now to these gardens because of that gentle old man and his wonderful drawings. He had done the very finest thing an artist can do—make a real place live in the imagination forever. That is genius, she thought. So many of the new illustrators were into a high-gloss slick illustration, dazzling in technique but yielding drawings that were so airless, they seemed literally to gasp for life. Somewhat the opposite was the retro fine arts trend, with illustrators intent on painting in a grand European tradition. But those drawings, too, lacked, if not life, soul. They seemed rather characterless. In either case, none of these illustrators could hold a candle to McCloskey or Sendak. Not one had any sense of how to really draw. They were great technicians, but most significantly they had no sense of narrative.

The boat pulled up to the float. Calista got out. It was settled. She would pack up a few things for Charley and herself and they would meet back in Cambridge and see whether their house was remotely livable.

"Are you sure you don't want to take the cats, Mom?" Charley said as she disembarked.

"I am sure."

"Do you think they'll be okay?"

"They'll be fine. I'll go over every day and check on them. I just don't want them in Cambridge. I don't need those cats in Cambridge. Those cats have an attitude."

"Mom, that's the whole point of being a cat—having an attitude."

CALISTA LOOKED at her son. He actually wore a little captain's hat to command this vessel and his fiery red hair stood out shaggy around his ears. A shadow from its bill sliced across the top part of his face so she couldn't see the lucid gray eyes. He had, of course, uttered one of the profound truths of the world. And with such ease, with such grace, he wore this mantle of wisdom. She wondered suddenly whether there were some great rabbis among their ancestors. It would seem that this kind of insight coupled with the grace, the very posture, must be genetic. It must come out of some august tradition of looking into the souls of things.

But as far as she knew, there was only one great "rabbi" in their past, their most recent past, and that was Charley's father, Tom Jacobs. *Rabbi,* after all, meant teacher, and Tom had looked into the soul of the universe. For he had probed the very beginnings of the universe, the beginnings of time. His area of expertise had been those first slivers of the first second after the big bang. And his major concern: When did time begin? Tom would often quote St. Augustine to his students: When asked what did God do before there was a universe created by Him, Augustine replied that time was a property of the universe God created and that time did not exist before the beginning of the universe. That, of course, was why the Pope was crazy about Tom—because Tom was the most eloquent proponent and explicator of the big bang theory and the big bang came the closest to Genesis and allowed for at least a cameo appearance by God.

The Vatican had had a conference on cosmology that Tom and Calista had attended. That was when the Pope had taken such a shine, as it 'twere, to Tom's ideas. Calista had loved Tom for other reasons. And now as she walked back to 16 Louisburg Square, she began to miss him just horribly. She missed Archie, too. But right now, she missed Tom more. It had been almost five years since his death, his murder in the desert. She would never get over it. She would always love him. She would always love Archie. Loving two men forever was not hard. Missing two men and knowing you would have to go on missing one forever was very hard.

Waves of heat shimmered up from the brick sidewalk as she turned onto Mt. Vernon from Charles Street and began the steep climb up Beacon Hill toward the cool green oasis of Louisburg Square. Its coolness as well as its tranquillity were perhaps just a mirage. Perhaps the lives of entire families that lived behind the elegant Georgian facades were nothing more than mirages.

SEVEN

As Calista stood in the alcove where her bed was and looked straight up at the sky through a hole in the roof that a baby elephant might fit, she did wonder what it was that had ever given her the notion she could manage even to camp in this house.

"Well, I think it might be okay for tonight. We can sheet that with some plastic, take the drop cloth off your bed. I mean, the weather's supposed to be good. No rain predicted." Michael Stephanotis laughed. "No shower, either!" he said, nodding toward the bathroom.

"You mean the water's not hooked up yet? I thought that was supposed to happen today."

"Well, they ran out of bends for the piping and Peter had to go out to Braintree to pick some stuff up. So he should have them tomorrow. And you know how Peter drives."

"I know. I worry about plumbers who drive Porsches and wear Armani suits."

"Mom!" Charley said in a genuinely shocked voice.

"I know, I know. I'm not politically correct. It's very hard to be when I'm dirty and tired and want my house back."

She sighed and looked around. There was plaster dust over everything. God forbid she should have a headache and want an aspirin. Nothing was where it should be. She had packed all the contents of the bathroom up in boxes because they were having to tear into walls behind cabinets to get into the piping. And then to save her clothes and books from dust, they had all been packed up and moved to a back room or the basement. But what else could she do? She might as well try it for a night. Maybe Michael's guys could move the television and VCR upstairs for her. Part of her intended therapy involved watching *Singin' in the Rain* and having a tot of Mount Gay rum—all in bed. A kind of two-step recovery program from murder.

Gene Kelly had been her first serious movie-star crush after Roy Rogers, who didn't count because he was strictly prelatency. No, Gene was genuinely sexy. She, of course, loved Fred Astaire for his nearly ethereal elegance, but Gene had that low center of gravity that gave him a very earthy grace. And his wit. The part in the rain number where he did the shuffle crossovers up and down into the wet gutter drove Calista crazy. And then there was Donald O'Connor's showstopping "Make 'Em Laugh." Talk about funny. No, she would definitely stay for a couple of nights. She could always go back to number 16 to shower. She had to look in on the cats anyway. And maybe for the weekend, she'd go up to Vermont. But she'd better call Lieutenant O'Leary and tell him where she was. He had said to keep in touch. So had Detective Brant.

"THEY WANT TO see me? The kids?... Yes, yes. I guess so. Well, tomorrow. I'm pretty tired now. Thank you for telling them that. Yes.... Okay, good-bye." She hung up. "Oh shit."

"What's the trouble, Mom?" Charley walked in.

"Oh, it's just that Quintana Kingsley's children and I guess her brother want to talk to me . . . you know, seeing as I was the one to discover her."

"Oh jeez." Charley sighed and leaned against the doorjamb. A shower of plaster dust sprinkled down into his hair.

"Well, I can understand it. It's just that it's not going to be exactly pleasant, and it looks as if I'm going to have to go to the funeral, too. It's Saturday," she said with a sour look.

"You were thinking about Vermont for this weekend?"

"Precisely."

Too bad the Kingsleys weren't Jewish, Calista thought wistfully. They'd never be buried on a Saturday.

SHE HAD BEEN ASLEEP for hours before she felt it: wet and cold right on her nose. She opened her eyes and stared up. Then she heard the unmistakable sound. Another drop, then another on her forehead. Slowly, the knowledge dawned. I am not singing in the rain. "Shit!" She sat straight up in bed. A rivulet of water from a crease in the plastic began to funnel down on her sheets. "I don't believe this," Calista muttered in the dark. She stood up to examine where Michael had tacked the plastic, but the rain was coming down harder. All she could say was "shit" and all she could think was that there was a literary term for this. It was either objective correlative or pathetic fallacy, but one minute you're watching *Singin' in the Rain* and the next minute you're being drenched in bed. That was the gist of it.

It was hopeless. She got up, spread the drop cloth over the bed, took her comforter, and threw it down with her pillow on the floor in Charley's bedroom, which was also a mess but didn't have a hole in the roof.

EIGHT

CALISTA WAS WATCHING Bootsie carefully as she spoke. Her head seemed to bend with the completion of each piece of information, each thought, as if this nodding was somehow helping her to digest it. It seemed to Calista that Bootsie was summoning all of her intellectual strength just to concentrate on the words. It was amply clear to Calista that Bootsie had been drinking steadily, probably since she first heard the news. A bemused look sometimes seemed to drift through the elongated celadon eyes. There was a large tumbler with gin or vodka that Bootsie rested her hand on lightly. She had been nursing it for a long time. It had not gone down that much since Calista had come over.

"See, Bootsie, did you hear what Calista just said? What the police told her—same as what they said to us." Gus Kingsley, Bootsie's older brother, leaned forward and touched her knee lightly with his hand in a tender gesture. Bootsie looked down at the hand that rested for just a second on her knee. Her face darkened and for the first time her glaze seemed to begin to crack. But then she looked up and stared through her brother. "Yes, I heard. Mummy didn't suffer much because the shears cut right through the aorta." Very slowly she turned her head toward Calista. "Comforting, isn't it?" There was a look of pure venom in her eyes.

Calista sat in the living room of Bootsie's large house in the Cottage Farm area of Brookline, Boston's first suburb. For those who wanted to be near the city but in a good public school system, Brookline was a premiere choice. Rambling old stucco and brick houses were set on large plots of land with big trees. Close to the great hospitals of Boston, it was popular with doctors. It had a large Jewish population now, but still the old WASPs, the ones who couldn't quite go the distance to the North Shore or pay the taxes on Beacon Hill, found a tranquil refuge here. Bootsie was one.

After her divorce, she had decided Brookline was just the place for her and Jamie. Of course, the family had a fit when she said he would attend public school and they insisted that he continue at Poulton Academy, where all Kingsley men had gone since it opened over one hundred years before. It was unthinkable for a Kingsley not to go to Poulton, which was dedicated to high thinking and plain living. It was the place where scions of cold roast Boston could meet, where bonds that would influence their business, intellectual, and social lives would be forged. The Kingsleys were unswerving in their devotion to Poulton Academy. They would no more think of not sending a son to Old Pulley, as it was called, than give up their pew in King's Chapel, their membership to The Country Club or, horror of horrors, not go to Harvard.

In fact, the Kingsleys felt that the Baldwins were positively bohemian for having never done more than a few of those very things. Will Baldwin himself had attended Poulton but had been thrown out in 1922 for mooning a teacher. Needless to say, he was not keen on having his son Archie go there. And although Will had gone on to Harvard, Archie had elected to go to Dartmouth. The whole lot of Baldwins were a bunch of agnostics, so King's Chapel had been out of the question for years. Finally, nobody played golf, so why belong to something like the Country Club?

Poor Bootsie, Calista thought as she looked around the spare but nicely furnished living room. She had tried so hard to escape all that. It was apparent from the Mies Van der Rohe chair to the glass coffee tables and stark white walls. There was an airiness to the room. Things had been peeled back to show the elegant moldings, the nicely curved double bay in the front of the living room. There were a few Oriental rugs and some truly spectacular Asian pieces, including four beautiful ink-wash Japanese scrolls from the Edo period. One depicted cranes in flight over a waterfall and another showed a mountain shrouded in clouds. These scrolls and a massive chandelier of the late Victorian period were Bootsie's major concessions to an older tradition in terms of style, along with a wing chair in which she sat now, her jaw tilted up, her head back. She held the scrolls in her gaze through half-closed eyes as she twirled the ice in her drink with her index finger. Gus stood behind her, resting his hand on her shoulder.

"Boots...Boots..." Gus spoke softly, patting her lightly on her shoulder. "Are you going to be okay?"

"Yes, yes, of course."

"Should I call Dr. Miles?"

"No, no...that's not necessary. Jamie..." She coughed nervously. A pained look crossed her face. She lowered her voice and muttered, "Jamie will be here. He'll take care of me."

"Yes, I guess so." Gus rose quickly. "Well, I better be going. Uncle Rudy's flight is due in soon. I'll just drive him directly to the Harvard Club. Then I'm afraid I have to go out to St. Bennett's. You know I always coach tennis on Tuesdays and Thursdays, and what with playoffs on the day when the funeral is scheduled, I better make some arrangements for the team." Gus was scratching his head and speaking to no one in particular. "Yes, I have to show Murphy the lineup for the playoffs, since I won't be there and . . ." Gus's voice dwindled off.

"You go and get Rudy. Then go out to St. Bennett's. That'll be fine," Bootsie said mechanically, and reached for her drink. She took a big swallow. Gus's eyebrows knitted together in a worried look. He gestured with his head to Calista as if he wanted to speak to her alone.

"Well, I better be on my way, too," Calista said, and jumped up. "I . . ." she hesitated. It sounded so dumb. "I hope that I've been of some help. I'm just so sorry that . . ." her voice faded. There was nothing she could say, absolutely nothing. Oh yes, she could tell them that she had been in the same place almost five years before when Tom was murdered, but what good would that do? Nothing, simply nothing at all.

Bootsie mumbled something as Calista left and seemed to try to wave good-bye with her thin white hand. It looked so delicate, that hand, like a brushstroke from one of the Chinese artist's scrolls. And then once more she remembered the strange children's drawings in the back hall off the pantries of 18 Louisburg Square. Suddenly, she wondered what had happened to the other Kingsley daughter. She remembered now that Bootsie had said some of the draw-

ings had been done by her sister. No one had
mentioned a sister at all since the murder. Surely if she
was alive, she would have been one of the "kids" that
had wanted to speak to Calista. Gus was now motion-
ing to her.

"Obviously, we've got a little problem here with
Bootsie." His voice was a husky whisper as he bent his
head down to speak closely to Calista. Gus Kingsley
was a tall man, early fifties, with a gangly kind of
grace. "Well, it's not your problem," he quickly
amended. "It's just that as you might have guessed,
she has a problem with alcohol. It understandably gets
worse under stress like this. She's a binger." He
paused. "I was a quiet but steady drunk myself."
Calista's eyes widened at this sudden admission. "I'm
a recovering alcoholic," he said simply. And then
Calista's question was answered. "Muffy, our other
sister, died of it."

"Has Bootsie made any attempts to recover?"

"Not really. You see, in a sense she was never as..."
He stopped and searched for a word. "As obviously
impaired as we were. And quite frankly, she didn't
drink as much. But lately, Mother and I both noticed
it's been getting worse. And we're worried about all
the pills she takes."

"What kind of pills?"

"Well, she does have some sort of thyroid condition. So she takes something for that. She claims that
the doctor said she could drink with these . . . but I'm
not sure if that's exactly the truth. Or maybe the doctor doesn't know quite how much she drinks. And
then she's always had insomnia problems. And Jamie's a real handful lately. So she's been a nervous

wreck over him. She mentioned that the doctor gave her something to calm her nerves.''

''Oh God,'' Calista sighed.

''Yeah, right,'' Gus said in a tired voice. She looked at him. He had very tired, shadowed eyes. They were almost unreadable. But she liked him. He had a simplicity about him, a directness. He seemed terribly concerned about Bootsie. ''Well, I must run. Pick up Uncle Rudy. You'll see him at the funeral. He's quite bizarre!''

''Oh!'' Well, maybe there will be something to look forward to at the funeral, after all, Calista thought.

Just then, a young boy about Charley's age came bounding up the steps. ''Jamie!'' Gus said, his face brightening. But Jamie whizzed right by his uncle. ''Might you at least say hello to Calista Jacobs here, the woman who discovered Grandma?''

''Hello,'' he said without turning his head. It was as spectacular a display of rudeness as only a profoundly angry adolescent could muster.

NINE

CALISTA STOOD nervously on the corner of Park and Tremont. She was scanning the people drifting along the paths that cut diagonally across the Common in the rising heat of the morning. No sign of Charley. She felt stupid standing there with his sports jacket, shirt, and tie on a hanger. Just where did he plan to change? A phone booth? It hadn't been her idea that he come to the funeral. He had volunteered, managed to find someone to fill in for him at the swan boats and would work a double-duty lunch break in return. Where there was a will, there was a way—and Charley wanted to go to the funeral, "scope it out," as he put it. She knew why. It was a challenge in the same way the electronic mazes of the computer challenged him. There was a code to be broken, passwords to be generated, access systems to be cracked. Suddenly, she saw him walking toward her. He certainly did not have the mien of one going to a funeral. He bounced along with an easy gait that defied both the rising heat and the occasion.

"Howdy doo, Tiggy-Mom."

"Try to restrain your ebullience, Charley."

"You look so Mrs. Tiggy-Winkle-ish—your hair is really out there."

"I know. It's the humidity." She handed him the hanger with the jacket and shirt, then touched the mass of silvery hair that foamed around her head. She tried to reanchor some of it with her industrial-strength barrettes. "Listen," she said, a bobby pin in her mouth, "where are you planning on changing for this event?"

"No problem." He took the shirt off the hanger, handed the rest back to her, and proceeded to slip it over his swan boat T-shirt. Within fifty feet of King's Chapel, he was knotting his tie. As they started up the steps, he put on the jacket. Calista had chucked the hanger into a trash can. They joined a throng of somber people. Under their summer tans, they all wore a strained look—not so much out of sorrow as from being called back to Boston from summer homes on the Cape, the Vineyard, Manchester-by-the-Sea, the coast of Maine, camps on tranquil golden lakes in New Hampshire or Canada for this tragic, yes, but ultimately confusing end to a life properly led. Indeed, Quintana Kingsley could have avoided all of this if she had gone up to Nohqwha, the family's lake retreat in New Hampshire. But alas, their house up there had been undergoing major reconstruction and was not ready. Perhaps it couldn't have been avoided even if she had gone away. There was no forced entry into the house. Nothing had been stolen. It looked for all intents and purposes as if Quintana might have known her murderer. So he or she could have achieved their goal at Nohqwha as well as at Louisburg Square.

Calista and Charley slipped into a boxed pew. There was a handsome family that looked as if it had just changed out of tennis gear across from her. Calista had forgotten this quaint detail of the first Church of England in the Massachusetts Bay Colony—the occupants of these boxed pews must sit facing one another. It was slightly unsettling given the occasion.

The rector began. A simple prayer from the Book of Common Prayer, as simple and spare as the clean lines of a dory. No room for ambiguity; perhaps that was the whole point. It was a prayer about accepting the blessings of life with grace and basically shutting up about the mysterious ways in which God works; plain New England homespun. No kvetching here. Shut up: That set the tone for the rest of the service. These people didn't know what they were missing by not being Jewish, Calista thought. She looked over at Charley. He was discreetly scanning the mourners. They all sat behind stony faces. Occasionally, an eye brimmed; there might be a sniffle or two. That was all. Calista spotted Bootsie. She sat in a pew just under a north window. Although deathly pale, she possessed a radiance; she seemed created out of nuances of light and shadow that at certain angles became dazzling. As Calista looked at Bootsie, it struck her that she seemed not quite real, but indeed like a creation of fluid brushstrokes. She could have been a portrait by John Singer Sargent. She had that ethereal yet slightly agitated quality that one associated with his women subjects: light dancing on surface, a high-strung nervous energy. It had once been said that Sargent's women were "the product of an age of nerves." That had been an era when nerves, and high-strung tension, had been elevated to a near art form. It had been just before the suffrage movement got under way, a little before Elizabeth Cady Stanton. There had been nothing but nerves for these women. They had done it well, with great style and grace; it had not been kvetching.

Even from a distance, Bootsie's eyes were remarkable, great enormous pastel smears amongst the light and shadow of her face. She stood between her son and a very elderly man. Next to the man was Gus. One could pick out the Kingsleys. There was a strong family resemblance that ran through, indicated by wide-set eyes in faces that often seemed a tad small. Kingsleys also favored high foreheads and rounded chins, with a somewhat pinched look about their noses. Of course, who knew whether the look was Kingsley or Parkington, Quintana's family. It was hard to sort these features out.

But who were all of these people at the hub of the hub, anyway? It was Oliver Wendell Holmes who had declared back in 1858 that the Boston State House was the Hub of the solar system. The name had stuck. Boston was, most Bostonians thought, the most civilized city in the world, and these people gathered in the chapel where George Washington had worshiped, with a bell made by Paul Revere, were the most civilized of the civilized. The pews were spiked with Saltonstalls, Welds, Cabots, Lodges, Forbes, and Perkins—and Baldwins. Not Nan and Will, but Calista thought she had spotted a cousin of Will's. There was a whiff to all of them—many looked overbred and underfed. The middle-aged matrons wore their darker summer wear from Talbots and some carried their Nantucket lightship wicker pocketbooks with the scrimshaw medallions on their covers. The older ones stood erect in sagging suits excavated from dry-cleaning bags, most likely Falk's, a Brookline cleaner favored by old families. Nan Baldwin had told her that once upon a time when you took your clothes to Falk's, they came back wrapped in thin paper with a tag that read: "If you send your clothes to Falk's, you can be sure these clothes will not hang next to someone's whose acquaintance you would not want to make."

There was most certainly an elitism, but that could not explain it all in Boston, the Hub. It was an elitism that had grown out of privilege. There was a difference, however: The privilege was not to be enjoyed for its own pleasure. Rather, with it there was a concomitant tradition of responsibility. If a person was born into one of the first families of Boston, that person was obligated to set a tone; there had to be certain standards, and these standards involved realizing your duty toward others. It was a sense of stewardship that came with the facts of privileged birth. Calista had no idea whether such values still persisted in many members of the Kingsley family, or other's families, for that matter. Blood had thinned out often along with brains and money over the generations. However, that sense of stewardship and responsibility was definitely alive and well in Nan and Will Baldwin and their son Archie and his siblings. They had the imagination to branch out, to see a broader world. But in many ways, the narrow world of Boston was still a very tight one, and Calista wondered whether indeed the Hub moved in relation to anything else.

The service was mercifully short. Quintana's life was not one that lent itself to elaboration or embellishment. She was not a Harriet Hemenway or a Minna Hall, pioneers in the turn-of-the-century environmental and suffrage movements and founders of the Audubon Society. And she certainly did not have the style and the money of a Mrs. Jack Gardner. Her life had revolved around the Chilton Club, the Friday-afternoon symphony, the Horticulture Society, and the annual Ellis Antiques Show.

The most colorful flourish of the funeral was an arrangement on the altar of three obscure lilies and a shaft of wheat from Ikebana Unit Number 9, a Japanese flower-arranging society to which Quintana Kingsley had belonged. And there were amidst all these Brahmins two or three Oriental faces. During the eulogy, there were several references to the sea because of the Kingsley-Parkington connection with Salem and shipping. Quintana's Colonial forebears had been heavily involved with coastal trading, and the Kingsleys of that generation had started out in the Derby wharf countinghouses of Salem and then went on to own clippers that sailed to Canton in the China Trade. Thus, the rector concluded his eulogy on the long, privileged, but simple life of Quintana Kingsley with a quote from an Emily Dickinson poem: "Exaltation is the going of an inland soul to sea . . ."

Calista loved this poem. Would those words not give some comfort to any grieving relative? She looked over toward Bootsie. Bootsie was no longer a composition of light and shadow. Her face had hardened into a venomous mask, rigid and taut, ready to crack not from grief but hatred. Calista inhaled sharply. It was a shocking face.

TEN

It was announced at the end of the service that guests were invited back to the home of the deceased's brother Diggory Parkington on Marlborough Street. "Let's go," Charley whispered.

"Well, I think I should, but really, Charley, I don't want you getting fired."

"Don't worry. I'll only stay for a little bit."

It was a venerable old building, a stone's throw from the Public Garden and one of the few on the entire street not condo-ized or owned by a college or some other institution. Built of gray stone, tall and narrow, with the stern rectitude of a Calvinist minister, the austerity of the exterior gave way to the something else almost immediately. As soon as a person stepped through the door into an octagonal foyer, one was ambushed by portraits of Italian cherubs in oval recessions in the walls. Of course, thought Calista as a uniformed maid directed her to a powder room on the second floor, the house was probably bought and decorated during the time of Mrs. Jack Gardner, who had built an Italian villa in the Fenway to house her haul of art acquired from Europe under the exquisite connoisseurship of Berenson. But it was Calista's guess that the Parkingtons not only lacked the style but the nerve of Mrs. Jack. There was immediately detectable a slight disharmony in terms of proportion and aesthetics. This was confirmed as she waited outside the powder room in a small drawing room on the second floor. There were several bucolic court paintings of the Watteau school juxtaposed with Oriental embroideries and geegaws from the China Trade. The woman who had sat across from her in the pew came out of the powder room and gave her a terse nod and a smile that could possibly have been measured in millimeters. Calista was set to give her a very warm hello. After all, they had shared the pew on an occasion that should have lent itself toward something a bit more congenial in terms of a greeting. Boxed in at King's Chapel in that sort of intimacy, even if formal and imposed, should count for something. Well, forget it.

Calista went into the powder room and tried to do something with her hair. All these WASPs with their straight hair like shining helmets on their well-shaped heads, and here she was with this froth of gray—no, silver; Archie said it was silver. She took out her pocket-sized can of hair spray—hair Mace she called it, for it was more of an act of subjugation than coiffing. In two minutes, the enemy was contained in a fairly attractive nimbus of silvery curls piled atop her head, with a few discreet tendrils falling around the edges. She took a pee, washed her hands, and went downstairs.

Diggory Parkington, a frail-looking man the color of parchment paper, was greeting guests while leaning on a walker. A nurse stood at his side. There was really no way to avoid him, but Calista worried exactly how she would explain herself. Would the knowledge that she indeed had been the one to discover the body be too much for the old soul, who looked ready to blow away with the first riffle of a wind?

"And who might you be?" He leaned forward. His bald skull had an intaglio of blue veins and Calista could imagine an aneuryism blowing up in front of her very eyes.

"Calista Jacobs, just a friend of Quintana's through gardening—Japanese gardening."

"Oh, an Ikebana gal!" He shook her hand warmly; a gracious smile, and then she moved on.

As she walked through a front parlor into the living room, she spotted Charley talking with Jamie McPhee by a table with platters of food. She scanned the room for Bootsie and spotted her, drink in hand, talking animatedly to a middle-aged man. She seemed propped up by the sheer animation of her talk. Her hands flew in antic gestures. A coquettish rictus twitched across her face. She would turn her shoulders this way and that in a constant series of minute adjustments, almost like a fashion model trying to arrange herself in the camera's lens. But it was all a jangle of nerves masked by poses and chatter and gesture.

"Here, how about a drink?" Calista felt a light touch on her elbow. It was Gus Kingsley. "The last thing she needs," he said, nodding toward his sister. "This is Pimm's with a slice of cucumber. It can be quite restorative on a day like this."

"Oh, thank you, thank you so much. Has she really been drinking all morning?"

"Actually, I don't think so. It might very possibly be the pills."

"This all sounds terribly dangerous. Have you talked to her doctor?"

"Oh yes. Everyone has talked to her doctor. And he has tried to wean her from the pills. But she still finds ways of getting them, and she is not inclined to do anything about the drinking. It's just a really difficult situation and it's not doing any good for Jamie. I just met your son, by the way—Charley. They are over there talking together. Very nice young fellow."

"Oh, thank you. You know your mother had asked if maybe Charley could get Jamie a job on the swan boats—that's where he's working this summer."

"Oh, that would be terrific. . . ." Gus's face brightened.

"Gussy!" Two long, elegant, and tanned arms snaked around Gus's middle.

"Bambi, dear."

I don't believe these names, Calista thought. She turned. Bambi was none other than her pew mate. Great. Oh well, no WASP princess called Bambi was going to undo her. Calista extended her hand immediately before Gus had a chance to introduce her. "Calista Jacobs." Then she turned to Gus. "We shared a pew." No getting out of it, cutie pie.

Bambi's mouth opened partway, just to that point on Calista's oven called "the broil position"—for the door when you want to run convection.

"You're not the one who does the children's books, are you . . . that Calista Jacobs?"

"Yes."

"Oh my Gawd! I don't believe it. Wait till I find Maisie and Tigger. You are their absolute favorite."

Great. So now you can smile at me and act civil instead of like upstairs, where it looked as if you thought that I might pee on your head instead of in the toilet. Calista assumed that Maisie and Tigger were children and not pets. "And you're Archie Baldwin's friend, aren't you?"

"Yes."

"Ah Gawd, he is so handsome." She ran her long fingers up across her forehead in one of those calculated gestures that people of little substance often use to punctuate their conversations. "He's older than I am, of course, but we all had crushes on him—you know, back then, Waltz Evenings and deb parties."

"Archie never cottoned to that sort of thing, as I recall," said Gus. "Never went to many, unless he was roped in to it."

"Yes, I would imagine that would be true. It fits," Calista said.

"So bright, though!" Bambi said, leaning forward. Again it was a gesture meant to convey understanding of Archie's work and career, yet it masked the fact that this woman knew absolutely nothing of what Archie did. This was, of course, the art of small talk. It let the conversation run on with no one getting into deep doo-doo.

"Where's Archie now?" Gus asked.

"Guatemala—Batan Grande, a Mayan site...." She was starting to lose Bambi, she could tell.

"Listen, dear." Bambi was slipping her arm through Gus's. "I really came here on a mission: to abduct dear Gussie to come over and see Grummy in the library." She turned to Calista. "Gus has always been a favorite of Grummy's, my grandmother, and she can't walk. Grummy was Queenie's cousin. So I hope you don't mind me taking him off like this...."

"Oh no, not at all."

"I'll see you, Calista," he said as Bambi led him away.

Bambi tossed a broad smile over her shoulder at Calista. "It's great meeting you. A real celebrity!"

Celebrity my foot, asshole. Calista smiled back sweetly. Just then, she remembered whom Bambi reminded her of—Jordan Baker, the athletic Long Island beauty in *The Great Gatsby* who cheated at tennis. And she bet dollars to doughnuts that Bambi was cheating at something else here. She didn't believe for one minute that bit about Grummy. Oh maybe she was in the library, but there was something about the way Bambi leaned into Gus's body that suggested the library was just an interim stop to someplace else.

Calista stood there trying to look occupied with her drink while simultaneously taking in more of the room. The room was a grand salon with marquetry parquet floors, worn Oriental rugs, twenty-foot-high ceilings, and a massive fireplace. She moved toward a long table supported by griffins on which some food had been set out. Cucumber sandwiches, brittle little crackers with some sort of repulsive-looking paste smeared on them, and a ham that had been hacked at most brutally by an inept carver. She couldn't help but recall Quintana, a mere seventy-two hours before, ministering with her delicate instruments to her ancient plants. But then her mind was flooded by the horrible image of the shears, the blossom of blood spreading on the chest. It had not been spreading, however, when she had discovered Quintana. It had already stopped. So why, Calista wondered, did her mind always see it in motion—the bloom unfolding like time-lapse photography of a blossom opening on a plant?

She took another sip of her drink and looked around some more. She was standing near a tall Palladian window with elaborate velvet drapery. In the middle of the window, there was a palm in an immense chinoiserie pot. It had a bad case of aphids or mites. She wasn't sure which. The lower fronds were desiccated and beginning to wither. As she looked down, she spotted a dead mouse nestled in the bottom of the drapery fringe that brushed the floor. To one side of the window were two hand-colored lithographs of something Egyptian. She moved closer to examine them. One was the Great Temple of Ammon in Karnak; the inscription on the other was the Grand Portico of the Temple of Isis in Philae. They were exquisite lithographs by none other than David Roberts, a nineteenth-century Scottish lithographer. Calista had studied folios of his work at the Tate in London. She would guess these to be the most valuable pieces in the house. As she gazed around the shabby splendor of the room, she realized that what she was looking at was the real thing! This, in fact, was uncorrected Ralph Lauren. Ralph reinvented the past, leaving out the dead mouse, velvet drapes worn so thin that the sunlight came through, the aphids on the palm. Lauren's vision was always more perfect than the past ever had been. Truly the pluperfect! But this untouched history, this peculiar *tableau vivant* of cold roast Boston, was terribly exotic in its own way. And what, thought Calista, was that poised in an arched doorway like some strange hothouse plant? The sight did not just catch her eye but arrested her entire attention. The man was the most peculiar-looking creature Calista had ever seen.

"Mom, I've got to go now or I'll be late. That kid Jamie is going to meet me over there later. I think they might hire him."

Charley had come up behind her and was speaking quietly in her ear, but Calista could not take her eyes off the figure in the doorway. "Charley, over there in the doorway, do you know who that man is?"

"Man?"

THE FIGURE WAS most definitely odd-looking and certainly seemed to fall between genders. Small, quite thin, the gentleman stood erect in an intriguingly cut suit, the jacket of which seemed midway between a Victorian frock coat and a shorter, more casual jacket. Beneath the jacket, there was a fairly sumptuous-looking waistcoat in a muted apricot color. The effect was sheer elegance. But the gentleman who wore it defied imagination. His hair was parted down the middle and obviously dyed, almost a burgundy color. His eyebrows leapt like small minnows above a pair of permanently startled-looking eyes. From Calista's vantage point, he reminded her of a deer just at the moment when it catches a whiff of the hunter. He looked about to bolt. Calista, however, hoped fervently he would not. She was inexorably drawn to him. Whoever was he? She felt a small tap on her wrist. A little voice scratched the air.

"My mom said you wrote a book we sort of like..." Calista looked down. There was a small boy of seven or eight. He stood waist-high and had the same golden blond hair as his mother. "She said we should come over and talk to you."

"She did, did she?" Calista replied in a distracted manner. Shit on Bambi! Just when things were getting interesting.

"Yep," said another little voice. Standing by the boy was a beautiful little girl of perhaps five.

"I've read all your books," said the little girl.

"No, you haven't, Maisie. You haven't read *The Boy Who Could Fly,* because we lost it before you were old enough for it. So just shut up." Then he turned to Calista. "Our mother said we should ask you what you are writing a book about now."

"Oh, she told you to ask that, did she?"

"Yep," both children answered.

"Well, how about you ask me a question that you want to ask and not your mom? A question of your very own."

"We don't have any," the boy said, and they both stood as still as small statues, looking up at her.

Great. How was she going to dump these kids? She really wanted to work over to the other side of the room and meet the peculiar little gentleman.

"You know," the little girl said suddenly, "you don't look nearly as old as your hair."

Calista bit her lip and suppressed a chuckle. There was hope for Maisie. "You know, dear, that's a marvelous observation. Maybe you'll grow up and be an artist someday."

"Hah!" The little boy laughed harshly.

Well, screw you, sonny, Calista thought. "But in the meantime, I see a very old lady in the corner and she looks as if she might enjoy some of those cookies they are serving. It might be nice if you took her some and a glass of tea."

"Oh, that's Grummy," Tigger was saying, "and she's half-crocked and she won't drink tea. They wheeled her out here so she could get away from our mom. She and Mom are always having fights."

"Oh," said Calista. The woman wore an ancient dress that involved layer upon layer of black crepe and lace. She even wore black lace gloves and a hat with a spotted veil. She was Miss Havisham togged out in widow's weeds instead of bridal finery. "Does she always dress this way, or is it just for the funeral?"

"Always!" Maisie's immense blue eyes opened even wider.

"Ever since her husband died," Tigger said. "And that happened before we were born, before Mummy was born."

"Oh dear," said Calista.

"He shot himself," Tigger offered. "With a duck-hunting gun. Blew him right to pieces, Mummy said."

Calista looked down at the two beautiful little children. "My goodness." She was thinking how boring her stories must sound next to these of Mummy's. "Well, I bet she would appreciate cookies to wash down with her uh . . ."

"Brandy," Tigger offered. "Brandy and lemonade. That's what she drinks. C'mon, Maisie," he said, tugging on his sister's hand. "This is boring."

Well, just get me in some black lace and give me a little brandy lemonade and a duck-hunting gun, Calista thought. But only briefly. She began making her way across the room.

"I AM SOOOO GLAD you made your way to our side, my deah!" The little minnow eyebrows shot up with genuine delight. "I have been admiring your hair from afar."

"Oh, why thank you."

"And as Oscar Wilde once said, only a fool would not judge from appearances." He then giggled rather maniacally.

Calista was taken aback. Who was this dear soul with his quick wit and the most beautifully tied Windsor knot she had ever seen? She was utterly charmed. She extended her hand. "I'm Calista Jacobs."

"Calista Jacobs. Two lovely names. What could possibly connect you with anyone in this room?"

"Well, it's tenuous, but significant, I guess. I'm staying in the Baldwins' house."

"Oh my heavens." He slapped his pink cheek with a small white hand. "You're the one who discovered poor old Queenie—" his voice dropped "—shears and all!" He made a small grimace with his tiny mouth as if he was tasting something bad. "Well, I'm Rudy Kingsley, Queenie's brother-in-law, but before we go any further, let me introduce you to Titty."

Calista nearly choked on her Pimm's. "Who?"

"Titty, darling." He turned, bent over, and tapped on the shoulder of someone sitting in the armchair next to him who was engaged with another very elderly woman who looked more like a soggy tea bag than a living, breathing human being. Titty turned from the tea bag and looked up at Calista. It was a face that was simply unbelievable. Pudgy and wrinkled, she had bulging eyes that peered out from under very thick eyelids. With a flattened nose, the face appeared slightly reptilian. She was virtually neckless and her puffy jowls rested on a shirred collar reminiscent of Good Queen Bess. Unfortunately, Titty had decided to wear eye makeup. So a touch of lavender with flecks of gold floated across the thick lids. She looked like a gilded toad. "Ah!" she exclaimed in a voice that seemed squeezed out of her. "The lady of the hair."

"The lady of the hour, Titty."

"Queenie?" The small eyes behind the lavender lids swam with momentary confusion.

"Calista Jacobs, the one who discovered Queenie," Rudy whispered sotto voce.

"Oh my goodness!" The pudgy hand slapped a jowl. "How terrible for you, my deah. Oh heavens, and she's not even family. How awful for someone to have to become mixed up with us." She pulled out a hankie from somewhere and began to wipe beads of perspiration from her forehead. Whatever had she meant by that last remark? Calista wondered. "I hope you'll be all right. I mean, it must have been so shocking."

"Well yes, of course, but I'll be all right; that's hardly the issue. Unfortunately..."

"Yes, Queenie will not be all right. It's absolutely unfathomable. I just can't understand it."

"Look, look at Bootsie," Calista said suddenly. She spotted Bootsie. She was standing against the heavy velvet drapes and seemed almost to be receding into the deep folds. Her eyes, however, were feverish and they were looking directly at Bambi, who was standing close to Gus, across the room.

"That poor, poor girl." Rudy sighed.

"Oh Boots?" Titty said. "Yes, poor Boots. So fragile."

"Is she okay?" Calista asked. Bootsie's eyes were no longer locked on Gus and Bambi. Instead, they were darting about the room.

"She looks like she wants to get out, doesn't she?" Rudy said.

"Don't we all?" Titty replied.

"Let me go over and rescue her," Rudy said. "Bring her back over here to our little oasis of sanity. By the way, Calista, Cousin Titty and I believe ourselves to be the only sane ones of the whole crew." He leaned forward as if to huddle with Calista and Titty. "And that's not saying much—me being an old queen."

"And me a failed debutante!" Titty broke in.

CALISTA HAD the strangest feeling. In this stuffy old Victorian house, it was as if she had climbed up onto the mantel and looked into the mirror; and the glass, just as it had in Alice's story, became "all soft like gauze, melting away like a bright silvery mist" while she, Calista, had magically passed through it into another world, entered another dimension. Nothing seemed to be what it really was and these two very curious creatures—one, this...this Red Queen—were to be her guides! She watched Rudy as he scurried across the room toward Bootsie and gently led her over to Calista and Titty. Would the clocks start talking next? The pictures come alive, the cherubs jump from their frames, the bosomy court ladies spill from the oval panels and accost the gentlemen? Would the pharaohs at the Temple of Karnak climb from their tombs?

"Calista! Isn't that the most marvelous name. Well, as you know, I'm a sucker for anything Greek. We need to get everyone here a refill," Rudy announced, snapping his fingers to flag down a serving girl. "Pimm's here for Calista? What are you drinking, Boots—vodka?"

"No, no, just some white wine." That was interesting, Calista thought. From what she'd seen yesterday and what Gus had said, she would have guessed Bootsie to be into higher-proof stuff.

"Titty, I know you—sherry. Gawd, darling, how you do it in this heat, I'll never know. And just two fingers of scotch on the rocks with a twist for me." He nodded at the serving girl. Calista liked Rudy's way with the woman who brought the drinks. There was no condescension. It was strictly business, but there was a gentleness and respect for the young woman and the job, which couldn't have been an easy one. This was a man used to being around servants and running a household.

"Now you must tell us all about your name. As I was saying, I just love anything Greek—"

"And your hair..." Titty broke in.

"Oh come on, guys." Calista laughed. She couldn't believe it, but she was actually enjoying herself quite a bit, and she had dreaded coming.

"No, we're serious." Rudy rolled his eyes.

"Well, if I tell you that, you have to tell me about your tailor and your beautiful tie."

"Oh, I'm so glad you noticed." Rudy looked down at his magenta-and-blue tie with the tiny design. "Boots, darling, it's a Guards tie, belonged to an old intimate of mine. One only wears a Brigadier tie after six o'clock or at the annual wreath-laying in the Guards Chapel. I felt the occasion warranted it."

Calista was sure that Bootsie's eyes would spill celadon tears. She leaned forward and kissed Rudy on the cheek. "Thank you, Uncle Rudy," she whispered. Then she said, "You know, the least interesting thing about Calista is her name and her hair. She is a wonderful children's book artist."

"Oh my word...how marvelous."

Rudy and Titty were awash in convulsions of praise, although neither one had ever seen her work. "I knew you didn't fit in here; I just knew it!" Titty was saying. Apparently, in her mind, this was the highest compliment one could give.

"Tell me, dear, have you done any of the Greek myths for children?" Rudy was asking. Suddenly, it burst upon Calista who Rudy Kingsley was. All those statues, the lovely Greek torsos, the lovely Greek boys, indeed some of the major Hellenic pieces in the Museum of Fine Arts had been donated by R. W. Kingsley years ago. She had heard about him. She was sure Nan and Will Baldwin had mentioned him, now that she thought about it. She must call them tonight. They had already called, anxious about her safety and any news she might have about the murder.

"Oh my goodness!" Titty moaned. "She's coming our way."

"Who?" Calista asked.

"The meanest lady in Boston."

"I'm getting out of here," Bootsie said. "If she asks me about that fucking portrait one more time..."

"Oh Gawd no! She's still on that?" Rudy sighed.

It was the lady in black lace being wheeled by her attendant toward them.

"Hello, darling Cornelia!" Rudy trilled.

"Don't you look ridiculous." The old lady growled and proffered a heavily powdered cheek for a kiss.

"Aren't you afraid I might have AIDS, darling?"

"What's that?"

"Ye gods!" Titty murmured.

It was at this juncture that Calista decided she should go. But neither Rudy nor Titty was letting her slip off without making a date. "Tomorrow noon, luncheon at the Ritz."

Why not? Calista thought, and accepted enthusiastically. It might be murder that had brought them together, but Rudy and Titty were about the most interesting people she had met in a long time.

ELEVEN

"TITTY? HER NAME IS actually Titty?" Charley blinked in disbelief. They were back on Louisburg Square, eating Chinese takeout on the small terrace. Calista was grateful that an immense hedge of yew blocked the Kingsleys' greenhouse from her sight.

"You have to get used to it with these people. They all have funny nicknames—especially the women."

"Who was their dad, Walt Disney?"

"Well, I'll tell you one thing, Titty and Rudy are great. I think Gus is very nice, too, actually. So is Bootsie, for that matter. She just has a little drinking problem. What's her son like, by the way?"

"I don't know. He's a little weird. But he showed up to talk to them about working. He's got the job, as far as I can tell. They really do need people."

"How do you mean, weird?"

"I don't know just...you know, weird...like it's hard to explain just weird...you know..."

Calista had heard it all before, a kind of teenage aphasia, an inarticulate loop of monosyllabic jargon—*weird, cool, major weirdness, sucks*. These words were then punctuated at frequent intervals with *you know*. One became used to it as an elemental narrative form in what passed for conversation. Put these kids in a majorly cool nineteenth-century drawing room—like, you know, Jane Austen's and, you know...so much for literature. *Pride and Prejudice* down the toilet along with *Barchester Towers, Mid-*

dlemarch, and the rest of the majorly talky books of manners and morals.

They cleaned up after dinner. Charley helped administer the various medicines to Piss and Moan, then retired to his room, Archie's old room. Three nights a week, he was sys op, a systems operator on Channel 1, a computer bulletin board. He could sys-op out of wherever he happened to be as long as he set up the access. And he made twice as much money doing this as he did pedaling swan boats, but Calista had insisted that he do something in addition to computer work this summer. She lived in constant fear of raising an electronic nerd, and Charley had made great strides in the past few years, particularly since Archie had come into their lives.

Shortly after Tom had been killed, Charley had gone into a kind of withdrawal and seemed to derive all he needed from wandering the electronic mazes of computers. His best friends were electronic buddies on the other ends of modems. The world they shared was on bulletin boards, where they swapped information and played games. He was smart and he was skillful. From the time he was twelve, he had been programming freelance for departments around MIT and Harvard. When he was thirteen, he had worked in a summer program for talented Cambridge youth at the Martin Institute, a big cancer-research center. He had written a code with his friends Matthew and Louise for imaging crystallography in its application for protein folding in cellular structure. He had also become pale and soft. No more totally indoor summers, Calista vowed; hence, the swan boats.

Calista went into Will Baldwin's study, where she had set up her drawing board, and began to work on

The Emperor and the Nightingale. She had read many versions of the tale and then retold it in what she felt was a sparer way than some that seemed overly embellished. She was searching for a cadence both in words and illustration that came closest to haiku, or at least something that suggested East and not West in terms of storytelling. She had completed a dummy and now was beginning to work on the second big spread, the one that would have Quintana's needle juniper shrouded in fog. She took out the sketches she had made in the greenhouse on that last afternoon. She wanted the branches of the juniper to melt out of the mist. The negative space in this was more important than the positive. Somewhat like the enigma of Quintana, she suddenly thought. Indeed, the notion was so provocative that she put down her brush, which she was just preparing to dip in the ink wash.

What did she actually know of Quintana Parkington Kingsley? In so many ways, all of these Brahmins with their carefully constructed lives conducted in time-honored patterns carried out in venerable institutions and clubs seemed almost interchangeable. A tiny little world rotating in a tight orbit that moved in a peculiar rhythm related to nothing else. These lives were well documented in one sense because the orbits were so small and so predictable. There were no secrets, or were there? Calista picked up a page of her dummy, with a line of text running across the bottom. "*'Like bells of glass!' exclaimed the emperor. 'Like silver chimes! You must come and live and sing in my palace.'*

"*'But,' replied the nightingale, 'my song is far better among the green trees, the notes more beautiful in*

*the fog of the morning, the rhythms dance with the
stars of the open sky.'"*

Why did these lines suddenly have such resonance
for Calista? Yes, it was a story of control, perfection,
artifice, and finally genuine risk. It was about losing
something. Why suddenly was she seeing those handless pictures of Bootsie's? The arms chopped off into
stumpy nothingness swam in her mind.

There would be no drawing tonight. She needed to
think. She went downstairs and poured herself a huge
glass of ice water. The Chinese food had made her incredibly thirsty. She undressed and put on a light
wrapper and went out onto the balcony with the ice
water. It was a thick August night. The stars sim-
mered in the sky. The moths seemed to sag in their
swirling flights around the halos of outdoor garden
lights. Calista thought about Bootsie, hopped-up eyes
darting, darting as if she was trying to escape. She had
seen that look before. Once years ago, she had gone to
a reading by the poet Anne Sexton. Sexton was reading her poetry to the accompaniment of a jazz ensem-
ble. The group was called Anne Sexton and Her Kind.
It was an experience to hear her, to watch her. The
throaty cigarette-thickened voice, the mad eyes sliding about the room as if to seek out the exits, the heat
from her soul nearly palpable.

Calista got up suddenly. In the library downstairs,
there was a shelf of poetry. Nan Baldwin was particularly fond of the confessional poets. She found them
"refreshing." That, of course, was why Nan was not
like half the women Calista had seen at Diggory Parkington's on Marlborough Street that afternoon.

There was a row of Anne Sexton's books. Calista
went right to *Transformations*. She owned the book

herself. The poems were blistering reenactments of Grimm's fairy tales. As one of the foremost illustrators of fairy tales in the world, Calista was more than familiar with them. They were not all good poems by any means. They were indulgent often, superficial and a bit facile at times, but they were also unequivocally a dark plunge into the very belly of the fairy-tale beast. She opened the book right to the poem she wanted: "The Maiden Without Hands."

> *Is it possible*
> *he marries the cripple*
> *out of admiration?*
> *A desire to own the maiming....*
> *Lady, bring me your wooden leg*
> *so I may stand on my own*
> *two pink pig feet.*

The terrible words floated across the page with their immutable blood-drenched truth:

> *Once*
> *there was a cruel father*
> *who cut off his daughter's hands*
> *to escape from the wizard.*
> *The maiden held her stumps*
> *as helpless as dog's paws*
> *and that made the wizard*
> *want her. He wanted to lap*
> *her up like strawberry preserve.*

Calista finished the poem and shut her eyes tightly. Something before murder had happened in this family. She was sure. Countless little murders, ones where there is no corpse—because the corpse is hidden, hidden in a facsimile of life. How clever.

And then out of the thick heat of the night, out of the soft charcoal darkness, another image floated toward Calista. She could barely perceive it. A boat with white flowers? No, with clouds, winged clouds? No, feathers. A swan boat. Would that make sense? No... no. She got up and found her sketch pad and flipped back through the pages. Here it was—the suggestion of a swan, in a tiny thumbnail sketch done with graphite and charcoal melting out of the smudged night—wings, a slender neck, created by the absence of darkness, by Calista rubbing with an eraser and sometimes with her own saliva.

"One could think of whores and not imagine the way of a swan..." Or was it "One could think of swans but not imagine the way of a whore..."? Did it come from Sexton? She thought so. She looked through *Transformations* but could not find the line. She went back to the shelf and searched in the other books. Still she could not find it. It had to be there someplace. She was sure. She would look again tomorrow. She was too tired now.

TWELVE

"PEOPLE HAVE sometimes called Oscar House a living museum. But I myself take offense at that," Rudy said primly, and patted his mouth with a beautiful paisley handkerchief after taking a sip from his martini. They were at a window table in the Ritz dining room, overlooking Arlington Street and the Public Garden. Rudy was well known at the Ritz. He had told Calista as soon as he sat down that although he always stayed at the Harvard Club, he ate most of his meals at the Ritz.

"Well, if you take offense, that's it!" Titty said in her small voice. "You dreamed the whole idea up. You can't imagine how lovely it is, Calista. On occasion, they make exceptions and allow women visitors."

"Oh, we certainly would for Calista. I can't think of a better candidate. You understand, I rather see Oscar House not as a living museum, and certainly not a memorial to Oscar Wilde—I mean I had to call it something—and although Wilde died in 1900 and I was not born until...well, some few years later, we did overlap in one small but significant way." Rudy's eyes glinted and fine lines creased the corners of his mouth as he smiled softly. Then his eyes seemed to grow dim, but the smile stayed. It was as if he were stepping back in time, through scores of years.

"One of Oscar's last lovers was my first. It was, shall we say, a seminal experience. Hence, Oscar House. I think of it as an academy, a place where young men—and now many have grown old—can come and think and play and study amongst beautiful things. But they were not just students. They were and are curators to all of these wonderful antiquities. It was required that they learn the art of conservation; the business of cataloging and assembling and displaying. Many of my 'graduates' have become curators and directors and appraisers around the world; speaking of which, I must try and contact Leon while I am here, even if I can't get down to New York.''

"Leon? Leon Mauritz?'' Calista asked.

"Yes, my dear. Do you know him?''

"I've met him just a couple of times. But Archie deals with him quite a bit.''

"Of course, Archie Baldwin would—New World antiquities. And there's been so much looting. You can bet Leon will know who the buyers are.'' Rudy paused. "Yes, Leon is interesting in that sense.''

Calista knew exactly what Rudy was talking about, for she had often heard Archie on the subject of Leon. For all intents and purposes, Mauritz operated scrupulously within the law, and particularly within the confines of the new ones prohibiting the selling of antiquities; he had, however, a profound knowledge of those who did not. As Archie had said more than once, with Leon there was only one side to be on—his good side.

"Well, I did not mean to digress here with Leon,'' Rudy resumed. "As I was explaining about Oscar House: Over the years as my collection grew, many of these pieces went out on loan to museums. You see, the residents of Oscar House lived amidst all this art and they were trained to care for it and were ultimately inspired by it.''

"It's a theory, an aesthetic theory that Rudy has. He's written articles on it. The positive benefits from living in the midst of beauty, caring for it and all that."

"There's even a biofeedback doctor who has come to study the effects of it in terms of respiration and metabolism. I don't quite understand it, but apparently there is an ideal physiological set point for each body, and Dr. Watkins feels that the ideal proportions, et cetera, of Hellenistic art, in particular, can, in fact, induce healthful body rhythms.

"Even more than an academy, I think of Oscar House as a kind of library, along the lines of the great library of Alexandria. You know, a miniversion devoted to the antiquities and cultivating the kind of thought and aesthetic that can inspire creative minds. I founded it with my first real profits."

The waiter had just arrived and began to serve. Calista had cold salmon; Titty, the Ritz chicken salad; and Rudy, scrod. He looked down at his plate with the perfectly cooked piece of scrod, golden and plump in its thick crust of bread crumbs.

"This, of course, is a major reason for coming to Boston—scrod. The most unprepossessing of fish, called cod most other places, its numbers declining daily. But caught by our forebears for centuries and shipped salted-down in Kingsley vessels in the triangular trade. Ah, scrod!" Rudy's voice swelled with the encomium. "Well, cheers, ladies!" He lifted his martini in a jaunty salute.

"Rudy, what did you mean when you said your 'first real profits'?" Calista asked.

"Well, my dear, in our family, as in so many of these old Boston families, the fortunes were made in the last century. Substantial enough, they were nursed along and sometimes indeed did grow . . . but—"

"Rudy," interrupted Titty. "I can tell you're going to be much too modest about all this. To make a long story short, Rudy was the only person of his generation, possibly the last two generations, really to make money." Titty set down her fork. The gilded eyes sparkled and she raised her hands to emphasize her point. The chubby fingers spread out in a fanlike gesture. "I mean really make money. How much was it, Rudy, with that drug firm in the Midwest?"

"Don't be coarse, Titty."

Titty dissolved in giggles over this. "You see, the whole point was that Rudy was supposed to be a fairy and fairies weren't supposed to have any head for money, and Kingie, Quintana's husband, was . . . you know—what's that word they use now for virile?"

"Macho," offered Calista.

"Yes. That's it, macho. And machos are supposed to make money. You know, do everything."

"Titty has a way of oversimplifying things," Rudy commented.

"Well, the point is that Kingie never made a dime of his own and our own little fairy here—" she turned and patted Rudy on the shoulder "—has made all the dough!"

"Did you do it all through the stock market?" Calista asked.

"Oh heavens, no. A lot through the art world. I began collecting stuff just for that purpose—you know, things that I knew I would never want as part of the family."

"That's what he calls his antiquities—the family."

"Like what?"

"Oh, for example, I never really liked de Kooning—but I knew his stuff would catch on. Same with Rothko. Then I made an awful lot in real estate."

"You see, they hate to admit that someone with—as they always said—Rudy's tendencies could make money and be a good businessman."

"Business fairy," Rudy said, and they both were seized by raucous fits of giggles. Rudy then took out the beautiful handkerchief from his breast pocket and wiped the tears from his eyes. "Oh my dear, you have no idea what it was like, what it is still like in one of these old families."

"No... no," said Calista softly, and she thought of the handless maiden and "a desire to own the maiming."

"Are you all right?" Both Rudy and Titty leaned forward at once, alarmed by the sudden change in Calista's face.

Calista bit her lip lightly. "What happened to Bootsie?" There was almost a stricken look in Titty's face, and Rudy reached out and patted her plump hand that lay as limp as a dead fish on the peach tablecloth. "And Muffy, Bootsie's sister? She died of alcoholism?"

Rudy squared his shoulders and looked straight ahead. "She died because she put a rope around her neck and hung herself." Titty squeezed her eyes shut as if to banish a terrible picture.

"I'm... I'm..." Calista stammered. "I'm so sorry I brought this up."

"There is no need to be sorry," Rudy said dryly. Titty gave him a furtive look. Rudy now sighed deeply. "There is a long history of troubled women in our family, and one cannot help but wonder if in some way Quintana's death is a continuation of that trouble."

"Troubles!" Titty seemed to come back to life. "You're sounding positively Irish, Rudy. You know, one always thinks of the Irish as so emotional, but when it comes to the really major things, Northern Ireland, for example, they refer to it as 'the troubles.' Or I remember a lovely Irish lady, a seamstress I used to go to. She referred to Hitler as 'the problem.' She had a sister in County Clare—you know, back then nobody knew how far Hitler might go. 'The problem'! she called him!" Titty's voice rose with indignation.

"I'm sorry, Titty dear. I didn't mean to belittle."

"Oh, Rudy, of course not. I know you better than that." She now reached over and patted his hand.

"Well, do you think that all this somehow relates to Quintana's murder?" Calista asked.

"Oh, it's hard to imagine." Rudy shook his head.

"Do the police have any ideas?" Titty asked. "I mean, obviously robbery was not a motive and there is no sign that the person broke in."

"Well, that is a moot point in a sense," Rudy offered, "seeing as she was working in the greenhouse, to which there are numerous access ways through the Connecting Gardens, no doubt."

"Exactly," said Calista. "If you could get into the gardens, it would be no trouble getting into the greenhouse. There are two doors—one directly out into the gardens and the other connecting to the house itself."

"So we cannot assume that she must have known who it was and simply let the person in. A stranger could have gotten into the greenhouse easily enough and found her there," Rudy said.

"But why would a stranger come and murder her there if he didn't want to steal something?" Titty said.

"Oh Lord, if she had only gone up to Nohqwha. She could have stayed at Bambi's on the other side of the island until the construction was over."

"I don't think Quintana cared for Bambi any more than the rest of us."

"What's with Bambi?" Calista asked.

"Oh nothing really—I guess. Except she's rather like her grandmother Cornelia. And people can never forgive women like Cornelia."

"Why?" Calista asked.

"Because she survived unscathed," Titty said simply.

SURVIVED WHAT? The question was left begging. But Calista didn't quite have the nerve to ask it. Rudy and Titty together presented a strange mixture of resignation, bitterness, and nerves that discouraged Calista from prying. These vague references to histories of troubles were not to be dismissed with a pat diagnosis of alcoholism. They were holding something back. She was sure. But now was not the time to push.

Calista returned to 16 Louisburg Square. She worked for the rest of the afternoon. Charley came home and reported that Jamie had indeed shown up for work and been hired. Charley had plans to go to a concert on the Esplanade with Matthew. Matthew would come back and spend the night with Charley. Calista was glad. The more people in the house, the better she felt.

THEN WHY HAD it taken her forever to fall asleep? And when she did it had seemed like only a minute before she heard the god-damn cats. She got up and staggered downstairs, silently cursing the felines. They were both standing in an ivy bed screeching at a sliver of a moon. "C'mon, c'mon, guys. Calm down." She carried a saucer of milk laced with sherry. "Piss, come here. You lead the way. C'mon boy."

Oh God, Calista thought. She really didn't understand cats at all. She picked up Moan and began to carry her toward the back door. She hoped Piss would follow. Then suddenly, it hit Calista. The last time, the only other time the cats had freaked like this in the middle of the night in the garden was the night of Quintana's murder. Had something, in fact, set them off—someone coming into the Connecting Gardens, over the walls, or perhaps from another house? The thought struck her forcibly. Anybody could have access to the gardens, just like herself, from another house. They wouldn't even have to go over the walls— just walk out a back door. She stood frozen to the ground. She looked around. The houses looked summer-vacant. The automatic lights turned on every evening. Calista subconsciously even knew the patterns of how the owners varied the sequence of when the clock timers would go off in the various rooms— to confuse would-be thieves, to suggest occupancy.

She clutched the cat tighter and began to walk toward the Kingsley greenhouse. The door was slightly ajar, not necessarily as if someone had just walked through but, rather, as if it had not closed properly. No wonder. There was one hinge separated from the door frame. It didn't look as if it had been forced. The hinge was old and rusty, one screw missing, the other screw half out of the hole. Moan was now calmed down and purring ever so softly in her arms. Piss stood on the low stone wall and looked disapprovingly at them. But Calista felt strangely emboldened.

She wanted to see the greenhouse again. She looked
over her shoulder at Piss and thought, Fuck you, then
stepped through the door. She could get through sideways without even moving it.

Inside, it had all been swept up and washed down.
Not a trace of the shattered needle juniper, nor a drop
of Quintana's blood left. The Crime Scene people had
obviously gotten all they needed. So why was she here?
What more was there to find? Or was there something to look at again? She knew what it was. She
wanted to see those pictures, the handless drawings of
Bootsie's and Muffy's. They held a key, not to the
murder but to the family.

She had given up thinking that these families were
simple. How could she have ever thought that? Look
at Archie's family. There were enough nuts in the
Baldwins—certain branches of the family, that was—
to start a small posh mental clinic. So, she told herself, she was not really trying to solve a murder but,
rather, do a little ethnographic research and maybe
just help somebody, somebody like Bootsie, who
seemed so terribly vulnerable. In these pursuits, was
she not following some age-old practices of previous
generations of Bostonians? Was there not a touch of
the settlement-house ethic here—repairing damaged
souls? Why was she so sure that Bootsie had been
damaged?

Calista had been walking slowly through the rows of
dwarfed plants toward the connecting door to the
main house when suddenly she heard footsteps. She
froze and gripped Moan to her chest. The steps became louder. She heard a door from the pantry open.
There wasn't time to get out of the greenhouse. Where
would she hide? There was hardly camouflage among

these stupid dwarf plants. In a corner, she spotted some fifty-pound bags of peat moss and fertilizer for spreading in the Connecting Gardens, no doubt. She rushed over. There was just enough room to wedge herself and Moan behind them. She crouched and tried to steady her breathing. Her heart was pounding ferociously and Moan, unlike herself, evidently found it soothing, for the dear old cat had nestled close to Calista's breast and for all intents and purposes seemed to have fallen asleep. Whoever it was had now entered the greenhouse. Calista could hear the click of heels on the brick. The knowledge dawned slowly. Those clicks must be from a woman's shoes—high heels. Just at that moment, they stopped within a yard of where Calista crouched. She could see the legs. Long and well shaped, they were sheathed in stockings with seams! Who wore stockings with seams anymore? Maybe prostitutes with garter belts. Calista's eyes opened in disbelief. She indeed spotted the buckle at the end of a strap. The woman was crouching down near the spot where Quintana's body had lain. She was running a gloved hand over the bricks as if searching for something. With her skirt hiked up, the buckle at the end of the strap showed and then popped. "Shit!" the voice muttered. Then with her right hand holding up the top of the stocking, she hitched the garter buckle to the fabric. There was something very sexy about the entire move. Maybe that's why men went crazy for straps and garters and all that outmoded paraphernalia. The woman then got up, continued out the back greenhouse door, and into the Connecting Gardens. Piss went nuts and began screeching again. But the figure hurried on. Calista rose up a bit and had a clear view. The woman was dressed in a somewhat old-fashioned-style dress or suit that showed off an hourglass figure. Her shoulders looked fairly broad, but her waist was very narrow and so were her hips. The hair appeared light in color and brushed her shoulders. She carried a tote, which jiggled against her hip as she tottered across the Connecting Gardens. Maybe it was the uneven bricks or perhaps her heels were too high, but she reminded Calista of herself when she had first worn high heels as a youngster and was not used to the new balance required for walking. She then disappeared around a hedge. Presumably, she went out through one of the tunneled alleyways that opened onto Pinckney Street. Only residents had keys to the doors at either end. Calista herself had Heckie's, the Baldwins' manservant.

Calista came out from behind the peat and fertilizer bags. She felt stiff and almost cold, although her body was sweaty from sheer nerves. The temperature must have dropped. When the cooler air hit her perspiring skin, it sent a chill through her. She was standing near the place where the woman had crouched. What had she been looking for? She began to walk toward the door, still clutching the sleeping Moan, when she spotted the silvery thing wedged between two bricks. She bent down and picked it out. It was a garter buckle, separated from the strap. Calista held it lightly and tried to figure out what the significance was. All she could think was that somewhere in Boston there was a lady with a great figure running around with one stocking about to fall down. No wonder she had said ''Shit'' when the other garter popped. Was this evidence? Evidence of what? Evidence perhaps that she, Calista, had illegally entered the Kingsley house and had seen a stylish woman there at 2:30 in the morning. This was going to be a hard one to explain to the police.

THIRTEEN

"DO WE REALLY HAVE to eat lunch with him?" Matthew was asking Charley as they headed toward the swan boats. It would be two hours before the boats opened for the public, but it took nearly all that time to get them wiped down, organize the ticket rolls, and go over the scheduling changes.

"Well, hopefully Art will put him on a different shift so our lunch breaks won't be the same," Charley said.

"I mean, it's not that he's not nice. But he's just so weird. He's kind of a heavy presence to have around." Matthew paused. "Especially in this heat. Why aren't we working in an air-conditioned office?"

"Because our mothers were afraid we were becoming nerdy, and apparently fresh air is an inhibitor of nerdiness. I'm sorry I got you involved with this Jamie guy, but I guess I sort of felt sorry for him. He does strike you as kind of a terminal loser."

"There's just something kind of dark about him. I don't mean dark in a bad way, like evil, just, you know—heavy, depressing. Like I mean, I know his grandmother got murdered and everything, but I still think he's just plain weird."

"No doubt about it, but you should see the rest of his family. They're all weird. His mom's an alcoholic—at least that's what my mom told me. And did I tell you about this lady who my mom says is really charming and she likes a whole bunch?"

"No. Who's that?"

"Get this: Her name is Titty—Aunt Titty."

"Titty!" Matthew gasped. "As in boobies, breasts, knockers?" He stopped dead in his tracks on the sidewalk that led from the Charles Street gate to the pond. They were right in front of the statue of Edward Everett Hale. "I need support," Matthew said, leaning on the pedestal. He began to laugh hysterically. "Titty! Titty!" He was screaming. "They named her Titty. How could parents do that to a kid?" He was doubled over and tears were running down his cheeks. A businessman walking by briskly with a briefcase glanced their way.

"It's funny, Matthew, but not really that funny." But then Charley began to laugh, too. They had both collapsed just under Mr. Hale's feet and walking stick.

"I don't think we should ever complain again about something our parents might do," Matthew said, gasping. "I mean, look—we've got these nice solid plain names, and who cares if we have to pedal two tons of fiberglass swan around in ninety-eight degrees of heat—piece of cake next to TITTY!"

"Nothing to live up to," Charley said, and started laughing again.

"Or out to," Matthew said, cupping his hands in front of his chest to indicate enormous breasts.

"Oh gross."

They finally picked themselves up. "Well, at least Jamie doesn't have a weird name. So what's his excuse?" Matthew asked.

"Well, his parents are divorced, and as I was saying, his mom's alcoholic and his grandmother just got murdered. So that's a nice little starter kit toward weirdness. But I get the feeling he was this way before.''

"He's so silent and he's always biting his nails—you notice that?"

"Yeah, and sometimes it's almost like he doesn't hear you. I swear it's like his mind is totally elsewhere. He gets this totally far-off look in his eyes.''

"Why did you ever tell him about this job?"

"Well, I don't know. I mean, we *are* short of help. It means we don't have to do double trips and can actually take full-size lunch breaks, and you know, I was just standing there with him and, as you noticed, this guy isn't really talky. I was sort of grasping at straws for conversation and it just came up.''

"You know, Jacobs, you really might have a career as a social worker.''

"Forget it. I don't want to have to spend my days talking to weird people.''

"Well, maybe you should join the clergy. I mean, you have this do-good streak. Become a rabbi.''

"I don't think rabbis or any other ministers have a do-good streak. Besides, I'm an agnostic.''

"How can you be an agnostic? You're Jewish.''

Charley stopped again. "Hold it right there. You can too. My grandfather said so. I am a Jewish agnostic.''

"Impossible.''

"Not at all: You eat Jewish; you think Jewish; you basically follow the Ten Commandments. And if you believed in God, you would only believe in one.''

"Sounds kind of half-baked to me.''

"All agnostics are half-baked. My dad was an agnostic—sort of.''

"What do you mean 'sort of'?''

"He basically believed that God was a simplification of a lot of laws that underlie particle physics—a lot of laws and stuff we haven't discovered yet. I think my dad really did believe in God. I think he thought God was at the bottom of Cygnus II and a lot of other black holes he spent his life studying. I know he thought there was a God particle in there somewhere."

"A God particle," Matthew mused.

"Yeah, that's what we agnostics think. It's not that we don't believe in God. It's just that we don't believe the God particle can be explained—at least not in a church or synagogue, or not for a moral benefit."

Charley, Matthew thought, was truly amazing sometimes. He didn't know where he got these ideas. But they popped up all the time.

CHARLEY HAD just finished unloading his fifth boatload of "swannies." He saw Matthew, who had been working the ticket line, standing off to one side with Jamie. There was a tall, slender man standing with them as he walked up.

"Oh, hello, Charley Jacobs, right?" He leaned forward and extended his hand. "Gus Kingsley, Jamie's uncle. I was just in this neck of the woods and I thought I might stop by and take Jamie for lunch. But he says he already has plans."

"I think that's an excellent idea," a woman said, coming up suddenly. "Why don't you let Jamie be with his new friends? You really don't belong here," she said quite pointedly.

"Mom, what are you doing here?" Jamie's dark eyes never looked up from the asphalt path. Then, under his breath and barely audible, he added, "What is everyone doing here?"

"Uh...well..." Matthew was saying. "We didn't mean to—"

"Nonsense," Bootsie broke in. "You fellows have your plans. There is no place around here for us."

"Then what are you all doing here?" Jamie spat out the words, turned, and, hunching his shoulders, walked off in the opposite direction.

Bootsie looked off, following him with her eyes. She raised her hand and lightly touched her cheek. It was a gesture of confusion mixed with utter despair. Gus, aware of the two boys standing there rather dumb-founded, tried to recoup from the awkwardness of the moment. "Well, I guess we adults have a knack for just marching in sometimes at the wrong moments." He reached out to shake both Matthew's and Charley's hands and gave them each a very earnest gaze. "I'm sorry, boys, really sorry." He looked again almost questioningly into Charley's eyes, and Charley could not help but wonder what he was looking for. It seemed to be more than understanding. Bootsie, meanwhile, was busy lighting up a cigarette, her eyes darting about like a freaked starling in a sudden gust. A genuine loony-tune, thought Charley.

FOURTEEN

IT WAS Friday morning and the weekend loomed ahead like a great two-day yawn. Charley and Matthew had the entire weekend off, their first all summer. Matthew had invited Charley down to the Cape, where his parents had a home. Calista was chained to her drawing board. Her plans were to really push for the next four days and then take a long weekend in Vermont beginning the following Thursday. But at the moment, she was feeling terrifically sorry for herself. Everyone else was someplace summery and having fun. Her own parents had called up to urge her to fly out to Montana, where they rented a cabin every summer for two weeks of fly-fishing on the Madison River. Nan and Will Baldwin called every few days with tempting invitations to come up to Mount Desert Island. But Calista was behind, and Janet Weiss, her editor, was nervous.

Nothing was cooperating, however. In the humid thickness of the August morning, the India ink full of shellac was hardening up faster than usual. It seemed as if every fifteen minutes her pen was getting clogged and she was having to take a razor blade to it. Then to add to that, she was working on vintage Whatman paper, the kind people killed for. Calista had not had to kill for it. Her dear old friend and mentor Emma Plotkin, a consummate children's book artist, had died at the age of eighty-six the previous winter and had actually willed to Calista and another young artist a stash of Whatman board bought in the year 1952. It was the paper that had inspired Calista to do this retelling of *The Emperor and the Nightingale.* Old Whatman, a cold-press-plate paper, was rather like red wine; it got better with age. It had a soft buttery yellow cast. It absorbed the ink perfectly for the feel that Calista was striving for in this story. It seemed to be paper looking for the right story. And Calista knew the Chinese fairy tale of Hans Christian Andersen, full of nuance and quiet passion, was the story. But it had also been problematic.

She was not just serving the story to the paper, however; this was a tribute to Emma. She felt Emma's spirit hovering around her always when she came to work on the book. And although that spirit was a benign one, it was nonetheless inhibiting. For one thing, she had a very limited supply of this paper—just enough for three books. So she couldn't screw things up. This was why it had taken her so long to get going. Every morning, there was half an hour of agony before her drawings seemed to loosen up, her hands relax. She didn't even work on the paper for the first forty-five minutes. She did a series of sketches and scribbled on other stuff she had around. But now the goddamn shellac was getting hard as nails in the ink. The fisherman pulling in his nets under the moon in his boat on the lake where the nightingale sang did not look right, not at all. Just then, the phone rang. Calista picked it up.

"Rudy here, dear. How are you doing?"

"Ecch!" Calista made a sound halfway between a snort and a whine.

"Not good. I can tell. How about a jaunt to the country with Titty and me? We have to go up to

Nohqwha to check on the work Queenie was having
done. It's apparently finished, and Gus can't make it
and Bootsie isn't in any shape to. It's so nice when octogenarians can be helpful. I've got a car and a
driver.''

"Well, I could certainly drive you. No need for you
to spend that sort of money," Calista found herself
saying while staring at the fisherman with his nets.
Jesus, the moon didn't even look right in this drawing. She better quit while she was ahead. "How long
are you going for?"

"Oh, we'll come back tomorrow, late afternoon."

"All right," she said.

AT LEAST IT wouldn't be the whole weekend. It might
be fun and maybe it would give her a chance to talk to
Titty some more. She had never exactly figured it out
after reading that Sexton poem about the handless
maiden. She thought again of those drawings. There
was indeed a sense of mutilation in this family, of
perhaps countless little murders, or corpses—so well
hidden because they came sheathed in the accoutre-
ments of life. And then she thought of the nightingale
she would soon be drawing—the real living, breathing one that the emperor wanted to possess completely and the bejeweled artificial one with its
glittering plumage studded with diamonds and rubies
and its mechanical song locked in its breast, to be released only when the emperor wound the key. Both the
poem about the handless maiden and *The Emperor
and the Nightingale* were stories of control, or the lust
for perfect and complete control.

She had found the Sexton poem with the swans and
the whore. It was called "Song for a Red Night-

gown." She had read it and thought of Bootsie. But she still did not know why. She could not understand what the poem meant. But when she came to the lines "One could think of feathers and/not know it all. One could/think of whores and not imagine the way of the swan," Calista thought of Bootsie. She knew that there was a link between this poem and Bootsie and possibly the death of Quintana Kingsley. She felt that Titty knew part of the answers she sought. There was so much to sort out: swans and nightingales, red nightgowns and whores, Brahmins and bonsai. And survivors—what was it that Titty had said about Cornelia and Bambi being survivors? Where did the survivors fit in with all this?

THERE WAS NO DOUBT about it: Rudy knew how to do things in style. He would not hear of her driving. He had rented a Bentley, and one of the stewards from the Harvard Club who had the weekend off had been hired to drive. Commodious and well upholstered, it was much more suited for the two octogenarians than Calista's Subaru or her old VW Bug that she hung on to simply because she could not bear to part with it. Archie had felt it terribly dangerous and bought her the Subaru as a Hanukkah present—at least that was what he'd said it was for. Titty, who was of ample proportions, would have found the Subaru a squeeze, however. So the three of them were now riding north in splendor on Route 93 toward New Hampshire. Rudy was sitting in the front seat with the driver and had an array of maps spread out before him. He also carried a compass. He and Titty were having a spirited discussion on how they used to get to Nohqwha seventy years earlier.

"No, we'd take the steamer from India Wharf, and in the morning we'd wake up at the Isles of Shoals and then Talbot would pick us up in the coach."

"Titty, you're all wrong. When Talbot worked for my father, they already had the Studebaker."

"Studebaker—that's a very modern automobile, Rudy. I think it might have been a Packard."

"Well, it wasn't a coach, I'll tell you that. I think maybe when we were infants, my parents had a man-servant named Apollo who used to drive their coach. And then he became their chauffeur. That's what a lot of these old coachmen did."

"Well, in any case, that last part always seemed to take forever. I just remember jumping up and down in what I picture as a coach, asking when we were going to get there."

"Now will you explain to me once again how you and Rudy are cousins?" Calista asked.

"My mother's sister Abigail married Tad Kingsley, Kingie's and Rudy's father. Abigail and Tad were much better off than my parents, of course. But Abigail convinced Tad to lease us some land at a very low cost. My father, Horace, was an architect and built a lovely camp on it."

"Is it still there?" Calista asked.

"No, no. It burned—when was that, Rudy?"

"Oh, before the war, I think."

"Wait—when was Pearl Harbor?"

"Oh, it was long before that, Titty."

On and on they went, trying to reconstruct an evanescent past, with details that had seemed to wash away like watercolors, having left unreadable but nonetheless indelible stains.

They stopped for lunch near Lake Ossipee, at a spot Rudy remembered. Malcolm, their chauffeur, got out the hamper from the trunk. Calista was helping Titty out of the car.

"There's no picnic table, Titty. Will you be okay on the ground?"

"Oh, we brought Titty's portable chaise," Rudy said from the rear of the car. "Malcolm will be right there with it."

"Isn't he a dear?" Titty sighed. "And have you ever seen anything more adorable?" She gazed with rapture at her cousin, who was standing by the trunk with his walking stick as he supervised the unloading for the picnic.

Calista had to admit she hadn't. Rudy was an elfin picture of sartorial perfection in his pale tan poplin knickerbockers, pink-striped shirt and red suspenders, an ascot of tiny checks tucked in the neck of the shirt, and, to top it all off, a bright white cap with a small brim.

Malcolm brought the folding chaise over for Titty and he and Rudy set it up. Titty eased her great bulk into it.

"Comfy, my dear?" Rudy asked.

"Of course—fit for a queen."

"Yes." Then Rudy turned to Calista. "I was once at Cowes Week with Lord Abington—very close to the Queen Mum, he is, and she was there, too. We took tea with her on the royal yacht, and instead of a deck chair, she had one of these. I immediately called up Hawes and Groot. They are actually sailmakers but have done very well in safari gear and that sort of thing; they can do anything with canvas or Dacron, and they'd done the Queen Mother's chair. So I ordered one for Titty.''

"You always take care of me, dear." She reached for Rudy's hand and pressed it to her plump cheek. It was the tenderest gesture.

"And I always will." Rudy looked down on his cousin with a look of pure love. He then reached into the cooler. "I'll be the wine steward. It's so much fun doing it outside," Rudy said. "Malcolm, you get the rest ready. We're going to serve the vichyssoise in those big goblets. No spoons required. You can just drink up, kiddos, and let's see, we have loads of smoked salmon sandwiches—some with the dill sauce, some without. And there's potato salad." Rudy stopped and slapped his cheek. "Oh Gawd, that's rather redundant, isn't it? Vichyssoise and potato salad! How'd I ever do that? You know, aside from losing one's looks, getting old is really a pain in the old arse when one makes slips like these. I know this isn't the worst—here, try this, darling." He had just uncorked a bottle of wine and was pouring some into a glass for Calista. "It's a Montrachet. Anyway, as I was saying—" He stopped abruptly. "Oh, I shouldn't complain. I've really had a wonderful life against all odds."

"Against all odds?" Calista asked.

"Oh yes, my dear. It really is against all odds when you're born into a family like this."

"Absolutely." Titty nodded and held out her glass to Rudy. He poured the wine.

"You're born into what is commonly thought of as great privilege. It's really, however, something to overcome. You must make your own luck and tiptoe through the privilege. So it is against all odds and despite all privilege.''

"Oh, I like that, Rudy!" Titty exclaimed, and raised her glass. "Here's to figuring out the odds and tiptoeing through the privilege."

At this point, Rudy began tiptoeing through the grass, his wineglass aloft, and singing an improvisation to the tune of "Tiptoe Through the Tulips." The improvised lyrics had to do with bloodlines, Cabots, Welds, and Saltonstalls, China Trade and opium fortunes, Beacon Hill and sailing ships. Titty was laughing gleefully and Calista was thinking what fine company she was in and how much nicer this was than trying to keep her India wash from clogging her pens.

"You see!" cried Titty, almost beside herself. "You see the Welles Club missed something with you."

"If I'm going to dress up like a woman, I'm not going to wear one of those god-awful tarty corsets, darling. Give me a Givenchy." Rudy ran one hand down his side and pinched his svelte waist. "Audrey Hepburn was always my dream."

"What's this about the Welles Club?" Calista had heard of the Welles Club, along with the Tavern and Somerset clubs. It was one of the handful of clubs to which membership was requisite if all else was to fall into its proper place for a proper Bostonian. These archaic old clubs were at the very heart of the Boston social structure. Unlike New York men's clubs, the Boston clubs eschewed the plush masculine comforts for the most part and were distinctly austere in their decoration of the rooms where merchant princes and scholars could meet. But despite their overt simplicity, they possessed a majesty that was awesome in the scheme of things. And once a year, the Welles Club, as did the Tavern, let down its Puritan guard to put on a show.

"They call it the 'Frivolities' at the Welles Club. The members dress up as chorines and tarts and dance. You know, rather like the Hasty Pudding Club."

"Oh how stupid," Calista said. Hasty Pudding and all their folderol used to drive Calista and Tom nuts. Luckily, very few serious physics students were in the Pudding.

"More than stupid, I think." Rudy had his legs curled under him and was sipping his wine ruminatively.

"How do you mean?" Calista asked.

"It is an interesting question." Rudy spoke slowly. "Why do clubmen dress up like women?" He paused and plucked a blade of grass. "It would seem that this phenomenon is a peculiar concatenation of urges, insecurities, and...and, yes, I do believe in some cases, mean-spiritedness."

Calista was watching Titty, who was rapt with attention.

"This dressing up," Rudy continued, "the way they do it is essentially a mockery, yet it's something they need to do. I have seen it close up. I worked the lights backstage at the Welles; never would get out there myself. But I saw those men. They never felt more masculine than when they were flexing their muscles in tutus and stuffing their jockstrapped cocks into bloomers. They were mocking, putting down the other sex. But at the same time, they were saying, 'There but for the grace of God go I.' And yet..." He paused again. "And yet, some craved it. And what have they done in those shows? They have created a *tableau vivant* not of femininity but of humiliation. They want to toy with humiliation—it is, after all, a direct escape from the burdens of their caste, the exigencies of their pedigree.''

"It's sick!" Titty exploded.

"Very—their whole notion of masculinity is sick, if you ask me." Rudy huffed, made a moue with his lips, and shrugged. "I trace it back to our dear relative."

"Cotton." It was a statement, not a question.

"Yes, indeed, Titty. The Reverend himself."

"Oh," Calista suddenly recalled. "Queenie had a portrait of him, Cotton Mather."

"Yes," said Titty, "and it is the one Cornelia is lusting after. Both sides of the family are directly related to the old creep."

"We got a double dose, as it 'twere," Rudy said, and stretched out his legs. "I always loved what Marion Starkey, the historian who wrote about the Salem witch trials, said about Cotton Mather."

"What was that?" asked Calista.

"As I recall, Miss Starkey suggested that if the witchcraft experience hadn't happened, Cotton Mather would have had to invent it, given his zeal for discovering witches. It was not something he would have foregone, she said; for it was, in fact, 'the scarlet thread drawn through the drab New England homespun.' Rather like the kick those fellows get with their corsets.''

"Yes," said Titty. "And of course, women are always the victims.''

"Always," Rudy said quietly.

FIFTEEN

THE HOUSES AND summer bungalows became sparser and the woods thicker. The road grew narrower and soon the tar turned to dirt. Ahead, Calista could glimpse a patch of sparkling water. "There it is—Lake Sachem!" Rudy exclaimed.

"I hope Hoops is there with the boat," Titty said.

"Oh, he will be. Has Hoops ever failed?"

"True," said Titty.

"We need a boat to get there?" Calista asked.

"Oh yes," Rudy said. "You see Nohqwha is on an island in the middle of Lake Sachem."

"It must be a big lake," Calista said.

"Oh it is. And the island is big, too. Do you know why it is called Nohqwha?" Rudy turned around in the front seat to talk to Calista.

"No idea. Why?"

"It's an old Seneca tale, one of those stories about the small one, the runt of the litter, winding up the all-powerful one. In this story, the little boy runs off to where he shouldn't go, a dangerous land, and he hears what he thinks are people calling, 'My Father! My Father!' And he fears that they are going to kill his father. But in truth, it was not people at all. It was frogs singing the frog song—*'Nohqwha! Nohqwha!'* This story caught my grandfather's fancy and—you know, this was back in the days of romance about the Indians—many of the great Adirondack camps had Indian names. So Grandfather named our place

Nohqwha. There are lots of frogs around—frog tapestries, weavings, little frog statues, door knockers. You know how a lot of people get about their summer places—little themes, leitmotifs, secret handshakes—all very Cub Scouty, really. So our totem, so to speak, is the frog.''

Calista wasn't sure. Her vacation home in Vermont did not have a name. She never had thought of naming it. It didn't have a theme, either. ''Well,'' she said, ''I was always crazy about Jeremy Fisher. For years, I've been trying to buy one of Beatrix Potter's studies of Jeremy. No luck.''

''You don't say?'' Rudy turned around and lifted a minnow eyebrow. ''You deal with Ropes and Fremont, Kensington High Street, for that sort of thing?''

''Yes. How'd you know?''

''Oh, the things I know are surprising, my dear,'' he said cryptically. ''Ah! Here we are, and there is our good fellow Hoops.''

THEY HAD ARRIVED at a pier that stretched out into glassy dark water. When Calista stepped outside the car, it was slightly chilly. It was wonderful. She could feel the heat, the fumes, the grit of the city peel off of her like layers of old skin. The scent of spruce was in the air.

''It feels wonderful!'' Titty sighed and stood resting her weight on her tripod cane. A slight breeze now riffled the water. At the end of the pier, Calista spotted a shell—double-ended, slightly wide for a true racing shell, but with more flowing lines than a rowboat. It was precisely what she had been attempting to draw that morning, just hours before. It even had a little birch canopy. This was a sign, she decided, that it had indeed been wise for her to leave her drawing board and come to New Hampshire, to Lake Sachem, and glide in a boat across the mirrored water to Nohqwha.

Calista was big on signs that permitted her to do what she really wanted to do. The first time she ever slept with Archie, it was a sign that she needed to move on to something else when she had been stuck on a drawing for *Marian's Tale,* a revisionist telling of Robin Hood. It had actually been a drawing of Marian shooting a bow and arrow that had her stumped. When Archie had arrived on that hot summer night, Charley was away and she was wearing running shorts, with no underpants underneath. What could have been clearer? This lady needed to get laid by someone who cared about her and whom she cared about deeply. So she just invited him into her study, and the next thing she knew, they were on the floor and Marian was still on the drawing boards, looking envious. She finished the picture the next day. It was lovely on all counts.

Hoops, although decrepit in appearance, had a sprightly gait and quickly loaded their bags into the boat. Titty's chaise was unfolded. It fit perfectly into the middle section of the boat. She looked like a benevolent toad queen surveying her domain. Rudy reclined in a slant-back low seat in the bow, looking positively louche. Calista decided he was one of those people who despite rather bizarre first impressions and general appearance can actually fit in anywhere and look as if he belonged. Calista sat on a seat in the stern under the birch-bark canopy and felt as if she were a character in one of her own fairy tales.

ONCE UPON A TIME, thought Calista, this had been a tent, or perhaps two or three on platforms with canvas flaps. But now what loomed before Calista as they walked from the pier up the pine path was a rustic creation that blended elements of a Swiss chalet with an American frontier log cabin. A fanned gable thrust out over a deep front porch. The rail of the porch was a spectacular intaglio of bent, peeled birch limbs. On the second level was another balcony with equally intricate railwork. Living trees had been incorporated directly into the porch structure of the house, with two great hemlocks on either end forming posts. The simplicity of the rustic log-cabin design combined with an ornamentation that was clearly Swiss was pure Adirondacks style and indeed perfect for this woodland-lake setting.

"Oh, they did a marvelous job on the upper verandas, Hoops."

"Well, sir, they spent a heck of a long time steaming that wood to make it bend. They knew what they were doing."

"Real craftsmen."

"Too bad Mrs. Kingsley couldn't see it. She was a passel of nerves about those verandas. Think it was where Mr. Kingsley used to romance her."

"Yes, yes," said Rudy somewhat hastily. Calista caught a glimpse of Titty and her breath locked in her throat. The eyes behind the thick lids were glittering, hard little slits, like narrow windows that showed a hatred that was so intense, it seemed to sear the very air around them.

Calista's bedroom was a Spartan affair just to her liking: a narrow pine bed, a chest of drawers with a small partially deglazed mirror above it, a braided rug on the floor, a small desk, a dear little twig night-stand supported by curved birch branches. On top was a reading light and a book of Rupert Brooke poetry on a crocheted doily. How odd! Calista thought, picking up the book. Who ever read Rupert Brooke nowadays? But as she opened the book and a pressed corsage fell out, she knew. This had to have been Muffy's book. It was as if time had stopped here and she had an uncanny sense that this was Muffy's room. This must have been Muffy's room. She looked around with renewed interest.

She heard a gong clang two times.

"Oh my stars and garters!" squeaked Titty, who stood outside the open door to Calista's room.

"What's that?" Calista asked.

"Rudy—Uncle Rudy, camp director of Nohqwha. He loves doing this. Two gongs mean time for a swim."

"It's kind of chilly, isn't it?"

"Of course it is. But why should that stop you? We're in the woods, lovey, plenty of plain living and high thinking. It will clear the brain, and if you don't do this, they might give you a physic or, worse yet, an enema." The eyes narrowed again to the little slits with the hard light. But then she laughed merrily.

"Are you going swimming?" Calista asked.

"In a manner of speaking," Titty replied.

TITTY'S MANNER OF swimming was to recline in an Avon inflatable life raft and be rowed around in front of the swimming beach by Hoops, while trailing a languid hand in the water. Meanwhile, Rudy paddled about in a bathing suit, the style of which had last been seen at the Brighton Pavilion circa 1912, with a bathing cap and goggles. Calista wore a tank suit.

"Oh God, I'm jealous!" Rudy said when she had appeared on the beach. "You're so long-waisted. I would be long-waisted, too, if I was taller. Hee-hee," Rudy cackled, splashing water up on the beach. "Come on, sweetheart, in you go. I'm eighty-one years old and skin and bones. If I can take it, you can. It's marvelous for circulation. You know, I have no blood-pressure problems. Thank God—all those old coots who take those blood-pressure medicines can't ever get it up."

"Don't talk dirty, Rudy!" Titty flicked some water toward him.

"Do you do water ballet, Calista?" Rudy asked, swimming over to her.

"I used to in college. As a matter of fact—" she lowered her voice "—forgive me for talking dirty, but we used to call ourselves the Wet Dreams."

Rudy began to laugh so hard, he nearly sank. When he had recovered, he asked Calista to show him some tricks. She remembered something called a back dolphin and another maneuver called a tuck, which she executed most imperfectly. But by Titty's and Rudy's applause, one would have thought she was Esther Williams.

AFTER THE SWIM, they sat on the porch, wrapped in thick dark green terry-cloth robes monogrammed with frogs intertwined with the letter *N*.

"I like a girl who likes her bourbon," Rudy said as he looked at Calista. He liked Calista. He thought that had he not been born the way he was, this would have been precisely the kind of woman he would have

wanted to share his bed with, his life. He liked her
sharp wit, her irreverence, and her long, solid legs and
hooded dark eyes. Her easy style, too. She was so different from anything he had ever encountered. She
was not theatrically bohemian like all those artsy-
fartsy Cambridge types so often were. He chuckled to
himself when he remembered what that ass Bambi had
said after meeting Calista—or had it been Cornelia?
They were so interchangeable, those two. But one of
them had called her "socially fascinating." What
they'd really meant was, How could a Baldwin have
become involved with a Jew? "Socially fascinating"
was a code for things that were not WASP and Brahmin in Boston. The Kennedys and the late Judge Louis
Brandeis were considered "socially fascinating."

Just before dinner, Rudy descended the great staircase in cream-colored knickers and a Norfolk jacket;
then Titty followed in something that looked like a
well-tailored pup tent with a beautiful nubbly woven
shawl. All Calista had brought was jeans. But instead
of a sweater, she had brought an old Chanel jacket
that belonged to a suit she had picked up in Filene's
basement. She decided she'd better wear it, since it was
the only slightly dressy thing she had brought. Calista
liked odd combinations and this was one. The faded
denims actually went rather well, if unexpectedly, with
the jacket, which was a white wool the texture of cottage cheese and had the characteristic Chanel braid
trim and gold buttons.

"Darling, I adore it," exclaimed Rudy as she appeared in the dining room. "Chanel—you know, I
knew her very well. We shared a lover at one time." He
studied her. "Would you mind if I suggested one
touch? I have just the thing for your neck. You have a

lovely neck, but it looks cold sticking out of that collar, and believe me, this room isn't warm."

"Certainly. I forgot to bring a scarf or a turtleneck."

"It's upstairs. Be back in a flash," Rudy said.

"Here, dear." Returning, he held out a silk ascot in a tiny plaid, the most beautiful Calista had ever seen.

"Oh, how elegant." It felt like water between her hands.

"Marvelous texture, isn't it? Woven from English silk rep, mills in East Anglia. That is where all the best silk for ties comes from."

"The colors!" marveled Calista.

"Yes, such clarity. You see, that is because the weft is floated on the surface of the material instead of being woven in."

"I've never seen this plaid."

"Well, it's actually popularly known as the Prince of Wales check. Look closely and you'll see it's a very fine grain overcheck printed on a Glen Urquat plaid. But there's a departure in the usual colors. These, I would call a custard and rhubarb."

IN THE DINING ROOM, one end of the long wooden-planked table had been set with three plates—all emblazoned with the Nohqwha logo of an *N* intertwined with frogs. There was a small fire crackling in the huge fireplace that was built from cyclopean rocks. Candles on a massive chandelier over the table had been lighted. Dinner was served by Hoops and observed by a half dozen elk heads mounted on the wall. It was simple: roast chicken, wild rice, sugar snap peas, salad, and apple pie. After dinner, they moved to the built-in bench seats by the fire. There was a chaise of peeled poles polished with beeswax and heavily cushioned for Titty. Then it was brandy and soda for Titty and Rudy and soda without brandy for Calista; for indeed, she felt as smooth and relaxed as the English silk rep and did not want to deal with the headache brandy often gave her. A few yawns, some vague references to an early-morning swim, and then good nights all around. It was perfect.

SIXTEEN

SHE SLEPT WITH the shutter slats open so the chilly air and the spruce scent could come through the window. She used the extra blanket and wore socks to bed. As soon as her head hit the pillow, Calista fell asleep.

When the first gray light of morning seeped through the open slats, she awoke. Alert, refreshed, and—who knew—possibly ready for that early-morning swim. When she looked at her watch, she saw that it was only five o'clock. She felt restless after just two pages of *Barchester Towers* and one absurdly treacly poem of Rupert Brooke's about an old love.

She looked around the room that had been Muffy's and wondered whether she had been like Bootsie. It suddenly occurred to Calista that perhaps there were other artifacts and mementos of Muffy's aside from the Rupert Brooke book with the pressed corsage. The notion of this was enough to get her to an upright position in the bed. She looked about. There were half a dozen little built-in cupboards and an odd-shaped closet in the corner under the eaves, with the top of its door slashed off at an angle. Why not explore? She swung her legs out from under the covers.

The first built-in was empty; the second had a dead mouse and some old tennis shoes; the third, a stack of old newspapers. She took them out and found ferns pressed between the pages of a *Boston Evening Transcript,* a paper long expired. She went over to the small closet, which looked as if it had been built for dwarfs.

It was quite dark. On the floor, there was a large
cardboard box. She pulled it out. In faded gold scroll
was the name Priscilla's of Boston. Of course, Priscilla's was the famous Newbury Street wedding-dress
couturier. Brides and debutantes were her clients.
Muffy and probably Bambi had bought their gowns
for these major events from Priscilla. Calista doubted,
however, that a wedding dress was in the box. She slid
her fingers under the edges of the top and lifted it.
''Oh!'' she gasped.

Her first instinct was actually to put the lid right
back on. There was this sense of trespassing. She
knew, in that instant, as she looked down on the
handless drawing, that she was approaching an edge,
an abyss, and within that abyss there was a terrible
secret, a secret that had devoured, a truth that had
killed.

But should she look? She was becoming a tres-
passer in the darkest woods of a shadowed mind. She
slid the picture over. There was another, and another.
All three were very similar to the ones she had seen in
the hallway off of the Kingsleys' pantry on Louisburg
Square. But it was the fourth one that made her blink.
The background was black, with bars of white falling
across in rhythmic intervals. Then descending from the
top of the paper were three pendulous pink shapes.
Calista looked across the room. Slats of light fell
through the shutter, across the bed, and onto the floor
in an identical pattern to the ones in the picture. This
would be the child's view, and of course the child
would try not to focus on the swinging pink genitalia,
but... She raised her hand to cover her mouth, to hide
a secret, to say ''Sshhh!'' Her hands trembled as she

set the drawing down on the floor. There were dozens of slat drawings.

She hadn't even heard the door open, but the slats of light on the wood floor were suddenly cut by a clawed shadow.

The voice was terrible. It was thick, deep, and barely human. "You guessed. I knew you would." Titty loomed above Calista—immense and dark, her eyes cold reptilian slits.

SEVENTEEN

LEON MAURITZ groaned and drummed his fingers on the inlaid edge of his desk. "What do you mean that the nose was chopped off in the same way? Be precise. You mean it was the same tool as used on the kouros at the Met?" He paused and listened, then resumed. "This is an honest error that anyone could have made. The problem is that you shouldn't have touched it in the first place, given the talk.... Yes ... yes ... I know.... Well, the infrared studies should help with that.... Yes, dear. Look at that thing in Indianapolis with the mosaics ... that's infinitely worse, and it was financed by a bank. The woman was strictly an amateur. Yes, yes, I know ... yes ... well, don't. Life's too short. Okay ... good-bye, dear."

Mauritz hung up the phone and sighed deeply. He was not a therapist. He was a consultant and sometime dealer in antiquities. It wasn't his fault that the Getty had walked into it with the damn kouros figure. It really had been stupid for them even to look at that statue, because there had been a whiff about it for years. And now the new technology for sniffing out these whiffs of fraud was proving about as reliable as the Bible, at least in the case of the dubious origins of the kouros. Quote any Scripture you want and prove your point. So much for science here. It was very difficult to pin anything down with these marbles of the fifth and sixth centuries. It wasn't like paintings, where pigments and techniques, as well as paper and canvas, had varied distinctly over the years. Stone was stone. The phone rang again. God, it was Saturday, and naturally, Griselda his secretary wasn't in. He hesitated. He just had a sense before he picked it up that this next call would also not be an altogether-pleasant one.

"Hello." The voice was unnaturally high-pitched. "Mr. Mauritz?"

It was Madame X, as he had come to think of her, for she would not reveal her name. "I was able to obtain the second netsuke."

"But I thought you were not interested in selling."

"I am not interested now. But at a later date perhaps, and I felt you might get me in contact with such collectors at that time. I mean you've been so helpful thus far."

"Well, you hope I have been."

There was a pause. "What do you mean?"

"Well, frankly, madame, I usually don't deal in this way. It is highly irregular for a person to call up, insist on anonymity—at least to this degree—and then only verbally describe the object over the phone. If the first netsuke is indeed as you have described—but I can never be sure of that without seeing it, or at least photographs—but if it is as you describe, then I say it is worth something, if you have its mate. It is the pair that counts; separately, they are nothing."

"Yes, yes. I understand."

"So I will not at this point give you any contact."

"Would you hazard a guess as to what the pair might be worth?"

Mauritz closed his eyes. There was a joke among Jews. It seemed applicable now. "Please God," prayed the old Jew from the shtetl that had just been

wasted by the czar, "next time, choose someone else."
"Well, Madame," Mauritz continued, "if indeed
these are the signed Tomotados, genuinely signed Tomotados, I would think they would fetch together one
million dollars."

"Thank you. I'll be in touch."

LEON MAURITZ stared at the phone. He didn't like this
business with the netsuke at all. It reeked. He wondered where the call had come from. Possibly New
York or San Francisco; more likely, Boston. There
were small cadres of people in Boston who were gaga
over Asian art. Most of them tended toward the awful China Trade stuff—Canton and lacquer *tsatskes*.
It might have been worth a call to Archie Baldwin or
the inimitable Jack Thayer, both scions of Boston
Puritan princes. But Archie was in some jungle, God
knew where, and dear Jack had died two years before—a death that almost palpably impoverished the
world that knew him. There was, of course, Rudy
Kingsley.

Rudy had been Mauritz's first "older man." The
affair had been brief but satisfying. And they had remained friends. Rudy had taught him as much as
anybody about Greek antiquities. Indeed, the first
whiffs on the kouros had been wafted by Rudy. When
was that? Back in the late fifties. God, time flies. Now
he was practically the age Rudy had been at that time.
Well, it was irrelevant, because Rudy was in England.
He planned to go over in September. He might mention it if he had time to get down to Oscar House. In
the meantime, he was feeling quite depressed and he
had yet another funeral to go to for a young art dealer
who had succumbed to the dread disease.

EIGHTEEN

"I TOLD RUDY THAT I knew you would," Titty was saying. Calista's whole rib cage seemed to shake with the thundering of her heart. She was down on the floor, looking at the drawings. This woman could easily crack her on the head with that pronged cane. She had to play for time.

"I guessed what, Titty?"

"Well, about Muffy, of course, and what he did to her and to Boots, I'm sure. It runs in the family, don't you know?" She suddenly appeared terribly tired. The color had drained from her face. She looked absolutely gray, like an immense, wrinkled Hubbard squash. Calista looked down at the drawings of the slats of white against the dark with the pendulous pink loops. "You mean—" she spoke quietly, her voice barely audible "—he raped her and Bootsie?"

"Yes." Then the tiny voice seemed absolutely strangled. Great tears rolled out of the slitted eyes.

"And you, too?"

"Oh no, not Kingie. His father, Tad."

"He raped you?"

Titty nodded, her chin quivering.

"Did you tell anybody?"

"Only Rudy. See, Rudy had suspected because he had an older sister. She had died here one summer. She was just twelve or thirteen at the time. But Rudy had suspected that he had done something—you know what I mean—to Sassy. He used to hear cries and whimpers. But she would never say anything.''

''So did you and Rudy tell your parents?''

''No. You see, first of all, we were the poor relatives—only here by the grace of Tad and Abigail. They handed over the land and built the house for us. It was one of those dollar-a-year things. And my parents would never have believed it. They thought Tad was God.''

''Couldn't Rudy have told them?''

''Yes, I have been asking myself that for—what, seventy years now?'' Rudy stood in the door in a silk dressing gown and velvet slippers, looking frail as a leaf. ''I finally did tell them, but it was too late.''

Titty looked up at Rudy. ''She figured it out, dear. I knew she would.'' He came in and sat down on the bed by Titty and put an arm around her shoulders.

''Just from these pictures, you figured it out, my dear?''

''I'm not sure,'' Calista said honestly. Had she figured out what she thought, or had they thought she had figured out murder? ''I really don't know how it happened. I guess I first started thinking that something might be wrong when I saw the handless pictures in the pantry at Quintana's, the ones Bootsie and Muffy drew.''

''Handless pictures?'' Titty said vaguely.

''Yes, like these.'' Calista shuffled back through the pictures on the floor and held one up. ''See.''

''Oh yes, I see!'' Titty said, leaning forward with intense interest. ''These are just like the ones I drew in Dr. Schlemmer's office in Vienna.''

''Dr. Schlemmer . . . Vienna?''

Rudy now spoke. "Yes, you see when Titty was about twenty, she had a complete nervous breakdown. Her parents sent her to Switzerland to some ridiculous hospital where they gave you mud baths and laudanum—that was basically the therapy."

"And sleeping," Titty added. "Sleeping was a big part of it."

"Well, it was ridiculous. Then when I heard them making sounds about a lobotomy, I was just horrified. Freud by now had a wide reputation, and I knew someone who had studied with an associate of Freud's, Wolfgang Schlemmer. I hustled Titty right out of that Swiss joint and down to Vienna to be psychoanalyzed."

"He was wonderful," Titty said. "You never heal from something like this, but you find out ways to go on living. You discover that there is more to life than being a victim. That's the most important part. You learn how not to be a victim. Dr. Schlemmer did that for me."

"But I just can't believe it," Calista was saying, and even while she was saying it, she knew it sounded dumb. Everyday there were articles in the paper about abused children. "And you say it runs in the family?"

"Oh absolutely," Rudy said. "In an odd way, it is probably why I am a homosexual."

"What do you mean? Were you abused?"

"Oh no, not sexually abused. I am gay for a lot healthier reasons than that. But you see, you must know about America and particularly Boston of that time. If you read the nineteenth-century historians, you will come to see that American males felt they were the most male creatures on earth. How this

translated in terms of the young males of lineage in
Boston meant that not only were they superb sports-
men, played games, knew how to drink, and had some
inclination toward scholarship but it was all bound up
with class and the Brahmin sense of stewardship. You
eschewed ostentation and lavish expenditure, for in-
stance; it was not only inappropriate in the Puritan
sense; it was slightly foppish. You avoided atmo-
spheres of money like Bar Harbor or Newport, for
example. It was not considered fit or socially responsible for people of advantage to flaunt it in such ways
as they did in New York. Embedded at the center of all
of these notions was an archetype of masculine behavior. You went to the frontier, like Parkman. You
explored the Arctic perhaps; as a boy, you read *Rob-
inson Crusoe* and *Two Years Before the Mast*. You
supported the arts, but you did not become an artist.
You might have salons for artistic types, but you did
not sleep with them or let them borrow money. At a
certain point, usually by November of your freshman
year at Harvard, you were taken to a reputable
brothel—there was one in Quincy—where you were
initiated into the mysteries of sex, which you came
away from totally underwhelmed and perhaps slightly
embarrassed. After that, you visited the brothel in-
frequently and found Irish girls clerking downtown in
department stores with whom you could try out your
sexual skills for free. Parsimony being a virtue, of
course. Then you retreated to places like Nohqwha for
bracing masculine weekends of blood sports. This was
all considered the essence of manliness in Boston, because all this was done properly by proper Bostonians
in the Hub, and it was around the Hub that the earth
revolved; for although Rome might be the Eternal

City, it was Boston that was the center of the universe. And its men were responsible for maintaining the torque that kept the Hub revolving.

"That, of course, was a very narrow definition of virility as far as I was concerned—a xenophobic version, in fact. I didn't consider it manly at all. I hated this cultish worship of Parkman. I hated their blood sports. That's why I always wear bright colors and red braces in the country. I want to alert the animals: 'I'm here. Run! . . .' Not that I'd shoot any of them, ever. I hated their stupid games. I loved beautiful objects. I loved the classical nude sculptures. They aroused me, yes, but I loved them for what they said about men during a golden era in civilization. And I loved the love between men. I always hated that psalm that said 'The Lord delighteth not in any man's legs.' My rationale for that is that God's a woman and she's lesbian. So now you ask, Was I sexually abused for my attitude? No. But my father loathed me. He couldn't believe I was the way I was. I was a blight on everything he valued. He hated me as a child dressing up in my togas and running around in the woods up here. Oh, it was fine for the men on their manly retreats to go swimming nude, but let me show up with a bedsheet I had fashioned into a toga and with a wreath of birch leaves on my head and it was as if I had marched stark naked into a waltz evening in Boston and pulled Mr. Hooper's dong.

"I suppose, however, being a total outcast within one's own family constitutes some kind of abuse. In any case, my father certainly was not going to let this kind of thing happen with Kingie, although Kingie was older and had none of my 'tendencies.' But Father decided to imbue him double strength with all that virility, to give him the manliness that I lacked, in addition to his own. I know that Kingie knew what was happening in that bedroom with Sassy, and I am almost sure that Kingie became part of the abuse. It was his initiation into manly pleasures—try it out on your sister.''

Calista felt almost numb. ''So it is a tradition.''

''Yes,'' said Titty.

Rudy sighed and crossed his legs. ''Well, let's say that they never thought of it as an aberration, a pathology. My homosexuality yes, but having intercourse with a daughter or a niece—no. But in the final analysis, yes, it became a tradition. It was very easy for Kingie to carry on with it. You must understand that we are families steeped in tradition. So anything that has been done before in this sense has a patina of rightness about it. It is condoned.''

''It's sick,'' said Calista.

''But it's tradition. They worship tradition.''

''But what about the women? Didn't they suspect? Didn't they do anything about it?''

''I honestly don't think my mother suspected,'' Titty was saying. ''And if she had, I don't think she or my father had the imagination to know what to have done. They felt beholden to Tad and Abigail. But it would never have gotten that far. They were experts at denial. They raised it to an art form in all matters.''

''But what about Abigail? Your mother, Rudy?''

''What about Abigail?'' he said with contempt. ''It is true she never knew, until I told her.''

''So you did finally tell her?''

''Yes. When the talk began years later about the lobotomy. I was furious. Almost murderous, to tell you the truth, and I blurted it all out. I suggested that rather than a lobotomy for Titty, how about castration for Tad. That was the last I saw of either of my parents. They cut me from their wills.''

"They did?'' Calista's eyes widened. Rudy nodded. ''Then how did you make all this money?''

"Well, I had already come into part of my trust fund by my twenty-first birthday and had doubled that. They also couldn't touch the money that my grandmother Eloise had set aside for me. I was a favorite of Eloise's and, although I am not sure she was ever told the entire story of my disinheritance, I always had the oddest sense that she knew all about the circumstances. Even beyond that, I began to wonder if my grandfather's death was in reality the suicide they claimed it to be. I was not the first to wonder if he had not been helped along. It was shortly after he and Eloise had separated.''

"Separated?'' Calista said. "Wasn't that unusual for those times?''

"Divorce was unusual, but not separation. As I have grown older and with the benefit of emotional distance, I have concluded that this tragic tradition of abuse began with my grandfather Theodore, and—who knows—possibly before. But Eloise, my grandmother, was the only woman to ever do anything about it. There had been a daughter, Marella, whom she had suddenly, and for no apparent reason, whisked out of the house and out of Boston. They went to Paris and then to Florence to live together. They became part of that circle of American expatriots toward the end of the last century. It was an interesting group. John Singer Sargent and his family were part of it. You know, Sargent was born in Florence. Of course, Eloise had a lot more money than the

Sargents. But they would traipse about to the various spas and cities in a strange nomadic existence. Marella and John Singer became quite close. I even think she entered the atelier of Carolus-Duran with him in the 1870s in Paris. And Marella willed to me two Sargents, which are now in the Philadelphia Museum of Fine Arts. But back to the story. Marella became the heir not only to two Sargents but to the lion's share of grandfather Theodore's estate. It was disproportionately large, her share in comparison to Tad's. You can bet this was Eloise's doing. Eloise was very cunning. It was after one of her trips back to the States that grandfather Theodore was found dead of a self-inflicted gunshot wound. Blew his head off with a duck-hunting gun—that is the weapon of choice among our kind for suicide. Samuel Warren used a duck gun, too.''

Calista was absolutely dizzy with all that Rudy and Titty had been telling her for the last twenty minutes. She looked down at the drawings again and then picked up another piece of paper on which something was scrawled. ''What about Queenie? Did she know what was going on?''

''I'm sure. But again, she would deny on a very deep level. I do remember once when they came over to England, Queenie and the girls, Muffy and Bootsie. They visited me and then I took them on a wonderful trip through the Hebrides and the Orkneys. Queenie never said a word to me about anything specific. But there was this feeling of putting something behind, of fresh starts. As a matter of fact, she was very interested in grandmother Eloise and at one point I think we toyed with the idea of going over to see

Marella in Paris. She was very old at that time, however. She lived to be well over one hundred.''

Calista picked up the piece of paper she had been holding and looked at it more carefully. It was in the wobbly hand of a child just learning to write cursive.

"What's that?" Titty asked, leaning forward to get a better look.

"I'm not sure," Calista said. "A poem maybe."

"What does it say?" Titty asked.

"'Little Mother, Little Mother,'" Calista began to read. "'Gone away, gone away. Away, away I float. Leave just those parts behind. From the cage with bars of moonlight, bars of sunlight, I fly on my wings unbroken.'"

Titty had raised her hand to her mouth as if to stifle a cry. "That's what Kingie used to call Muffy, 'Little Mother.' It made my skin crawl. It was when I first heard him call her that that I began to suspect. I should have done something. But I didn't know what to do. That...that poem..." Titty pointed a plump, shaky finger at the paper. "That describes it perfectly. You see that is exactly what you do. You float out of your body. You take your brain and leave the rest behind. You imagine you're elsewhere, anywhere else but where you are. You teach yourself to endure, not to protect yourself, but just to get through it. If there is one thing an abused child learns how to do, it is to be abused. You become nothing more than a vagina. But your mind is somewhere else all the time."

"This is horrible. Just too horrible. And Queenie just let it happen?"

"Yes," said Rudy quietly. "She would never risk facing it. She would never risk divorce. She was a very conventional person, you know. She had made, after all, what was considered to be a superb marriage by all counts. And that was what determined a woman's fate in Boston of that era."

"But her children?"

"They suffer, and if they don't die from it, they begin to hate. Bootsie did hate her mother. I hated Aunt Abigail almost more than Uncle Tad."

"What happened to Muffy? Did she hate, too?"

"Of course. She hated most of all. The only way she could kill the big mother was to kill the Little Mother." And Calista saw hate swell in Titty's face.

THEY TOOK A WALK, then took a swim. Titty gathered some wildflowers. They did all the things that one was supposed to do at a summer place. But it all had changed from yesterday. It was as if there was a presence. The island, the woods, the house was full of little ghost girls fleeing, screeching in their silent terror as they were invaded, penetrated. This was where childhood had been slaughtered—at Nohqwha.

They returned to the house to pack up their things and go back to Boston. Calista heard the phone ring outside the bedroom as she was packing. A minute later, Rudy appeared at her door.

"A new development," he said. Titty was just coming down the hall.

"About Quintana?"

"Yes, a possible motive."

"What?" Calista and Titty both asked.

"Apparently, something is missing. Two priceless netsukes are gone."

"Netsukes?" Calista repeated.

"Yes. The toggle worn on the Japanese sash, the obi, by which the obi cord could be tied up and secured. Some are quite valuable and there are people throughout the world who collect netsukes quite passionately."

"But...but..." Titty stammered. "The police said nothing was missing, and Boots and Gus didn't think anything was, either."

"Well, they are quite small. They might have just overlooked them. Boots and Gus were in no state, of course, at that time to be taking detailed inventories."

"Yes, yes. Something that small is easy to overlook," Titty said.

Unless, of course, Calista thought, one was a connoisseur of Asian art and knew what to look for first. It was almost as if Rudy was reading Calista's mind.

"Of course, they might not be of any real value at all." A nervous shadow flickered across his face.

NINETEEN

"SO YOU DON'T have a father?" Jamie stared hard into his sandwich with a concentration it did not require.

"No, he's dead. Why did you ask?"

"Oh, I don't know. I just kind of wondered."

Kind of wondered my ass, Charley thought. This was the first vaguely personal thing this kid had ever said to him. The kid was a total zombie. Charley regretted the day he had ever met him, let alone told him about the opening on the swan boats. But he was caught in this terrible bind. This kid seemed irreparably damaged to Charley and he couldn't put his finger on it.

"You got a father?" Charley asked.

"Not around."

"Where is he?"

"California. He's got a new wife and new kids—brand-new everything." Jamie laughed bitterly. Yeah, thought Charley, they are all brand-new and you really are damaged old goods, aren't you?

"You ever go see him?"

"Naw...uh...he comes here sometimes."

"So it's just you and your mom." Charley decided to be bold.

"Yeah...yeah, just me and Mom."

"Well, that's almost the same as me. Me and my mom, except when Archie's around."

"Who's Archie?"

"My mom's friend—like boyfriend."

"They sleep together?"

"Yeah."

"Is that like weird for you? I mean, you know, like him not being your dad or stepdad."

"Naw. I mean it's not like she's had this string of boyfriends revolving through her bedroom. At least Archie's the only one I know about who's spent the night at our place, and I really like him a whole bunch."

"That's cool."

No, thought Charley, it's not just cool. There's something more going on here with Jamie. He was going to push it. "I guess, you know, maybe it is kind of weird thinking about your parents or your mom doing it . . . sex, I mean."

Jamie got up quickly and brushed off his pants. "I wouldn't know. My mom's too tanked most of the time to do much of anything." He laughed again and headed back toward the swan boats.

A FILIGREED SHADOW played across Titty's jowls, which rested comfortably in the nest of pearls encircling her throat. She was squashed into a wing chair with a teacup and saucer poised above her formidable bosom. "In the middle of August, there is no more discreet place than the Athenaeum. And I have always sought discretion," she said cryptically. "It's all part and parcel of the syndrome, so to speak."

Every Wednesday, tea was served at the private library, and Titty had called Calista to join her. Calista was familiar with the Athenaeum and had often used it for research. It had proved particularly helpful for tracking down some of the original Robin Hood source material when she was working on *Marian's*

Tale. It was the most august of Brahmin settings, with its marble busts gazing down from lofty niches, its neoclassical detailing and soaring Palladian windows. Calista was intimately familiar with the moldings throughout the library. They were the most exquisite in Boston and she had done painstaking sketches of them for the palace of the Beast, in *Beauty and the Beast,* a story that she had avoided illustrating for years before she was so terribly uncomfortable with its sexuality. However, once she had decided on the neoclassical motif with a decidedly pre-Raphaelite look to the landscape and characters, she had been more comfortable. It struck her as very odd now that here of all places, the Boston Athenaeum, she was discussing incest with a descendant of one of the most revered families of the Commonwealth. For although Titty's parents had not been nearly as wealthy as the Kingsleys or the Parkingtons, their lineage was equally dazzling and had its fair share of Adamses and Cabots and indeed Reveres and Brattles. Now Titty was telling her a horrific story about a trip to Newport when she was just fourteen or fifteen.

"Yes, we usually went down there for a week every summer, although Newport was somewhat frowned upon by many Bostonians. It was really a New York place. Vanderbilts, you know, that ostentatious crowd. But anyhow, both through my parents and Rudy's, we had relatives there. They gave the most lavish parties. The great flower of Newport was the American Beauty rose. Everyone grew them in those garish gardens they favored down there. You know, those homes were really in such bad taste. Big piles of pink Italianate stucco. In any case, every Newport hostess would try to outdo the others. They all loved splendor and they devoted their lives to creating it—chandeliers with crystal drops the size of oranges; everything overdone, overripe. There was one party where the host hung fourteen-karat-gold fruit from the branches of all the trees in the garden to create a *bois doré*. At another party, servants dressed as water nymphs, mermaids, and Tritons swam in the blue-tiled pools; they would rise up dripping from the pools and offer bowls of fruit to the guests. But as I was saying, the American Beauty rose—well, Newport felt it had an imprimatur on that flower. So it was always part of some party motif. And it certainly was the main theme at a Vanderbilt ball the year I was first allowed to attend. Five other young lovely girls and myself were to be part of the decor.''

Calista visibly winced. ''Yes, dear, I know. This was way before women's lib.'' Titty took a sip of her tea and continued. ''Well, we were led in wearing our lovely white gowns with satin ribbons wrapped round our wrists. It was supposed to be a kind of daisy chain, I suppose. Or rather, a rose chain, for we were then tethered, each of us to a rosebush.''

''Oh how awful!'' exclaimed Calista.

''You have no idea how awful, especially if you had been violated as I had for the previous five or six years. I felt as if I was a stain on this beautiful tableau; that I didn't belong in the company of these pure, flawless creatures in their white gowns; that I must have stuck out like a sore thumb; that my terrible secret must show. You see, that is the most awful thing. Ever since Tad had begun doing these horrible things to me, I felt that although it was a dreadful secret, everyone knew or suspected and that they blamed me. Even the fireflies on the screens knew my terrible secret; they were the same fireflies that were on the screens in the boathouse where Uncle Tad often took me. But worst of all was the feeling that in some strange way Uncle Tad had given his permission for other men to treat me this way. It was confirmed on that night at the Vanderbilt ball. A cousin of Tad's, one I had never met from Connecticut..." Titty's voice dwindled off.

Calista reached forward and took Titty's hand. "I was so angry," Titty continued. "I was desperate, and Rudy wasn't there. But I was sure that Aunt Abigail knew about it. I was just sure. And she was happy that it was this cousin and not her husband, Tad, this time. I could have killed her. So I can understand now how maybe—" Titty's voice dropped very low "—Bootsie could have perhaps murdered Queenie...but we must protect her no matter what."

"It doesn't look good with this netsuke theft...but then again, it seems so...so..."

"So what?"

"Obvious, I guess. I mean, Bootsie is the one who knows Asian art in the family, the one who has the connections."

"Not necessarily. Diggory and his sister-in-law Cornelia know a thing or two. They collect scrolls, I believe."

"But they're so old. And they certainly don't need the money. Does Bootsie?"

"I have no idea what Boots's financial condition is. She must get something from her former husband. I know that Rudy has given her some stock. But that's Rudy, forever generous."

"What about Gus? Has he given any to Gus?"

"I would imagine. Gus can't make much on that prep school teaching salary." Titty paused. "You know, perhaps I shouldn't say this, but Rudy always suspected that Gus might have tendencies.''

"Tendencies?'' Calista asked.

"You know—homosexual—gay, as they call it.''

"Gus?'' Calista's eyes widened in surprise.

"Oh nothing overt like Rudy. Good Lord, Kingie would have killed him if he had ever given the slightest hint. It's just a feeling that Rudy has had for a long time.''

"Well, actually, that might be a relief, considering the family history of heterosexual abuse of young girls.''

"Yes, yes, I always thought so,'' Titty said primly.

TWENTY

As CHARLEY PEDALED the swan boat to the dock, he noticed the dapper little man in a blue blazer with a crest on the pocket and a cap on his head. He looked like an illustration from one of his mom's children's books. He looked familiar, too. It dawned on Charley as he was stepping aboard who the little man was. The man managed to get into the last row of benches, the one directly ahead of the swan seat where Charley sat between the two large wings and pedaled.

"Charley Jacobs," the man said, and turned around on the bench, offering his hand. "Rudy Kingsley, a friend of your mother's."

"Yeah, I know. What are you doing here?"

"You bear a striking resemblance to your mother. It's the coloring, I think, and the shape of the eyes. Yes, that's it." The boat was almost fully loaded and the attendants on the pier had begun to shove it along manually. Charley began pedaling. A grandmother and her granddaughter had taken the seat next to Rudy. "I always say a trip to Boston is not complete without a swan-boat ride," Rudy said expansively. "Except, of course, if it is winter. Here, madame." He spoke to the woman next to him. "I happen to have bought some extra peanuts. Would the little girl like to feed the ducks?" They were most appreciative and soon became engaged in the feeding activity. Rudy then turned to Charley.

"I have arranged with the head boatman back there, or whoever that person is who seems to be directing things, for you to take an extended lunch hour tomorrow. You do own a jacket and tie, I presume?"

"Yes, sir."

"Wear it. Meet me at Locke-Ober's at twelve-fifteen. I'll be upstairs in the Ober Room, at the table in the northeast corner. It's my table."

"Northeast," Charley said vaguely.

"Take a compass if it's a problem. They do still teach geography, don't they?"

"Oh yeah, sure."

"Jock, the maître d' will be on the lookout. And by the way, don't mention anything to your mother about this—just yet."

Charley leaned forward a bit and pedaled harder as they were circling the duck island. "What's this all about, sir, the lunch and all?"

Rudy turned around. His face had a look of puckish delight. The minnow eyebrows leapt toward the neat brim of his cap and his lips moved around each letter of the word elastically. However, no one would have ever suspected the word this extremely effeminate dapper little gent was spelling. It was *M-U-R-D-E-R*.

"LOOK AT HIM. Wasn't he beautiful?" Titty said, pointing to a faded photograph of Rudy at about the age of ten or eleven. Calista and Titty had taken a cab back to Titty's duplex on the corner of Dartmouth and Commonwealth Avenue. The apartment had a bewildering array of the detritus of over a century of New England materialism. To the untutored eye, it appeared to be a confusing collection of stuff, which,

although seemingly unconnected, did have a kind of
pattern that could have spoken only of the inclina-
tions of merchant princes and Puritans.

China pug dogs stood sentry duty beneath an elab-
orately carved mantel. A vermilion Japanese fan filled
the fireplace. There were vitrines displaying porcelain
shepherdesses and willowware side by side, as if in
defiance of any dictums charging that never the twain
shall meet. Shawls were draped across the back of love
seats. Legions of tufted and tasseled footstools were
scattered about as if awaiting Titty's swollen feet at
anyplace she might decide to sit. Embroidered cush-
ions and Oriental rugs were everywhere. An immense
silver service stood on a sideboard. The service involved tiered trays supported by drooling silver grey-
hounds. Calista looked up from the photo album, her
gaze falling upon the dogs. Titty observed her.

"'Majestic bad taste,' that's what Rudy calls that
thing. To tell you the truth, I don't know how it
wound up here. It did come down through my mother's side of the family, presumably before they lost all
their money in the crash of '73. You know, the Crédit
Mobilier and all that." Calista's American history was
shaky, but Crédit Mobilier did ring a dim bell. "I
would think," Titty continued, "it would be worth
more than those netsuke things taken from Queenie's. My God, if you'd melt that thing down ... well,
maybe I should." Titty giggled. "It's hell to dust. Be
worth more as silver bars.

"Oh look! There's a picture of me and Rudy. I
think I'm Diana the huntress," Titty said, pointing to
another photograph in the album she had open on her
lap. There was a photo with curling edges of two
somber-looking children swathed in sheets. Titty had

dark curls and was carrying a bow. "I think those were my mother's furs draped over my shoulder." Calista turned the page. She felt something quicken.

"Oh dear," said Titty, "these are really out of order."

Calista bent closer. "What in the world?" she whispered. There was something very strange, very wrong about the picture.

"That's the Welles Club 'Frivolities,' my dear. When the gents dress up like women—or tarts."

"They don't even look human," Calista said in a soft voice. Titty reached for a magnifying glass. "Let's see. The date on this is 1924. Goodness, I wonder why I'd have this picture. I guess my father must be in it. Ah yes! There he is. Uncle Tad's not in this, but there's Kingie looking quite lissome."

It was all true what Rudy had said about this penchant for dressing up being ultimately a mockery. There was an element of something downright despicable in this picture. The grotesquely painted faces, the hips thrust out to the side, the corsets and fishnet stockings, the snickering expressions. But there was something else, something terribly disturbing about the picture independent of the smirking mockery. It triggered a vague response in Calista's brain, some image, some dim memory, some fragment of a picture, shard of a half-understood dream. What was it? She stared hard at the picture. "That's Kingie?" she asked.

"Yes. Quite handsome, wasn't he? Looked a lot like Rudy, but taller. He wore that corset well, what with his hourglass waist. All of the Kingsleys really cut such marvelous figures. Rudy didn't get their height, but you saw him in his bathing costume."

"Yes, very svelte," Calista said.

"Too bad I didn't get any of the svelte genes." Titty laughed.

But Calista wasn't really hearing her. She was lost in a maze of half images, shreds and slips of thoughts, but nothing would come together. She had to see Bootsie again. Surely she could go over on the pretense of something about Jamie and Charley and the swan boats.

TWENTY-ONE

CALISTA HAD BEEN scouring the old soapstone plank in the counter by the kitchen sink for well over five minutes.

"Mom, I think that's clean by now," Charley said.

"Oh . . . yeah, I kind of forgot."

"Forgot what? You seem a little spacey." I am a little spacey, Calista thought. For days, she had been wrestling with whether to tell Charley about her midnight visit to the Kingsleys' greenhouse where, hiding behind the fertilizer bags, she had seen the woman. It had been bad enough trying to figure out what to do before she went to Nohqwha, but now with the discovery of the missing netsukes, it was worse. She had possibly witnessed a crime and not just an intruder. When the woman had stopped to fix her stocking, she had a bag, and in that bag could have been the netsukes.

"I got a problem, Charley," Calista suddenly blurted out.

"What?" Charley asked.

"Hold on a minute." Calista ran upstairs. When she returned, she unfolded a handkerchief on the kitchen table.

"What is that?" Charley said, staring down.

"It's a garter. You know, for ladies' stockings."

"Oh. Oh yeah." There was a slight blush that crept across Charley's face. Not that he was such a prude. But as Calista had suspected, Charley had probably looked at some magazines with pictures of women in garter belts, something beyond the Victoria's Secret catalog. "So?"

"So." Calista sighed and began to tell him the story of how she and the garter had crossed paths in the Kingsleys' greenhouse.

When she had finished, Charley looked steadily at her. The gray eyes acquired that strangely luminous quality, so like Tom's, which on others might suggest that all the circuits were down, but Charley's, to the contrary, were in high gear. It was their deep-think look. He drummed his fingers on the table in a rapid-fire staccato. "You're right, Mom. You got a problem." Charley was thinking how Rudy had asked him not to say anything to his mother about their meeting the next day for lunch. He wanted to explain things first. But things were getting really complicated. His mom could, in fact, be implicated in this. What was it? Withholding evidence or something? But was it evidence?

"What makes you think that this person was there to steal these Japanese things that night? It doesn't make sense. Why didn't she take them at the time of the murder? Why revisit the scene of the crime? Isn't that more risk?"

"Yeah, yeah..." said Calista slowly. "Unless..."

"Unless what?"

"I'm not sure." Calista rubbed her forehead and dug her fingers into her brow.

"Don't do that, Mom. It really makes me nervous. I'm always scared that you're going to gouge your eyes out."

"I'm sorry." How did kids like Charley dare criticize their parents for these little habits? One would think that here, old Charley—whose sneakers sometimes smelled so badly that on occasion she had to spray them with Glade, or who thought nothing of wearing jeans that hung in shreds around his knees—could give a little more latitude in reference to certain parental characteristics. "It's just that I keep losing my train of thought. There is just something that is not fitting here."

"Like a person coming back after the big crime to steal something—yes, very illogical. Doesn't fit."

"No, it's more than that." She stopped again and rubbed her brow. To hell with him. "But if it is illogical, why would they do it?"

"Oooh, Mom! That's great. You're thinking mathematically!" Charley said with a burst of enthusiasm. He had just then decided for sure not to tell his mom about his meeting with Rudy until after the fact.

"I am? What do you know!" said Calista, somewhat mystified.

"Yep."

"I thought mathematics was all logic."

"It is...but how do you know what logic is until you figure out what is illogical?"

"Oh."

"It's just like Zorn's lemma."

"What?"

"Zorn's lemma. Dad told me about it a long time ago. But when I was doing that independent thing in set theory last semester...well, it was a big part of it."

"Lemma, not dilemma?"

"Yeah, lemma. See, Zorn was this really cool guy and he thought up this very basic thing that is fundamental to algebraic structure theory. It sounds real simple. It says that given an infinite number of sets, it is possible to make a new set by choosing one item from each of the other sets. Sounds simple, doesn't it?''

''Not really.''

''Oh, yes it does,'' said Charley dismissively. ''That's the elegance of the whole thing. Deceptively simple. It is really the equivalent of the axiom-of-choice set theory, but more ramifications. It cannot be derived from any of the other axioms in mathematics and yet it is totally universal. Cool, huh?''

''Well, if you say so. But I don't understand how Zorn and this—'' she held up the garter gingerly ''—come together.''

''Me, neither. That's sort of the beauty of it. It's one item from a set. A set that we have posited as being illogical. You said yourself, 'If it is illogical, why would they do it?' The set appears to be syncretic, but that is only if you look at it one way. Implicit in your question is why would they do it? This is a kind of lemma-esque proposition.''

''Oh, Charley, you've lost me.''

''No I haven't, Mom. Your question was mathematically legitimate, even if you were assuming an illogical stance. Look, you keep doing the illogical part and I'll do the logic. We can work this out. And remember this, Mom.'' He held up his finger, his eyes were burning bright.

''What?''

''There are an infinite number of sets.''

''And I'm supposed to find this comforting?''

FOR MATHEMATICIANS, infinities were an aphrodisiac. Calista thought of mathematicians as intrepid wanderers in rimless worlds, realms without confines, undaunted by notions of multiple and simultaneous universes. That was Charley. That was Tom. But she was one who needed edges, perimeters. She was bound to a two-dimensional, finite world. She worked in an arena that could be measured in inches. Books that came in trim sizes of nine inches by eleven, or possibly, if she was feeling very expansive, eleven by twelve. But often she worked in much smaller spaces. And within the paper's edges, she sometimes drew borders to limit the universe of the narrative further, to contain her story.

She lay in bed now, thinking about what she and Charley had discussed. Tortuously, she was trying to make the connection that the photograph from the Welles "Frivolities" had triggered. The sets could not be that limitless. If they were, there was no hope. But the limited sets pointed to Bootsie. Bootsie, with a double motive now: Kill the mother who had let the abuse happen; and, in some kind of ironic revenge, steal the family jewels. *Family jewels*—the term became freighted with dreadful meaning. Despicable families doing heinous things generation upon generation. Yes, it would be enough to make one murderous. She had not yet told Charley about the sexual abuse. It was so sad. Somehow, it seemed sadder than murder. But she would have to tell him sooner or later if his mathematical inquiries were to come together. Charley had said she should stick to the illogical and he'd take care of the logic.

She smiled to herself in the dark. How blessed she was. And then suddenly, she felt a sharp twinge deep, deep in her mind. It was familiar, but it had been a long time since she had missed Tom with that degree of sharpness, fresh as if it were just yesterday that she

had heard the awful news of his death. The terrible
realization that he was no more. There was again that
kind of lurching disbelief that seizes you when you
realize that you will never see someone again. Those
moments when you catch yourself thinking, Oh I want
to tell him that—or, Won't he love this? Had it been
all the talk of the mathematics? It was sharp and keen,
this kind of missing, and she had not had it in years.
The jolting roller-coaster ride of grief had smoothed
out, subsided into a kind of overwhelming sense of
loss, which seemed duller and less profound. There
had been fewer and fewer sharp twinges, no more
mistakes of expecting him to come through the door.
You knew now. You knew so well now the meaning of
never. You had grown accustomed to it and you hated
yourself for doing just that. But you were accustomed and, what was worse, you realized that life is
infinitely shabbier in the long, dull ache of missing.
This was terrible. She had never let herself be so self-
indulgent. What about Archie? He had been a wonderful lover, companion, and father for Charley. But
at this moment, Archie seemed farther away and more
abstract than Tom.

TWENTY-TWO

FOR A SECOND TIME, Charley found himself getting dressed as he crossed Boston Common. He had pre-made his tie that morning so he could just slip it on over the oxford-cloth shirt that he had neatly folded in his backpack. He had stepped beneath the fringed shade of a weeping willow to pull off his T-shirt and change into the other shirt. His mom would have died, but people had exposed worse than that in the Public Garden and the Common.

The bells of Park Street Church were just beginning to chime as Charley reached the corner of Tremont and Park. He continued up Tremont for a short block and then cut into Temple Place, a narrow alley that led directly into Winter Place. Over the entrance was an immense lock with a keyhole and scrolled design. The black-mullioned windows that faced the small, narrow street were half-curtained with lace. Charley straightened his tie and went in.

"Mr. Jacobs." An elderly man in a jacket and white bow tie was at his elbow immediately. "Mr. Kingsley is expecting you. This way, please."

Charley had never seen anyplace like this. He'd been to the Ritz a couple of times when his mom's editor, Janet Weiss, or Ethan Thayer, the publisher, came to town, but this was different. There was leather, beautiful wood, sparkling silver, polished brass, and stained glass. All this was reflected in the flash and glint of mirrors. Nothing really fussy, but it was a lit-

tle intimidating. They went up a set of stairs. The light
became dimmer, the draperies heavier, and the carpet
thicker. Charley followed the man into a beautiful
room of gleaming dark wood with touches of dull
gold. Rudy stood up as he approached the table. He
was dressed in a cream-colored suit. His bow tie was a
pale peach color, with darker checks. In the eternal
twilight of the room, Charley couldn't tell, but he
thought that Rudy Kingsley might be wearing makeup.
Oh well, it takes all kinds, he thought. He shook
hands.

"Welcome, dear boy. Have a seat. Hope you don't
mind eating up here out of the hubbub. I find it more
restful, more discreet for our subject matter. And alas,
I really find that eating lobster bisque under Mademoiselle's tits does something to my digestion."

"What?" Charley's eyes widened.

"Oh, of course. This is your first time to Locke's?"

"Yes, sir."

"Well, downstairs in the bar, there is a famous nude
painting. For some unknown reason, for generations
she has been called Mademoiselle Yvonne. For years,
they used it as an excuse not to seat women downstairs. Then there was the famous liberation of the bar
back in August of 1970."

"What happened?"

"A woman, a professor from MIT, called up and
made a reservation for Dr. So-and-So. She failed to tell
them that the Dr. was herself, a woman."

"So they seated her."

"Absolutely."

"Now, how about a drink for the young man," said
Rudy as a waiter arrived.

"Sure."

"I trust you're not taking in these yet?" He nodded at the two glasses lined up one in front of the other, with clear fluid and olives resting on the bottoms. It did seem a curious arrangement to Charley.

After Charley had ordered a Coke and the waiter had left, Rudy leaned forward and whispered, "Martinis! A delight to be anticipated, my dear, when your palate has developed and your innards have already gone to hell. This is the only way to drink martinis, lined up like this. Jack Benny would always drink from the second one first. Do you know why?"

"No."

"Well, he always said the second one goes down so much easier than the first." Rudy leaned back and laughed, his eyes crinkling into mirthful slits. There is something very likable about this weird little man, Charley thought. "But that's not why I do it," Rudy said. He lifted one of the martinis. "Have you ever seen a lovelier liquid in your life? Isn't it like liquid candlelight? And then if you order two of them, you get these lovely reflections and the play of light off the crystal and the gin in a room like this...aahh!" Rudy sighed. In a soft voice, he began to recite.

> There is something about a Martini,
> A tingle remarkably pleasant;
> A yellow, a mellow Martini;
> I wish that I had one at present.
> There is something about a Martini,
> Ere the dining and dancing begin,
> And to tell you the truth,
> It is not the vermouth—
> I think that perhaps it's the gin.

"Ogden Nash," he said. "A verse for almost every occasion—except murder, I believe. And that, of course, is why I have invited you to lunch."

RUDY WAITED, however, until the waiter had brought a Coke for Charley.

"Now, as I was saying—about Queenie, Quintana Kingsley, my sister-in-law. You have heard, I trust, about the latest development in the case—the theft of the netsukes."

"Yes." Charley felt something turn inside him. Should he tell Rudy Kingsley about his mom's midnight adventure? Of course not, but he hoped that Rudy wouldn't suspect that he was hiding something.

"Your mother tells me that you are quite ingenious with computers."

"Well, I mess around with them."

"She tells me that on occasion—very special occasions—you are most skillful at cracking into systems." A deep red flush began to crawl up Charley's neck and across his face. He felt his pulse quicken. He was no good at small talk.

"Don't call it *crack*. Call it *hack*. Crackers are evil hackers."

"Well, this is certainly not evil. I just want you to browse around, see what's happening."

"Passive monitoring," Charley said. It wasn't a question; it was a statement. "I don't mess anything up."

"Right. I just need some information."

THEY ORDERED and then Rudy explained what he needed.

"Hopkins, Bishop and Creeth," Charley said. All those law firms sounded the same. At first, he thought it sounded like his mom's lawyers, Haverford, Phillips and Beame. "You don't by any chance know what kind of system they use?"

"System?" Rudy asked. Just at that moment, a waiter came with their first course. Shrimp cocktail for Charley, lobster bisque for Rudy.

"Operating system for their computers."

"Oh, I have no idea, dear boy."

"It's probably VAX, with a UNIX system. I can find out. A friend of mine did a lot of work setting up systems for law firms around here. So what am I looking for?"

"Well, basically, information about the Kingsley estate. Young Harley Bishop still does a lot of work for me. So I am in their files—if you need me as camouflage."

"Do you have any documents with you, any paper stuff at all?"

"Oh no, I'm afraid not. It's all back in England in my office there."

"Where are these guys located—the law firm?"

"One Post Office Square. Why, are you planning on walking right in?" Rudy raised an eyebrow in bemusement. "I thought you could do all this over your electronic wires."

"I can. But some preliminary trashing might help."

"Trashing."

The waiter arrived with their main courses. Charley blinked as the waiter set down Rudy's plate. There was a mound of dark reddish brown stuff with something on top that looked as if it had died.

"Something wrong, Charley?"

"What is that stuff?"

"Roast beef hash with poached eggs on top."

"Oh." What would people think of next? He dug into his chopped sirloin. He had specified to leave off the mushrooms.

TWENTY-THREE

JUST AS CHARLEY HAD thought: In an alley behind Post Office Square, there was a loading dock. Two Dumpsters sat side by side at one end. This would probably be fruitless, but one could never tell. The biggest payoffs in terms of this activity came if one trashed the telephone company. Phone phreaks did it all the time. They could get access codes, discarded manuals, old papers containing passwords, whatever might help them in ripping off service from the baby bells. But then the phone companies started shredding documents with a vengeance when they realized what was happening. Phone phreaks were weird; they didn't just enjoy stealing service, gabbing their heads off and messing up switching stations, but, in addition, they absolutely loved to taunt their victims. Their methods in and of themselves, though, were appealing.

Charley did not see anything wrong in going through folk's trash as long as it wasn't to steal or for blackmail. He might get lucky and find some account information. It was so easy. You could do it in broad daylight. He took off his jacket, tie, roughed up his hair, and began muttering. Most likely, he looked like a somewhat cleaner-than-average homeless person looking for returnable cans or edible garbage. Hopkins, Bishop and Creeth did not believe in shredding—at least not phone logs and phone bills. He took handfuls of paper. He had no idea whether any of it would help him, but Charley liked to be thorough. Just as soon as you decided you didn't need something was exactly when you needed it. This was not going to be a phreaking job—at least not so far, but he wasn't going to leave any base uncovered.

CHARLEY RUSHED HOME after work. Luckily, his mother wasn't in. He sent E-mail to Liam Phillips, a computer jock for the Martin Institute, a genetic-research outfit where Charley had worked in an intern program one summer. Liam wrote beautiful code for all the wanna-be Nobel laureates at Martin. He had also been the computer consultant to law firms throughout the country, a specialist in programming for lawyers and writing code for time-keeping programs, so every minute increment could be billed and accounted for.

Later that evening, Charley, in the thick heat of the August night, sat naked at a desk in his bedroom at 16 Louisburg Square. He had Eric Clapton's *Unplugged* playing softly on his CD player. Liam had left a one-word message: UNIX.

This would be pig-easy now for Charley. He picked up the phone and dialed a number.

"Mr. Kingsley, please."

"Just one moment, sir."

Charley waited. There was the click. "Yes?"

"Hi. It's me. Can you call up that Harley guy and ask him for a copy of some document—anything. Tell him you want it on disc because you want to send a copy through Internet to your London office."

"Yes."

"Tell him you got a friend at Harvard in the computer lab that can do it for you, but you just want to see it first."

"I have many friends at Harvard."

"Yeah, you got me. And I still got my dad's old access code; so it's not like you're lying. I mean, I am a legal user on the Harvard system."

"I trust, however, that you are not really going to Internet this."

"No, but if we need an excuse, we got it."

TWENTY-FOUR

"NO...NO, GUS, I just can't believe it.... Yes. Do you mean that? Okay, yes.... I mean, it's just so ridiculous. Do you think I should get Jamie out of town?... Yes. I guess you're right; that would arouse more suspicion... yes, yes, okay. Good-bye."

Bootsie McPhee put down the phone. How had it all gone so wrong? Jamie! Never! How had this happened? Oh God, she needed a drink. But she needed to think, too. Gus had actually said he would help her. Time to let bygones be bygones, he had said. She laughed out loud harshly. Bygones! So that's what he called it. Well, she had little choice. Hadn't it all started out to protect Jamie? Was it so strange now that it was coming round full circle, so to speak, to this? Maybe she should talk with Rudy? But Gus had said not to. Anything was premature at this point. A panic welled up inside her. She could feel it fluttering and hot, pressing inside her rib cage. There was only one thing that could quell it, smooth it out so she could think. She had to be able to think. She went into the kitchen and took the bottle of vodka from the freezer, where she kept it. She poured two inches into a frosted glass and put in three cubes of ice. She set the glass on a small silver tray. A halo of condensation formed on the tray around the base of the glass. She loved that part. Then carefully, she sliced a thin peel of lemon. Bootsie had her rituals. They were important. It was just a question now, as her hands began to

shake slicing the lemon, if it was penance or ritual?
Was she delaying the pleasure or prolonging the pain?
She set down the lemon and the knife and grabbed
hold of the countertop. Her face clenched. Tears, the
first in years, squeezed from her eyes. How had every
fucking thing gone so fucking wrong in her entire
fucking life, and now . . . now just when she needed to
be strong for Jamie? Gus said he would be right over.
He had to help her. He really owed it to her. Now she
really needed him. Oh God, how had it come to this?
Hurry, Gus, hurry! she prayed. "I am praying to
Gus!" she blurted out loud, her voice cracking with
astonishment.

THE DOORBELL RANG. She didn't bother to wipe her
face. What would he expect, after all?

"Oh my goodness!"

"You?" Bootsie gasped, perplexed. What was Calista Jacobs doing on her front doorstep?

"Bootsie, is something wrong?" How stupid,
thought Calista. Something was obviously very wrong.
"Are you sick? Can I help you?"

"Oh no, no . . . just uh . . . some upsetting news. Come
in? Do you need something?"

Well yes, Calista thought but so much for the whole
ruse of just being in the neighborhood—what the hell,
she might as well do as she had planned. "I . . . I was
just in the neighborhood and thought I'd drop in and
say hi. I think it's great that Jamie is working with
Charley at the swan boats. He really enjoys Jamie."
Was this sounding as hollow and forced to Bootsie as
it was to her? This was so stupid. Why had she ever
decided to come here? But Calista had begun to see an
inexorable course. Just that morning, a homicide de-

tective had paid a call. It was about the recent netsuke theft.

Oh, they were clever. They had never directly mentioned Bootsie's interest in Oriental art, but Calista
could read between the lines. And she had a gut feeling about Bootsie. She just couldn't believe that she
had murdered, and, in particular, she couldn't believe that even if she had, the motive would be money.
There was too much baggage there, and money was
not going to make up for the terrible abuses in the
past—the abuse by her father, the outright neglect by
Quintana of her daughters in their tragic predica-
ment. It added up to hatred, yes. Calista could believe that Bootsie had a deep well of hatred, but she
did not believe that it would lead to murder. Those
haunting handless pictures were part of her belief.
Bootsie was a profoundly incapacitated person; to take
up those shears and plunge them into her mother's
chest with her own two hands would be beyond her; at
least Calista thought so.

Bootsie stood now in front of Calista, swaying
slightly, her face blotchy and her eyes vague and un-
focused.

"Yes, isn't it wonderful about Jamie. Come in!
Come in!" A new animation crept into her voice.
"Oh, I am so happy that he and Charley were able to
get together. I mean, Jamie has needed something like
this." Bootsie was talking a mile a minute. She seemed
to be making a spectacular recovery from whatever
bad news she had just received. "Jamie was telling me
that Charley is quite the computer buff. You know one
of my objections to Poulton Academy—that's Jamie's school—is that it's so old guard and locked into
such ridiculous traditions that they do very little with

computers. I really think that I may have him change next year...now that there is no one to object. To hell with Diggory.''

Calista could barely keep up with the stream of verbiage issuing forth. ''Would you like some coffee? I still have some left from breakfast or tea, or here's a great idea. It's so hot, maybe I'll put some ice in a glass and we can have iced coffee.''

''Fabulous!'' Calista said. She felt as if she were drowning in the rushing stream of words. She followed Bootsie into the kitchen. Bootsie got a glass out and filled it with ice cubes and poured in the morning's coffee. ''Sugar, milk?''

''A little of both would be fine.''

''Great,'' said Bootsie. ''I'll just pour mine in here.'' She took the coffeepot and poured it into a glass on a silver tray that already had ice in it.

They went out to the living room. Calista took a sip of the coffee. She sat directly across from the Japanese scroll that depicted cranes in flight over a waterfall. Muffy's poem came back, shards of it like slivers of glass:

''Little Mother, Little Mother... Away, away I float. Leave just those parts behind. From the cage with bars of moonlight, bars of sunlight I fly on my wings unbroken.''

Terrible little mothers, Calista thought, mutilated little mothers. Bootsie was rattling on about Jamie—how she felt he would profit from going to just a regular public school, Brookline High. More in touch with the real world. But Calista just kept staring at the cranes in flight. ''You like the scroll?'' Bootsie asked, finally breaking out of her nonstop talk.

"Yes. It's quite lovely. So tranquil." Would it be possible to segue, as it were, from Japanese scrolls into incest? Calista wondered. She felt desperate for Bootsie. Perhaps if Bootsie could know that someone else knew, someone who cared, someone who could understand her anger and yet know that she would not have murdered . . . But how could Calista do this? She was just an interfering person who had happened to live next door to the scene of a terrible crime. Those pictures . . . could she ask her about the pictures? But if Bootsie had never been able to talk with Rudy or Titty about this, why would she talk to Calista about it?

"Of course, now with the netsukes being stolen, I guess that moves me into the category of prime suspect, doesn't it?"

Calista gasped.

"Don't look so surprised. With my interests and connections, it's natural." Bootsie spoke almost casually.

"But . . . but . . ." stammered Calista. "You said it really wasn't much of an interest."

"I said that?" Bootsie raised her eyebrow.

"I thought you did."

"Well, it's not a career," she said, lifting her glass for a swallow. She held it to her mouth for a moment before drinking and looked over the rim, the celadon eyes cold as ice. "It doesn't pay . . ." She paused. "Unless you get into something like the netsukes."

Calista was speechless. Just then the doorbell rang. "It's my brother. I've been expecting him." Bootsie jumped up.

THEY WERE DELAYED in the entrance hall. Calista heard a low rapid-fire exchange. Then Bootsie and Gus both walked into the living room with expressions of cheerful well-being that looked like pancake makeup applied with a backhoe. Calista felt alarms going off in every part of her brain. Now both of them started talking nonstop about Jamie. Bootsie sat in the wing chair, her head lolling back, her eyes looking slightly feverish while both she and Gus did a red-hot jig of praise for Jamie. They tossed bits and pieces of talk back and forth while Gus paced around the room, behind the chair where Bootsie sat, neither one of them ever making eye contact with each other. But it was as if every word and glance was being directed toward Calista. "Wonderful boy." "Great idea, Brookline Public High." They were God-blessing Charley and the swan boats all over the place. Relentless talk about computers, summer jobs, college boards, extracurricular activities, on and on until Calista wanted to scream, Stop, you idiots! Don't you know that your mother has been murdered and you, Bootsie, are fast becoming a prime suspect? You said as much yourself. Why all this talk about Jamie? Isn't it time to get down to business here?

"Oh, I just remembered—I have to make a call," Gus said suddenly.

"Use this phone right here," Bootsie said, "unless it is private."

"No, not at all. It's just about the coaching schedule. I coach tennis out at Longwood and at St. Bennett's. Very hectic, come summer, with all the tournaments. I've got to call someone from Longwood now."

Bootsie, in the meantime, had brought over a book of nineteenth-century Japanese scroll paintings to show Calista. They were very beautiful. And Bootsie obviously knew her stuff. In the background, she could hear Gus talking. "No...no...every Tuesday and Thursday, I'm occupied out at St. Bennett's. It's the only time we can get court time. So I always just spend the night out there in a dorm. It's hardly worth the trip back into Boston. Yeah, yeah. Sorry, Dan, but that's the schedule."

BY THE TIME Calista had finally wrenched herself free of Gus and Bootsie, her head was spinning with their ceaseless chatter. Had they both taken amphetamines or what? Gus had made another call to discuss his tennis-coaching schedule. There certainly had been no opportunity to open up any sort of discussion with Bootsie about her past. A soft drizzle had begun to fall. As Calista walked up Charles Street, she wondered how she had ever been so presumptuous as to think she could have gone in and begun talking about all this stuff with Bootsie.

The wet brick smell rose from the sidewalk. The rain came down harder. It felt good. She was not wearing a jacket and soon her blouse stuck to her skin. She felt cool at last. Ringlets of wet hair plastered her forehead and there were rivulets running down to her eyebrows. She turned up Mt. Vernon Street. The trees dripped and the windowpanes in the tall brick houses were slick. If you squinted just so, the inky green of the trees, the dark cobbles of the street, and the brick smeared into a slide of rain-dark colors. It was a very sensual, timeless world. Perhaps she could slip through a loophole into another history, another universe. If there were multiple universes, there could be multiple and simultaneous histories. If only time were not linear but curled back on itself in loops so that there was no such thing as "progress" or "advancement" in a chronological sense, then there would be this place where time stood still, at the center of things, where you could meet another aspect of yourself in this motionless place with complete understanding. Just supposing, thought Calista, I have a nineteenth-century counterpart who lived on this hill. She turned into Louisburg Square and continued her thought: Instead of being products of time, we would be nuances of, say, light or passion; then time and chronologies might be irrelevant.

Just ahead, Calista spotted a cluster of dark umbrellas at the end of the walk of number 18, the Kingsleys'. A dark car was pulled up. Calista approached.

There was the meanest lady in Boston, her mouth a trembling red slash. A nurse held an umbrella over her to shield her from the rain. "What do you mean we can't get in? We don't have the right set of keys? I thought you squared this with Gus, Harley, you fool! Bambi, call Gus now."

"I tried, Grummy. There was no answer." Bambi looked away from Cornelia Parkington and spotted Calista approaching. "Oh hi! We can't reach Gus— although I know this isn't his day for coaching at St. Bennett's. You don't by any chance have a key to the Kingsleys'?"

"Who's that?" growled Cornelia.

"Calista Jacobs, Grummy. You know, the one who is the Baldwins' friend and is staying there this summer."

"The Jewish one?"

Holy smoke! thought Calista. Had she actually heard that correctly? The shrewish one perhaps? Bambi colored and Harley stopped his intense perusal of the set of keys he was holding. He coughed loudly. "I think we should be going."

"I think we should not," barked Cornelia. "I want to check on that painting. If they stole those Japanese things out of here, it is not secure. If anything happens to the portrait, I'm going to hold you responsible. Figure out a way to get in, Harley."

"I can't break in Cornelia."

"Call Bootsie," Cornelia snapped. "She might have a key."

Harley groaned. "Let me run down to Charles Street. There must be a pay phone down there."

"Oh, don't do that," Calista said. "Come on into the Baldwins'. You can use the phone."

"How kind of you," Harley said.

"Uh . . . would the rest of you like to come in out of the rain?"

"Oh no, that won't be necessary," Bambi replied quickly, rolling her eyes in a manner that indicated good old Grummy could drown out here, for all she cared.

Harley followed Calista in to number 16. "There's a phone right in there, in the study."

"Oh thank you. This is very kind of you . . . and er . . . uh . . ." Calista knew what was coming. "Don't mind Mrs. Parkington she's just a . . ."

"An ignorant bitch." Calista finished the sentence. She would not tolerate excuses in such matters.

"I wasn't going to put it quite that way . . . but—"

"Well, I did. So you don't have to now."

Harley blinked at her through his horned-rimmed glasses as if perhaps he was seeing something for the very first time. He then turned and went into the study to use the phone. "Busy," he said. "Do you mind if I try again?"

"No, not at all. Be my guest," Calista called in. She was sorting through the mail.

"Uh . . . is this your work here on this board?"

Calista walked in. She had set up a drafting table by the window. On it was a half-finished painting of the artificial bird that had been made to replace the nightingale in the story. Calista had painted it sitting on a silk cushion set beside the emperor's throne.

"Yeah."

"You do this for a living? Oh, by the way, I'm Harley Bishop, attorney for the Kingsleys."

"I'm Calista Jacobs, and yes, I do this for a living."

"Why of course. I have heard of you. I believe my children, when they were younger, read your books. Why, you're famous!" His face seemed to brighten and he looked at her again. "What is this picture for?"

"*The Emperor and the Nightingale.* It's a spread where they've just brought the mechanical one to the emperor."

"Gee, I'm not sure whether I'm familiar with that story."

"Oh it's an old Andersen tale, basically about power and obsession with perfection and art and artifice—perhaps a tad like Cornelia out there."

This reference seemed to bring old Harley back to reality. "Oh, I'll try Boots again. God, I hope she has a key."

He dialed the number. "Ah, Boots! Harley Bishop, dear. I'll tell you why I'm calling. Dear Aunt Cornelia...yes, you guessed it...having fits about the Mather portrait. She just wants to check on it. We can't get in. My keys don't seem to work. By chance, do you have one? Splendid...what? Oh, there is one here? Yes...yes. Well, as a matter of fact, I'm standing with Ms. Jacobs right now. Calling from Will Baldwin's study. Terrific."

THERE WAS A KEY hidden behind the greenhouse in the back by the hedge. Calista took Harley out through the Baldwins' back door to the Connecting Gardens. He was back in less than a minute, just as Charley Jacobs came walking through the front door.

"Oh hi, Charley. Meet Harley Bishop. He's a lawyer for the Kingsleys."

Charley nearly gulped, but he recovered fairly quickly. Was this weird or what? He hadn't even hacked in yet and here was this guy. He even had a fragment of a copy of Harley's phone log upstairs, culled from the Dumpster in the alley behind Post Office Square. Rudy Kingsley was supposed to have the disc this afternoon. God, he couldn't have blown it yet. He trusted there was some other agenda going on here.

"You're drenched, Charley. Maybe you'd better go upstairs and dry off."

"Yeah, and I have to meet...uh...Matthew...soon. They let us off early because of the rain."

"Will you be home for dinner?"

"Uh...no."

"Nice meeting you, Charley," Harley said as Charley turned to go upstairs.

"Oh, nice meeting you, Mr. Bishop." This was absolutely too weird. Wait until Rudy heard this.

"Well, I better go. I can't thank you enough, Calista." He shook her hand. His grip lingered. This guy's going to call, Calista thought. Damn it. She always could tell when they were going to call. He was attractive in that tight-ass WASP Elliot Richardson way. Not the way that appealed to Calista. Shoot! She wished Archie would come back. This was one complication she simply did not need. And no denying it: She was horny as all get out.

TWENTY-FIVE

"YOU DON'T SAY, Leon . . . no . . . my this is a coincidence . . . but totally unanticipated. So you say that it was a woman's voice and she insists on anonymity? And you're sure that she most likely did not have the second netsuke at the time of her initial call? Interesting . . . Oh! My young friend has just arrived. Yes, I'll be talking to you, and you keep me posted if you get any other phone calls from Madame X."

Charley had been shown to a smaller room off the library at the Harvard Club on Commonwealth Avenue, where he found Rudy.

"Welcome to my Boston office. Quite convenient. We have everything here one needs to carry on business—phone, fax, copy machine down the hall."

"You got the disc back to them?"

"Yes, I messengered it to Harley first thing this morning."

"I just met Harley."

"You what?" Rudy's pale eyes widened in surprise.

"Get this: He was at the Baldwins' house, using the phone. Mom let him use it because he had come with some old biddy to check on some picture in the Kingsleys' house and his key didn't work."

"Cornelia had him over there." Rudy's face darkened. "At two hundred and fifty an hour, Cornelia is hauling Harley over to number Eighteen to check up on that ridiculous painting." Rudy pulled a saffron-colored silk handkerchief that appeared to be the size of a small towel from his pocket. He sank onto a settee, rolled his head back, and began to mop his brow.

"Are you all right?" Charley asked. Just his luck for this gay geezer to have a heart attack on him.

"I'm fine. Believe me, if there is such a thing as reincarnation, I think I would honestly prefer to come back as Tammy Faye Bakker than as a member of this family. Every day is a trial; every day one must use one's wit and grit just to survive the sheer outrageousness of this family and their peculiarities, their neuroses. It eats you alive if you don't. So what do you wind up with—the survivors—people like me and Cornelia. But I swear if that bitch wasn't wheelchair-bound, I wouldn't put murder past her."

"You wouldn't?" Charley asked.

"Throughout her life, this woman has committed a thousand and one little murders, little bloodless murders."

"What do you mean?"

"Oh, my dear boy, it's too complicated to go into."

"But she's from the other side of the family, isn't she? She's not directly related to you?"

"Not exactly. But as with all these Boston families, the genealogies get intertwined at certain points. This is really the source of the problem over the Cotton Mather portrait. Both families, the Parkingtons and the Kingsleys, can trace a lineal descent to that loathsome man. You know, he was best known for his zeal for hunting down witches and his experiments in curing the afflicted girls—pseudoscience being the last refuge of pinched minds. The problem was, the best witch was yet to come."

"Cornelia?" Charley said.

"Yes, and Bambi, her granddaughter, would be a close second. Anyhow, enough of that. Weren't you supposed to bring your computer?"

"I did," Charley said, taking off his backpack.

"In that? It fits in there?"

"It's not a mainframe, just a laptop. Have you called Harley and had him load the disc up to show the changes?"

"Yes. Actually, it was his secretary, Mildred."

"It doesn't matter who it was just as long as we got it into the system."

"Well, yes. I did it rather smoothly. I just called up and told them that the accession number on the small gold minotaur must be followed by a letter indicating a new system we were trying out with Greek antiquities of a certain size. I also corrected a small detail concerning a tax benefit over a gift to the Tate. All quite convincing, I thought."

"Social engineering," Charley said.

"What?"

"Social engineering. I knew you'd be great at it."

"What is it?"

"What you just did with Mildred. It is a hacker's best tool. You pose as someone else or you make up a phony question that gives you a foot in the door."

"But really, Charley, *you* did that, or at least you're going to get us in."

"No. I created the door, a back door. You got your foot in it through your social-engineering skills with Mildred. I couldn't have done that. It's not my thing. I've got friends who can. You talk real smooth and your accent and all. It helps. There's this woman, Barbara, she's really famous. She was actually a prostitute, but she was queen of the phone phreaks.

She got right into the heart of the Pacific Bell system. She downloaded a whole set of missile-firing parameters and maintenance schedules for intercontinental missiles. She knew exactly how the Pentagon was connected with the Bell system. She worked with a gang out of L.A., but she was the perfect social engineer. Well, seeing as she was a prostitute, maybe it came with the territory." Charley had a bemused look on his face. Rudy nearly burst out laughing. He had never seen anything quite so quixotically charming as this boy.

"Okay now, are you going to show me how it works?"

"Sure enough. Let me plug in."

IT TOOK CHARLEY less than a minute to plug in his laptop and modem, then boot up. He dialed the number for Hopkins, Bishop and Creeth.

"What's that?" Rudy said excitedly. He had pulled up a chair next to the table where Charley was working. He leaned forward and recrossed his legs. The gray screen had brightened.

WELCOME TO HOPKINS, BISHOP AND CREETH. WARNING: THIS SYSTEM IS FOR THE EXCLUSIVE USE OF HBC FIRM EMPLOYEES ONLY. ANY ABUSE WILL BE PROSECUTED UNDER THE COMPUTER INTRUSION ACT 1039.

"That's supposed to scare us," Charley said.

"But it doesn't?" Rudy replied, his voice swelling with excitement. He wiggled in his chair and recrossed his legs again.

"Right. We're tough dudes here."

"Oh, this is so exciting, Charley. I can hardly stand it."

Charley was excited, too. There was nothing quite like the high of busting into a bureaucracy. Their sheer smugness was adrenaline into the veins of any technocowboy riding through cyber space. Give those kids with the funny haircuts and the plastic pen holders white hats, spurs, and chaps and they would carry on the best of the American frontier tradition. Only now it was an electronic frontier. Nonetheless, these kids were absolutely soaked with a heroism as old as the country, a heroism associated with cowboys, mountain men, and original thinkers who had stood up against rigid no-balls institutions; it could be the Bell system, the Pentagon, Wall Street, NASA, big industrial complexes, or fat-cat law firms—mainframe guys. But all of the guys in these places set themselves up as an "information priesthood"; they treated knowledge and information as an elitist commodity—just like their fucking elitist clubs, one of which Charley now sat in, and the university in which his late father had held the Cowles Chair of Particle Physics.

USER NAME:

"What's Mildred's last name again?"

"Hennessey."

Charley typed in her name.

PASSWORD:

BIJOU

"That's French." Charley looked up.

"I know," Rudy replied. "Is it going to work?"

"Of course. Eighteen months ago, I could have set up a program to generate passwords randomly to get Mildred's word. But a lot of places now have programs that can detect when that is being done. These folks probably don't. They seem old-style. They don't monitor this thing at all. I can tell. But better safe than sorry. This is the cleanest way possible.''

''I still don't understand what you did exactly.''

''It was easy. On that disc you gave me, I created a backdoor into the system. I wrote a little virus in a computer language—C plus, plus.''

''But a virus? That makes me nervous.''

''Don't worry. It's not destructive and it's containable. I'll delete the whole thing when we're through. No trace. Besides, even if it got loose, it wouldn't hurt anything. Not terminal. I just made it so that this password of mine, *Bijou,* is recognizable along with whatever Mildred's other word is. Think of it like a Trojan horse—that's what they sometimes call them— to get us into the city. Okay. Get ready. Here we go. What do you want to see?''

''Call up Elliot Kingsley's will.''

Charley raked through the files. There were nearly one hundred documents under Kingsley. He found the file Rudy had asked for.

Rudy got out his reading glasses. ''Yes, just as I remembered. Quite standard. It passes to the widow first. And now that will pass on to the kids through Quintana. They should have put part of that in an irrevocable trust. I told Kingie that before he died. Taxwise, it would have been beneficial, and, of course, it precludes squabbling. Okay, dear boy, let's go to Quintana.''

''Oh man...there's a lot here,'' Charley said, looking at the files listed. ''Lot of action in the last year.''

"Lot of action in the last two months," Rudy said. "This could be interesting."

IT TOOK HOURS, and for Charley, it was not that interesting. He felt like a digital drudge, but Rudy was fascinated. "That bitch! Wouldn't you know that Queenie would be that kind. Changing her will just slightly every three weeks and probably calling everybody in for little family dinners to announce the favored heir of the month. But she certainly seems to have favored Gus consistently. She always was soft on him. Poor Boots. Let's call up Boots's file and get a peek at some of her assets."

Charley found a file for Bootsie.

"Well, isn't that sweet," Rudy said sarcastically. "Queenie gave the main house of Nohqwha to Bootsie."

"That's not good?" Charley asked.

"Not for Bootsie, I don't think. It is not a repository of happy memories—to say the least. It was where her sister Muffy hung herself, for one thing. And how would Bootsie ever maintain it? Her portfolio, at least what I see of it here, looks rather pathetic. Her major asset is the Brookline house. She apparently has a second mortgage out on that. See, I told Kingie that if he had set up an irrevocable trust, real estate like that could have gone into it and it would have relieved Bootsie of a terrible burden. What else does she have to show here? Good God, railroad stocks! How they treat the women in this family! Look, her best stuff is what I gave her years ago—a rental property in the South End, Charming Shoppes—those clothes for chubby ladies are still doing well. Good grief—she's still got the Wang. I told her to get rid of that."

At 10:30, Malcolm, the steward, arrived with a tray—Lapsang souchong tea and a plate of smoked salmon for Rudy; Coke and home fries for Charley.

"Gee, these are fat," Charley said, picking up one of the fries. "Not like McDonald's." He took a bite of one of the fries. "Did you ever hear about Fry Guy?"

"Fry Guy?" Rudy repeated.

"Yeah. He's this incredible kid from Indiana. He's in federal prison now. I mean, I don't want you to think I would actually ever do anything like this, but the guy really has style."

"Yes?" Rudy said. "I'm waiting." He slid his thumb under his suspenders.

"Well, this kid, he's in the Legion of Doom."

"Legion of Doom? Is this going to be an S and M story?"

"S and M?"

"Sadomasochism."

"Oh no no noooo, nothing like that. This was all good clean fun till he got busted. Well, there's the phone-sex part."

"Phone sex?"

"Yeah, Tina in Queens—but I'm jumping ahead."

"Well, by all means, don't do that. Let's savor the story." Rudy leaned forward and stabbed a slice of smoked salmon. He arranged it on a piece of dark rye and then took a tiny spoon and spread some mustard sauce on it. It was all so dainty and neat, Charley felt kind of gross by comparison. He had just dribbled some catsup on his shirt from the fat fry.

"Well, anyway, the Legion of Doom is just this underground bulletin board. You know, a pirate board. I explained to you about these electronic bulletin boards. Pirate ones, you know, do stuff that is either slightly illegal—copies of games or manuals, stolen passwords, how to get into systems—or all the way illegal, like getting credit card numbers. Some of the boards are really heavy, anarchistic boards.

"*Phrack,* a phreak hacking magazine, shows up on a lot of these boards. It is considered by the feds a major bad-attitude outfit, along with the Legion of Doom. In any case, Fry Guy was a typical Legion of Doom dude. He lived out in Indiana. He was just about sixteen years old, and he is considered like majorly wicked now by the feds."

"What did he do?"

"Many things. He got his name from one particular stunt when he lifted a password or something and logged in through a local McDonald's to their mainframe. He did some social engineering, came in as a manager, and gave two of his friends nice raises."

"And he got caught?"

"Well, finally, but not for that. He actually got caught for receiving stolen goods through electronic credit-card fraud. He was an expert at raiding information from credit card-reporting agencies. He really broke track in a whole new kind of wire fraud."

"His mother must have been so proud," Rudy said dryly.

"He knew all the tricks of switching stations. He combined his credit card know-how with his switch tricks, and man, the guy could have had Wall Street by the balls. But see, like a lot of phreaks and crackers, they just can't shut up; they have to brag. He was so full of himself. But with each job, it was like he was driven to top his last performance."

"I'm waiting for the phone sex," Rudy said primly, and took a sip of his tea.

"Here it is: Southern Bell is notoriously slipshod in their security. There was a probation office down in Florida somewhere and it seemed as if every call that was for that office somehow got switched to a phone-sex worker named Tina up in New York."

"Good God! How did that happen?"

"Fry Guy. It was really before he got into the heavy stuff of stealing money through wires. He was just having some fun. But you know, it would be bad if someone was having a heart attack and you called nine-one-one and all of a sudden you got switched to Tina. Fry Guy got into the central switching station for Bell South and reprogrammed the works. They got kind of paranoid when they found out what he had done to their 'state-of-the-art' digital switching station. Actually, Legion of Doom guys had been traipsing around in Bell South switches for months before that. It was Fry Guy who just pulled off the ultimate stunt."

"Where do you draw the line on this sort of thing?"

"You mean me personally?"

"Yes, you, Charley Jacobs."

"I told you, I don't trash as in crash and I don't steal. But I don't buy this shit of theirs that there's like, you know, a priesthood that can control knowledge and information completely. I'm thinking it out, have been thinking it out for a long time. What is the meaning of the words *intellectual property?* I hate the notion of forbidden knowledge. I know that nothing I have ever done electronically has hurt anyone, deprived them of anything—information, money—anything."

"So you do have this rather rough-hewn ethos, rules."

"Yeah, ethos. Rules, I'm not sure. Rules are for rodents, as they say. But yeah, I got standards—moral standards. The best hackers do. You never hear about the best hackers. They're very adult. They don't brag. They've got beautiful skills. They don't go in for fancy hardware. They get these banged-up junkers and they make them hum like Porsches. It's like my dad's friend Freeman Dyson, this physicist at Princeton. He had this totally cool idea about going into space—this was years ago, before anyone had ever done it. He was a lot older than my dad, but Dad had had him as a professor when he was at the Institute, and he said that Dyson hated all the money that NASA was spending. Dyson's idea of a great spacecraft was something that people put together in their backyards—you know, bits and pieces of old junk, scrap hardware. One of his designs had the thing powered with atomic bombs—can you believe it? It was before people were environmentally aware, needless to say. But my dad and I used to make rockets like that, not atomic ones, just things pieced together with cardboard tubes, the kind that come inside toilet-paper rolls, and chicken wire and we messed around with crystal radios a lot. That's really the way it is with the best hackers: They slap their machines together with gaffers' tape, old chips, fishing line. I got some of my mom's fishing line in this thing. You wind up with something fabulous. 'Digital dragsters,' they call them."

"But what about the rules? Why are rules for rodents?" Rudy asked.

"Well, rules are more concrete. They deal with real things. See, you got to understand where we are now isn't quite real." Charley gestured at the computer screen. It showed a letter concerning changes in Quintana Kingsley's will.

"What do you mean not real?"

"It's cyber space. Cyber space isn't real."

"Are you saying it's a state of mind?"

"Sort of. But it's not real like a glove or a hat is real, or even money is real. You can't hold it in your hand. Cyber space is electrical space. And it is a place where things do happen that affect people and the world. It used to be like this dark narrow tunnel with two-way traffic. It was the space between two telephones. You could talk, one person to the other, transmit and receive. But now, in the past thirty years—well, twenty years—it kind of crossbred or maybe interbred with computers. It's like a whole new species has evolved. The space is no longer this narrow little tunnel. It's like this weird bright place with these electronic tentacles stretching out everywhere. Cyber space is to the electronic landscape what the rain forest is to earth—a virtual powerhouse; the rain forest for bio diversity—oxygen and all that; cyber space for information. Both are primal generating systems."

"Very interesting," Rudy said. "Well, we better get back to what we're looking for."

"You want me to download these files here—the changes in the will—to my computer?"

"Yes. I suppose that might be helpful. Evidence, I guess." Rudy's voice dropped. There was a slight melancholy tinge to it that Charley could not miss.

"What's wrong?"

"It just seems that there is a pattern here of favoring Gus over Bootsie. Bootsie looks virtually, or comparatively, penniless. And it's difficult for me to explain to you, but Bootsie has very substantial reasons to be profoundly angry with her family.''

''So you think this gives her a reason to kill her mother?''

''Possibly. But certainly to steal those netsukes. If she were cut out of the will and is indeed in such bad financial straits as she appears to be here...well, the netsukes, I am told, could get her close to one million dollars.''

Charley whistled low. ''Not looking good for Bootsie.''

''No, it isn't. But there is one thing that troubles me.''

''What's that?''

''I can't quite put my finger on it at the moment, but it has something to do with the actual theft. It is possible that the pair of netsukes were taken at two difference times. That doesn't quite make sense.''

Charley shifted nervously in his seat. He thought of his mom and her visit to the greenhouse when she had seen the woman intruder. Maybe he should tell Rudy.

''Look at this,'' Rudy said. ''On July twenty-seventh, little more than a week before Quintana was murdered, she changed her will to favor Gus substantially. Talk about the lion's share. He stood to inherit three million in cash assets and stocks—and that is not counting the house on Louisburg Square, which could easily fetch close to another million. Not fair. It would make me mad.''

''But maybe it made Gus impatient. Maybe he wanted his hands on that money. This could be a motive for him, too, you know,'' Charley said.

"Yes, that's true. But Gus wasn't desperate. He had already been favored. See, being older than Bootsie, he had already come into a trust at fifty."

"Will she get one when she turns fifty?"

There was a knock on the door. It was Malcolm. "Mr. Kingsley, could you step out here a moment?"

"Why of course, Malcolm." Rudy turned to Charley. "I'll be right back."

When Rudy Kingsley walked into the room five minutes later, he looked ten years older. Pale and shaking, he sat down. He put his hand lightly on Charley's arm. "You were asking will Bootsie come into a trust when she is fifty—unfortunately she will never be fifty. That was the police. She hung herself tonight. Jamie discovered her. There was apparently a note confessing to the murder of Quintana."

"Jamie found her?"

"Yes. I have to get right over there for the poor kid. Perhaps we should tell your mother. There are very few stable women in this family. I think that your mother might prove helpful at this point."

"Yeah," Charley said softly. He had this inexorable urge to cry. This wasn't cyber space. This was real—so real. This was just like a few years ago when the unbelievable news about his own father came. This was horrible. He wanted his mom.

TWENTY-SIX

CHARLEY HAD insisted on coming with her, and Calista didn't like the idea one bit. On the other hand, leaving him by himself was not at all appealing. He had seemed to shrink before her eyes; he was as pale and wispy as a little kid, his eyes full of fear. It had brought back too much and he needed to be near her. And Calista needed to be near him. They were strong together. The thought struck her as odd. But it came in response to this last horror. She wondered whether the Kingsleys had ever been strong together. They seemed thoroughly blown apart; atomized—this was their natural condition. And in that condition, they thrived on one another's weaknesses and vulnerabilities. Deceit and distrust were at the core of family dynamics, the twin handmaids of their peculiar family neurosis. *Neurosis* was too nice a word. They were sick all right, but they had let it go on—eating up the family, innocent victims like Bootsie. She supposed Bootsie wasn't so innocent. Apparently, there had been a note confessing to her mother's murder.

WHEN THEY ARRIVED at Lockwood Street, an ambulance was just pulling away. Good, Calista thought. At least there won't be a body around. Malcolm was driving them. Rudy and Charley had swung by Louisburg Square to pick her up and then they had continued to Brookline. There were three police cars pulled up and a BPD van. Lights were flashing and a uniformed police officer met them coming up the walk.

"I'm Jamie's great-uncle, Rudy Kingsley, and these are close friends. How is Jamie?"

"There's a doctor with him now. You folks can go right in. He's in the living room still."

"Still?" asked Calista.

"That's where he found his mother. She hung herself from a lighting fixture."

CALISTA GASPED as they entered the living room. Although the body had been removed, her shock was as profound as if it was still there, swinging from the noose that hung from the thick brass arm of the chandelier. A kitchen stool was directly underneath the chandelier. The noose seemed strangely obscene, derisive of the fine taste and style of the room. Calista realized with a jolt that bordered on anger that Bootsie had hung herself directly across from the beautiful Japanese scrolls. She half-expected those cranes to metamorphose into nightmarish gargoyles and come screeching out from their tranquil flight, leaving the waterfall behind to churn with blood. The room had changed in a distinct yet unnameable way. Everything had disintegrated into disorder, confusion, chaos. Or was there an unknown order here, a pattern? Had Bootsie's life been ordered toward this end—no matter what? She remembered Bootsie sitting in the ivory brocade-covered wing chair, her head tilted back against the braided piping that edged its contours. She looked at the scroll again. The cranes flew on and the waterfall cascaded in another world, one far away, of order and purpose. That world was still intact. Calista did not know which was more real.

And then she saw Jamie sitting rigid on the sofa where she herself had sat a day before.

Rudy had gone over to him and had put an arm around his shoulders. But Jamie stared ahead, his eyes unblinking, his head bent forward toward that noose as if trying to comprehend the lopsided oval, the space of nothingness that had ended his mother's life.

There were people walking about in circular patterns vaguely familiar to Calista: a photographer, a woman with a clipboard, another one with a tape measure. There was the crackle of voices coming over transmitters and cellular phones. Charley sat down on the sofa on the other side of Jamie. Calista moved with him. She was not aware of walking. It was rather as if she were a magnetic filing in Charley's wake. She felt herself crouching in front of Jamie. She was very aware of Rudy's scent—toasted almonds. It was a cologne that he wore. And she saw his thin, wrinkled hand with its age spots stroking Jamie's forearm. She heard herself telling Jamie that he should come back and stay with them for as long as he wanted, until his father came or whatever.

It was all like a dream and it felt no more real than if she had been a figure in one of the ink-wash scrolls. She heard a police officer ask to talk to Rudy. It was very odd. She could hear more than one conversation. It was as if a sudden clarity had washed through the room or through her brain. They were talking now about time of death, 5:00 p.m.; she heard the words *open and shut*. She presumed that these modified the word *suicide*. It was as if the sentences in which they were speaking were being parsed as she listened. Modifiers floated out with clarity: direct objects, adjectives, adverbs—*instant, instantly*. They had used both words. She listened carefully. That would be important. It would be nice if they could tell poor Jamie that his mother had died instantly, that it was over within a fraction of a second. Then a silent harsh laugh crashed through her brain. Yes, how nice, a derisive voice muttered. After years of pain to have it all end quickly—is that the reward? A swift and sudden death by your own hand? There was a note, yes. Detective Froines had the note.

TWENTY-SEVEN

"WHAT DO YOU MEAN he can't be reached? Everybody is someplace; therefore, everybody can be reached. This is the last decade of the twentieth century. Making contact with an extraterrestrial is just around the corner."

"Jamie's dad is on a safari with his family and he is in the one region at this time where he is totally inaccessible."

Rudy closed his eyes and pursed his lips as if to damper down his own dismay.

"I have a feeling this whole fucking family has been inaccessible to its children for aeons. Shit, this is absolutely preposterous," Calista fumed.

"I know, Calista. I know too well."

Titty, who had remained quiet, sighed heavily. "The poor child." She nearly moaned. "I thought it was bad being a girl in this family, but I guess in the final analysis, no one is really safe."

Calista looked up at Titty. She knew on one level what she meant, but on another, there was something very unsettling about it. Titty was right. It had been the girls who had been the victims, or so it was believed, until now. But why had she found what Titty had just said so disturbing? There was something prodding at the back of her mind. She knew she was not thinking this whole thing through the way she ought to be.

"Has he eaten anything?" Rudy inquired.

"What? What did you say?" Calista asked. She had not been listening. The notion of females as victims was disturbing her in a new way, as if there was some new wrinkle in it.

"I said, Has Jamie eaten anything yet?"

"Oh yes, we have made some headway on that front."

"He still won't see a doctor, I take it?" Rudy asked.

"No. He actually won't see anybody except us. Gus came over. So did Bambi. One of his teachers from Poulton called, but Jamie wouldn't talk to him. It puts Charley and me in sort of an odd position. I mean, why will he not see or talk to any of them but here he is with us? Not that I mind it."

"Maybe he's finally around some sensible people, a family that knows how to be a family. Did that ever occur to you?"

"Well, maybe. He even walked over with Charley to the swan boats this morning."

"Has he cried at all?" Titty asked.

"No."

"That's the most worrisome thing of all, I'd say," Rudy replied.

"You've talked to the police?" Calista asked suddenly.

"Yes." Rudy took out a handkerchief and wiped his brow. "I read the note. She made it quite clear that she had killed Quintana, and said she could not go on living."

"She didn't say why she killed her?" Calista asked.

"I guess she didn't feel it really required an explanation. It was a remarkably terse note. There was nothing about Jamie in it at all."

"I think that's weird," Calista said. "And I think it's even weirder that she would kill herself where she did, where Jamie could find her so easily. She might have been alcoholic and mentally damaged, but I just can't believe she would do this terrible thing with such total disregard for Jamie."

"Yes, but no telling what state she was in," Titty said.

"I do wonder," Calista said softly.

"Wonder what?" Rudy asked.

"What state she was in?"

JAMIE JUST NEEDED some clear space, time to think things out. He had lost count of how many times they had been around the duck pond. Jamie sat in the very back of the boat, just in front of Charley, or if it was a full load, he stood next to Charley while he pedaled. Art, the supervisor, didn't seem to mind. He would tell Art that he would take care of bedding down the swans that night. He actually enjoyed that part of the day best. You swept out the floor between the benches, made sure there were no weeds on the paddle blades, then wiped down the swans, their heads, the lovely curve of their necks, the wings. Now, however, he just stared ahead and listened to the sound of the water churning through the paddle wheels as Charley pedaled. Had his mom really thought that he had killed Grandma? Is that why she wrote that note and then killed herself, to protect him? He had to sort this thing out. It was so confusing. He was getting things all mixed up. He had found that letter when he had taken out the trash before he had gone to work that morning, the morning of the day his mom had killed herself. It was a rough draft, printed out from

his printer but not complete. What had surprised him
was the "Dear Gus." His mother would never call Gus
dear, even if it was the standard way to begin a letter.
She hated her brother. And although hardly loving,
hatred was certainly not the tone of this letter. Desperate—that was the tone. He had the letter tucked
away in his pocket now. He did not need to take it out
to remember the words.

Dear Gus,
I am willing to put the past behind. You are
right—the damage is done and nothing in terms
of legal redress can repair what you have done to
Jamie. I thought the worst had happened, but
this is worse. I cannot believe that the police have
any kind of evidence that could link him to
Mummy's death. I still can't quite follow what
you are saying that led you to believe this, but
promise me you will let me know anything else
you hear. I guess you're right about it being too
early to bring in Harley. I don't know where to
turn. I guess, for better or for worse, we're stuck
with each other. It's like a bad joke. Our entire
lives have been a bad joke, Gus. Maybe you have
been as much of a victim as Muffy and I were.
You're sick. So am I, but please help me save Jamie. He is all that I have to live for....

Live for, but then she died. That was the part that
Jamie just could not figure out. And was he supposed
to die now? Or was he supposed to kill? Where had
this stuff come from about him killing Grandma? He
stared straight ahead. They were approaching the island where the ducks lived. The little babies, mere

fluff balls earlier in the summer, had fledged their wings. They weren't swimming as close to their mothers. They were paddling out in larger circles, until she would come and shoo them back. Those ducks were saner, better off than he was; there were parts of nature so uncomplicated and so straightforward as to be almost brave in their simplicity. The truth overwhelmed him.

Suddenly, Jamie realized that he was through with being sullen, angry, damaged. He hated those words. He wanted to be brave. Within seconds, it became very clear to him: The past had been bad, but it had been bad largely because he was not in control; the future was going to be worse, if that was possible, but it was and he knew it—worse things were about to happen to him. He was being set up for something terrible, just as his mother had been. She had not killed herself to protect him. She had, if anything, died in vain, and he was still unprotected. He was going to have to kill or get killed. He had had it with the other way; he had had it with stupid anger and blaming. It didn't matter anymore. He had to be brave. It was very simple if he looked at it that way. He just had to keep his focus and keep it simple. He had to forget right now, once and for all, the years of humiliation, the horrible things that Gus had done to him.

TWENTY-EIGHT

SHE HAD BEEN sound sleep; she had not been dreaming, at least she didn't recall dreaming. But when she opened her eyes, she could see that noose so clearly—the twists of it. Calista got out of bed and walked to a window. There were curtain cords. She took them and began to twist them. Her left hand was the steadying hand. She made the twists with her right hand counterclockwise. Was this common? It seemed the natural way to do it if you were right-handed. She tried to twist it the other way, clockwise. It didn't feel right. She tried to reverse her hands and use her right hand as the steadying hand and use the left to twist the rope. That was almost impossible. She spent the next twenty minutes trying various knots with the curtain cords. Calista knew a lot of knots and a lot about knot tying, for she tied her own flies for fly-fishing. Those were often very specialized knots. But take the most basic kinds of knots used for tippets, such as a barrel or a surgeon's knot, and take the most elemental part of, say, a barrel knot, where you must wind one end around the standing part. If you were right-handed, you did it one way; if left-handed, you did it another. The string either wound clockwise or counterclockwise. She realized, of course, that in terms of statistical value, her control group was rather small. She would try it tomorrow with Charley, not Jamie. She stared at the knot she had just tied. A new realization began to creep into her mind as she pictured the noose hanging from the chandelier: What did it really matter whether the twists were clockwise or counterclockwise? The knot itself was meticulously, perfectly made. For a woman who was usually well into a quart of vodka by midday, this seemed to constitute a fair bit of manual dexterity.

THE PHONE RANG a little after seven. A scratchy voice on the other end cawed, "I understand you're keeping him."

"Who? . . . Who is this?"

"Cornelia Parkington, Diggory Parkington's sister-in-law and Bootsie's aunt. I want to know why Jamie's staying with you. It's not appropriate."

To say this conversation was going poorly was an understatement. What's more, there seemed to be very little hope of getting it back on any "appropriate" track. Calista felt the anger swelling in her. "I would say that there have been a lot of inappropriate things going on in this family for a long time, particularly in recent weeks. I would suggest that you talk to your lawyer, Harley Bishop, concerning Jamie's staying here. But if you want to know why he is . . ."

"Yes I do," Cornelia snapped.

"It's because he wants to." She was about to say good-bye and hang up, but Cornelia barked again.

"And there is the matter of the Cotton Mather portrait."

"What?" Calista was stymied. What in the world could that have to do with Jamie?

"He cannot touch that portrait. It comes down through my branch of the family."

"Fuck Cotton Mather!" Calista slammed down the phone.

Ten minutes later, Harley Bishop called up. "I'm sure we can work this out, Calista."

"As far as I'm concerned, there is nothing to work out. I am not keeping Jamie here. He elected to stay here. It would seem most appropriate to speak with him, but I think he's still asleep. Should I have him call you when he gets up?"

"Yes, yes, do that, and Gus would like to see him, too. Please tell him that."

"I will."

"And . . ." Harley's voice rose just slightly. Here it comes, Calista thought.

"I know, given the circumstances, this might seem inappropriate." Calista rolled her eyes. What was this obsession with appropriateness? "But would you be interested in meeting me for a drink this evening? I should be finished at the office around seven-fifteen. And I'm really so intrigued by your work as an illustrator." Baloney, Calista thought. "I'd love to talk to you more about it and just thought perhaps a drink at the Ritz . . ."

Calista's instincts were to say no, but this was the Kingsley family lawyer. Charley and Rudy had told Calista about Charley's electronic peregrinations through the Hopkins, Bishop and Creeth computers and what they had found in terms of the recent will changes. She supposed she might be able to gab a little about children's book illustration and then, as Charley would say, do some social engineering and perhaps find out something else. She still simply did not believe that Bootsie had killed Quintana. She was beginning now to doubt Bootsie's suicide.

"Okay, but listen, one thing."

"Certainly."

"Keep that old bat out of my hair."

"You mean Cornelia?"

"Precisely. And more important, keep her out of Jamie's hair. The kid just does not need her right now. He needs his dad, wherever he is."

"We're trying on that front."

"Okay. See you around seven-thirty at the Ritz."

No sooner had she hung up than the phone rang once more. She hesitated picking it up. It might be Cornelia at the other end. She could picture her talons grasping the receiver. Oh would that the bitch's wheelchair roll into the Charles!

"Hello."

"Rudy here, dear. May I come over right away for breakfast? In the confusion, there is an important piece of information I entirely forgot about. Make sure Jamie is up and functioning as well as can be hoped."

"Yes. Yes, of course."

"YOU ARE SURE of this?" Calista asked, pouring herself another cup of coffee.

"I am not sure, but Leon Mauritz is fairly sure. However, the important thing is—" Rudy turned to Jamie "—your mother was an expert in this area. She, of all people, would know that those two netsukes were most valuable as a pair. Only a neophyte would steal just one."

"So then why would they steal just one?" Calista asked. "I mean, if they were sitting there together on the shelf, why not take two, even if the one was slightly damaged?"

"The only reason I could think is that the person was trying to set up a motive for the killing of Quintana—robbery. It would appear perhaps that the robbery was interrupted if one was left behind.''

"Interrupted?" Charley asked. "But she was murdered in the greenhouse and the netsukes were in the living room.''

"True." Rudy paused and closed his eyes. He tapped a pencil on a piece of paper. He made a number 1 and underscored it. "But what we do know, or, according to Leon, what we can be ninety-nine percent sure of is that the netsukes were taken at two separate times and—'' he then wrote down the numeral 2 under the one ''—number two, whoever took the netsukes was not an expert in Asian art. Number three, Leon's caller was a woman.''

Calista looked nervously across at Charley. He swallowed. The time had come for her to tell what she had seen in the greenhouse on that night shortly after Quintana's murder.

"Wait a second," she said, "I have to show you something." She got up and went to the pantry. She opened up an empty tin canister used for sugar. Inside was a small plastic bag and in the bag was the garter.

She held out her hand with the plastic bag containing the garter. "I found this in the greenhouse a few days after Quintana was murdered.''

Calista told the story of the woman she had seen walking through as she hid behind the bags of mulch and fertilizer.

"So, in short, you witnessed, or possibly witnessed, the theft of the second netsuke," Rudy said. He then turned to Jamie. "Does the description sound anything like your mother?''

"No, not at all. For one thing, I don't think my mom wore garters. I mean, I think she just wore those pull-on kinds of stockings."

"Panty hose," Calista offered, then added, "and probably not in eighty-five degree summer heat."

"Yeah," said Jamie. "And, like Uncle Rudy said, she was an expert. She would have taken both of them and not just one."

"I guess I should tell the police about this, but I suppose they could get me on withholding evidence."

"Well, we should really ask Harley," Rudy said.

"Oh God, I'm having a drink with him."

"You are?"

"Yes. He called and asked me this morning."

"I presume it has something to do with all this."

"I don't know why you presume that. Why, is he married?"

"The last I heard, he was."

"Oh dear, I should have known."

"Listen, Calista. Hold off telling him right away. I want to figure a few more things out."

"So do I," said Calista. "I've been thinking about that Lieutenant O'Hare—was that his name? One of the detectives the other night?"

"Something Irish," Rudy answered vaguely.

Jamie listened to Calista and Rudy talking. Everyone was trying to help him, trying to help his mother, as much as one can help a dead person, clear her name. They were convinced that his mother had not killed his grandmother. He knew that he should tell them about the letter. But if he showed them the letter, then he would have to tell about Gus and the things Gus had done to him. He wasn't sure he could do that yet. He knew he had to be brave. But this was another kind of bravery.

Calista looked over at Jamie. A little tick had begun to kick around his jaw. His eyes shifted nervously and he picked at the bag with the garter. Something was disturbing him. She didn't know what. But the garter was triggering something.

"Oh, by the way, Jamie, when Harley called this morning, he said that your Uncle Gus wanted to see you."

"Well, I don't want to see him," Jamie barked, then colored deeply.

EVERYONE LEFT—the boys for the swan boats, Rudy for a special meeting at Harley's office to talk to him about the meager estate that Bootsie had left and how he might supplement what was left for Jamie. Calista began to clear away the dishes, her mind turning over the meaning of everything she had learned so far. She picked up the piece of paper on which Rudy had scribbled his notes concerning the netsuke thefts. There were three points: The thefts had occurred at separate times, the thief was not an expert, and finally, the thief was a woman—a woman who wore garters. There was a fourth point, however! Why hadn't she ever thought of this before? She ran to a calendar hanging on the wall over the sink. Yes! The theft had occurred on a Thursday. She turned back the calendar. Quintana had been murdered on a Thursday, the first Thursday in August. She flipped the calendar forward. And Bootsie McPhee had committed suicide on a Thursday. Somebody had Thursdays off. But there was one person who didn't. She had heard the alibi more than once—clearly, deliberately, articulately. Gus Kingsley was always at St. Bennett's on Thursdays; ergo, he could not have done it. He couldn't be a real suspect. St. Bennett's was in New Hampshire, over two hours from Boston. Gus always spent the night when he coached there. The man doth protest too much—about Thursdays. Could she break his alibi? But then where would that get her? The person she had seen when she was in the greenhouse was a woman. Bambi! Bambi and Gus. Was that stretching it? They had seemed rather close when she had seen them together at the reception after the funeral. And hadn't Bambi, too, known Gus's schedule? When they were all on the sidewalk in the pouring rain trying to get into number 18. They were just cousins. Are cousins that familiar with one another's schedules? Maybe cousins who are lovers are. Then where did that leave Cornelia? Calista's stomach turned at the thought of that crone. And what was the motive? Only Bootsie really had a motive. She had the anger, the anger over the sexual abuse she had suffered; the anger over being virtually cut from the will. What the netsukes were valued at was not insignificant. But could or would Bootsie really hang herself? And then there was the noose itself.

Calista put down a dirty coffee cup in the sink. She went to the telephone.

"Lieutenant O'Hare, please. This is Calista Jacobs. Tell him I have some information about the recent suicide of Barbara McPhee." This, of course, was stretching the truth. But Calista had dealt with the police before. She knew they wouldn't return her call unless she left the distinct impression that she knew something they didn't.

A HALF AN HOUR LATER, she walked into the Boston police station on Berkeley Street. She was shown immediately into an office. With Lieutenant O'Hare were two plainclothes detectives—the woman who had been at the house following Bootsie's suicide, and a middle-aged man. They were introduced as Detective Froines and Graham. They looked at her with expressions that were a blend of expectation and calculated indifference. It was an odd mixture. At the same time, there was the distinct feeling that they were going to be very polite and prepare her for some inevitable disappointment: prick pinholes in her theories and watch with ill-concealed satisfaction as the air went out of the balloons.

"So you have some information, Ms. Jacobs?"

She resisted any fudging. She knew they expected her to have sudden doubts, to begin to back off, to declare that the information was perhaps a bit marred, knicked, less than perfect. Well, to hell with them.

"Do you still have the noose that Barbara McPhee used to hang herself?"

"Yes," the woman, Detective Froines, said. "It's in the crime lab."

"Could you get it?"

"Is there a reason for this?" she asked.

Calista opened her eyes wide and said nothing. This woman had an attitude. Maybe she should introduce her to Piss. Lieutenant O'Hare cleared his throat nervously and punched a few numbers on his phone. He leaned toward the intercom screen. Keeping his eyes on Calista, he spoke into the box. "The Brookline suicide. Send up that noose you got from down there. And the photographs, too."

IT WAS JUST AS Calista remembered. Basically, it was a clinch knot with five turns—same knot she often used to tie tippet onto a fly. And the turns were going clockwise. Calista reached into her handbag. She drew out several lengths of twine that she had found in the Baldwins' utility closet.

"I want you to do something for me." She put on her reading glasses so she could see the twine better. "First of all, are you all right-handed here?"

"Not me," said Detective Froines.

"Okay. Now, do you all know how to make a clinch knot? It's used a lot in fly-fishing. I do a lot of fly-fishing." They were watching her, rapt with attention. She was not the usual witness in any sense of the word. She did not appear too eager or too nervous. She worked calmly and efficiently; there was a thoughtfulness to her that bordered on studious. And she was very attractive despite the fact that she wore no makeup, had a mop of silvery hair, and was dressed as chastely as any female police officer.

"I'll demonstrate this knot. It's easy. You'll all get it on the first try." She smiled primly, but underneath the smile, the half glasses, and the mop of hair was a very sexy den mother. That was what O'Hare decided. "Okay," Calista continued. "You take your twine, one end in each hand. You're going to want to form a loop down at the bottom. If we were fly-fishing, you'd be leading this through the eye of a fly. Yeah, you got it, Lieutenant. So do you, folks." She looked over at the two detectives. "Next, I want you to take the piece that is on top and wrap it around the standing part of the leader, say five times. Okay." She looked around. They had begun to wind. Yes, it was just as she'd thought. "All right. You got your five turns; now just bring that end back and pass it through the loop.'' Calista held hers up.

''So what are we supposed to do now?'' Detective Froines asked. ''Hang ourselves?''

''Detective, look at your noose. It's different from ours.'' Detective Froines slid her eyes first to her partner's, then to O'Hare's, and finally to Calista's. She didn't get it. But O'Hare did.

''Lisa's is like the one used in the suicide. Its turns go the opposite way from ours.''

''Exactly. We're right-handed. We hold the twine, the standing part of the loop, with our less dominant hand, the left. We use our right hand for the finer motor work of making the turns. It seems that the tendency a hundred percent of the time, in this small control group and with other people I have tried this on, is to make the turns toward your weaker hand— the left hand in all our cases, except for Detective Froines, who is left-handed.''

''So?'' Lisa Froines asked.

''So Barbara McPhee is right-handed. That noose—'' Calista pointed to the tray from the crime lab ''—was made by a left-handed person.''

''And you feel this is conclusive evidence that Barbara did not commit suicide?''

''Did you check the alcohol level in her blood?''

O'Hare reached for a file. He opened it and ran his eyes down a top sheet. He whistled. ''Point two was the level.''

''You think she could have tied that knot even if she was left-handed?''

''Someone else could have made it,'' Detective Graham offered.

"And she could have conveniently found it and then hung herself?" Calista asked.

"It's possible," Detective Graham said. But there was a slight constriction in his voice that suggested substantial doubt.

"Somebody else did make the noose. That is becoming fairly clear," O'Hare said. "As to whether they hung her or she hung herself . . . well, that's another question."

"But the bruises on her neck are completely consistent with those of hanging and not murder," Detective Froines said.

"What are you talking about?" Calista asked.

O'Hare got up and walked from behind his desk to the table where another tray from the crime lab sat. He picked up a manila envelope and took out eight-by-ten glossy prints. He walked over to Calista. The top one showed a curve of white, with a dark inverted V. This was not an abstract design, not a Mark Rothko painting, not calligraphy. The pieces came together slowly for Calista. This was a neck, a human neck through which life had been shut off, extinguished, broken, asphyxiated. It was Barbara McPhee's neck. But Barbara McPhee, the one whose parents had welcomed to the world forty-five years ago and precisely nicknamed Bootsie, no longer existed; the one whose father had raped her and whose mother had let it happen no longer was. Or rather, she was a collection of bruised, decomposing tissues and bones, leaking chemicals on a glinting metal tray in a refrigerated room. No more cute names. The neck and the body it belonged to, the person it had housed, had become a case. The number was 99-6750.

But this is Barbara McPhee's neck, Calista had to keep telling herself. O'Hare was speaking softly, almost gently.

"You see, when it's murder, the bruise mark goes straight across." He slid his finger in an imaginary line across the neck, parallel to the bottom of the page. "In a suicide, the marks look like an inverted V, just the way they do here. Look, you might be able to understand it better from this next picture." He took out a photograph from underneath. Calista swallowed. This picture showed more of the head. The jaw was completely exposed. Wisps of hair curled around her ear and the rope mark went straight up through these wisps and behind the ear. The jaw was cocked up to show the bruises. Calista leaned closer. The angle of that jaw was odd but familiar—not the angle so much as the pose. She closed her eyes briefly. She remembered those life-study drawing classes she had taken, years of drawing nude models. The models would hold the poses for as short as thirty seconds sometimes. It was an exercise in developing visual memory and skills in quick contour drawing. She had seen this pose before. Not in a life-drawing class, but in Barbara McPhee's living room: Bootsie sitting in the wing chair, her jaw tilted up as she leaned her head back, looking at the scrolls through half-closed eyes, twirling the ice in her drink with her index finger. And Gus, standing behind her, resting his hand on her shoulder. But he had to dip his hand down to rest it on her shoulder. For the back of the wing chair was high. And if...

"Are you okay, Ms. Jacobs?"

"Fine, just fine. But tell me one thing. Wouldn't an inverted V bruise be formed if someone was standing behind the victim, who was, say, sitting in a high-backed chair, and then slipped the rope down around her neck and then pulled up—presuming the victim's head was several inches lower than the murderer?''

"Yes."

"Then you have to look at the rope," Detective Froines said. "There should be abrasions on one side of the rope and you would see strands of the rope sticking out." She picked up a sheaf of papers and shook them slightly with a loose twist movement. "There is no report of that kind of abrasive action on the rope itself here. We check for that automatically." She looked steadily at Calista as if to say, I know my job, toots, and you are strictly an amateur.

This lady did have an attitude. But attitudes never undid Calista. She bit her lip slightly and concentrated on her next move. "You know, you're probably right. But that chair was upholstered in a silk brocade, an ivory on white. Silk is so smooth. It's hard imagining it roughing up a hemp rope like this. But the rope could certainly mess up the fabric of a chair like that—or at least rub it a little."

"That's a point," O'Hare said. "Lisa, why don't you and Bill go over to Brookline and take a look at the chair Ms. Jacobs is talking about. See if there are any rub marks, and in the meantime, maybe we should send this noose over to Michael and have him take a look at it through the electron microscope for foreign fibers."

Ha! thought Calista, and resisted looking triumphantly at Detective Froines. But she could not resist one last question.

"Might I go along with Detective Froines and Graham?"

"I can't imagine how that would help," Froines said, looking to O'Hare. "I think we'll be able to find the chair in the living room on our own, Ms. Jacobs."

Bitch.

TWENTY-NINE

CALISTA HAD JUST driven through the two stone pillars that marked the entrance to St. Bennett's Academy. She checked her watch. Two hours and forty-five minutes from Boston. And the traffic hadn't been bad. She proceeded up the long, winding drive. There were signs directing visitors to the admissions office, administration, the athletic center. She took the turnoff for the athletic center. To the right of the parking lot, she saw tennis courts, but they were empty. She walked into the field house. It was elaborate. To think that Cambridge public schools had to cut back on hiring school librarians and this place had signs pointing to an ice-hockey rink, a Nautilus room, and another directing one downstairs to a swimming pool. The indoor tennis courts were apparently through the double doors directly ahead. There were several kids playing on the courts. A coach was watching carefully from the sidelines. There were some other kids sitting in the bleachers, holding racquets, apparently waiting their turn on the courts. Calista hoped that she wouldn't have to meet an adult. She could do this better with kids. She slid into the bleachers.

"Pardon me," she said to a young boy with tousled blond hair. "I'm looking for Gus Kingsley."

"Oh, Mr. Kingsley is only here on Tuesdays and Thursdays during the summer," the boy said.

"Oh dear... what a disappointment." She sighed. "I don't know whether I can get up here next Thursday, or Tuesday, for that matter. Do you know about what time he's apt to be here?''

"Ah well, he usually comes in the afternoon and stays overnight, because he lives all the way in Boston. Practice is from three till nine—we break for dinner.''

"Oh," Calista said. "Does he go right back to Boston first thing in the morning on Fridays? I might be through here again on a Friday and could catch him.''

"Jeez, I don't know. Sukey over there would have a better idea of when he's around. He's the custodian here.''

Sukey spoke slightly more English than Calista spoke Japanese.

"Yes, yes, Mr. Gus always here Tuesday and Thursday... always... always. Never miss practice. Never miss practice.'' Sukey smiled broadly and swung his arms, mimicking a double-handed backhand. "I like to watch him myself. He can play with both hands. Velly good left or right!''

"Left or right!''

"Yah! Yah! Double backhand like Chris Evert.''

Holy shit, Calista thought.

"Is he ever late?''

"Rate...no, no...bus rate sometimes. Yah, bus very rate Thursday. Kids must come from Manchester— and oh, there's Billy. Billy favorite of Mr. Gus. He tell you—me no speak so good English.'' He motioned Billy, a rather sullen-looking boy, over. "Billy is in dorm where Mr. Gus stay when here.''

"Hello, Billy," Calista said. "I'm a friend of Gus Kingsley's and I can't seem to catch up with him. Apparently, I come the wrong days.'' She'd work into this easily and not ask Billy right off the bat whether Gus had been there last Thursday. She'd ask about other times first. "Tell me—I know he's always here on Thursday. Is there any chance of ever catching him very early on a Friday morning before he leaves?"

An absolutely distraught look passed over Billy's face. "Uh...I wouldn't know."

"Oh, I thought, since you were in his dorm..."

"My room is nowhere near his," he said fiercely. Calista blinked. The kid was desperate. This response was so out of kilter. She knew then instantly that he was lying. He had to be. She was as sure of this as she had been of anything in her life. But why would a kid in a summer program in a New Hampshire prep school lie or cover up for Gus Kingsley? How could a kid be involved with this? She must proceed very cautiously. The last thing she wanted to do was scare this kid off. But he was obviously very frightened.

"Well, oh no...I mean..." She ran her fingers through her hair in her best Mrs. Tiggy-Winkle fashion, hoping to look like something in between a kindly hedgehog and a distracted mother. She was very good on the latter. "I just thought I might be able to get through on Friday morning and catch him. But maybe a Thursday. Sukey was saying something about a late bus on Thursdays—"

Billy cut her off. "Sometimes the bus is late on Thursdays, but Mr. Kingsley is never late. He's always here. Always. I saw him myself last Thursday. He was here at five."

"Oh yes, yes, of course," Calista spoke mechanically. "Then maybe I'll try to be here then."

"Yes. He's always here on Thursdays."

The bus on Thursdays was apparently often late. Did this back up tennis practice and could Gus count on it being late? And why had Billy blurted out that he was here at five? She hadn't asked for a specific hour. Why five? Five was the estimated time of death of Barbara McPhee. It had said just that on the lab report from the crime lab. Right under the case number, there were two times: time of death, listed at 8:30 p.m., and estimated time of death—5:00 p.m. Eight-thirty was when Jamie had discovered his mother's body. Five was when Barbara had ceased to be Bootsie, had ceased to be a mother, and had become case number 99-6750.

THIRTY

WHEN CALISTA got back to Boston, there was a message from Lieutenant O'Hare on the answering machine, asking her to call. She would have to hustle if she was to make drinks at 7:30 with Harley. And she didn't know whether Charley and Jamie were planning on eating at home this evening. They were supposed to have gotten the afternoon off from the swan boats because there was a private party that night and they were going to be working late. She'd leave money for them to order a pizza. She had begun to get undressed while being put on hold for Lieutenant O'Hare. When he finally picked up, she was naked and felt compelled for some idiotic reason to grab her robe from the back of the chair to cover up.

"Ms. Jacobs?"

"Yeah."

"You wanna come work for me?"

"How come?" she asked. She had put the robe on upside down and one sleeve was dragging on the floor.

"You were right. Somebody yanked her off. The back of that chair had rope fibers and rub marks all over the edging material—you know, that fancy braid stuff they use to upholster the edges of furniture."

"Hah!" She tried not to gloat.

"You have any suspects in mind?"

"Yep."

"Who's that?"

"Her brother, Gus Kingsley."

"Why?"

"Well, he's ambidextrous for one thing." He can play tennis lefty or righty.

"But what would he use for murder? For yanking off his sister? We need something more concrete. A piece of physical evidence that would link him to the scene of the crime." Calista thought of the garter, but that, of course, was from the scene of a different crime. She wasn't quite ready to let that one go yet.

THIRTY-ONE

CHARLEY LOOKED UP from the piece of paper. Jamie knew what was coming next. He wasn't sure if he could do it. "What did he do to you?"

Jamie wanted to say it was a long story, but that really wasn't the issue. It had started a while ago, but in many ways it was a simple story, now when Jamie looked back on it. It was a story of power and weakness. He had been ten and they had gone to Nohqwha for a fishing trip. Gus said it was part of being a man at Nohqwha. There had always been all sorts of secrets at Nohqwha and ceremonies. When you were six and could swim to the raft, you could go out in a canoe. When you could turn over the canoe and roll it back up, you could go out by yourself in it. When you were fourteen, you got to go duck hunting with the men in the fall. When you shot your first deer, they rubbed the blood on your head and threw you in the lake, if it wasn't frozen. These were weekends when no girls or women were allowed. Gus had shown him the sweat lodge that they had built just like the Indian ones and told him how the men sat naked in it and sweated out the impurities, especially the alcohol. Gus had said that the whole family drank too much. That he was smart and knew when to quit but that most people didn't. He hoped that Jamie wouldn't do that. He loved Jamie and had a lot of high hopes for him. He hoped that since Jamie's father had moved so far away, Jamie would come to think of Gus as a kind of father, someone whom he could always come to. And it would be his honor to raise Jamie in what he called the best of the Kingsley manly tradition. He used the word *manly* a lot. This was all part of being "manly," he had said—taking off your clothes and sitting naked in the woods, in the stone circles and in the Indian sweat lodge. This was how you must learn your body and its amazing powers.

So they would sit there and masturbate. That was how it had started, and then Gus would ask him to touch him. And when Jamie didn't want to, Gus had said, well, he would touch Jamie. He hadn't expected his uncle to do what he had done, to put it in his mouth. It didn't feel bad; it felt good. Then it had just gotten out of control and Gus had said that part of being a man was learning how to give pleasure; that he had learned how to give beautiful pleasure to his sisters. His father, Jamie's grandfather Kingie, had taught him. And his father before him had given pleasure. It was all part of a "manly" Kingsley tradition going way, way back. Jamie thought about all of this. How would he ever explain it to Charley. It was beyond comprehension. There was no explaining it. Better just say it.

His voice sounded very thin and far away, as if he were in space, in a place with no air, no atmosphere. "My uncle touched me, then he took my dick in his mouth, and then I took his, and then he raped me. And he's been doing it since I was about ten years old. And then my mom found out and she threatened to kill him and she went to Grandma and Grandma didn't believe her and then Grandma got killed and then my mom committed suicide and that's it."

Charley didn't know what to say. He felt his heart racing. He had heard about this kind of stuff; he'd read about it. But here was someone, a kid just his age, standing right in front of him telling him about it. He didn't know what to do, what to say. He felt Jamie's shame. Yet another part of his brain was telling him in a very adult voice that there was no shame for Jamie in this. It wasn't his fault that he had been abused. But no matter, Charley knew that there had to be shame; he knew how he would feel—ruined, ruined for life, totally destroyed. He would want to die. He should be giving a pep talk to this kid. He should be telling him he had his whole life ahead of him; that he could put this behind him; that it was over; that he could grow up and be a productive citizen. Wasn't that what they always said? Wasn't that supposed to be the goal now for kids—a contributing member of society, of civilization? Productive citizen? It all sounded like such a load of crap now.

"Wh…" The word would not even come out whole. He started again. "Why did you tell me this?" Charley hoped it didn't sound like, Why me, poor little old me? But he was genuinely curious. And although not quite aware of it, implicit in the question was another one? What are we going to do here?

"I told you." Jamie spoke slowly. He was adjusting to this new feeling of letting his terrible secret out. He had told his mother, but it wasn't the same. She was so helpless and her outrage so futile. Her anger was more like a debilitating disease than anything else; it was just like her alcoholism. It ate at her. This felt better. Jamie began again. "I told you because I think that Gus is setting me up for something."

"It sounds from this letter that he's setting you up to take the rap for your grandmother's murder, or at least your mom thought so."

"Yeah, that's the point. I've thought a lot about this. I think that he wanted her to think that I did it and then maybe it would drive her so crazy that she would commit suicide and confess to it in order to cover up that I did it. My mom, you got to understand, spent half her life in a bottle of vodka. She could be made to believe almost anything and would get more and more paranoid the more she drank."

"You actually think that your uncle could have convinced her that her own son killed his grandmother?"

"Not convinced her, but scared her shitless."

"But I don't understand. What motive could he have manufactured, or you?"

"None for me, but I think he had plenty."

"You mean you think that he murdered your grandmother?"

"Yes."

"What was his motive? Why would he want to do it?"

"Money—money and the fear that my mom would really blow the whistle on what he had done to me. She had already told Grandma and I think Grandma was on the brink of changing her will to give a lot more to Mom than she had planned to. This was really earth-shaking, because Gus had always been Grandma's favorite. And to tell you the truth, I'm not sure if Grandma was that upset about what he had done to me. I don't think she believed it. At least that was the sense I got from Mom."

"Then if she didn't believe it, why would she change her will to favor your mother?"

"Because my mom was threatening to make a stink in public; she was going to go to a lawyer, and not that idiot Harley Bishop. She was going to go to the DA. That really scared the shit out of Grandma. Grandma Queenie believed that there were only about three times when a person should get their names in the paper. When they were born, when they got married, and when they died."

Charley whistled low. This was incredible. "So you think that in order to shut up your mom, she was going to buy her off?"

"Yes."

"But you said your mom was tanked half the time. How did she get it together even to think about the DA and go to your grandmother and read her the riot act? I mean, that takes a certain amount of sobriety."

"Mom had her clear periods. She had a clear one starting in late spring—May, June, well into July. She was determined to do something about this. But then I don't know, she just kind of started crumbling again."

"So let me get this straight. You think that your grandma really would have changed her will to avoid publicity?"

"Yes."

"But if she changed it, wouldn't that have given your mom a motive? I mean, then she could have gotten all the money before your grandma changed it again. You know, she did that all the time." Charley quickly bit his lip.

"How do you know?" Jamie said. His voice was shot through with tension.

There was no beating around this one. Charley knew it. He had blabbed too much. "Because I hacked into Hopkins, Bishop and Creeth's computers. Your Uncle Rudy asked me to."

"You did?" Jamie was stunned. "Uncle Rudy asked you?"

"Yep."

"What did you find?"

"That your grandmother changed her will about as often as some people change their socks. And in the last will, we found everything was in your uncle's favor still."

"It was?"

"Yep. You want to see?"

Charley walked over to the desk in his bedroom. He booted up his computer and punched in the numbers on the keypad of the telephone. For twenty minutes, they read through the various letters, wills, and amendments to wills that composed Quintana Kingsley's file at Hopkins, Bishop and Creeth. Charley leaned forward suddenly and peered harder at the screen.

"There's something new."

"New?"

"Well, at least I don't remember seeing this when Rudy and I were going through the file the other day. It's dated August 1."

"That's two days before Grandma died. Open it up."

Charley and Jamie read the short letter from Quintana Kingsley to Harley Bishop requesting the following amendments to her will so that the bulk of her estate be held in an irrevocable trust for her only grandson, Jamie, with his mother and Rudy Kingsley as the principal executors. The last part of the letter glared on the screen.

For reasons that I do not want to go into in this letter, or at any future time, I think that this is the best arrangement for all parties concerned. I know this is a move that Rudy had urged Kingie to make years ago. There is no fool like an old fool, and Rudy is no fool. I am afraid that perhaps I have had the dubious honor of having been both an old and a young fool throughout my life. I can never make amends at this late date for past errors, but I can try to avoid making new errors. I shall be in first thing Friday morning to sign the papers necessary for the irrevocable trust and the newly amended will. Sincerely yours, Quintana Kingsley.

Charley looked up at Jamie.

"She was dead by Friday morning," he said quietly.

"Yes. So it remained unsigned and the last will, dated July twenty-seventh, was the one in which Gus got it all."

"We've got to tell Rudy this," Charley said.

"And we have to tell Rudy the rest, too," Jamie said quietly.

THIRTY-TWO

THERE WERE a lot of horses' asses at the Ritz bar, most of them hanging on the wall, jumping hedges. However, it could have been worse. Calista was always happy that the Ritz bar was not one of those places that went in for paintings of drooling dogs and bleeding pheasants. The portraiture in general tended to favor well-groomed lapdogs—terriers, corgis, the occasional dachshund. The portraits of people had a marked affinity for the austere—a Thoreau-like young man looking simultaneously contemplative and ethereal due to a particularly wan pallor. This gentleman faced a Hawthornesque Puritan maiden walking through a woods. The picture always reminded Calista of the scene in *The Scarlet Letter* where Hester and Dimsdale finally had words seven years after having nookie.

The best thing about the Ritz bar was that it was one of those rare places that seemed to be a little universe unto itself, a tiny independent solar system, totally oblivious to any other gravitational systems or forces. It had its own unique light, a warm, redolent amber glow; its own weather, crisp yet warm; its own season, forever autumn.

She spotted Harley Bishop in a far corner. He stood up as he saw her coming across the room. He had already ordered a drink, a martini. Despite his horn-rimmed glasses and button-downed demeanor, there was a look of clear anticipation on his face. It was not just sexual. This guy wanted more. Calista had sensed it immediately from the first time she'd met him, in the rain on Louisburg Square. This guy was looking for someone to change his life. He was the late George Apley waked up and realizing that although he had done everything just the way it should be done, maybe just maybe, he should have considered an alternative.

Alas, Calista had neither the time nor the inclination for this kind of rehab work. She had already begun to pity the poor woman who would eventually take Harley on and the poor wife he would most likely be leaving behind or hurting in some way despite the best of intentions. A little dirge to be sung for such lives. Calista remembered now the part from the Marquand novel when Apley questioned his very existence. Fragments of those lines came back: "'Have any of us really lived?' he asked. 'Sometimes I am not entirely sure; sometimes I think that we are all amazing people, placed in an ancestral mould.... [But] There is no spring, no force'."

"HELLO, CALISTA. I'm glad you've come." Harley Bishop reached for her hand as if she was extending a lifeline.

Their drinks came, a second martini for Harley, a Campari and soda for Calista.

"Well, here's to!" Harley lifted his glass and she, to be polite, did the same. But what were they drinking to? And why in the hell was she here? Why was he here, for that matter? He was married. And Calista herself was as good as married to Archie. Well, she knew why she was here. It was not because she was horny. It was because she wanted to find out all she could from Harley about the Kingsleys, starting with Gus. How to begin? But he was already beginning.

"I went over to Barnes and Noble today and looked at your books. They are quite marvelous."

"Thank you."

"I was wondering..."

"Yes?"

"Sometimes, I almost felt that I was catching a glimpse of you in an illustration, but just rarely. Do you ever draw yourself in?"

"All the time."

"How fascinating. I was right, then. I thought I saw a little bit of you in the eyes of the cat in *Puss 'N Boots.*"

"Oh yes, that's my most obvious appearance in any of my books."

"Well, where else?"

"Oh, you have to look hard." Calista smiled. Her hooded dark eyes crinkled. Harley leaned forward. There was something very spellbinding about her eyes, glinting with a kind of sorcery that seemed to come from another world—a world of gnomes and giants and evil fairies."

"Well, where should I look?"

"Sometimes in the scariest and ugliest parts of the pictures." He realized she was dead serious. He took a big swallow of his martini and set it down. "Did you see my book *Snow White?*"

"Yes, yes. I do believe I did. Were you one of the Seven Dwarfs?"

"Oh no, worse." Calista laughed. Again the dark eyes sparkled, full of merriment. "Remember the evil stepmother?"

"You weren't her?"

"Oh no—she was pure Leona Helmsley. Well, with a touch of Nancy Reagan for leavening purposes. But remember her mirror?"

"The mirror?" Harley said vaguely. "You mean when she says 'Mirror mirror on the wall'?"

"Yeah, the frame."

"The frame?" His brow knitted.

A child would have never missed this, but a person who spent seven hours a day doing estate law might. "Yeah, the frame was made to look as if it was carved. It had all those death's-heads and . . . well, some sort of suggestive phallic shapes, lots of writhing bodies— very Hieronymus Bosch."

"You're in the frame."

"Yep, one of the death's-heads. Look in the forest, in the bark of some of the tree trunks. You'll see me there, too—same death's-head just transposed to the bark of the tree."

"My, my! You're a very interesting person."

Calista smiled warmly. "No, I'm really not, not at all. You see, I get all my fantasies out and down on paper—in ink and gouache and watercolor and acrylics. What's more interesting and more dangerous are the folks who don't." She paused. Harley looked nervously into his drink, as if wishing that the olive sitting in the vortex of the glass would suddenly jump up and say something. "Folks like the Kingsleys," Calista added.

"I'm not following your drift here, Calista."

Go for it! a little voice in the back of her mind seemed to mutter, and the voice was not hers, but Archie's. Time to call a spade a spade, Cal. "Did you know that generations of Kingsley children, girls, and young men have been sexually abused throughout their younger years by Kingsley men?''

Harley blanched. His lips began to tremble. ''As legal counsel for the Kingsley family, I must caution you before you proceed any further with this discussion or these accusations.''

''Who's going to sue me? Kingie Kingsley? He's dead. As is his father, Tad, who passed on this marvelous tradition. The victims, too, except for Titty, are dead.''

''Titty—was abused?''

''Yes. She told me herself. And Rudy knows about it all.''

''Rudy knows?''

''Yes. But I really didn't come here to discuss that.'' Harley seemed to sag in anticipation of something worse. ''I don't think that Barbara McPhee killed herself.''

''Bootsie didn't commit suicide?''

''Harley—'' Calista leaned forward ''—I don't want to sound melodramatic about any of this, but could we call her Barbara? She hated that name Bootsie. Bootsie is like a name you give a pet. I happen to think that Barbara was a real person, although her family never treated her that way. So I just feel better calling her Barbara.''

Harley's eyes looked steadily into Calista's. Then he settled back into his chair and stared down at his knee. He looked totally forlorn and depressed, deeply depressed. He had come to this meeting with such anticipation, such excitement. His own life had become so vapid with Joanie; his work life so constricting; his children so removed. He didn't even know what love was anymore. Or had he ever? Then on that dreary

rainy day on Louisburg Square, this woman had appeared, as tantalizing as any creature Ulysses had encountered, with her wild silvery hair and hooded eyes
full of sorcery. She had appeared like the sexual witch
that had haunted their musty Puritan past, a glorious
succubus. God, he had ached whenever he thought of
her. And now here she sat, still beautiful in this very
odd way, but so sensible, and not righteous, but just
and wise in ways he never dreamed. Nothing scared
her, either. He had just threatened her—well, warned
her—that he was legal counsel from the most distinguished of all Boston law firms for one of the oldest
of Brahmin families and she hadn't flinched. Rather,
she'd very politely reminded him that the perpetra-
tors of these abuses were dead, as were all the victims
save for Titty. Harley Bishop had thought he was going to come to this meeting at the Ritz and maybe
change his life. That wasn't going to be, and she had
told him a worse tale. What was that she was saying
now?

"I don't think she killed herself. I think that Gus
killed her."

"Gus?"

She had to work carefully now. She could not reveal that Charley had busted into Hopkins, Bishop
and Creeth's computer. "Would he have stood to gain
anything from his mother's immediate death?"

Yes, thought Harley, everything if Quintana
Kingsley died before the meeting in his office on that
Friday morning, as indeed she had.

THIRTY-THREE

"MADAME X, how delightful to hear your voice. I'm so sorry to have had to rush you off earlier. But all to your benefit, my dear."

Leon Mauritz signaled his secretary, who immediately put through a call to a number in Boston.

IN A PRIVATE ROOM at the Harvard Club, Rudy Kingsley stood with four distinctly scroungy young men whom Malcolm had let in through the rear door that afternoon. When the phone rang, it was as if a current had passed through the five people. Calista, Jamie, and Liam stood in a semicircle around a man in his late twenties seated in front of Charley's laptop. This was Phink Tank, the hottest phone phreak in the Northeast. Like many phone phreaks, Phink Tank had worked deep in the bowels of the baby bells as a consultant. He was an expert in AT&T hardware and digital communications. Since college, he had been the local technical backup for the AT&T 3B2 system, a monster multiuser UNIX platform 3 with 3.2 gigabytes of storage. Phink Tank knew this system in and out; he was legendary for his expertise. He had written an elegant code-scanning program by the time he was eighteen and he was, to boot, a wily operator. For years, since the breakup of Ma Bell, he had been sucking away at AT&T and UNIX. He had a mess of corporate code, but he never sold it for a penny. He was an electronic Robin Hood—stealing from the monolithic pavilions of phone technology and redistributing it among the poor, passing around a source code that supposedly was kept under well-guarded security but that in reality was about as effective as a rusty chastity belt on Madonna. But most important, he was quiet about his underground work.

As a consultant at AT&T, he was adequately paid but got no benefits, no insurance, no retirement program—no nothing. He hated the idea of intellectual property; he hated these fat cats. He didn't cause harm like Fry Guy, but he liked playing Robin Hood with software.

Of course, if the company had found out, they would have been outraged. He was a "field niggah" in the company and he was supposed to come in through the back door and not eat with the good silver. Tonight, he sat in the Harvard Club and when the call came through from Leon Mauritz's office, he began his fine dance through the switching stations. He punched a few more buttons on his phone keypad. Within nanoseconds, he was into the system as a technician.

"These Centrex lines are incredibly insecure. They operate off of standard UNIX software and this new generalized automatic remote thing—the one they call GARDEN—is a crock. You don't even need a trashy Radio Shack One Thousand to reprogram the switching station. You just log on as I have done here, as a technician. Okay, listen up."

Leon Mauritz's voice came through a box. "I have a prospective buyer, very enthusiastic."

"Oh really!" the female voice trilled. Rudy's brow creased. It was not a voice he had ever heard before.

"Who is this man?" the voice asked.

"What makes you think it's a man?" Leon replied. There was a pause. One could almost sense the caller's surprise. "It is," Mauritz said quickly. "I just don't think we should jump to conclusions about these things."

"Right, of course." But there was a quaver in the voice that had not been there before.

"This person insists on seeing the netsukes within the next forty-eight hours." Rudy lifted a triumphant fist and shook it in the air. Leon was coming through just as he knew he would.

"Oh..." Another pause.

"Is there some problem?"

"No... this is just rather sudden and I hadn't expected things to happen so quickly."

"Well, where are you? My client is prepared to fly anyplace."

"More hesitation. "Uh... New York..."

Rudy's eyebrows shot up.

"Good. Let's say day after tomorrow. My office at four p.m."

"No. I shall call and tell you where by four o'clock."

"Fine. Just as long as it's within the next twenty-four hours."

"He better be serious."

"Madame, I don't deal with people who aren't."

"Well, tomorrow, then. You'll hear from me. Good-bye." There was a click as the caller hung up and the connection was severed.

"I got the number. It's a seven-two-three exchange. That's Boston; maybe Back Bay."

THIRTY-FOUR

CALISTA WALKED out of the Ritz bar, heading diagonally across the Public Garden toward Charles Street. She wasn't sure Harley had believed her. But maybe it didn't really matter. It seemed as if Lieutenant O'Hare was beginning to. Her head swirled with thoughts. She paused to look at the beds of tuberous begonias. They were thick and velvety, brilliant crimsons and magentas. She did not notice the simply dressed but elegant woman stopped at the opposite bed to admire the evening primrose. Calista began walking again. The woman followed.

Calista thought about Billy. She was sure he was lying. But why would a kid in a summer program in a New Hampshire prep school lie to cover up for Gus Kingsley? How could a kid be involved with this? Unless.... She stopped in her tracks. Children, young people, had always been abused by Kingsley men. Was it possible that? Astonishment crept into her slowly but surely. With an inexorable certainty she began to feel a new truth.

She was at the far corner of the gardens. Bronze ducks were set in the asphalt path to commemorate the Robert McCloskey classic children's book *Make Way for Ducklings*. The elegantly dressed woman paused near a bed with concentric circles of gaily colored petunias when Calista stopped. Is it possible, thought Calista, that Gus is abusing this boy? And if he is doing that, could he have done something to Jamie, as well? She lifted her hand toward her mouth. The possibility of this truth was awful. Was there no end to it all? The woman's shadow slid up behind her. Calista took off jogging. She must call Rudy. She must tell Lieutenant O'Hare to go out to St. Bennett's.

Calista was very good at running in heels. The woman was not.

THIRTY-FIVE

HE COULDN'T BELIEVE that he was doing this at his age. But then again, wasn't that precisely the point? His age. Eighty-one years. It had been a good life. Wonderful friends, some truly splendid lovers, and pots of money. He had nothing to lose, but they had so much to lose. And Jamie, poor boy! Still, they could call him a fool for trying this. But he was an old man now and he did not want young, innocent people getting hurt.

It had been sticky with Calista. She had wanted to know why he couldn't meet with her immediately. But if he had told her, she would have wanted to come along. She was that kind—a tad reckless. She had told him about what the police had discovered about the so-called suicide. Very clever of her. Now as he sat crouched behind the standing Edo screen, his back began to hurt. He had taken two Motrin already. God, getting old was a pain. He had selected the camouflage of the screen because from it one could see the living room, the front hall, and the staircase going to the second floor. Rudy had had a hunch that at least one of the netsukes was here and not at Gus's place. Here where Bootsie would never find it, but where he could have arranged for the cops to find it—that is before he became aware of how much the pair together would be worth. So Rudy was prepared to wait it out for Gus. And then what? He had tried to get through to the police, the Lieutenant O'Hare Calista had mentioned. His best hope would be to get through this next part with no confrontation. He had brought an old revolver that he'd found over at Queenie's just in case things got dicey. Of course, the thing looked like something left over from the Crimean War.

If he could just confirm that it was indeed Gus, then follow him to New York and the meeting with Mauritz. By that time, good God, he should be able to get through to the police. Ah! A noise—the distinct sound of a key turning in the lock. He heard footsteps. They were coming into the front hall.

Rudy blinked, but he wasn't fooled for a moment by the heels, cream-colored pleated skirt, and matching linen jacket. The hips appeared very slender, the shoulders wide, and the calves muscular as the figure mounted the stairs. It was Gus. He should have known that Gus might have this bent. Hadn't Kingie started to get very naughty at those Welles Club "Frivolities," almost to the point of embarrassment on the part of some of the other members? Seemed like Kingie had liked keeping the clothes on a little too long after the event and began some rather embarrassing flirtations with Albie Belmont's youngest boy.

There was a ring at the doorbell. Rudy froze. Who in the world could that be? What was supposed to happen now? He certainly hadn't planned on this contingency. He wondered if Gus had. Would he open the door? There was no sound from upstairs. But then once more, he heard the click of the lock's tumblers.

"Yoo-oo! Rudy, are you here?"

Good Lord, it was Calista Jacobs! "I got this extra key from Titty."

"Oh . . . oh my . . . I'm sorry. . . ." Calista looked up at the top of the stairs. There was a woman in a cream-colored suit. She began coming down the stairs toward Calista. Then it all seemed to happen very quickly. Fragments of images swirled through her brain like the bits of colored glass in a kaleidoscope. A pattern arose. There was the picture of the Welles Club men all tarted up for the "Frivolities." There was Kingie with the hourglass waist—he wore it so well, Titty had said. And so had the lady in the greenhouse, the lady with the garter! Like father, like son. The realization exploded in Calista's brain. This was no lady. This was Gus and he was going to kill her.

THIRTY-SIX

"YOU JUST COULDN'T stay away, could you?"

Calista was thinking as fast as she could. She had to convince him that he would never get away with this, that too many people already knew.

What could she say? Where to begin? Could she pretend that the cops knew everything for sure? That there was plenty of evidence? She'd just have to wing it.

"You know...uh...you don't think anybody knows about you, do you?" She didn't wait for an answer. Just keep talking. Every word, every syllable meant delay; delay was good. "You gotta think this through, Gus."

"You have to think it through, Calista!" he said, moving toward her.

"No...no...you don't get it. Everybody knows, you see, Gus, just everybody. They know you killed Queenie. And...uh...they know about the money, all that stuff with Harley Bishop and the will, and the cops got the picture fast on Barbara's death. They've got it all figured out, Gus. They've got evidence." She was almost panting. It felt more like sprinting than talking, but it might have to be a long-distance race.

"Like what kind of evidence?"

She shouldn't say they had prints. He might have been wearing gloves. She thought fast.

"Fiber stuff...it's not like fiber optics that they do; it's this other kind of fiber stuff...you...you..." she stammered. "You left fucking fibers all over the place!" She almost shouted the words.

"She's right, Gus." Both their heads swiveled as Rudy stepped out from behind the screen, holding the gun. In one swift gesture, Gus tore off his wig, threw it right into Rudy's face, and lunged, knocking Rudy down like a paper doll. Gus had the gun and, wheeling around, he grabbed Calista. "Rudy!" Calista screamed. A thin trickle of blood seeped from just above his ear. Had he been shot? She hadn't heard anything. Suddenly, she was aware of this excruciating pain in her arm. Gus had it twisted up behind her.

"You're coming with me."

"Where?"

"That's your car."

"Yes."

It was close to midnight. There was not a soul out on the streets. He was immensely strong.

"I want Jamie."

"I don't know where he is."

"I do."

"Where?"

"He's finishing up at the gardens. Probably wiping down the swan boats—late party, right?" He laughed harshly. "See, I'm no dunce. I figure things out."

"Oh yeah!"

He took the butt end of the gun and knocked her in the jaw. It hurt worse than anything she could imagine. Her whole face and the inside of her skull clenched in a spasm of fierce pain. She tasted blood.

"No smart remarks, Calista. Else you die now and I get the kids later."

She could hardly register what he was saying through the pain. Did he say "kids"? Was he going after Charley, too? They were walking down the front steps toward the car. He was opening the door. He had wrestled her into her car.

"Where are your keys?"

"In my sweater pocket."

He jammed his hand into the pocket and took out the keys.

"Okay, now drive!"

"I can't!"

"What do you mean you can't?"

Her words sounded thick and far away. "I hurt too much." Her whole face hurt so badly, she could not move it.

"You will!" He pointed the gun at her temple. She started the car and pulled away from the curb. He sat close to her, the gun thrust just under her throat. He helped her steer with his other hand.

The pain was unbearable. She could not think, let alone talk.

But time played funny tricks. She couldn't remember the route or the drive. But suddenly, they were there, at the gardens. It was after midnight. She was being propelled along the path toward the pond. There were a few people out for a late night stroll, but did she and Gus look any different? He had the gun pressed against the small of her back. He was rasping in her ear. The words came out in a hot, rapid-fire way. He was telling her what to do. How did he know the boys would still be there? She wasn't sure herself. The party was definitely over, but the swan boats were not tied at the far end where they left them for the night. That meant that the cleanup crew was still working. Charley and Jamie and Matthew were the cleanup crew. They got paid extra for it. So they would be here.

Gus had figured everything out. There was a growing sense of dread welling up from the pit of her stomach. She stumbled. He yanked her up. She had just one thought: She could not allow anything to happen to the kids. Nothing. She would kill before she allowed those kids to be harmed. She would not only kill; she would die for those kids. She had all to lose and nothing to gain—unlike Gus, who had all to gain and nothing to lose. The thought gave her a strange comfort. There was some sort of peculiar logic to it that made her feel superior, stronger—more ready for the fight. Now what the hell was he saying?

"You have to go over there and call to Jamie." She could barely talk let alone call out. "And remember, I'm going to be right behind you in those bushes. I'm a good shot, Calista. And don't worry—I won't shoot you; I'll shoot Charley."

Her pain dissolved instantly and a rage began to creep through her. They were near the entrance to the swan-boat pier.

"You got that?"

"Yeah," she mumbled. Her teeth felt as if they were swimming in blood.

SHE WALKED THROUGH the gate and was just stepping onto the pier. She could see the boys mopping down the boats.

"Mom?" Charley said, looking up.

"Get down, Charley!" she screamed.

There was a huge blast, an acrid smell. She saw Charley fall backward into the water.

"Charley!" she screamed, and ran toward the boat. She heard a click, then another. Two of her teeth hit the pier. Then it was chaos. Gus came charging out of the bushes. Matthew and Jamie ducked for cover. Calista was on her belly, sprawled across the floor of a swan boat.

THIRTY-SEVEN

THE SERGEANT and his partner looked at the old queer sitting in the wing chair and wondered who in the hell he had tried to pick up. Wearily, Rudy began to explain again.

"Look, I don't have time for this nonsense. I tell you that nothing has been stolen—except the two netsukes."

"What?"

Oh God, why had he mentioned that? Now he was going to have to give a lecture on Japanese art to this none-too-bright-looking boy in uniform. "I am telling you that this is the home of my late niece, who was murdered. But on the police files, it said it was suicide, apparently until this morning when Lieutenant O'Hare confirmed my friend's suspicions."

"O'Hare?"

"Yes, Lieutenant O'Hare, and there is a Detective Brant who is working on the case of my sister-in-law."

"What case is that?"

"Mrs. Elliot Kingsley. She was murdered a few weeks ago."

"The Beacon Hill case."

"Yes!" There was a flicker of light in the young cop's eyes. Two neurons connecting, Rudy prayed. "I'm telling you there is a crime in progress right now. This lovely woman has been abducted by a homicidal maniac—my nephew. I don't know where they went, but he is terribly dangerous."

"I'll put in a call to unit Three-four."

"And try to get O'Hare."

RUDY HAD COME to just as he heard Calista's car drive away. He had sat up and tried to put his thoughts in order. He was still trying to put his thoughts in order as he followed the two cops down the steps of Bootsie's house.

"You say you are staying at the Harvard Club?"

"Yes, but why?"

"We'll take you back there after we take you over to Mass General."

"Why in the world would you be taking me to Mass General?"

"That gash is going to need some stitches. In a man of your age, it might be more serious than you think, sir."

"And who cares if it is? I am eighty-one years old. Can I not impress on you two young gentlemen the importance of finding this maniac? He has kidnapped somebody."

"Well, we've called it in."

"Look, fellows, I don't care if I die. But we have to move fast. Listen to me for just a second." He touched the younger cop's lapels in an infinitely gentle way. The cop found himself strangely moved by this man's selflessness, a selflessness that he seldom encountered in his job.

THIRTY-EIGHT

"CHARLEY!" Calista scanned the water. Where could he be? The pond was barely three feet deep. Then she saw him. "Charley!" His head was above the water.

"Don't worry, Mom. I'm okay. I felt something hit me, but I'm not bleeding. It just knocked me off the boat. But God, you are! What happened to you? You've got blood all over your face."

"Charley," she whispered hoarsely, "it's Gus. He's after us, all of us. He's totally insane. He's got a gun." She suddenly heard the creak and wash of the pier.

"I'm coming after you. Goddamn it. Jamie! Jamie!" Gus shouted in a hoarse voice.

"Quick, get in the water, Mom!"

Calista slipped over the side. The water felt cold. But it was not very deep. She had to crouch. She saw Jamie and Matthew under the stern of the boat ahead. Then she saw the boat suddenly lurch. Gus had stepped on it. The boys seemed to disappear.

"Where'd they go?" Calista whispered.

"Under the paddle wheel, between the two pontoons. There's a groove. We've got to do it, too."

She felt Charley dunk her and then pull her into a space. She broke through the water. Their heads seemed to be in a dark box between the two pontoons that formed the understructure of the swan boat. The boat began to rock wildly.

"You're here! You're here! I know you're here," Gus cried, then he jumped to another boat.

Charley stared at his mom. She could see his horror over her appearance. But she was curiously detached. She didn't even feel the pain in her jaw anymore. But the gears in her mind were starting to click in, take hold. Was it possible that the gun had blanks? Charley had said he had been hit, but he wasn't bleeding. She drew closer to Charley. She cupped her hands over his ear. "Where were you hit?" she whispered.

Charley then cupped his hands over her ear. "My left shoulder. But it just aches a little."

She felt down the left side of his neck to his shoulder. "Right there!" Charley whispered. "I think it was the surprise that made me fall rather than the bullet."

Calista thought he might be right. Then Charley, enveloped by his mother's growing calm, became curiously detached, too. He was thinking. He was contemplating cause and effect and the convention of linear events as they are linked through cause and effect. But Charley remembered his father talking about oddities of time; places where time flowed backward or raindrops were suspended for eternities and never hit the ground; occasions when cause and effect became separated and no longer were part of a logical conjunction. Places that disobeyed the known laws of physics and time, like black holes. Perhaps he and his mom had fallen into one of those 'tween places.

It was very odd. Calista had always wondered how she might act in a situation like this. This calm that followed the shock was mesmerizing, and strangest of all, she felt the presence of Tom. Had it been just barely a month ago that she had been so depressed about missing him, missing him forever? It seemed weird. Why miss him when he seemed so near? He did seem near. She must think now and not just revel in his nearness.

The gun had not shot Charley. Yet they were proceeding as if it had. Cause and effect had been disrupted, disjointed. This was one of those universes that Tom had lectured to his students about in the core-curriculum physics course. It was the lecture following the one about special relativity, which explained the ins and outs of Einstein's theory as it related to such phenomena as time dilation, which occurred when one was traveling near light speed. Tom would give a lecture called "Jacob's Weird Places," in which he would upset all notions of conventional physics, including relativity, and begin to imagine realms where time stopped altogether, or flowed backward, or where time was not at all linear, or never a quantity at all, but a quality. Calista felt she had entered one of Tom's weird places. And he was right beside her.

Once more, she cupped her hand over Charley's ear. "I'm going out. I'm going to distract him. Can you get through this groove to where Matthew and Jamie are?"

Charley nodded.

"Okay, now listen. When you hear me start carrying on, you boys make a run for it. There's got to be a cop around here someplace."

Charley felt calm. His mother was doing just what she should. She was reversing the cause-effect cycle. He could picture it just like the boxes in a cartoon sequence. Box number one: Charley gets blown into the water. Box number two: His mom blows out of the water; the gun would turn back, the gunfire be redirected.

CALISTA HAD ducked under and out of the paddle-wheel box. It was very hard to swim in such shallow water. She only needed to get over to the shore just beyond the pier. She was almost there. The concrete sides of the pond began to slope upward. She staggered out. She could see Gus still on the boats. He stood sleek and dark among the swans' gracefully curving necks.

"Help! Police!" she yelled at the top of her lungs. Gus wheeled around. She raced across the grass. He came running toward her. She swerved at a statue and then headed toward Charles Street. God, he was gaining on her. No wonder. She was drenched, her sneakers full of water. She didn't dare take time to kick them off. It was only one hundred feet to the corner of Beacon and Charles. She heard a tremendous grunt and something hit the pavement behind her. She turned to look. "God Bless Robert McCloskey!" she muttered through her mouth, dribbling blood and bits of teeth. He had tripped on a bronze duckling and was flat on the ground. She kept running.

Then she heard shots. And the night was illuminated with blue flashing lights. Calista stopped. She was confused. "Tom!" she called softly. She was trembling. The flash of glitter and blue light limned the trees. There were cars on the grass. How odd. Right by the KEEP OFF THE GRASS sign, there were three cars with sirens. The world had dissolved into absolute chaos. "Tom?" she called again. But he was gone and there was this strange little elfin man coming up to her, putting his arms around her.

"It's all over, Calista. Sergeant, bring me a blanket, please, and yes, call an ambulance... She seems to be bleeding from her mouth. Don't worry, dear.

Charley's here. Jamie's here. The boy Matthew is here.''

But Calista was crying. Oh, how she missed Tom again. She would have to go on missing him for the rest of her life. He had been with her. He had!

And then she remembered nothing.

THIRTY-NINE

THERE IS A special glory to an early-autumn day with the crispness in the air and the light refulgent and golden, gilding every blade of grass and rimming every cloud in a shimmer. Calista reclined on the wicker chaise lounge in her newly finished conservatory and looked at a plant her mother had sent her, hoping to goodness she could keep this one alive. The light fell through glass panels onto the jewel-colored octagonal tiles. The plumber was supposed to come today and hook up the little pool, which she preferred to call a "grotto" at the other end of the room. Charley couldn't wait to buy goldfish for it and she herself had ordered some waterlilies, a particularly hearty variety that she had read about in *Horticulture* magazine. She thought about Jamie. His father had shown up quicker than they had anticipated and he seemed genuinely grieved by Barbara's death and Jamie's own particular tragedy. But most important, Jamie seemed really pleased to see his dad. He had left with him just the day before yesterday to begin a new life, hopefully a much better life, in California.

Calista looked around the room. It had turned out nicely and it would be lovely in all seasons, but especially come January, when it would offer a sunny oasis in the long New England winter. At this point, Calista couldn't wait for winter—for winter and for Archie. He was supposed to be coming home in two days. She had refused to let Charley or the elder Baldwins call Archie or bring him home early. It was ridiculous. He was supposed to be home within a week after the frightful events in the Public Garden. No sense getting him all upset. Everything was fine, after all—well, almost fine. Calista took the glass of lemonade and delicately slid the special straw through her teeth. There were a few gaps now. That made it easier.

She heard someone coming in through the front part of the house. It must be the plumber, she thought. Charley had stuck around to let him in. She took a sip and went back to her book, *Barchester Towers*. She wondered whether she could be hauled around on this rig à la Signorini Neroni. She was feeling quite languorous and almost Italian in this setting, what with her grotto about to be hooked up.

"Hello!"

Calista looked up over her reading glasses.

Archie!

Only it came out "Awshie."

Certain consonants were impossible with her jaw wired shut. She started to raise herself from the chaise, but then Archie was there all over her, cradling her head, her fragile Humpty-Dumpty head, in his arms, kissing her face.

"Tell me where it doesn't hurt...so I can kiss you."

"It dushn't matter. Kish me where it hurz. Kish me all over."

This was heaven. She buried her cheek in his neck and smelled him. He smelled so good, and the wonderful blue eyes, crinkled, slightly tired, full of worry, worry for her. His rough short gray-brown hair scratched her forehead. She pushed him away and ran her fingers over his face. She couldn't quite believe it. But here he was, every wonderful bit of him. How often she had drawn those great cheekbones, cheekbones to die for, the angular jaw, the gentle slope of the eyelids. Oh God! She was one lucky woman.

"There was this package outside for you."

It was postmarked from England. "Oh, it mush be frum Rudy."

"Rudy?"

"Long story." Calista opened it. There was a narrow box.

"Turnbull & Asser. My goodness," said Archie.

She lifted the lid and unfolded the tissue paper. There was a beautiful pink shirt and an ascot, the colors of which could only be described as rhubarb and custard. She took a card out of the envelope.

I figured you were about my size. So they made one up, a "bespoke shirt," as they say, for a dear friend and in the colors of the regiment to which another dear friend of mine belonged.

With much love, Rudy.

"Ah, how schweet." Calista sighed. Then she caught sight of something by Archie's leg. She had remembered him carrying a box when she had first looked up from her book.

"Whassh dat?"

"A rare orchid, my dear, from the rain forest."

Calista's neck turned red. Archie loved to watch Calista blush. It always started as a red flare on her neck and crept toward her jaw—her poor old jaw.

"The one you shaid reminded you of me—"

"Certain parts."

"Oh boy, Awshie."

"Yes, darling, a dirty mind is a joy forever!" He kissed her again.

THAT EVENING, before they got down to dirty, Archie brought out a bottle of Veuve Cliquot that he had put on ice. Veuve Cliquot was Calista's favorite champagne. She had always loved it, even before she became a widow. Nobody had noticed then. But Archie knew how the widow loved the Veuve and he had made sure to stop on his way from the airport and get the Grand Dame. The most distinguished of all the *cuvées* in its fetchingly curvacious black bottle. Charley joined them. Archie poured the sparkling liquid into three glasses. Calista slipped a straw into hers. They lifted their glasses in a silent toast. They took their sips. It was wonderful.

She closed her eyes and savored it in the back of her mouth for a second before swallowing. She thought how lucky she was to be drinking this champagne in the company of all these good men—all three.

"Still good with the straw?"

She remembered the words of the old monk Dom Perignon on the occasion when he first tasted the liquid he had invented.

"Issh like drinking the schtars! I mean..." She paused. "Stars!"

She said the word with painful clarity.

Buried In Quilts

(First Time In Paperback)

Sara Hoskinson Frommer

A Joan Spencer Mystery

WHERE THERE'S A WILL...

Joan Spencer, violist and manager of the Oliver Indiana Civic Symphony, is busy with preparations for the group's performance at the hugely popular annual quilt show. But when the body of show organizer Mary Sue Ellett is found under a quilt, the competition takes on a sinister tone.

Joan suspects Mary Sue's death had to do with a missing will that the entire Ellett family has been circling like vultures to locate. But looking for cold, hard motives among the soft down turns up some surprising stitches—and the handiwork of a devious killer.

"Entertaining..."—*Publishers Weekly*

Available in June at your favorite retail stores.

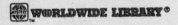

Take 3 books and a surprise gift FREE

SPECIAL LIMITED-TIME OFFER

Mail to: **The Mystery Library™**
3010 Walden Ave.
P.O. Box 1867
Buffalo, N.Y. 14240-1867

YES! Please send me 3 free books from the Mystery Library™ and my free surprise gift. Then send me 3 mystery books, first time in paperback, every month. Bill me only $3.94 per book plus 25¢ delivery and applicable sales tax, if any*. There is no minimum number of books I must purchase. I can always return a shipment at your expense and cancel my subscription. Even if I never buy another book from the Mystery Library™, the 3 free books and surprise gift are mine to keep forever.   415 BPY A3U5

Name _____ (PLEASE PRINT) _____

Address _____ Apt. No. _____

City _____ State _____ Zip _____

---

* Terms and prices subject to change without notice. N.Y. residents add
  applicable sales tax. This offer is limited to one order per household and not
  valid to present subscribers.

© 1990 Worldwide Library.

MYS-596

Die Dreaming
Terence Faherty

First Time in Paperback

An Owen Keane Mystery

ALMA MURDER

Ex-seminarian turned seeker of lost souls—especially
his own—Owen Keane attends his tenth high school reunion
and finds himself the butt of a practical joke by the old gang.
Vengeance being the operative mood in his "morning after"
state, he starts asking sticky questions about a decade-old
secret that has shadowed the lives of everyone involved.

What he discovers is shocking, but pieces are missing.
Not until the twentieth reunion do they fit together. One of
the gang has been murdered, and Owen is determined to
unravel the tangle of lies that cost a man his life—and now
may cost Owen his own.

"Rich and surprising..."—*Publishers Weekly*

Available in July at your favorite retail stores.

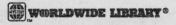 **WORLDWIDE LIBRARY®**

DREAMING

PRAISE FOR THE SECOND EDITION

"*Radical Focus* is a must-read for anyone who wants to accomplish out-sized results. Christina does a great job showing both the why and the how of OKRs. Avoid the all-too-common mistakes by reading this book first."—**TERESA TORRES**, author *Continuous Discovery Habits*

"Everything good I've ever learned about OKRs I learned from Christina Wodtke and Radical Focus."—**JEFF GOTHELF**, author of *Lean UX*, *Sense & Respond* and *Forever Employable*

"A master at getting things done, Christina offers a radically focused way to achieve one's goals through disciplined use of OKRs."—**IRENE AU**, Design Partner at Khosla Ventures

"It has been five years since Christina published the first edition of Radical Focus. The book has gone on to become a favorite for thousands of product people working to learn how to empower their teams, and utilize the OKR technique... I think you will love [the second edition.] It will inspire you.."
—**MARTY CAGAN**, author of *Inspired: How to Create Tech Products Customers Love*

PRAISE FOR THE FIRST EDITION

"Busy grinding without purpose is the secret death of too many startups. In this memorable story, Christina gives us a glimpse of a more satisfying kind of startup—still hard and chaotic but full of purpose and the chance to build something great."
—**JAMES CHAM**, Founder Bloomberg Beta

"This is a book I wish every business owner, designer, strategist, marketer, student, and content creator I have ever worked with would read. It is brilliant in its ability to teach important lessons while keeping the readers engaged in a story."
—**ABBY COVERT**, Information Architect, Etsy

"Finally, a parable I could relate to! The real message is that OKRs work and *Radical Focus* is a great implementation guide to the world of OKRs, making it easy to deploy and see the exceptional results you're after."—**DAVID SHEN**, Launch Capital

"I'd recommend *Radical Focus* for anyone wanting to build not just great products but great organizations."
—**RYAN SHRIVER**, Director of Technology at SingleStone

"Our VP at Nest bought a copy for everyone on the team."
—**SCOTT RUFFNER**, Product Manager at Nest

"This book is useful, actionable, and actually fun to read! If you want to get your team aligned around real, measurable goals, *Radical Focus* will teach you how to do it quickly and clearly." —**LAURA KLEIN**, Principal, Users Know

"Someone once told me that 'problems are just opportunities that haven't presented themselves'. Since I was introduced to OKRs, they've been an invaluable tool for me, and our company. Christina's ideas have been instrumental, allowing me to better navigate the often ambiguous approach to goal setting and along the way creating a more open and accountable team and a clearer path for myself professionally. I personally can't thank her enough for the guidance."
—**SCOTT BALDWIN**, Director of Services, Yellow Pencil

"*Radical Focus* illustrates how to implement OKRs in an engaging, compact, realistic story. Best of all, Wodtke proves OKRs can be fun!" —**BEN LAMORTE**, OKRs.com

Radical Focus

RADICAL

Achieving Your Most Important Goals
with Objectives and Key Results

F CUS

A business book in the form of a fable

CHRISTINA WODTKE

*Dedicated to the dreamers, always unsatisfied,
always sure the next time it will actually be good.*

*Dedicated to the executioners, who know
the way to make things happen is to make them happen.*

*Dedicated to my beta readers,
who made me think maybe this could be a book.*

*Dedicated to the editors of the world.
Without you, I'd look dumb.*

*And, as always, dedicated to Amelie.
Because Amelie.*

PRAISE FOR THE SECOND EDITION

"*Radical Focus* is a must-read for anyone who wants to accomplish out-sized results. Christina does a great job showing both the why and the how of OKRs. Avoid the all-too-common mistakes by reading this book first."—**TERESA TORRES**, author *Continuous Discovery Habits*

"Everything good I've ever learned about OKRs I learned from Christina Wodtke and Radical Focus."—**JEFF GOTHELF**, author of *Lean UX*, *Sense & Respond* and *Forever Employable*

"A master at getting things done, Christina offers a radically focused way to achieve one's goals through disciplined use of OKRs."—**IRENE AU**, Design Partner at Khosla Ventures

"It has been five years since Christina published the first edition of Radical Focus. The book has gone on to become a favorite for thousands of product people working to learn how to empower their teams, and utilize the OKR technique… I think you will love [the second edition.] It will inspire you.." —**MARTY CAGAN**, author of *Inspired: How to Create Tech Products Customers Love*

PRAISE FOR THE FIRST EDITION

"Busy grinding without purpose is the secret death of too many startups. In this memorable story, Christina gives us a glimpse of a more satisfying kind of startup—still hard and chaotic but full of purpose and the chance to build something great." —**JAMES CHAM**, Founder Bloomberg Beta

"This is a book I wish every business owner, designer, strategist, marketer, student, and content creator I have ever worked with would read. It is brilliant in its ability to teach important lessons while keeping the readers engaged in a story."
—**ABBY COVERT**, Information Architect, Etsy

"Finally, a parable I could relate to! The real message is that OKRs work and *Radical Focus* is a great implementation guide to the world of OKRs, making it easy to deploy and see the exceptional results you're after."—**DAVID SHEN**, Launch Capital

"I'd recommend *Radical Focus* for anyone wanting to build not just great products but great organizations."
—**RYAN SHRIVER**, Director of Technology at SingleStone

"Our VP at Nest bought a copy for everyone on the team."
—**SCOTT RUFFNER**, Product Manager at Nest

"This book is useful, actionable, and actually fun to read! If you want to get your team aligned around real, measurable goals, *Radical Focus* will teach you how to do it quickly and clearly." —**LAURA KLEIN**, Principal, Users Know

"Someone once told me that 'problems are just opportunities that haven't presented themselves'. Since I was introduced to OKRs, they've been an invaluable tool for me, and our company. Christina's ideas have been instrumental, allowing me to better navigate the often ambiguous approach to goal setting and along the way creating a more open and accountable team and a clearer path for myself professionally. I personally can't thank her enough for the guidance."
—**SCOTT BALDWIN**, Director of Services, Yellow Pencil

"*Radical Focus* illustrates how to implement OKRs in an engaging, compact, realistic story. Best of all, Wodtke proves OKRs can be fun!" —**BEN LAMORTE**, OKRs.com

Radical Focus

RADICAL

*Achieving Your Most Important Goals
with Objectives and Key Results*

F CUS

A business book in the form of a fable

CHRISTINA WODTKE

Dedicated to the dreamers, always unsatisfied,
always sure the next time it will actually be good.

Dedicated to the executioners, who know
the way to make things happen is to make them happen.

Dedicated to my beta readers,
who made me think maybe this could be a book.

Dedicated to the editors of the world.
Without you, I'd look dumb.

And, as always, dedicated to Amelie.
Because Amelie.

CONTENTS

FOREWORD
TO THE
SECOND EDITION

I t has been five years since Christina published the first edition of *Radical Focus*. The book has gone on to become a favorite for thousands of product people working to learn how to empower their teams, and utilize the OKR technique.

But much has been learned about this topic in the past five years.

It's no secret that many product teams have struggled to get the value out of the OKR technique that they had hoped. Why is that?

When you read Christina's book, you'll find that it is really about two major topics.

The first describes a culture of empowerment. It's at the heart of the first half of the book, the fictional case study.

The second describes the OKR technique, and how that technique can be used to help empower your product teams with problems to solve (the objectives), and shift the focus of their work to outcomes (the key results).

It is tempting to just try to apply the OKR technique, without embracing the broader concept of an empowered product team. Applying a technique is easy. Changing culture is hard.

Unfortunately, what too many people don't realize is that this particular technique depends on a culture of empowerment. It emerged from companies that already had this culture of empowerment.

I have seen literally hundreds of companies that have tried to superimpose the OKR technique on top of their top-down, command-and-control culture. In this case, the result is both predictable and not pretty. It's come to be known as "OKR Theatre."

Some leaders understand that it's really the culture change that matters, but they hope that applying the OKR technique will serve as a stepping stone to an empowered team culture.

But that's like thinking you can buy a pair of high-performance skis as a stepping stone to actually learning how to ski. Of course, buying the skis is the easy part; those performance skis are useless unless they're on the feet of someone that's already put in the effort to learn how to ski.

For those that are willing to put in the effort to embrace a culture of empowerment, I think you will love this book. It will inspire you, and get you started on your journey.

Marty Cagan
February, 2021

INTRODUCTION TO THE SECOND EDITION

Is it too soon for a second edition?

As I write this, it's almost five years since *Radical Focus*, the first book written about the Objectives and Key Results approach to goal setting and achieving was published. I wrote "The Art of the OKR," the blog post that set me down this route, in 2014. A lot has changed since I wrote that post. I've given dozens of talks and helped over a hundred clients. I don't even dare guess how many conversations about OKRs I've had, and I've seen a wide variety of struggles people have trying to achieve their goals. Goal setting methods have been around for a long time. Most people have heard of KPIs and SMART goals at some point in their career. What's fresh about OKRs is they come with a framework for actually achieving those goals after you set them.

When I wrote the first edition, I was writing for start-ups. I had only seen OKRs work with small companies that had found product-market fit and were trying to grow. But the phone calls I got were from all sizes of organizations, from a one-man consultancy to behemoths such as Pepsico and Walmart. I developed new approaches to OKRs to deal with the heterogeneous environments I was working in. But the core of OKRs— a focused goal, both inspiring and measurable, tracked regularly— never changed. OKRs supercharged R&D groups, helped small teams of intrepreneurs[1] explore new markets, and aligned multiple innovation efforts spread across multiple departments. OKRs work for anyone trying to do more than just conduct business as usual.

But along with the OKR methodology's rise to popularity, there sprung up a lot of people who decided they would profit from it without changing the work they actually did. Software companies rebranded project management approaches and called them OKR software, even though OKRs are all about monitoring results and not the roadmaps of tactics a team might try (admittedly best would be both). Consultants charged companies to learn how to "do OKRs right," but often didn't really understand what makes OKRs work. Worse, a few consultants were willing to water down elements of the OKR framework the moment the client pushed back on some of the more difficult aspects of OKRS. And finally, a lot of self-congratulatory blog posts talking about committed OKRs and task Key Results muddied the methodology water. Some days it seemed like the very things that make OKRs work were the first to be tossed out the window.

---

[1] Entrepreneurs are start-ups; intrepreneurs are start-ups within an existing company.

I've spent my time since 2014 teaching at my new position at Stanford, writing *Pencil Me In*[2] and then *The Team that Managed Itself*, which explains the other two legs of a successful management approach. Too many leaders asked me how to do performance reviews with OKRs, and after talking to them I realized there is a dearth of easy-to-read books on good management practices. But after I published it, I realized it was time to return to OKRs.

Is it too soon for a second edition? I fear it's almost too late. It's time to pin down the core ideas that make OKRs work so well and suggest ways they can effectively be used in nontraditional ways. I worry OKRs will end up on the trash-heaps of management fashion along with extreme programming and Six Sigma.

I haven't changed the fictional case study much, but the back of the book is twice as long and includes advice for both start-ups and giant corporations.

I hope this second edition will help you learn what aspects of OKRs matter, learn where to change the methodology to suit your culture, and, most of all, achieve the goals you set. Life is too short to start work on your dreams "tomorrow," for tomorrow never comes. You might as well start working to achieve your goals today.

---

2 A book about Visual Thinking which teaches you to draw and how to draw many key business approaches such as storyboards, wireframes, and that consultant favorite, 2×2s.

FOREWORD TO THE FIRST EDITION

When Performance Is Measured by Results

By Marty Cagan, founder of
the Silicon Valley Product Group

I was extremely fortunate to have started my career at Hewlett-Packard as an engineer during their heyday, when they were known as the industry's most successful and enduring example of consistent innovation and execution. As part of HP's internal engineering management training program called "The HP Way," I was introduced to a performance management system known as "MBO"—Management by Objectives.

The concept was straightforward, and based on two fundamental principles. The first can easily be summed up with the famous General George Patton quote: "Don't tell people how to do things, tell them what you need done and let them surprise you with their results." The second was

7

captured by HP's tagline of that era, "When Performance Is Measured by Results." The idea here is that you can release all the features you want, but if it doesn't solve the underlying business problem, you haven't really solved anything.

The first principle is really about how to motivate people to get them to do their best work, and the second is all about how to meaningfully measure progress.

So much has changed since my time at HP. The technologies are dramatically more advanced, the scale and scope of systems we build are several orders of magnitude larger, teams move much faster, generally with superior quality and performance, all delivered at a fraction of the cost. However, these two performance management principles are still at the foundation of how the best companies and teams operate.

The MBO system was refined and improved at several companies over the years, most notably Intel, and today the primary performance management system we use is known as the "OKR" system—Objectives and Key Results.

Unfortunately, another thing that hasn't changed is that most teams still don't operate with these principles.

Instead, groups of executives and other stakeholders all too often come up with the quarterly "roadmap" of features and projects and then pass them down to the product teams, essentially telling them how to solve the underlying business problems. The teams are just there to flesh out the details, code and test, with little understanding of the bigger context, and even less belief that these are in fact the right solutions. Teams today are all too often feature factories, with little regard for whether or not the features actually solve the underlying business problems. Progress is measured by output and not outcome.

This book is intended to help all organizations start operating like the best organizations. I have seen these techniques deployed successfully in organizations as large as a sixty thousand employee company to as small as a three-person start-up. Large or small, if you've worked hard to hire smart people, this system will help you unleash their potential.

INTRODUCTION
TO THE FIRST EDITION

*Every published writer has had it—the people who
come up to you and tell you that they've
Got An Idea. And boy, is it a Doozy. It's such
a Doozy that they want to Cut You In On It.
The proposal is always the same—they'll tell you the
Idea (the hard bit), you write it down
and turn it into a novel (the easy bit), the two
of you can split the money fifty-fifty.*

— Neil Gaiman, "Where Do You Get Your Ideas?"

In my years in the Silicon Valley, I've had a similar experience to Neil Gaiman's: I sit down with a new entrepreneur with "a big idea" and they ask me to sign an NDA. A nondisclosure agreement usually swears the parties to not talk about the ideas, or copy them. These kids are convinced that their idea is so precious and amazing that the hard work has been done. Nothing left but to get a-coding!

I usually refuse. Ideas, like NDAs, aren't worth the paper they are printed on.

I almost never hear a new idea. In fact, it's rare I hear an idea I haven't thought of myself, unless it's in an industry I'm unfamiliar with. It's not because I'm a genius (I'm not). It's that ideas are easier to come up with than you think. What's hard—really hard—is moving from an idea to reality. It's hard to find the right form of an idea, a form that will let consumers see its value, understand how to interact with it, and feel excited enough to pay for it. That is so hard that it often takes a team of people to do it. And that's when the level of hard goes even higher. Suddenly you have to find a way to hire the right people, get them all focused on the right thing, and make sure no one forgets why they got together in the first place in this world of interesting (and profitable) other things to do.

The writers. The musicians. They struggle, and they only have to manage themselves! The filmmakers and the entrepreneurs have even a greater challenge. Yet somehow these people manage to fight against the long odds against them to make their idea take form. How do they do it, when so many others fail to make it past the "I've got an idea!" stage?

It's not important to protect an idea. It's important to protect the time it takes to make it real.

You need a system to keep you—and your team—aimed at your goal when the world seems determined to throw shiny objects at you.

The system I use is made up of three simple parts. One: Set inspiring and measurable goals. Two: Make sure you and your team are always making progress toward that desired end state. No matter how many other things are on your plate. And three: Set a cadence that makes sure the group both remembers what they are trying to accomplish and holds each other accountable.

Inspiring and Measurable Goals

I use OKRs for goal setting. I'll go into those in detail throughout the book. In short, this is a system originated at Intel and used by folks such as Google, Zynga, LinkedIn and General Assembly to promote rapid and sustained growth. O stands for Objective, KR for Key Results. Objective is what you want to do (launch a killer game!), Key Results are how you know if you've achieved them (downloads of 25K/day, revenue $50K/day). OKRs are set annually and/or quarterly and unite the company behind a vision.

The Objective is inspiring and motivates those people who don't dig numbers. For those who do love numbers, the Key Results keep the Objective real. I know I've got a good Objective when I leap out of bed in the morning eager to make it happen. I know I've got the right Key Results when I am also a little scared you can't make them.

Tying Actions to Goals

When I first started learning about productivity systems, I heard of the Important/Urgent matrix. It's a simple four-square with two axes. The first is important and unimportant. The second is urgent and not urgent. We should spend time in important-and-urgent, and do. We should spend time in important-but-not-urgent and *not* in unimportant-but-urgent, yet ... urgent is so ... urgent! It's mentally quite difficult to drop things that don't matter (especially if someone is nagging us). So a solution is to time-constrain things that are important but not urgent, thus making them urgent.

Let's start with a personal example. Let's say you have been meaning to sign up for a personal trainer because you suck at getting to the gym. Yet week after week goes by and it never seems to happen. You could try making your health an Objective for a quarter, and Key Results involve muscle mass, weight, and emotional well-being. Each Monday you set three tasks to complete against the goal. One might be, "Call a personal trainer." Next you find someone to hold you responsible. A friend, a coach, or a spouse are all good picks. Now, if you don't complete it, you will be held responsible by someone.

In a work example, it might be any number of things, from optimizing a database to creating a faster site and increasing customer satisfaction, to redoing all your material with the new brand so your company doesn't look unprofessional. The OKRs set goals. The weekly priorities remind you to achieve them.

As well, if you review the priorities each week, you discover what conditions allow you to achieve them. And, more valuable, what keeps you from getting things done. In my experience, many people fall into two camps of misestimating: those who think they can do anything and constantly overestimate what they'll accomplish, and those who sandbag. As a manager, learning who is who lets me know who to push and who to question. As well, tracking lets the employee learn to know themselves better, a good outcome all by itself.

Cadence

Starting every week with a public setting of priorities is powerful. You commit to the team and to each other to make the Objective occur. A Friday celebration of what's been accomplished is the second bookend of a high-performing team's week. This commit/celebrate cadence creates a habit of execution.

Beware Greeks Throwing Golden Apples

When I was a kid, one of my favorite Greek myths was that of Atalanta. She was the fastest runner in Sparta and did not care to be married. Her father, being worse than medieval—ancient Greek—did not agree to that plan, and set up a contest in which young men would race to win her hand in marriage. She begged to also race, to keep her freedom. Her father agreed, to keep her placid, never thinking she might win.

The day of the race, she was so amazingly swift, she might have won. Except a clever lad, Hippomenes, managed to lay hands on three golden apples and rolled them into her path each time she started to pull ahead. She kept pausing to pick them up, and Hippomenes beat her by a nose. If she had only set some clear goals and stuck to them, she might be ruling the city footloose and fancy free!

Every start-up will run into golden apples. Maybe it's a chance to take the stage at an important conference. Maybe it's one big customer that asks you to change your software for them. Maybe it's the poisoned apple of a bad employee who distracts you while you wring your hands over what to do about him. A start-up's enemy is time, and the enemy of timely execution is distraction.

By setting good goals and committing to working toward them each week, while celebrating your victories, a company can have amazing and focused growth. No matter what kind of apples roll across their path.

The Executioner's Tale

My book is a fable of a small start-up that almost didn't make it. Hanna and Jack start out as dreamers. They start out being really good at having an idea. They are good at hoping everything will work out well. They soon find out that a good idea is not enough; they need a system for making dreams happen.

By the end of the tale, they are no longer just dreamers. They are executioners.

THE
EXECUTIONER'S
TALE

THE EXECUTIONER'S TALE

Hanna sat at her desk, hunched over her keyboard, her shiny black bob hiding her face from the rest of the office. To them, perhaps, their young CEO looked like she was focused on the monitor. Perhaps going over last quarter's numbers, which were not anything like what they should be. But she wasn't looking at any number in the Excel sheet she had open. Her hands sat flat on either side of her keyboard, and only she knew she was trying hard not to face-plant into it. How the hell did she get here?

The company had a viable market, but couldn't figure out how to get out of its own goddamn way and grab it. Her partner was a whiny diva. Her new CTO was some kind of methodology cultist, and she was going to have to fire someone for the first time in her too-short career.

Why had she wanted to be an entrepreneur, again?

Six Months Ago ....

Once upon a time there was a start-up.

This start-up had a vision to bring delicious artisanal loose-leaf tea to fine restaurants and discerning cafés.

There were two founders, Hanna and Jack. Hanna was first-generation Chinese-American and loved the tea she grew up with at her parents' house. Her mother had run a small restaurant in downtown Phoenix for years, and her family cared about good food and good tea. She studied business at the Stanford Graduate School of Business, and she hadn't been so lucky finding nice tea in Palo Alto. Hanna despaired of getting a nice cup of Longjing after a fine meal.

Jack was British and he was miserable at cafés that could poach an egg perfectly yet thought Earl Grey was a who and not a what. Jack was at Stanford, too, studying the design of human-computer interaction. Jack loved technology when it meant carrying fewer books in his book bag or a spell check that caught his sloppy typing. But he drew the line at tea in little bags. He did not consider that progress.

Hanna and Jack met one day at the university bookstore café. Jack was loudly moaning over tea in packets. Hanna, standing behind him in line, laughed and showed him the tin of green tea she had in her purse. They quickly became friends. Hanna had known she would be an entrepreneur since she was a little girl. She came from a family of entrepreneurs. Besides her mother's restaurant, her father had his own accountant's office, and Hanna's aunt had started her own law firm. Entrepreneurship was in her genes. She hadn't known what kind of company she wanted to start until she met Jack. They agreed to take an entrepreneurship course the spring of their senior year, and after graduation they were ready to go.

Jack and Hanna knew there were plenty of great tea producers. So they decided they would connect the people who grew great tea with fine restaurants and cafés that were snobbish about coffee but ambivalent about tea. They named their startup TeaBee. And because they went to Stanford and had made the right connections, they managed to raise a little money to make a go at it.

Hanna took on the title of CEO and Jack that of president, but really Hanna owned the business and Jack the product. They found a small office near Highway 101 where the rents weren't quite as bad, and had a happy six months furnishing the office and giving away tea at tech meet-ups. They hired a few engineers, and Jack made a very pretty website where buyers could find tea producers and order tasty tea. Hanna closed a few deals with local restaurants. Jack talked Hanna into hiring a visual designer on contract to make a sexy logo, and they even got a part-time CFO to make sure the books balanced. The office hummed quietly with keyboards typing and murmurs of voices.

But they started to feel a little uneasy. While they had another year of money before they'd need to raise another round of funding, they still worried about why it was taking so long to build a marketplace. They had many, many little tea producers signing up, but only a few buyers. A lopsided market is not a profitable market. Like good founders, they decided to go out to try to sell more tea themselves, in order to learn more about the psychology of buyers.

One day, Hanna came back to the office with a very big order from a restaurant supplier. This restaurant supplier sold tea to all kinds of restaurants, big *and* small, as well as canned goods, dry goods and coffee. Jack was both happy and alarmed. He was happy to see so much money about to come into the business, yet this was not "to plan." They were here to connect fine dining and fine tea! Did this restaurant supplier care about tea? Did it care about quality?

"Jack," Hanna sighed. "The restaurants don't want to set up accounts with us. We're too new. They don't trust us. The suppliers are more willing to try us out, and they will place our tea in restaurants. The tea growers still get more business. Let's just see how this plays out."

Hanna Finds Another Great Customer

A few days later, Hanna used her mother's Rolodex to close another deal with another restaurant supplier. She pulled into the parking lot outside their office and sat in the warm car for a moment, her hand on the keys still in the ignition. TeaBee's mission was "Bringing great tea to people who love it." Perhaps not the sexiest mission, but clear, she thought. Did it matter if she sold to a restaurant or a restaurant supply company? It shouldn't, she decided. She pocketed her keys and headed into the office.

The office was warmed by the same sun that made her car a bad place to hide. Hanna threw her blazer over the back of her Herman Miller chair. They'd bought the iconic chairs, as well as a couple of whiteboards, at a sale held by a start-up that had run out of money. All start-ups are built with the bones of past failures. Google's offices were once Netscape's, which were once Silicon Graphics'. You had to be optimistic or crazy to ignore the proof that launching a start-up had only slightly better odds than winning the lottery Hanna figured she and Jack were a bit of both.

She found Jack in the back of the office, where they had a long table set up. The team had lunch together there and held impromptu meetings when their one conference room was occupied. Jack stood next to the new designer he had just hired. Ann? No, Anya. Jack slouched to try to have an easier conversation with her. He was about six-two, and towered over little Anya's five-five. Hanna joined them, and Jack straightened a bit with a sigh.

On the table before them sat several cardboard boxes with different colored labels on them.

"Hanna, have a look. I think this blue is rather lovely, but I'm afraid it won't pop on the shelf. This orange is stronger, but maybe it's not a tasty color? Blue is terribly trustworthy." Jack could talk about colors for hours. Add in typefaces, and you could lose half a day. Hanna had no idea why he thought they had needed to hire a graphic designer. Jack seemed knowledgeable enough. But he'd insisted it wasn't his bag, and she'd given in. Anya pushed forward a dark red box.

"Um, yes, the dark red is nice," Hanna said. "I'm sure you two have it under control. Jack, I just wanted to let you know ... I closed Brightwater Supplies. They cover Modesto through Fresno."

Jack scrunched up his brow. "Fresno is ... north?"

Hanna laughed out loud. "South! You are so coming with me next time I head into the Valley." She pushed aside the packaging mock-ups and placed the contract on the table in front of Jack. She flattened it out, almost petting it. Jack looked it over. The numbers were ... impressive. Bigger than any deal they had closed so far.

"Hey, this." He tapped at a spot in the contract where lines had been crossed out, and a new bit written in. "What's this about not using the website?"

"It's too much work for them."

"Rubbish! I did usability testing on that."

"They looked at it and didn't like it. Don't freak out. You can go with me to see them in a couple weeks, when we do the check in. I'll just enter the orders in myself until you can figure out what the changes need to be. Perhaps you can get Erik to write an API so they can integrate it with their system? They order a lot of tea, and they order regularly."

Jack looked unconvinced.

"It's a boat-load of money and I'll do the work." Hanna took a deep breath. "Go back to work; don't fret."

She strode off to the kitchen to make a cup of tea, feeling upset. She had expected Jack to be excited. This was money. Not just money, but regular, hefty amounts of money. Yet he acted like she had brought in groceries, but forgotten the milk. She felt better, though, as soon as she entered the kitchen. The room was full of the tea samples from the growers, and she was always spoiled for choice. She poked through a pile of samples of green tea from a Washington farm she'd visited last week. She closed her eyes and pressed her nose into the bag, inhaling the scent of the tea, sweet, like dried grasses crushed underfoot on a hike. Then she realized she wasn't alone.

"Okay, that's embarrassing," she said, turning to Jack.

He waved his hands. "Oh, whatever. We all do that. Tenzo's stuff is aces." He plugged in the electric kettle, and pulled another mug off the shelf. He leaned against the counter and crossed his arms across his chest. "I'm not sure I'm good with these people."

"These people?"

"Suppliers. They put Lipton into three-star restaurants. They don't *care*."

"I don't know about that. They provide what the restaurants want. I convince them good restaurants want good tea. It's just customer development." She shrugged.

"The point of a start-up is to do things the right way. Excellent product, packaged excellently, sold to excellent customers. Not doing things the way everyone has been doing it."

"I thought the point of a start-up was to find product-market fit in order to grow a company that benefits the people who depend on it."

The kettle light went on, and Jack poured. "Yeah, yeah, that's what it says in the textbooks. It doesn't matter if you can sell, if you sell rubbish." He swirled the tea ball around for emphasis. "This is our chance to make a *difference*. We can make amazing experiences even more amazing. I know you are worried about the bottom line. Just don't forget what we are all about." He strode from the room, not waiting for her answer.

We're *about* ten months from running out of money, unless we close more deals, Hanna thought. If the tea is good, and the money is good, what is the problem?

Hanna Suggests a Pivot

A few weeks later, Hanna pulled Jack into their conference room. The room was nothing special. It had the proportions of a shoebox and was painted the shade of white that office park landlords seem to favor. Three of the four walls held elderly whiteboards, marred with traces of notes left by former tenants. Hanna found the fluorescent lighting mildly unpleasant, but at least it didn't flicker. Hanna had been in many rooms just like this in the two years she'd spent consulting between college and grad school. Those with flickering lights had made her crazy. It was not only annoying on its own, but a sign the owners were too neglectful or distracted to deal with them. She considered them an omen of doom.

Upon entering their well-lit conference room, they found it occupied by Erik, their lead programmer. He liked to sit in the windowless room and code.

"Um, Erik, we need the room."

"One second ..." Erik did not raise his sandy blond head from the laptop. Taller than Jack but much thinner, his lean frame formed a question mark over the gleaming silver computer.

"Sod off, Erik," Jack said, not unkindly, but firmly.

"Yes, going ... I'm standing up ... I'm walking." Erik rose, balancing the laptop on one arm, occasionally hitting a key. He exited without taking his eyes off the screen.

"Why does he hide in here?" Hanna felt irritable. She hoped Jack knew already what she was about to talk to him about, but she also had a bad feeling he didn't.

Jack shrugged. "He needs to focus. Anyhow, he's good, and we don't have a CTO yet ..."

This reminded Hanna of yet another problem. Technically, finding a CTO was on Jack's to-do list. But it seemed to Hanna that Jack didn't take interest in any part of the business that wasn't about design, and she wondered if she'd have to add it to her to-do list. She bit her lower lip.

They pulled up chairs at one end of the long conference table made up of two Ikea wooden kitchen counters Jack, Erik and their front-end developer Cameron had assembled one weekend, which made a handsome and affordable table. Unfortunately, they hadn't finished it, and anything spilled left a history. Hanna rubbed at a coffee stain with her finger while she figured out how to explain what she was thinking. The stain didn't fade.

Jack waited. Jack was good at silence.

"Jack, I've made several sales recently to restaurant suppliers." Hanna paused and Jack folded his arms across his chest. Okay, this wasn't going to go super easy. "Each sale has been the equivalent of closing ten to twenty restaurants. Because that's who they serve. I've been putting in the numbers for Aramaxx, and they are providing a lot of business for the tea producers. Jefferson Supplies has doubled their order. It's been so good, Tenzo Farms is even talking about adding staff!"

It seemed like Jack grew stiffer as she looked at him. She really hoped he'd just guess where she was going. Unless he had, and he didn't like it. Forward, then.

"This is a far better business. The sales cycles are just as long, but the suppliers are willing to try us out. Unlike the restaurants and cafés, where we can have five or ten meetings and they just want us to come back when we've been in business longer. I think we've got the evidence we need. I think it's time to pivot."

In their entrepreneurship class, they had learned that a pivot is a change in tactics without making a change in strategy. Hanna felt strongly this was exactly what needed to happen. They could still get great tea into the hands of consumers; they just needed to use the pre-existing relationships the restaurant suppliers had to do it.

Jack rocked back on his heels, nervously. "Look, I get it, about the sales cycle." He looked pleased with himself as he used the business jargon. "But I'm not at all sure the restaurant suppliers won't get the producers used to the custom, then try to push the prices down. What if they force the tea people to lower quality? What if they make garbage?"

Hanna chided him. "Solve the problems you have, not the ones you imagine." She had heard that a hundred times from her mother and laughed at herself for saying it now. "Jack, it's working. We are making the tea growers money. We are starting to make us money. And the suppliers will get dependent on us also. If it's mutually beneficial, they can't force us to do what we don't believe in."

Jack paused, and closed his eyes for a second. She saw his eyes move under his lids, as if he was dreaming. He did that sometimes, when he worked on a design. It was him working a problem through to the end. He opened his eyes.

"Whose labels will go on the boxes?"

"Really?" Her eyes widened. "That's a worry?"

"We've done a lot of work on it. We need a brand presence. Like Intel on laptops. It made them. You can't settle for being a secret sauce!"

"I don't know what they are thinking on packaging. They haven't asked for us to change." She shrugged.

"Hmm. Well. I can see your point."

His tone had Hanna far from convinced he did see her point. She noted he was grinding his teeth.

"I think it might make sense to consider focusing on the suppliers."

And there was his reluctant dance around the idea. Next would come the "but."

"But look, you don't know, and I don't know, what it's going to be like, working with these blokes."

And, out of facts, Hanna was stuck. She couldn't argue with nebulous fears and vague anxieties. Then she had an idea.

"Let's talk to Jim."

Jim Frost had been the first angel who had invested in them. He was a Valley veteran, and had seen many companies go under, as well as a few succeed. He was wise and insightful and, if anyone could help them figure this out, it'd be Jim. Jack and Hanna had both learned to trust him. He had introduced them to their lead programmer and was on the hunt for a CTO for them.

Jack sat with the suggestion for a second, then nodded. "A fresh pair of eyes never hurts."

Jim Is Holding Court at Starbucks

Jim Frost liked holding his meetings at Starbucks. He loved Starbucks. It was the kind of rags-to-riches story any investor would love. Starbucks had started by bringing high-quality, European-style coffee to one small Pike's Place café and charging three times the going price for a cup. Coffee used to be bottomless and a buck. Now it was a single cup of single origin and cost three. Starbucks had invented a market and then owned it. Now there was a Starbucks on every block, and Jim could even enjoy their coffee on an airplane. He wished he'd had a shot at investing in them. And he dreamed of meeting the next Starbucks entrepreneur.

Jim's next appointment came from the coffee bar with espressos in hand, and he rose and gestured them over. The two founders sat down. Dan was a slim, young, Indian man, Fred a freckled strawberry-blond with a Doritos-and-Coke-diet waistline.

Jim listened to them talk through their latest change in direction. Their fourth in eighteen months. When he had funded them, they were doing diet tracking. Then came gourmet health menus. Now they were focusing on healthy recipes. Jim suppressed a sigh while the entrepreneurs faked excitement about the new direction.

"Our beta users love the site!" Dan gushed. But there was no real excitement in his voice. Fred stared into his espresso as if it were a scrying pool. He didn't even try to meet Jim's eyes. The passion the two had brought to the original idea had foundered on the rocks of a disinterested market. Fred, especially, had loved the technology the tracker had used. Now it was gone, and he was stuck coding a website he didn't care about. He looked tired. And several pounds heavier. Dan was so stuck in hustle mode, he didn't recognize when it was time to turn it off and face their problems honestly.

Some entrepreneurs run out of money. Others run out of heart, Jim thought. These guys are going to do both.

Jim shook their hands, saying goodbye to both the men and his investment. Once a team ran out of heart, there was no reason pouring more money in.

When Jim saw Hanna's Civic pull into the parking lot, he wondered about these young entrepreneurs. Would Hanna and Jack be in Dan and Fred's shoes in another couple of quarters? Or would they be Starbucks?

Jack Really Hates Starbucks

They had to meet at a Starbucks near Jim's office, which always made Jack have small, quiet meltdowns inside. The strip mall that held it also sported a Safeway, a Shell Oil, a Taqueria, and a surprisingly good kaiseki restaurant.

Starbucks represented everything Jack found alien and confusing about Silicon Valley. Why did venture capitalists always want to meet at Starbucks, when there was better coffee to be had, and much better tea? Why did a Michelin-starred restaurant choose to be in a strip mall? Who needs this much parking? He'd never seen a lot more than half full.

Hanna pulled her aging Civic into a spot in front with ease and was out with her keys in her pocket before the engine had finished shuddering to a halt. Jack followed dutifully.

Seeing Jim cheered him up a bit. Jim sat on the back patio, where he usually held court. Jim was in his late fifties; a former Intel exec who had built two very successful start-ups, then moved into angel investing. His lined face told more stories of smiling on sunny golf courses than the stress of all-nighters, though life had handed him more of the latter than the former. He stood, shaking the hands of two young men, both dressed in identical blue dress shirts and khakis. Finishing a pitch up then, Jack thought.

Hanna touched his arm lightly, to hold him back. "I don't feel much like doing the social dance," she muttered. They slowed their walk, and the other entrepreneurs left. Jack and Hanna took their seats, greeting Jim. Jack found his seat still warm. They laid out the question of the pivot before Jim.

Jim sat back, and lightly ran his finger along the rim of his double espresso. Every time they met, he was drinking coffee. Yet he never seemed anything but calm, as if he'd stepped out of a yoga class.

"Back when I worked at Intel, we had a story we recalled when facing a hard decision. Back in the eighties, the Japanese were gaining market share in memory. As Intel lost more and more money, there was a ton of internal debate about what to do. Real brutal arguments," Jim said. "One day, Andy Grove and Gordon Moore were talking about it again, and Andy looked out the window at the revolving Ferris wheel of the Great America amusement park in the distance. He turned back to Gordon and asked, 'If we got kicked out and the board brought in a new CEO, what do you think he would do?' Gordon answered without hesitation, 'He would get us out of memories.' Andy, struck by the clarity of that simple statement said, 'Why shouldn't you and I walk out the door, come back in, and do it ourselves?'

"Well, you know the rest of the story," Jim continued. "That propelled Intel into greater success yet. After that, Intel would always use the revolving door test on really tough decisions. We'd think of what someone not burdened by history and emotion would do." Jim paused, and sipped his espresso.

"So kids, if you were hired as a new CEO, what would you do?"

Jack looked at Hanna, but she remained quiet. He knew what she thought.

Jack said, "I'd have to consider this direction seriously. It's good money. But I'm rather worried if we go this direction, we'll be pressured into lowering quality."

Jim asked, "And then what would happen?"

Jack replied, "I'd have to say no. I'd walk away first."

The three of them sat there in silence.

Hanna said, "I'd say no also."

Jack looked up from his untouched tea.

"I don't want to build a company selling a poor product," Hanna said. "That never works in the long run. If I wanted to sell bad tea, I'd work for Bigelow. Or Celestial Seasonings. We're here to change the world, not reproduce it."

Jack looked back into his cup. "I know. Dammit. I know." He'd heard it before; they had talked about it a hundred times. Yet, when it came to money, would she stick to her principles?

Hanna smiled now. "Well, dummy, we are here to get the tea to the people who like to drink it! Not let it grow old and disgusting in the warehouse. Like what you're doing here." She pointed at his cup.

Jack looked at his cup, and back at her, giving her a quick smile. When she talked like this, she reminded him of his sister. Yet Hanna was an MBA. In his department, they'd made fun of MBAs and their weird language: "exits" and "maximizing value." He always figured "value" was their code word for money. But that wasn't what he thought of when he thought of value.

Jack finally spoke. "It seems we've achieved the elusive product-market fit when we weren't paying attention. I suppose if I was the new CEO, I'd have to agree to commit to the pivot."

He saw Hanna's shoulders visibly relax.

"Good," Jim said. "Don't be surprised if you get some resistance from the team. It's typical. I recommend you consider using OKRs to keep things on track." He received blank stares from both the young entrepreneurs. "That stands for Objectives and Key Results. A lot of my companies use them to increase focus and team output. Each quarter, set a bold, qualitative Objective and three quantitative Results that let you know when you've hit your Objective.

"So, what do you think a good Objective would be for your group? Something tough, but doable in three months."

"Prove our value to the restaurant suppliers," Hanna quickly replied.

Jack interrupted her, "What do you mean by value?"

"Show we can deliver an excellent product that helps their business."

Jack paused, then nodded. Excellent product. That sounded right.

Jim asked, "How will you know you have succeeded?"

Hanna and Jack went back and forth. Finding a revenue-based Key Result wasn't hard. But agreeing on a metric that would represent the supplier valuing TeaBee was.

"No bargaining?" Jack suggested. "I mean, if it's that good, they won't haggle over cost."

Hanna rolled her eyes at that. "Look Jack, bargaining is just what you do in the business. Your livelihood depends on getting the best price. If my mom wasn't bargaining, I'd check for a pulse. Let's try a retention metric." Jack looked blank. Hanna continued, "Like reorders at 30 percent?"

Jim jumped in. "OKRs need to be hard goals. The kind you only have a fifty-fifty shot of achieving. You're trying to get the team to push itself. As your investor, I'd worry if 30 percent retention was all you're aiming for." This was a sobering reminder that Jim wasn't just a friend; he had skin in the game.

Jack jumped in. "One hundred percent reorders!"

Jim smiled. "Is that possible? It can be upsetting to set a goal that the team knows they cannot achieve."

Hanna stepped in. "I think 70 percent is possible. So far, everyone has re-upped, but that was with my prompting them."

Jack said, "That's something I want to stop if we can. We have a website after all. Surely they can use that to make their orders?"

Hanna replied, "They can't use it. It isn't really set up for their needs."

"Well, we'll put in some OKRs about fixing the site, too, then."

Then Jim's next meeting showed up, and he quietly extracted himself to another table, leaving them to work through the details.

Hanna and Jack discussed goals and metrics until they suddenly realized they were shivering in the shade of the late afternoon. The sun had dipped behind the Starbucks, and their tea was ice cold, but they had real goals they could both live with. They each went home to sleep on it.

Hanna Announces the Pivot

The next morning in the office, over a pot of Keemun, they reexamined the OKRs they had set the day before. They looked hard, but right.

Hanna and Jack called the team into the conference room. Hanna stood at the front of the room. She still felt awkward addressing a group, even though she'd been forced to do so every week in her entrepreneur class. Their three programmers sat in a row, all with laptops open. Anya, the designer, hid behind a cascade of hair as she drew furiously in a sketchbook. Naoko, the CFO for hire, sat quietly, a hand resting lightly on a pile of printouts of the latest sales. Hanna felt even more nervous, knowing these people were betting their future on Jack and her. No pressure, right?

Hanna took a breath, and tried to send it to her toes like her yoga teacher recommended.

"Hey guys." She looked at their faces for encouragement. Well, the faces she could see. Erik, the lead programmer, glanced briefly up from his laptop then returned to his work. Cameron and Sheryl, the other two programmers, stayed eyes locked on their code. Jack, sitting next to her, smiled at Hanna and nodded for her to begin.

"We've got an announcement. We're going to make a small, but we believe, significant pivot. We are going to focus solely on selling to restaurant suppliers." She took them through the latest events and through the numbers Naoko had brought with her.

Jack chimed in, "We are still bringing great tea from scrappy producers to fine restaurants. We've just found a more efficient and profitable approach."

Some in the team looked unhappy. Erik was particularly upset. For the first time, he looked up from his computer. "This is bull. This company was started to help farmers and small businesses! That's why I joined."

He was a Midwestern boy, and had come to California to attend Berkeley, but stayed to avoid the Kansas winters.

"These suppliers sell corporate teas. They don't care about the tea farmers! They just care about profit."

Jack replied, "It's good for those growers that they have TeaBee to protect their interests. We'll make sure they get a good price, while reaching new customers."

Hanna chimed in. "Besides, most of them aren't big enough or don't have sufficient consistent supply to interest the restaurant suppliers. When I talked with the restaurants, they were concerned with consistent delivery. When I talked to the restaurant suppliers, they viewed the little guys as too little to be worth the effort until TeaBee aggregated the offering. We can make sure we can always offer a good green and black tea at a minimum."

Jack finished, "Now the tea producers can sell more tea. And, better yet, they can predict how much they are able to sell and know when to hire or even expand. This could be really great for everyone."

The team seemed to get the change finally, though Hanna noticed Erik had his hand cupped over his mouth, as if to stop himself from commenting. She wondered what was going on in his head.

"Let's discuss what this shift means." Hanna drew a business model canvas on the whiteboard. "We've got a new customer now to consider—the restaurant suppliers. This means some changes. We're going to have to hire some salespeople and a strong customer service department. Our sales have been based on Jack's charm and my footwork." She got a couple laughs there, as everyone knew Jack disliked the sales part of the job. He liked to schmooze and he often found new clients, but closing the deal, negotiating prices, and getting contracts signed—that was all Hanna. "We need people who know what they are doing. Each sale will be in the thousands, not the hundreds. TeaBee is about to be high touch."

Next, they talked through the OKR process, and went through the OKRs.

Hanna led by writing the first OKRs up on the board.

Objective: Establish clear value to restaurant suppliers as a quality tea provider.
KR: Reorders at 70%
KR: 50% of reorders self-serve
KR: Revenue of $250K

Then she added another set of OKRs.

Objective: Build a valuable platform for restaurant suppliers to manage orders.
KR: 80% repeat orders placed online
KR: Satisfaction score of 8/10
KR: Calls reduced 50%

And then she added: "Objective: Build an effective sales team," with KRs on that, and "Objective: Build a responsive customer service approach," and added three more KRs to that goal.

The team discussed if they could hit the goals, and reduced reorders to 60 percent.

"After all," Erik said, "We can move that number up next quarter, right?"

As the conversation drew to a close, Cameron raised his hand. "But what about our current customers? The restaurants?"

"Oh, we can keep them," said Jack.

Hanna's head spun around. They could?

She opened her mouth to disagree with him, then stopped. They were already introducing so much change to the team. And it wasn't like they were going to go out and sell to new restaurants. She could talk to Jack privately later, perhaps, and form a plan to retire the restaurants gradually. She wasn't avoiding conflict. She was picking her battles. Right?

Hanna Attends a Tasting

Hanna was inputting orders for the distributors when she felt someone standing near her desk. She looked up. Jack stood there, with his coat on, holding several cardboard boxes.

"You about ready?" he asked.

"For what?"

"The tasting? At the XFlight Coworking space? You know? We need to go now, or we'll get clobbered by the traffic."

Hanna stared at him, moving her thoughts from numbers to words. "Look, I need to finish putting in these numbers or Systovore won't get their tea order."

"Why don't they use the site?"

"We talked about this. The site only lets you put in orders in increments of ten. At their size, they'd flip if they had to put in an order eighty times. Either fix the site, or leave me alone to finish this."

"I'll wait in the car."

"It's ninety-five degrees out there. The car will be an oven!"

"Don't let me die, then." He stalked away with the boxes, muttering to himself. "I hate being late."

Hanna growled, but closed the file she was working on and headed out.

They arrived in plenty of time to set up the tea samples. XFlight was a typical coworking space. It held six small start-ups of three or four people each in an open loft space. The desks looked Ikea, but the chairs were the usual expensive Herman Millers. It had a central kitchen that held a couple microwaves and a water dispenser. The glassware included branded coffee mugs and Mason jars. "Good thing we brought our own kettles and cups," Jack chirped happily. "No one seems to care about actual quality, just looking hip in this joint."

Hanna felt better, more focused. She had blared disco the entire drive up, and was still humming "Car Wash" to herself as she set out the small glass teacups her mom had gotten wholesale. She would do this one tasting, then tell Jack, no more. Jack was loudly socializing with the general manager of the coworking space, running interference for her. A natural introvert, she preferred not to do any more small talk than necessary for survival.

The evening progressed much as others like this had. They had done tastings at coffee shops and a couple bakeries. Jack managed to talk with everyone there, convincing people to try each tea. Hanna and the CEO of a travel app compared notes on angels they had each pitched. The tenants of the space left by eight o'clock, either back to their desks to code or off to find food. Hanna packed up, tired from interacting with humans and not relishing the drive back. Then she remembered she had one more order to put in. She sighed deeply and put down her box of cups.

"Jack?"

"Hmm?"

"Why did we do this?"

"We just closed an order with the office manager. Fifteen pounds a week! And our brand will be on the packages ... that could help recognition."

"Recognition with who? It's not like a restaurant supplier is going to be hanging out in this kitchen. That's our customer."

"Okay, then a VC? Anyhow, we got a sale."

"To a coworking space! It's not our focus!"

"They can self-serve on the website. What's your problem?"

"I'm doing more data entry every day! You are supposed to be running product. So fix product!"

"It's in the backlog!"

"Is that engineering for 'go away'?"

"No. Dammit. No." Jack backed off. He looked puzzled, as if confused by her show of anger. But he would be; they never fought. They didn't like fighting. She didn't like fighting, anyhow. She didn't like it now. "Look I'll just cab it home today. That way you get on the road faster." He was offering her a white flag.

Hanna swallowed her distaste of conflict. She had to say something. "No. Jack. Before you call a car, you need to promise me. No more tastings. We agreed on our OKRs. These don't move any of them forward. These are a waste of time."

Jack hesitated. He jammed his hands in his pockets, and then took them out again, as if chided. "These are useful. Networking." His voice was softer now, a hint of doubt entering his voice.

"No. I don't think so. "

And then suddenly, his attitude brightened. "Oh, you are nervous about the sales call with those Monterey blokes. Don't worry! I'll come along! Make sure everyone is chummy! Go! Chill out. Sleep." And he took the box of cups out of her arms and went out the door as her jaw hit the floor. He had completely dismissed her concerns. Chill out? Hanna couldn't chill out. And she certainly couldn't sleep. Not with another order of twenty different teas to type in.

Jack Commits to Quality

Jack got into the office by late morning. He slowly locked his bike to a rack in the back. Hanna was an early bird, and Jack didn't feel like rehashing last night's fight. She'd apologize and he'd feel bad, or he'd apologize, and what if she didn't forgive him? Anyway, he was going to feel bad. He just wanted to run a good company that made a good product.

He'd seen so many of his favorite product designs get ruined over time. Even his beloved smartphone was now big and clunky in his pocket, when it used to be a joy to hold. When he'd worked over the summer for a company he'd always admired, he saw how product managers and business analysts threw over quality for quick returns. Then he realized why everything got worse: money. The business folks pushed to get an uptick by end of quarter so they could bag a bonus. No worry for customer experience or the reputation of the company! He decided then that the only way to assure quality and stay true to a vision was for him to start a company himself. Now he worried he'd get pushed into becoming one of them, those executives he'd resented, and give up his principles to keep TeaBee going.

Perhaps if he just explained to Hanna why showing off their product quality at these tastings was so important. One needs a strong brand for strong word of mouth, and strong word of mouth meant getting tea into people's mouths! Then people would understand how good TeaBee was, and the money would sort itself out. That's what he'd do; he'd just explain it. She'd understand; she loved tea, too.

When he walked in, he noticed her chair was empty. That meant she was out selling. His shoulders relaxed. He hadn't even realized he was holding them tightly in. Well, conversation for another day. He headed over to his desk, but before he could sit, Erik waved him over.

"Hey man, I saw something cool, and I stayed up doing a prototype. Check it."

Erik sat back in his chair, his long legs sprawling beneath the desk. He gestured toward the monitor with his slim, yellowed fingers. Jack briefly wondered how many cigarettes he smoked a day.

Erik scrolled down the front page of the site. The navigation stayed put, while the rest moved. Then he kicked off the order form, which showed each field as soon as the last was correctly filled out.

"Pretty slick," said Jack, admiring the effects.

Erik shrugged. "Just killing time while waiting on the bulk order spec."

Jack's stomach tightened. "That would be on me. I'm about half there, but I had to stop for a bit. I was prepping for the tea tasting."

"Dude, don't sweat it!" Erik said. "Seriously. Those restaurant suppliers should suck it up and type in their orders. They're making enough money from ripping off farmers. Let them spend a little, create a data entry job at least."

The phrase "data entry" made Jack feel worse. "Hanna's been typing it in, not the suppliers." She'd been doing the work because he hadn't written up a technical spec so Erik could code the new functionality.

Erik seemed oblivious to Jack's stress. "Anyhow, I don't get it. Why are we making the middle man fatter? Wasn't the point to help the farmers? And the restaurants? You know, the indies?"

Jack liked meeting with restaurants. He liked doing the coworking spaces and the incubators. He did not much care for the corporate offices most of the suppliers had.

"I think Hanna wants to be the next Starbucks, sometimes," Erik finished up his rant.

"Yeah, I dunno," Jack finally replied "Seems like every time we meet up with an investor it's at Starbucks. That's what they want. The giant exit, the big return."

Erik nodded. "Well, good thing we're watching out for the tea growers. Somebody's got to."

"Yeah, mate. Right. The world has enough mass-produced garbage. We've got to show people what quality looks like!"

"Dude. Exactly."

Jack returned to his desk feeling better. They had good tea, the packaging designs were looking good, the website was solid. Hanna'd come around.

Hanna Talks Numbers

It was late into the afternoon when Hanna finally returned. Sunlight streamed past the flip charts an engineer had taped to the window to try to reduce the light.

She walked up to Jack, not even pausing to set her bag down at her desk. "Let's talk."

She walked to the conference room.

"We need the room, Erik," she said as she entered. Her tone brooked no argument.

He unfolded himself from the chair and carried his laptop back to his desk.

Hanna sat down. Jack sat across from her, keeping the big table between them. On the wall were the OKRs posters he'd made at the beginning of the quarter. He wondered idly how many they'd reached so far.

Hanna leaned forward. "Jack, you extended Anya's contract."

He blinked. "Yup. We aren't done."

"We can't afford her. We can't afford us! We are six weeks into the quarter. In a few months, we're going to have to go out and try to raise money again. But our numbers are not moving. I don't think anyone is going to invest."

Jack continued to stare at Hanna uncomprehendingly. He seemed unprepared for this conversation.

Hanna glared at him. "Do you look at the dashboards I send you? Jack!"

"Um, I'm not really a numbers kind of guy. But we closed XFlight! And the restaurant last week!"

"And we lost a restaurant the week before. They went under. They do that. We are revenue neutral. Look, we discussed this. We need the suppliers. Just two more this quarter, and five next. And we'll have strong numbers, strong enough to start fundraising."

"Can't we just get a bunch of restaurants?"

Hanna stared, speechless. She saw the moment Jack must have realized that they had had this conversation just two months before. But it was too late. She exploded. "We can't close enough restaurants in time. Not without hiring a lot of salespeople, and that will increase our burn rate. Restaurants are slow and cautious and take forever to close. And when we do close them, they order only a pound of tea a week. One supplier is worth one hundred restaurants."

Hanna burned with fury. "Jack, your refusal to pay attention to basic economics is driving me crazy. If you were a designer in some big company, maybe you could nap during the math part of the meetings, but for heaven's sake, this is your company!" Which wasn't going to be his for long if they went under. She slammed her hand on the table, causing it to shudder. Jack took a step back.

Hanna shook her head, frightened by her outburst, and sat down. She took a deep breath and continued, her voice low now, and more disturbing for the new calm it held.

"Jack, if we can't raise money, we'll have to let people go. You know my mom's restaurant? It wasn't her first. My grandparents had a restaurant before she did. That's where she learned how to run a place, and fell in love with the business. But during the economic downturn in the seventies, no one ate out. My grandparents tried to keep the place open, and they tried to keep the staff on. They didn't want anyone to not have a job when things were so tough. But things didn't get better fast enough. And the whole place went under. Maybe if they'd fired someone sooner and found a way to cut back ..." Hanna leaned back in her Herman Miller chair. It was comfortable but it was expensive.

She looked at Jack, showing none of the emotion she felt so keenly. "I can't make that mistake."

"What are you saying?" Jack asked softly. He looked concerned, maybe even a little afraid.

"I'm asking you to commit. Jack, what do you want from this?" She gestured around the room, covered with OKR posters, smiling customer personas, and website mock-ups. Jack's work on the company surrounded them.

"I guess I wanted a place to do things right. I wanted to find something wonderful, and find a way to help other people fall in love with it the way I love it. And I thought it would be fun."

He paused and leaned forward, elbows on the table, hands clasped in front of him. "And I thought it would be fulfilling. Every day I read the tech news and see people making things that change the world. I want to be part of that."

"Sometimes it is fun," Hanna replied. "But you can't do the fun part and leave the hard part to other people all the time. If we get this wrong, we will go under. And people will lose jobs. And no one will find out how great tea can be." She managed a grin that was only half a grimace.

Jack replied, "I'll go through the dashboards, okay?"

Hanna nodded. Jack sighed deeply, and Hanna wondered if he just wanted the conversation to end, or if he really planned to change.

Jack Eavesdrops

Jack sat at his computer with his headphones on. He had been listening to music, but it had stopped some time ago. He stared at Hanna's dashboard. What were these numbers? She had the OKRs, but where did they change? How much were they making? What did they have left? Nothing looked familiar, but he was embarrassed to ask. Anyhow, Hanna was out on a sales call until four. Maybe he'd suck it up and ask to have it explained if he hadn't figured it out by then. He figured if he just stayed with it, the numbers would eventually reveal themselves to him.

Through the headphones, he heard the murmurs of Sheryl and Erik. He assumed they were discussing some bug triage, but then he caught a few words. "Hanna." "Sell out." He couldn't help but tune in to their conversation.

"Yeah, typical MBA bull," he heard Erik say. "She just wants to make money."

"Maybe," said Sheryl. Sheryl was not a talker.

"Look. She's got us in the pockets of the big companies. She's probably setting up the company to flip. That's what they teach them in 'B-School.'"

Erik made scare quotes with his fingers around "B-School." Jack tried to hide that he was watching from the corner of his eyes. Yeah, he thought, an MBA doesn't teach you everything.

Erik continued, "Those people just drive revenues up, then they fire everyone to make a better bottom line. So they can get the biggest exit, see?"

That didn't sound quite so plausible to Jack anymore. That wasn't Hanna's story.

Then he heard Erik say something that chilled him to his bones.

"They won't be getting me with any 'cost-cutting measures.' I still haven't gotten the spec, so I've been making a few adjustments to the code in my free time. Good luck to any new CTO they want to hire. He won't be able to figure anything out."

Jack had heard stories of engineers who wrote confusing code so they could never be fired. He always thought it was a Silicon Valley legend. A kind of engineering boogie man. He was wrong. He closed the dashboard, and opened the spec. Then he reopened the dashboard in his second monitor. And he sat like that, eyes flicking back and forth between them, trying to figure out what to do.

Jack Gets More News

The office phone rang. It rang so rarely, Jack jumped. Hanna picked it up, coolly answering, "Hello, TeaBee, Hanna speaking." She paused, then continued, "Yes, fine, Philip!"

It was one of the restaurant suppliers! Jack sat at the edge of his seat. Maybe he could get her to ask for a testimonial to help with sales on the site. He hovered, in case there was a pause.

"I'm so sorry!" Hanna replied, her brow furrowing.

So much for a testimonial, Jack thought.

"Look, can we make it up to you? I can drive the tea over!"

Now a long break as she listened.

"I understand. Again, I am so sorry. Goodbye."

She hung up, and Jack walked over to her. Hanna let her forehead fall to her keyboard.

Jack waited to be noticed. He understood what it cost to be interrupted.

She looked up at him. "We lost Jefferson."

"What?"

"Too many wrong orders."

Jack noticed she was wringing her hands, tangling her fingers together and apart over and over.

"How is the bulk order flow coming, Jack?" she asked. "I can't keep doing the order entry."

"Um, I handed it to Erik yesterday. I figured he should have something to do."

"Yeah. He should." Hanna looked at him, her eyes going cold and empty. Her hands lay still in her lap now.

"Okay, you can call Tenzo Farms."

"What?"

"You can tell them that we won't have any orders for them. Jefferson was the only one taking matcha. They have most of Japantown. Tell Tenzo they are losing their biggest customer, and hope they haven't hired anyone lately to help with the increased orders."

Jack paled.

Hanna turned away from him. "Go," she said. "Go do it, Mr. President."

Hanna Gets Advice

Hanna stood outside the Starbucks, hesitating. She wasn't sure if Jim was the right person to go to for advice. But she didn't know who else to talk to. Losing Jefferson had shaken her, shaken her faith in herself. Jack couldn't help; *he* was the problem.

She bought two espressos and joined Jim on the back patio. He stood and smiled as she handed him one of the cups. "Where's Jack today?"

Hanna hesitated, then said, "I wanted to speak to you privately."

Jim's smile disappeared. His next words were kind enough, but his eyes flicked over her, assessing. "So what's on your mind, kiddo?"

Hanna began, nervously. "Well, we've got some challenges. I was hoping for some advice."

Jim gestured to go ahead.

"It's Jack." She took Jim through her litany of complaints. "And because of his insistence on farting around with these tastings and the packaging, instead of handling the technical issues we have, we've lost Jefferson."

She looked at Jim to respond, and it was as if the laugh lines around his eyes had been erased. His lips pursed slightly, then he laid both hands flat on the table. "He has to step into his role. Have you explained that to him?"

"Yes." Then she thought a second. "Maybe? I pointed out he was wasting his time." But she only mocked him about being president. That was not the same. "I think he knows."

"Hanna, it's not complicated. Tell him clearly. Then tell him again. When you are tired of saying it, people are starting to hear it. You've got to focus on the Objectives and Results, and you have to make sure he knows *his* role in getting there." He sipped the last of his espresso. "Know your role as well. Your job as CEO is to set the goals and have the hard conversations. Go be CEO."

"I'm worried about the next round." Hanna wanted so badly for Jim to tell her what to do.

Jim shrugged. "Push comes to shove, we can get in a more seasoned exec."

Hanna froze. Her stomach leapt into her mouth and the espresso burned the back of her throat. She briefly wished she'd stuck with the bad tea she usually got.

"I like you both personally, so I'm going to be honest. You've just told me you are falling apart. I'm your investor, not your mom. You get it together with Jack, or you remove him. You focus on fixing your numbers. Or I look for a way to get someone in to get the company to the next level. It's not complicated. You've got the beginning of something, but the Valley is littered with the beginnings of good things."

It was not uncommon. She'd heard stories. Founders replaced with experienced executives forced upon them by their investors.

"I'll get there. I mean I'll talk to Jack." The espresso was making her heart race.

"Good. I look forward to our next check in."

Hanna Gets More Bad News

When Hanna got in, it was late. Jack still sat in front of his computer. The office was otherwise empty. Everyone else had gone home, unless Erik was lurking about in a conference room. She put down her coat, and was about to sit down when Jack strode across the room toward her.

"What's up?" she asked. She wasn't ready to have "the talk" yet. She wanted to put together a game plan.

"We need to talk."

Hanna looked down, hoping to stall. "Now? I've got more orders to enter."

"I think Erik is sabotaging us."

"Is he ..." She looked at the conference room.

"No."

"That's crazy. Why?"

"I overheard him. He told Sheryl he was obfuscating the code for job security reasons."

Hanna sat down heavily, on top of her bag. She stood, removed it, and sat down again. Jack perched at the edge of her desk.

"Jack ..."

"I know."

He didn't know, not by half. "We need a CTO. Soon. Neither of us knows enough code to know if this is true." Her entire company was unraveling before her eyes.

"It's not about code. It's about Erik. I knew he wasn't behind the pivot, but this is over the top. He's gossiping." Jack swallowed hard. "He's saying nasty things about you."

"We should fire him. Can we fire him?"

"I don't know."

Hanna opened her laptop, hands shaking slightly. Too much caffeine, she thought. "So, did you call Tenzo?"

"I think we need to focus on Erik right now."

She knew then he hadn't.

"I ... I need to think. Let's sit down tomorrow. I need to digest this."

She felt utterly alone.

Jack Makes a Call

Jack spent the morning not calling Tenzo Farms. He'd never delivered bad news before. He'd never fired anyone. He'd never even told a client off, though he had wanted to many times.

He spent his afternoon not calling them as well. He knew he'd either have to call them by six, before they went home, or first thing in the morning. Hanna would be in his face tomorrow. He left his desk and headed to the Bayshore Trail.

Their little office was off the frontage road of Highway 101, in the swath of land between the road and the Bayshore Park. It was populated with a variety of start-ups, consulting companies, and odd businesses, from animal hospitals to educational services. A large bookkeeping company anchored one end, a tiny airport enjoyed by fresh-minted millionaires the other.

Everyone walked the bay when they got stuck on a hard problem. Hanna liked to have her one-on-ones walking on the trail, unless there was a confidential matter. He missed their walks here. It seemed like every time they talked these days it was confidential. But here was nature, a good antidote to days of humming screens.

He had thought that having a start-up was a good idea. Designers pretty much never founded start-ups, it seemed like. They were scared of the money thing. Now he wondered if they were really afraid of being in charge. He'd taken a year off between college and grad school and done a bunch of consulting. It was easy: Make the client happy. Now it was confusing. Who was the client? And no one was ever going to be happy.

He'd tried calling Jefferson to talk them into a second chance. That went over like a lead balloon. They were done. They'd told Hanna they were done, and they seemed annoyed by having to tell him the same thing. Jack worried Hanna might bust him for wrecking a chance to close them later.

In the end, he decided to do the call to Tenzo from his cell, on a bench, looking at the salt flats.

He dialed the number.

"Hi, this is Jack from TeaBee. May I speak with Atushi?"

"Hey! It's me. How are you doing? How are things in start-up land?"

"Hey. Um, well, not great."

"Okay. What's up?"

"Well. I have some bad news. Jefferson has stopped working with us. We are not going to have any more orders for matcha after the seventeenth."

Silence on the end of the phone.

"Are you still there?" Jack asked.

"I'm here," Atushi answered. "I just don't know what to say. Can we fix it? Was it a quality thing?"

"No. It was ..." Jack felt bile rise in his throat. "It was us. We ballsed up an order, and they cut us off. I'm sorry."

"Okay. Got it. So we'll have to adjust next month's ... we have a really good guy who was working part-time. We were talking about converting him." Jack heard Atushi's disappointment. "... but now ... sorry, that's my business. Thanks for letting us know quickly. Appreciate it." Atushi's voice was now firm, but not angry. Jack heard the pain, though. A small business was always teetering, he had learned. He was the one who had given it a nudge in the wrong direction today.

"Sorry, mate." Jack had nothing else he could say. He looked for some bit of cheer to offer but came up empty. "I'm sorry."

"Yeah. Me, too." Atushi sighed. "Talk later." And he hung up, not waiting for Jack's response.

Jack sat for a while. A heron landed in the small creek, a beautiful explosion of white wings on blue water. Jack found no comfort in it.

That was it, he decided. He couldn't just focus on product. He had to design the entire business. He had to understand the whole thing, and make sure every choice was the right one. For the first time, he realized TeaBee wasn't just deliciousness in a good-looking box. It was the people he worked with and the conversations they had. It was the plans they made together. It was even the damn numbers. His business was an ecosystem, and he was more a gardener than designer. He had to get better at his job.

He stood, jammed his fists in his hoodie pockets, and walked back to the office.

Out of Time

The call with Tenzo Farms lit a fire under Jack. For about a week. Hanna kept typing in orders, and got the front-end dev, Cameron, to double check them before she committed them. It was a slower process than before, but they couldn't afford to lose another supplier. Cameron didn't seem to mind. He sat next to her and flirted as he looked over the numbers. Hanna wasn't sure how she felt about that, but decided it was far from her biggest problem right now and ignored him.

Hanna left Cameron double checking the orders, running his finger along her monitor as he tracked each line carefully. She approached Jack, sitting at his computer. "So, we're launching bulk order flow this week?"

"Yes, yes. I am just changing a couple things after usability testing."

"The best is the enemy of the good," Hanna muttered.

"Huh?" Jack grunted, head down.

"Never mind. Just launch. I'll buy some Nukey Brown for the launch party." Newcastle was his favorite. Pricey, but it made him happy. Anything to get the damn thing out.

"We've got a tasting at Daily Bread tonight," Jack mentioned hesitantly.

"You are kidding me."

"Sorry, it was set up months ago!"

Hanna's eyes wandered to the OKR poster. Damn, it had grown invisible in the weeks it had been up. The next step now stared at her: "Robust Sales Team."

She turned back to Jack. "You have a tasting to run. I have Objectives to hit. Good luck with that."

She scooted back to her desk to get a job posting up. She paused again, trying to decide when to talk to him about what she learned from Jim. But maybe he was getting better on his own?

And quite suddenly, the end of the quarter arrived.

Numbers

Hanna pulled Jack into the conference room again to review their OKRs. Again they kicked out Erik, who bragged, "I've shaved half a second off the load time of the homepage!" When Jack told him to "sod off" this time, it was considerably less friendly.

Hanna laid out the printouts of their OKRs on the table and pulled out a red pen to circle misses. They looked at the reddening sheets of paper.

"Sales team?" asked Jack.

"Frank's great, but he's one guy. I didn't get the ad up until halfway through the quarter." She pointed at '50% of reorders self-serve.' "And this?"

"You know. We launched the new bulk order system last week."

"Yeah, I've got the usage numbers somewhere." She shuffled the papers around. "Okay. Hmm, 15 percent so far."

"Well it was new. I didn't want to piss off any of the customers. So I just told a couple restaurants and one of the suppliers about it."

Hanna let out a long, shuddering sigh. "I suppose that's right. I just wish we'd gotten it out sooner."

She paused, gathering her thoughts. "Have you got that satisfaction survey you ran last week? Did we get enough results to get a read?"

Jack pulled out a colorful printout of a survey with one hand, while chewing at the skin around his thumbnail. "Um, yes, I think it's enough responses. The results are ... they are ... uneven, I think I'd say."

"So, not that KR."

"No." Jack looked chagrined. Customer experience was *his* baby.

She pulled out the sales numbers. "I've been watching this one." She pointed to revenue. "Close, but not close enough. There was a little uptick here and I thought we had it." She pointed to the end of month two. "But then Jefferson ..."

The pain of the loss of Jefferson sat between them like a poisonous toad. They stared at the chart.

"So," Jack said. "Zero?"

"Zero." Hanna said. "We made zero OKRs." The weight of the red ink made her exhausted and angry. "This is bull-shit!" she yelled. "How did we not make any of the OKRs? I mean, I know we were supposed to make them hard, but it's like nobody even tried!"

It's like I didn't try, a voice in her head said.

It's like Jack didn't try, said another.

"Hey, we got the new branding system up!" Jack replied. "And we've been helping the restaurants with the website. We improved the checkout flow for them. But ..." his voice trailed off. "None of those things were things we agreed to focus on." He put his hands in his hoodie pockets, looking down at the papers in front of him. They both knew nothing *he* did was there.

Hanna stood looking at him, lips tightly pressed together. Then she turned on her heel and strode out of the conference room. She had to get out of that room. Only bad things happened there.

Jack chased her. "You can't walk out on this. We need to finish." He spoke in a low tone. The office was still full.

"Why? It's clear enough. We fucked up." Tears lurked behind her eyes. She had to stay angry or it was going to get embarrassing. "My mom always said, 'In times of crisis, people go back to the thing that made them successful. Even when it's not the right thing to do.'" Hanna knew she and

Jack were both scared, leading a company for the first time. "You focused on design and usability for the old customers. And I went out and sold, instead of building a team who could do it." Her voice rose, cracking with emotion. "And now we don't have numbers that justify investment. I don't think we can turn it around."

Suddenly she noticed the office had grown silent. Filled with embarrassed horror, she headed toward the front door, to escape to the bay.

Jack's cell phone vibrated in his pocket. He glanced at the display: Jim.

"Hanna, hold on!" he shouted, then answered. "Jim," he mouthed, pointing at the phone.

"Jack? Jim. Can you kids swing by the Starbucks? I am talking to a fellow here, and I think you ought to meet."

"Be right over! Fifteen minutes!" he said brightly.

Hanna glowered. "Great. Great. I am not ready to have this conversation. We didn't hit our numbers." Her voice rose again. Jack's cheeks now flushed with embarrassment, but she didn't lower her voice. She was too angry. "What are we going to tell him?"

"So the OKRs didn't work. I mean, it's hardly our fault. It's his system, we did it, and it didn't do anything. It's just another Silicon Valley fad."

"Jack, do you honestly think it was the OKRs' fault?" Hanna hissed.

"I can't say. It's a system that's supposed to help us kick arse. And we didn't kick anything."

Hanna lowered her voice. Her anger had become a deadly calm. "Something certainly didn't work."

She grabbed her jacket with the car keys and strode out the door. Jack followed, all eyes in the open office watching as their founders stormed out the door.

Hanna and Jack Meet a New Player

The drive to Starbucks felt too short. Hanna realized halfway there the car was silent; she had not even thought to plug in her music. Jack stared out the window, away from her.

Hanna slid her Civic into a tight space between two minivans, and Jack sucked in his breath to slide out of the passenger side. But he didn't complain as he usually did about giant American cars.

As they approached the back patio, they saw Jim sitting across from a dark-haired man in his late twenties, draped across the chair like he owned the place. He had close-cropped hair, dark aviator sunglasses, and a tattoo peeking out of his black T-shirt. As they got closer, they saw the T-shirt was of a My Little Pony version of Dr. Who, and the tattoo was the RSA-perl program. His nerd credentials were fully in order.

Who was it, Hanna wondered? Another seed investor? He'd never invest once they confessed their failure.

Jim waved toward the empty seats at the table. "Hello folks! I may have found your CTO."

"No pressure," the alpha geek grinned.

So this wasn't to be a numbers review, Hanna thought as she sat down. Her stomach unknotted slightly.

Jim introduced his guest. "This is Raphael. He just left SOS."

"The game company?" Jack asked.

"Yup," said Raphael.

"Congrats on the IPO," said Jack.

"It was okay." His grin widened, telling another story.

Jim made up for Raphael's lack of chattiness. "Before that, he was at a start-up that was bought by Google."

"Aqui-hire. And I worked on Orkut, so ..." He shrugged. Getting your company bought for the talent was still a respectable exit, and landing at Orkut, Google's first experiment trying to build a social network, was hardly embarrassing.

"So why aren't you on a beach somewhere?" Jack asked.

"I'm not done. Games are great. I had some juicy problems. But I want to do more."

Hanna took a look at Jack. Jack sat upright, listening intently.

Raphael went on, "I've been reading about the single original coffee that high-end coffee shops offer. It's allowing coffee growers to sell directly to roasters, at a much better price. It's improving lives in coffee-growing countries. I don't see why it couldn't be done for other markets!"

He paused and drank from his cup. "Jim has been telling me what you've already done, and I think this could make a difference in a lot of lives."

Jack began to throw off his doldrums. "Exactly ... instead of paying low prices for tea, and blending good and bad into mediocre, we can bring great tea to everyone!"

Raphael cocked his head. "Why does that matter to you?"

"I care about quality," Jack said. "I can't stand badly made things. My mum, she loved bargains. She'd buy anything as long as it was on sale. I had twenty pairs of jeans, none I could be seen in out of the house. And one pair of 501s, which I wore every day. If you can experience something well made, well designed, you know the difference. I know we can do that here."

Hanna had never asked herself why Jack was such a perfectionist. She'd just written it off as a designerly quirk. Now she saw he was on a mission as well. It just wasn't the same as hers. Maybe if she could get Raphael to join, she'd have someone sensible to partner with.

Maybe she could close the deal by sharing her passion.

She jumped in. "Plus, think of the people whose lives we'll change. For example, Wakamatsu Farms was founded by the first Japanese immigrants in California. It's now a cultural heritage site that has just started producing tea again. We'll be able to place that tea in restaurants to help raise money for restoration of their lands. And there is a family farm in Hawaii I was chatting with this morning who would love to be able to get their tea to more people. We can do that, if we can succeed."

"That's exactly what I mean!" Raphael pounded his fists on the table so that the cardboard cups shook. "Work that raises the bar! Work that makes the world better by giving entrepreneurs a way to compete against industry."

Hanna felt excited, and yet ... she also felt she was selling a lie. There was no way she could let him join without talking about their OKRs. And Jim should know, too. Better she bring it up than wait until he asked. She slid her hands under the table so she could turn her rings, fidgeting privately.

"There is something we should talk about, before we go any further. We set several critical goals last quarter, and we met none of them."

Jack shot her a look like she had just betrayed them. Maybe she had, but she couldn't bring Raphael in under false pretenses.

"We set five Objectives, one around value, one around providing a platform, one around sales and ..." She trailed off. She couldn't remember the other two. She looked to Jack. He shrugged. Well, it hardly mattered now. "We gave them all Key Results in the form of hard metrics. And we did not make any." She took a long breath, looking around the table, then back to Raphael. "I understand if that might make you think twice about joining us."

To their surprise, Raphael chimed in, cheerful as ever. "You're doing it wrong," he said. "No, seriously, I used them at my last two jobs. They work, totally. But five OKRs? You can't even remember them all. How can your team? Carville, the dude who ran the Clinton campaign, had a hard time keeping Clinton from doing his policy wonk thing. Every time he got on stage, he wanted to talk about education, foreign policy, energy, all that. And Carville said, 'If you say three things, you say nothing.' You know, keep it simple stupid. It's the economy, stupid. Focus on one key message. Same things with OKRs. Plus your weekly check-ins go on forever if you have that many Objectives!"

"*Weekly* check ins?" Jack queried. "We try to stay pretty meeting-free at TeaBee."

Raphael shook his head. "I get it, but you can't just set goals up and hope they happen. You have to execute against them as a team. That means check-ins. Just like the daily stand-ups and weekly planning we do in Agile. It can be a good, useful meeting if you have a framework you use every week to guide the meeting." He grabbed a napkin and unfolded it on the table. The creases divided the napkin into four quadrants.

He dug a Sharpie out of his laptop bag and wrote: "Objective," followed by three "Key Results." He then wrote "5/10" after each KR.

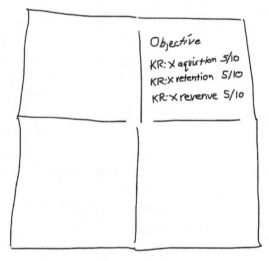

"Okay, so you got that the Objective is the inspiration for the quarter, yeah? And the Results are what happens if you do the right things. It's easy to forget them, though, because every day something cool shows up. So every Monday you look at them. And you ask, are we closer or farther from making these Results? We used a confidence rating at SOS. We'd start the quarter with each Key Result at five out of ten."

"Fifty percent confidence? A fifty-fifty shot at making it?" asked Hanna.

"Exactly. Goals aren't divided into regular and stretch goals. They're all stretch goals. And they need to be hard. Not impossible, just hard. Impossible goals are depressing. Hard goals are inspiring." Raphael looked around the table. Hanna was now leaning forward, and Jack back, the opposite of a few moments before. He continued. "So each week, you have a conversation. You say, have we gone up or down? If you are dropping to two out of ten from eight out of ten, you want to know why. What changed? Helps you learn as well as track."

Jack spoke up. "No way, mate. We've got tons to track. We can't just ignore our other metrics."

"I have to agree with Jack here. We can't just stop paying attention to everything," Hanna agreed.

Raphael shook his head. He moved his pen to the lower right and wrote: "Health."

"Hang on. Here, in the lower right, we put health metrics. These are things we want to protect while we shoot for the moon up here." He pointed to the OKRs.

Hanna and Jack glanced at each other, checking to see if the other was also confused. Raphael took a deep breath.

"Let me explain. Let's say we pick an Objective that's about radical pipeline growth. We're trying to get as many suppliers and distributors partnering with us as we can, right?"

The founders nodded in unison.

"Well, we don't want to forget our current customers in the rush to get new ones. So maybe we do this."

He wrote: "Customer Satisfaction: Green" in the lower right. "This way we force a discussion each week about whether our customers are still happy. Lots of stuff can go here."

He wrote "team health, code health, orders, revenue" in a list. "But just like with the OKRs, we want focus. So we'll pick a couple to talk about each week with the entire company, and we can review the rest less often, just us chickens."

"Customer satisfaction is a must," said Jack. "Maybe code health? We don't want bad code."

"Bad code can become a problem easily," Raphael agreed.

"No, look, guys," Hanna interjected. "Code is code, but we are more a relationship business than a tech company. Let's get real. I like the Objective to be around sales, but health of the team, or better yet the bottom line, really seems more important."

Raphael replied, "OKRs are the thing you want to push, the *one* thing you want to focus on making better. The health metrics are the key things to continue to watch. Making them the same doesn't make a lot of sense."

They made plans to have Raphael join them Monday as interim CTO, so he could try on the company and so they could try him out as well. But Hanna felt it was a done deal. He was their perfect technical cofounder. She felt a bit less alone.

The Executive Team

The Sunday before Raphael started, he met with Hanna and Jack at the Palo Alto Café. The little coffee shop was mostly empty at this early hour. While Starbucks and Philz had lines out the door with commuters filling up, the PAC's first customers were the TeaBee team and a dad watching his toddler climb under the secondhand wooden tables that furnished the place.

Hanna and Jack were rabidly loyal to the PAC. It was one of the few coffee shops in town that really cared about tea and had been TeaBee's first customer. It was typically quiet until ten, when families, retired folks and writers would settle in to while away the long hours of the day. It was one of the last few cafés free of entrepreneurs and VCs pitching each other.

The newly bonded executive team began planning.

"Shall we introduce Raph here at the team meet?" asked Jack, casually truncating Raphael's name.

"Why not," Hanna replied, "They just be wondering who he is otherwise."

"Yep. And maybe you could send an email announcement tonight," Raphael added.

And then Jack looked at Hanna, raising an eyebrow. "Erik?"

She thrust out her chin. "Go for it."

Jack ground his molars together, then spat out what they were both thinking about. "Raphael. There is a guy on the team. He's ... well, he's been messing with the code. Obfuscating it. So other people can't work on it."

"Fire him," Raphael replied.

"Well, we thought ... I mean ... you are the CTO now. You could look and see, then fire him if you can."

"Nope. You hired him, you fire him. I'll deal with whatever has to be dealt with after."

"But aren't you worried?"

"It's not a complicated system. If I need to, I'll rewrite it. But you cannot let a bad apple stay put. They poison everything, like the saying. You need to fire him and you need to do so by end of day tomorrow. Then walk him out. If he's done what you've said, you can't let him near his computer once he's let go."

Hanna looked at Jack. "You're head of product."

Jack looked at Hanna. "You are CEO."

Hanna paused, sipped her extremely excellent tea. She thought about her mother, and her grandparents. She thought about Tenzo and the other tea producers.

Then she said, "Damn right. He's gone." She took another pause and looked at Jack. "And if things don't change, you are next."

Jack wasn't sure she was kidding.

His first Monday, Raphael came in at eight. Hanna sat typing away at her desk. She gestured vaguely at him and went back to typing. Soon she smelled coffee, and she smiled. He'd found the stash Cameron kept in the freezer.

At ten, with the office full, Erik strode in. Hanna stopped typing. *Showtime*, she thought. She nodded to Raph, who was camped next to her on an empty desk. They got up and walked Raphael over to the engineering pod to introduce him to his new team.

"Is that coffee I smell?" Erik asked, accusingly.

"Not everyone can start their day with tea." Raph smiled.

"Don't I know it!" replied Cameron.

Erik frowned, his first insult having missed its mark. "Look, I get you've built some big-name games. But I gotta warn you, tea might look simple, but it's not. We've rolled our own system for order management here. It's hard to handle the rapidly fluctuating supply, but I've got an algo that predicts it."

"Good to hear," Raph replied.

"You are familiar with algorithm design?"

"I'm okay. I worked on search at my last two companies."

Hanna interrupted the interrogation. "Erik, can I talk to you about an issue in the conference room? Before we start the meeting?" she asked.

"Um, I just want to do a few more things."

"Now," Hanna insisted.

He shrugged and reached for his laptop.

She placed her hand lightly on the docked machine. "We don't need that."

Erik rolled his eyes with a "whatever" expression and followed her into the conference room.

Hanna sat, gesturing for Erik to do the same. Erik stayed standing.

"Erik, we know what you've been doing with the code. That's not acceptable here."

Erik jammed his hands into his jeans pockets. Hanna waited. She struggled not to say anything into the silence. She counted the seconds, keeping silent. He opened his mouth, but it seemed an eternity before he said anything. As if he was fitting words on his tongue until he found the ones that felt right.

"What you are doing with the company is not acceptable!" Erik spat out. "This is not the company I joined!"

Hanna began to prepare her next words. Before she could say anything, though, Erik started back in.

"The gamer guy? What is that? Prepping for an IPO? You bring him in just so you can raise another round? Do you care about the farmers? Do you care about people?"

Hanna was aghast. What could he be talking about? They were years from any kind of decent exit, much less an IPO.

"Erik, look. We've been pretty clear we've been looking for a CTO for a while ..."

"What is this place becoming? Unless we go back to dealing with restaurants, I quit."

He stood there stock still, daring her to argue. Demanding she beg him to stay.

She looked back at him, appraising all six-foot-five inches of tobacco-stinking, code-muddling, snake-in-the-grass anarchist. And when his shoulders drooped just a little bit, she replied.

"I think you misunderstand my point, Erik. You're fired."

When Hanna and Erik stepped out of the conference room, Jack and Raphael were waiting for them. Raphael had boxed up Erik's things while he was in the meeting, and he handed it to Erik as he walked by.

Erik looked startled. "Hey, can I get some personal stuff off my work laptop?"

Raphael looked at Jack, tilting his head slightly. Jack coughed, as if to clear fear from his throat, and replied, "Sorry. Because of the circumstances of your departure, we cannot allow that."

Erik leaned over Raphael, looming above the slight Hispanic man. "You are doomed, you know."

"Probably." Raphael shrugged. "It is a start-up."

Erik threw a last longing glance at the laptop, but he shambled toward the door. Hanna followed him out.

"We'll need to change the security code," Raphael said to Jack.

Jack stood there, letting the reality of it sink it. "Bloody hell. She did it," he said.

"She is the CEO. And Erik was endangering the company. We're too precarious, too new, to let things like that slide."

"I get that. I just think ..."

Raphael turned from the door to look him in the eyes.

Jack continued. "I'm going to step down as president. We don't need a president. But we need a head of product. What I really care about is making sure we have high-quality products." He paused. "But is that what TeaBee needs? I've spent so much time doing stuff we don't need, not paying attention to real problems. I don't know if I can really be CPO. Or VP of product or whatever it's called."

Raphael sat back on the edge of a desk. "None of us know if we can do it. That's why they say 'fake it until you make it.' You don't think I'd like to go hide in Notepad, just code for a while? Man." He looked down at his shoes for a moment, then back into Jack's eyes. "Just pretend you know what you are doing, and focus on your Objectives. Trust that the OKRs will keep you from sliding back into old habits. That's why I like OKRs so much. They hold me to my promises, even when I feel like sliding back into my comfort zone. Dude, we're all making it up."

Jack let out a long sigh. It felt good to know he wasn't the only one who felt like an impostor.

Raphael picked up a stapler off the desk, and turned it as he continued, "We need to commit to each other, and to our company and our goals. Then, we just execute like madmen."

And with a laugh, he stapled several times into the air.

Jack laughed, too.

Hanna walked back in.

"Well?" asked Jack.

"He's gone. Let's get going. I'm in a mood to get things done."

They headed into the conference room where the rest of the team waited.

Jack opened the meeting by introducing Raphael.

"Hi folks. If you missed the email last night, this is Raphael. He's coming on as interim CTO, and if we behave, perhaps he'll even consider joining permanently." There were a couple polite smiles from Naoko and Cameron, but many of the team had their heads down in their laptops. It was like talking to robots.

Hanna stood. "Folks, we're going to make more changes than just having Raphael join us. First, I'd like everyone to close their laptops. We need everyone's attention." She waited.

All laptops closed, except Sheryl's. "I'm just finishing up a bug ..." Sheryl said, holding up a finger.

"I think that bug will be there when the meeting is done."

The room sat silently until Sheryl shut her laptop.

Hanna opened up discussion on the OKRs from last quarter.

"Most folks did not hit their OKRs last quarter ..."

The team exploded into excuses.

"We had some problems with the performance of the site!" said Sheryl.

"We had to deal with wrong orders and late deliveries to Los Gatos!" Cameron chimed in.

"I don't think we're marketing right," Anya suggested.

"We didn't hire a second salesperson," added Naoko.

"And that's okay," Hanna interjected.

The team quieted.

"I mean, not okay, but rather … to be expected. I've been asking around." She nodded toward Raphael, "And it seems many teams fail the first time they try to do OKRs. It may take us another quarter to get our OKRs right."

Sheryl said, "Do we have time for this? We're too little for this kinda big company thing, aren't we?"

Hanna was ready for this. "Google started with OKRs when they were a year old, and it worked for them. Many small companies become big companies because of OKRs. And guys, we may not have made our OKRs, but we should be grateful they showed us we've got a problem with focus."

Silence. Hanna continued. "So we're making a few changes to how we do it this quarter. First of all, we are only going to have one OKR for the company. We need to focus on the one thing that will make or break us, and that is our relationship with the suppliers."

She looked around the room. The team's faces mostly looked blank, but Raphael's twinkling smile encouraged her to continue.

"Second, we will set OKRs for each group that tie back to the company goal. Third, we are going to set a confidence level for our Key Results. Each one should be five out of ten level of belief we can hit them. All our goals will be stretch goals. Most important, we are going to check in on our OKRs and what we are doing to accomplish them every single week, in this meeting."

The team still looked grim. Some, like Sheryl and Cameron, leaned forward in their seats. They were with her.

"We have a new format we'd like to use for our weekly status meeting. We'll be sharing our priorities and our confidence changes. This is not a report card. It's a way to help each other meet our goals and stay on track."

She drew a four-square on the whiteboard.

"From now on, we'll use this as our format. It shouldn't take you more than ten minutes each week to update this model. The first one may take a bit longer of course, but after that it's just edits.

"Here in the upper right we'll list our OKRs. As well, we'll list the confidence level we have that we'll actually hit them. Here are our company's from last quarter, as an example."

She wrote:

Objective: Establish clear value to restaurant suppliers as a quality tea provider.
KR: Reorders at 85% 5/10
KR: 20% of reorders self-serve 5/10
KR: Revenue of $250K 5/10

Then she continued, "Notice all my confidence levels are five? That's because I want them to be really bold, but not impossible. If we can hit two out of three, I'll be pretty proud of us. I'll update the company's confidence each week. Raphael will do engineering's, Jack will do product's, including design, Frank will do sales', and Naoko finance."

"I want you guys to feel free to ask why my confidence is going up and down. This is a discussion document."

Jack joined her to the left of the board.

"Here in the upper left, we'll list the top three things we're doing this week to meet the Objective. We will mark them with the priority, P1 for must do, P2 for should do. We won't even list it if it's less than that, and we won't list more than our top four. Focus!"

He wrote:

P1: Close deal with TLM Foods
P1: New order flow spec'd
P1: 3 solid sales candidates in for interview
P2: Create customer service job description

He said, "You may want to occasionally add a P2 if you think the group might want to be aware of some task you are doing, but the goal is not to tell people about every little thing. Just the big stuff, the stuff that they can help with, or at least should be aware of. We know you are working hard. We just want to make sure the right things are getting done."

Then he filled out the lower left.

"Here is where you'll give a list of the most important things that you're planning to work on next. This is just to keep us all on the same page, in case we need to buy servers or get marketing ready. List the big things that are happening in the next four weeks or so."

Finally, Hanna pointed to the right-hand bottom. "These are going to be our health metrics. We'll be driving the team forward pretty hard, so we want to make sure everyone is okay, not getting burned out or feeling left out. What do you think our second health metric should be?"

There was a vigorous conversation where people threw out things they thought should be tracked, like code health and customer satisfaction, but finally they committed to the happiness of the restaurant suppliers. That would keep everyone focused on the new customers.

"We'll set it red, yellow, or green. I know that is a bit imprecise, but we want to get a gut feeling about how we are doing and talk about how to fix it. For example, on customer satisfaction, red would be if we are losing customers, yellow if we think we are about to." She paused, feeling a little nervous. She had no idea how the next part of the conversation would go. "Where should we set it today?" asked Hanna.

"Yellow," said Cameron. Jack and Hanna turned to their normally easygoing engineer. "Um, well, when you guys are out selling, I answer the phone. Sheryl doesn't like to, and Erik's always got headphones on. Always *had*. And the suppliers, they ask me stuff about how the website works a lot. I don't think they actually like it."

Jack grimaced ruefully. He was supposed to be the one paying attention to users. "I know. We'll fix that this quarter."

"And team health is red?" Jack ventured. "Because of the changes?"

"Yellow," Sheryl retorted. "Erik wasn't as important as he thought he was. We'll see how new guy does." She smiled, and the team laughed as they realized she was joking.

Hanna finally relaxed. If the taciturn Sheryl was joking, maybe they had a shot at this working. "Okay, folks, now let's set this quarter's OKRs!"

Cameron frowned. "Aren't you going to give them to us? Like last quarter?"

"Nope," Hanna replied. "Let me ask you a dumb question. Should we replace this conference table?"

"Hell no," said Cameron.

"Why not?" asked Hanna. "It's wobbly, and if we hire two more salespeople, we're not going to all fit around it."

"We can't ditch it! I remember when we first moved into the office. It took Jack and me three hours to figure out the instructions and get it built."

"There you go. We value the things we make together. We're going to set our Objectives together. We're going to pick Key Results as a team. And we are going make them as a team, too. This is our company. We succeed or fail together."

And then the team went to work on their new OKRs and priorities.

Hanna, Friday, One Month Later

"Demo!" Raphael shouted. His engineers got up and started hooking up a laptop to the big-screen TV, and pulling chairs around it.

"That means everybody!" he hollered. "Come on you, sales!" He hadn't quite managed to remember everybody's name yet. And then, "Hanna, put down that spreadsheet and join us! Beer!"

Hanna had forgotten about demo day. Raphael had warned he'd be taking over the office Fridays around four. He planned to demo the work the engineers had done that week. She stretched, sighed at the work she now wouldn't be doing, and strolled over to the back of the group. A normal Friday was the founders working late, as various employees sheepishly left one by one. The week ended with a whimper, not a bang. Would today be different?

The engineers shared the code they'd written, demo-ing snippets from the new restaurant supplier support interface. Even the reticent Sheryl shared a rework of the database to allow for an API for the supplier reorder system. Hanna was relieved. Finally, work toward their actual Objectives!

Then as Hanna thought things were going to end, Jack jumped up. He gestured Anya to plug in. "We've got a few new directions for the restaurant supplier information pages we'd like to share."

Hanna was excited to view the mock-ups. Yet more progress toward their shared Objectives! As well, she'd been kind of wondering what Jack and Anya did all day. Seeing the design in various stages of completeness made her realize it was pretty complicated stuff. In fact, she felt better about both teams. Which made her wonder what everyone else did all day.

When they were done discussing the new designs, Hanna moved to the front of the group.

"Folks, this was great! But I know we've got more to share. Frank? Any sales?"

"Well, I've gotten a little company called Tasteco to sign."

Hanna barked an uncharacteristically loud laugh. "Damn! I've been after them forever! That gets us into the Midwest! Congrats!"

Then Jack interjected, "Well, Hanna? What have you been up to?"

Hanna shook her head. Only Jack could put her on the spot like that.

"I found us a part-time customer service person! Her name is Carol Lundgren, and she built E-Pen's customer service team. She's a mom who's putting her kid into preschool, so she's looking for a place that is willing to be flexible with her working hours. So we were able to scoop her up!" The team burst into spontaneous applause.

So the TeaBee team went on, drinking beer and sharing the week's stories. Hanna found herself giddy with all the amazing progress they'd made. And more important, the mood of the room had changed. It was hard to believe just a month ago they'd been moping around, feeling incompetent.

Jack came up to where Hanna perched on the edge of a desk and sat next to her, close enough to speak quietly and not be overheard.

"I ended Anya's contract early. Today is her last day."

"What? The mocks looked great!"

"Yes, but I can take over if we need any revisions. The work she was doing was not a P1. It wasn't helping the OKRs."

Hanna looked at the leaves floating in the bottom of her cup of Dragon's Fog. She thought perhaps she saw a tiny gallows and she frowned.

"Hey now! Don't fret! Designers are the hottest commodity in the Valley! She's already got another gig. If we don't focus on keeping this company afloat, she won't be the only one job hunting."

Hanna smiled softly. "You are singing my tune."

The team made Friday celebrations part of their weekly rhythm. Each Monday, they'd plan together and commit to each other. They would have the hard conversations a young company has to. And each Friday, they'd celebrate. Some weeks, when it felt like they were never going to make their OKRs, the Friday "wins session" (as they started to call it) gave everybody the hope to keep trying. It was incredibly motivating. Everyone wanted to have a win to share, and would work hard during the week to find one. The team began to feel like they were part of something magical.

Happily Ever After?

A quarter later, the team had a very different check-in. They had accomplished every Key Result. The team was jubilant and burst into excited chatter.

Raphael poured water on their excitement. "Hey guys, this isn't good. Are we sandbagging?"

"Sandbagging?" Jack asked.

"You know, setting goals we know we can make. To feel good about ourselves. Instead of setting real stretch goals."

The room fell silent. Hanna gritted her teeth. She silently prepared to overcome an inevitable morale drop.

Then Jack spoke up again. "Well then, we'll just have to set proper brutal goals this time. I've seen you on Fridays. We can kill it!" Hearing their dour Brit use Silicon Valley slang made everyone laugh. The team dug in and set their hardest goals yet.

Hanna, Six Months Later

The next quarter, the team gathered again to review their quarterly goals. As Hanna predicted, the team did not fit around the conference table. Carol sat with her customer service team at chairs against the wall, slightly behind the sales team. Mindy, the newest member of customer service, flirted unapologetically with Frank. But Hanna couldn't bring herself to worry. While this time around they had only hit two of the company's Key Results, they were two critical ones that Hanna had doubted were possible to achieve.

Jack nearly tap danced as he led the team through setting the next quarter's goals. Not only were the suppliers all reordering through the site, TeaBee had gotten their first new business lead through it.

Meanwhile, Raphael had flown down to Argentina and made connections with local farmers there. Now they had small producers of Yerba mate providing their herbal tea for the suppliers to buy. Sarah, their new head of marketing, had a game plan to create a Yerba mate craze.

It wasn't all celebrations. Sheryl had gotten bored, now that the hard problems were done, and she resigned. But she left on decent terms, and between the Friday celebrations and Raphael's tireless reminders of the company Objectives, the engineering team grew and thrived. TeaBee was a good place to work, and was becoming a good place for the tea growers of the world.

Hanna, One Year Later

Hanna sat at her desk, staring at her email. It was done. They had closed the Series A. They were funded! They were set for at least a year! She spun around in her chair to look for her boys. Jack and Raphael sat hunched over a monitor, and Raphael was pointing at something on the screen. "No smudging!" Jack scolded, and they both laughed.

Hanna sighed. Everything was easier now. Each week they shared their goals. Each week they pushed each other and supported each other. Each week, the numbers went up. She watched the guys talk back and forth about the new buyer dashboard, easily exchanging ideas. Even disagreements were easier now.

Hanna sat back in her chair and cupped her hands around her freshly brewed Longjing. Perhaps she'd save the good news. Tomorrow was the Friday wins session. It'd be nice to have the best news to brag about.

THE
FRAMEWORK

THE FRAMEWORK

Why We Can't Get Things Done

We all have things we really want to happen. Maybe it's a trip to Thailand or to go back to school. Yet year after year passes and that goal is still only a goal, and not a reality. If you are a CEO or a manager, you want things for your company. You want to move into that new market, or figure out mobile, or build a competency in an area where you are weak, such as design or customer service. Yet even in the most successful companies, the thing we have determined must happen, often doesn't.

Why is this? If it is important, then why doesn't it happen? I believe there are five reasons.

One: We haven't prioritized our goals.

There is an old saying, "If everything is important, nothing is important." Too often we have many competing goals that all seem equally important. And they may *feel* equally important, but if I asked you to stack rank them instead of choosing between them, you could probably put them in order of importance. Once you've prioritized them, choosing to work on them one at a time has a much higher likelihood of success.

It's the same with a company, only worse. With so many people running around, you are sure you can get many goals to move forward. But the reality is, running a company takes work all by itself. Each day people are running hard to stay in place: fulfilling orders, stroking customers, minding hardware. Add to that the background noise of a half-dozen goals, and you assure very little beyond the bare necessities will happen.

By setting a single Objective with only three Key Results to measure it, you can provide the kind of focus needed to achieve great things despite life's little distractions.

Two: We haven't communicated the goal obsessively and comprehensively.

"When you are tired of saying it, people are starting to hear it." —Jeff Weiner, CEO of LinkedIn

Once you have picked the goal you want your team to focus on, you have to reiterate it daily. But it's not enough to talk about it. You must weave reminders into every aspect of company life. Progress toward the goal must be marked in status meetings and weekly status emails. Projects must be evaluated against the goal. To set a goal and then ignore it is an easy recipe for failure.

By continually repeating the goal every Monday in the commitment meetings, in the weekly status emails, and in the Friday wins celebrations, we assure that the goal is in the front of everyone's mind and tied to all activities.

Three: We don't have a plan to get things done.

Once we know the one thing we must make happen, we think willpower is enough. "Just Do It," right? Wrong.

When people want to lose weight, they do better with Weight Watchers than willpower. When people want to get fit, they do better with personal trainers than willpower. That's because willpower is a finite resource. This was shown in a famous 1998 study by Roy Baumeister, in which subjects forbidden to eat a bowl of radishes were able to work twice as long on unsolvable math problems than those who had been forbidden to eat freshly baked chocolate-chip cookies. (I also learned that it doesn't take much willpower to skip eating radishes.) After a long day of not quitting your job, killing your coworkers, or hitting Reply All on that email chain, trying to turn down a slice of birthday cake is beyond anyone's will.

You need a process that helps you make sense of the work you need to do and keeps you on track even when you are tired. The process reminds you what to do, even when you don't feel like doing it. The original OKR system was just a way to set smart stretch goals. But the system around it—commitment, celebrations, check-ins—makes sure you continue to make progress toward your goals even when you feel more like eating a cookie.

Four: We haven't made time for what matters.

"What is important is seldom urgent, and what is urgent is seldom important." —Dwight Eisenhower

The Eisenhower Box is a popular time management tool. Most people focus on the lower right, where you stop doing what is unimportant and not urgent. But how many people take the upper left seriously and schedule what *must* be done? Urgent things get done, both important and unimportant, because we feel keenly the pressure of time. Unless we bring that pressure to other important things, they will continue living in the land of tomorrow. And because we live in the land of today, we never do them. Block out time to do what matters.

There is nothing as invigorating as a deadline. By committing every Monday to work toward the Objective, you assure you'll be held accountable to progress.

EISENHOWER MATRIX

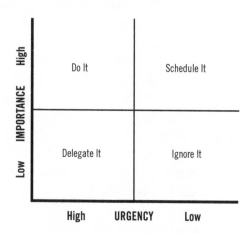

Five: We give up instead of iterating.

"Happy families are all alike; every unhappy family is unhappy in its own way." —Leo Tolstoy

When I work with clients to implement OKRs, I give them a warning: You will fail the first time. They do all fail, but they all fail in their own special way.

Maybe a company will find they have sandbaggers, and they manage to make all their Key Results in the first try, because no one ever sets hard goals. This is a company that is afraid to fail, and has never learned what a stretch goal really is. The next cycle, they have to push themselves farther.

Maybe a company is the opposite, and no one makes their Key Results, because they are constantly over-promising and under-delivering. This is a company lying to itself. It needs to learn what it is actually capable of.

The most common fail is not tracking efforts toward OKRs. I've seen any number of companies set OKRs, then ignore them the rest of the quarter. When the last week of the quarter shows up, they seem surprised when no progress has been made.

Successful companies are all alike in the same way: After they fail, they try again. They learn from the failure and adjust their approach. The only hope for success in any endeavor is iteration. This does not mean blindly trying the same thing over and over again. I believe that is the definition of insanity. Instead, you track closely what works, and what does not, and you do more of what works and less of what doesn't. The heart of success is learning.

A Path to Success

Making your goals is not complicated. It's merely hard. Hard like "eat less and exercise more." It will take discipline and practice.

- Pick which goal matters most, and not be greedy and unrealistic and try to do everything at once.
- Clarify conceptualizing that goal: What does it look like, when is it accomplished, what exactly do you want?

- State that clear, conceptual goal in all messaging, over and over, until everyone understands and pursues it.
- Make a plan that will keep you moving forward, even when you are tired and disheartened.
- Dedicate time to accomplishing the goal, instead of endlessly hoping for a tomorrow that never comes.
- Be ready for failure, ready to learn, and ready to try again.

Part One of this section is devoted to the core concepts of using OKRs, whether you are a tiny start-up or a group within a larger organization. Part Two focuses on implementation, exceptions, and variations of the core rituals.

We start our journey to our dreams by wanting, but we arrive by focusing, planning, and learning.

PART ONE:
The Fundamentals of Objectives and Key Results

This section of the book covers the key concepts of the OKR methodology.

WHY OBJECTIVES AND KEY RESULTS MATTER

While OKRs have been adopted by companies all over the world now, that wasn't the case when I first encountered them in 2011 at Zynga. Back then, Zynga was a start-up trying to change the world by connecting people through games. I can only speak to the time I worked at Zynga, but while I was there, it was one of the fastest growing companies in the Valley. Like any company, it had its dysfunctions, but I vividly recall how good Zynga was at accomplishing its goals and how it constantly got smarter as an organization. OKRs enabled Zynga to focus many disparate "studios"[3] on what was really important to the company as a whole, empowered those studios to make their own choices on how to realize that strategy, and enriched the company with proprietary information that fueled unprecedented growth.

How did Zynga find OKRs? The framework of what would eventually become Objectives and Key Results came from Intel, where Andy Grove implemented Peter Drucker's Management by Objective system. John Doerr, former Intel executive and now partner at Kleiner Perkins, evangelized OKRs to all the start-ups he invested in, including Google and Zynga. Both companies embraced the system and used it to unify and energize their companies. Many more companies have adopted OKRs, such as LinkedIn (which adopted OKRs after I had moved on) and General Assembly (where I taught in 2013). OKRs have been an effective accelerant to their growth. Over the last six years I have used OKRs in both my professional and personal life with great results. When I quit Zynga, I was burnt out physically and mentally. Today I am a bestselling author and I have my dream job teaching in Stanford's computer science department. OKRs work if you are a person or a company.

When I first left Zynga, I advised start-ups. I found again and again start-ups struggled with a painful and potentially deadly lack of focus. Even start-ups who had found product-market fit found it excruciating to get their employees to all work towards that validated vision. All start-ups are racing against the ticking clock of running

---

3   A studio was a small, self-contained team focused on building and improving a game. It usually had no more than fifty people and ran like a start-up, relying on the parent company only for things like cross promotion and IT.

out of funding. They have to get the kind of results that open up a VC's pocketbook before they start to miss payroll. How could I help these start-ups focus on what mattered? I think you know.

What are OKRs?

OKRs stands for **Objectives** and **Key Results**. The form of the OKRs has been more or less standardized. The Objective is qualitative, and the Key Results (most often three) are quantitative. OKRs are used to focus a group or individual around a bold goal. The Objective establishes a goal for a set period of time, usually a quarter. The Key Results tell you if the Objective has been met by the end of that time.

OKRs are a goal setting and achieving method. It's not a complex system, but it can be hard for companies to change their habits. When you are first adopting OKRs, be prepared to learn about your company's strengths and weaknesses. Then correct your missteps and try, try again.

In this book, I will talk about an OKR set when referring to a given group of an oObjective with its Key Results. I will refer to OKRs when we mean the methodology; which includes setting, checking progress weekly, and grading at the end of the time period (often quarterly).

How to Write a Good Objective

Your Objective is a single sentence that is:

QUALITATIVE AND INSPIRATIONAL

The Objective's job is to get people jumping out of bed in the morning with excitement. And while CEOs and VCs may jump out of bed in the morning with joy over a 3-percent gain in conversion, most mere mortals get excited by a sense of meaning and progress. Use the language of your team. If they want to use slang and say "own it" or "kill it," use that wording. If they say "delight" and "transform," that's the language for that team.

TIME BOUND

It's common to take on too much work or too little the first couple of times you use OKRs. But with practice you'll learn to size your objective. Early stage start-ups will rarely have an annual Objective (there are some exceptions, such as biotech, banking, and medicine) and usually just set quarterly OKRs. Larger companies need annual and quarterly OKRs. Examples such as "Bring our world-class product to the world" and "bring our world-class product to Canada" show how hard sizing can be. Can we really bring our product to all of Canada in three months? Or can we bring it to British Columbia? Maybe just Vancouver? You just have to make your best guess, and learn at the end of three months if you over- or undershot.

ACTIONABLE BY THE TEAM INDEPENDENTLY

This is less a problem for start-ups, but bigger companies often struggle with OKRs because of interdependence. Your Objective must be truly yours, and you can't have the excuse of, "Marketing didn't market it." This means some teams won't have OKRs but will instead use the company's or the product team's OKR sets to prioritize their support work.

An Objective is like a mission statement, only for a shorter period of time. I think of it like this: A mission is an Objective for five years, and an Objective is a mission for three months. A great Objective inspires the team, is hard (but not impossible) to do in a set time frame, and can be done by the person or people who have set it, independently.

Here are some good Objectives:

- Own the direct-to-business coffee retail market in the South Bay.
- Launch an awesome MVP that delights product managers.
- Transform Palo Alto's coupon using habits.
- and some poor Objectives:
- Sales numbers up 30%.
- Double our userbase.
- $2 million in revenue.

Why are those bad Objectives bad? Probably because they are Key Results.

Key Results

Key Results take all that inspirational language and quantify it. You create them by asking a simple question, "How would we know if we met our Objective?" This causes you to define what you mean by "awesome," "kill it," or "pwn." Typically, you have three Key Results, but I've seen as many as five and as few as one. Key Results can be based on anything you can measure, including:

- Growth
- Engagement
- Revenue
- Performance
- Loyalty

If you select your KRs wisely, you can balance forces like growth and performance, or revenue and quality, by making sure you have the potentially opposing forces represented.

"Launch an awesome MVP" might have these Key Results:

- 40% of users come back twice in one week
- Recommendation score of 8
- 15% email newsletter open rate

If you haven't worked with these metrics before, trust me, these are hard. If you don't have a baseline for a metric you wish to measure, just make a guess. By the end of the quarter, you'll be a lot smarter.

Basics of Setting Key Results

Start by looking at your Objective, for example, "Our customers love us so much they are our sales team." Now ask, "If our customers were our sales team, what numbers would move?" I often look at the Objective and see if there are words that could be quantified. In the example above, "love" becomes NPS[4] and "sales" becomes referrals. Both are measurable outcomes.

---

4   Net Promoter Score (NPS) is a management tool that can be used to gauge the loyalty of an organization's customer relationships. I don't particularly favor this approach to measuring customer satisfaction, but I do use it as an example as it is widely adopted. There are a lot of folks who think it's a poor indicator, so I recommend that if you are seeking a quality metric, shop around. https://hbr.org/2019/10/where-net-promoter-score-goes-wrong

KR: NPS >7
KR: Referrals +25%
KR: "How did you hear of us" survey results: Friends and Family up 20%

Using OKRs helps you move the team from output thinking to outcome thinking. It may take a few tries, but you will be more successful once you focus on outcomes.

I like to develop Key Results using a technique called "freelisting." Freelisting is a design thinking technique. To do it, simply write down as many ideas on a topic as you can, one idea per sticky note. You put one idea on each sticky so you can rearrange, discard, and otherwise manipulate the ideas you have generated. It is a far more effective way to brainstorm, and results in better and more diverse ideas. Make sure you give people a tiny bit too much time, so they move past the obvious and into the more innovative.

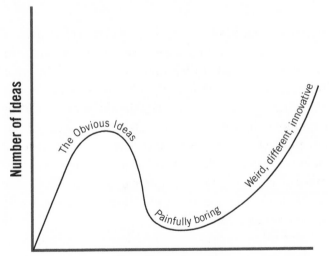

Then the team should stack rank the metrics. The metrics that are the best indicators of progress go at the top of the list and ones that are less trustworthy go to the bottom. Finally, think through the consequences of these Key Results. In *High Output Management*, Andy Grove talks about "pairing indicators:"

> Indicators tend to direct your attention toward what they are monitoring. It is like riding a bicycle: you will probably steer it where you are looking. If, for example, you start measuring your inventory levels carefully, you are likely to take action to drive your inventory levels down, which is good up to a point. But your inventories could become so lean that you can't react to changes in demand without creating shortages. So because indicators direct one's activities, you should guard against overreacting. This you can do by pairing indicators, so that together both effect and counter-effect are measured.

Sometimes your health metrics act as counter-balances to the OKRs, and I'll cover them later in the chapter. But sometimes you want to lend nuance to your Objective. Customers love us? Revenue might be one indicator, but so might customer service calls (they should go down). Want to sell more units, but don't want sales using deception to move product? You may wish to also set a satisfaction score. Common pairs include long term/short term, qualitative/quantitative, process/outcome, internal/external. These pairs make sure that, in the words of Grove, "both effect and counter-effect are measured."

Some things to consider as you develop Key Results:

- Do we have a baseline? You may have to measure something for a month or two before you are comfortable setting Key Results.
- How easy is it to measure? I remember talking to a group who wanted to fix their boring meetings. Attendance was suggested. I asked, "Do you really want to measure that?" They could have, but they chose not to. They believed no one would remember to do it.
- Is it a strong signal or a weak signal? How confident will you feel if this number is met?

CAN PROJECT COMPLETION BE A KR?

If you make a Key Result a project, you are locked into it even if it doesn't work. You don't want to commit to a tactic that may turn out to be a bad choice. Instead, you want to aim for an outcome. Let's pretend your OKRs look like this.

O: Customers love us so much, they are our sales team.
KR: New self-service help area
KR: Love-driven marketing with TV commercials
KR: Customer service completes sales training

It is completely possible to achieve every single one of those Key Results and not have any number you care about move. Revenue could stay flat. Acquisition could go down. Retention could do a belly flop. Once your team is checking to-do lists instead of watching metrics, you've institutionalized self-delusion.

ASK QUESTIONS ABOUT TASKS TO FIND THE REAL METRIC THAT MATTERS

When frontline teams set their OKRs, they will stick tactics in there. Engineers, designers, and product managers are solutions people. If you spot a task or project listed as a Key Result, ask a few questions:

- Why this project? Why is it important?
- What will it accomplish? What will change?
- How do you know if it's successful?
- What numbers will move if it works?
- How does that tie into the company's Objective?

If you get an OKR from your reports that looks like this:

O: New self-serve help area
KR: Better search
KR: New FAQ
KR: Forums

You can push and ask questions until it becomes this:

O: The company helps our customers succeed when they are struggling.
KR: "Did this help" rating rises 15%
KR: "Problem resolved" rating on FAQ improves 30%
KR: Peer-to-peer help forum has DAU of 2K (down from 10K)

Do the hard work of coaching people until you see that your reports are thinking in outcomes not projects. If a Result is a result, you can change your tactics until the numbers move. If a Result is a project, you have locked yourself into achieving it, even if you find out it's the wrong approach.

Key Results must be results for OKRs to empower teams.

KRS SHOULD BE DIFFICULT, NOT IMPOSSIBLE

OKRs are always stretch goals. Start by asking yourself, "On a scale from one to ten, how confident am I that we can make this goal?" A confidence level of one means "never gonna happen, my friend." A confidence level of ten means "easy as falling off a log." It also means you are setting your goals way too low (often called sandbagging). In companies where failure is punished, employees quickly learn not to try. If you want to achieve great things, you have to find a way to make it safe to reach further than anyone has before. If you only have a fifty-fifty shot of making this goal, it's probably the right level of stretch. If you've ever done yoga, the instructor encourages you to reach until you feel the stretch but not so far that you feel pain. If you feel pain, you are in danger of injuring yourself. It's the same with setting goals: Set goals too hard and the team may burn out and quit. Set them too easy and the company may become weak and die.

Take a hard look at your Key Results. If you are getting a funny little feeling in the pit of your stomach saying, "We are really going to have to all bring our A game to hit these ..." then you are probably setting them correctly. If you look at them and think, "We're doomed," you've set them too hard. If you look them and think, "I can do that with some hard work," they are too easy.

Some companies set committed and aspirational OKRs. "Committed" is what you know you can do and "aspirational" is what you hope you can do. This adds complexity to the goal-setting process. Throughout the book, I'm going to prod you to simplify your OKRs. OKRs work best when they can be held in people's memory. The more OKR sets you create and the more complex you make them, the more likely it is that the team will not remember them when they must quickly prioritize one activity over another. Don't over-complicate your goals.

THE METRICS FIRST APPROACH TO SETTING OKRS

Sometimes when setting your OKRs, a team member comes up with a Key Result first. Many people, especially those in business, product management, or sales think in numbers, not inspiring statements. But just like when a teammate suggests a task as a Result, you can have a conversation about what that number tells us. For example, your CEO demands that revenue grow to five hundred thousand dollars per month. You need to ask your CEO, what does that number tell us? Is it that we're ready to raise a series B? Is it that visitors are becoming customers at a high rate? Are users screaming, "Take my money, please?" Every number has a story to tell, and that story is your Objective. Once you have your Objective, you can ask yourself if there are other good metrics to watch. Let's say we decided on "ready to raise the next round." You might choose retention, conversion, or engagement numbers for the other KRs.

Having three Key Results is not required, but it is a good way to triangulate success. Retention balances revenue, to make sure your team isn't just squeezing a few bucks out of customers for a short-term lift. Let the Objective and Key Results inform each other.

Prerequisites

The OKR process is not a silver bullet. There are companies and situations where it is not the right choice for managing your company's efforts. For example, if you are considering adopting OKRs in order to better control your employees' activities, that won't work. OKRs are based on giving employees freedom to decide how to get to the outcomes you want. If you want to use OKRs to get ever-increasing productivity in a toxic culture, OKRs will just look like a new kind of whip to your employees. And if you are doing a dozen different things in a dozen different markets and are unwilling to give that up in favor of focus, well, good luck with that.

OKRs are most likely to work when a company has a strong mission and when the company hires great people and then trusts them to do great things.

First, Check Your Mission

Most start-ups resist creating a company mission. It seems like an exercise in big company propaganda and not something Lean and Agile folks should be fiddling around with. This is a waste. Almost all start-ups start with a mission, even if they haven't written it down. (And don't forget, big companies were start-ups once.)

If you think that you create a start-up to make money, you are misinformed. Ninety percent of start-ups fail, according to a recent study by Allmand Law[5]. If it's a payout you want, it's a much safer proposition to join a Wall Street consulting firm. But if you want to change the world—an already ridiculous goal—you can do worse than starting a company to do it. Which means you think the world needs changing. Which means you probably have a mission in your back pocket.

---

5 "Mapping Tech Startups," by Reed Allmand, https://allmandlaw.com/mapping-tech-startups/

ly started with the founders saying, "If only
.id figure out which teachers are actually good,"
wish there was an easier way to share videos with my
parents in Poland," or "I wish I could get decent tea at my
favorite café." Then a little poking around led to the realization there was a market that wanted the same problem
solved. Finally, that led to a mission, "Know who knows
how to make you know," or "Connecting far-flung families
through easily shared memories," or "Bringing great tea to
people who love it." They don't have to be great works of
poetry. They do have to be simple and memorable, and act
as a guide when you decide how to spend your time.

A good mission is short enough everyone in the company
can keep it in their head. Great missions are inspirational yet
directed. Google's early mission was so powerful that even
non-Googlers know it: "To organize the world's information
and make it universally accessible and useful."

Amazon's is: "We aim to be Earth's most customer cen-
tric company. Our mission is to continually raise the bar of
the customer experience by using the internet and technology to help consumers find, discover and buy anything, and
empower businesses and content creators to maximise their
success.," which, even if you forget the rest, you can remember the first part about being customer-centric. Zynga's is the
simple: "Connecting the world through games." And if you
get a coffee at Philz, you can ask anyone there and they'll
tell you their mission is to "better people's day."

Your mission is short and memorable. When you have a
question in your daily work life, the mission should be top
of mind to help you answer.

To make one, start with this simple formula:

We [reduce pain/improve life] in [market] by [value
proposition].

Then refine. As you can see from some of the shorter missions above, just value proposition can be enough.

Now I know you may change markets, or add a business model as you go along, but try to make a mission that can hold you for at least five years. In many ways, a mission and an Objective in the OKR model have a lot in common; they are aspirational and memorable. The key difference is time scale. An Objective takes you through a year or a quarter. A mission should last a lot longer.

A mission keeps you on the rails. The OKRs provide focus and milestones. Using OKRs without a mission is like using jet fuel without a jet. It's messy, undirected, and potentially destructive. Once you have a mission, selecting each quarter's Objectives is straightforward. You are no longer faced with a crazy world of possibilities. You can have a conversation about what will move the mission forward. You can fight about sequencing. But once the dust has settled, you can pick the one big, bold thing you will do because you know where you are going.

Second, You Need a Strategy

"Strategy is knowing what not to do."
— Michael Porter

Objectives and Key Results can only be set if you have a strategy.

All organizations balance resources between strategic activities and reactive activities. Strategic activities are planned efforts to gain traction in the market. Reactive activities are how you respond to the world around you; when you either try to recover from negative events or exploit positive ones.

companies, the 2020 pandemic was a disaster. ence organizers had to cancel their events or try m online. For other companies, the pandemic meant unprecedented growth. Online meeting tools had more demand than they could handle. It is very easy to end up in reaction mode all the time, between life's tiny disasters, like a well-established company suddenly deciding to move into your market, and world-wide disasters such as the economic collapse caused by the pandemic. Strategy is what you do to make the company resilient. It's what you choose to do rather than what you are forced to do by external forces. While a company can be made or broken by external events, their long-term survival depends on having and executing a strategy.

Let me show you an example.

When a company begins, they start with a small market of early adopters they can really delight. But at some point, they run out of new people in that market to convert to customers. They have a critical decision to make: Do they start trying to acquire people in a new geographic location or a new demographic, or do they meet another need for the market with which they already have a relationship? After research and experimentation, they will pick a direction. The OKRs will come out of that. Will it be, "Bring our world-class product to the world" as an annual Objective and "bring our world-class product to Georgia," as your quarterly, or will it be, "Solve all a business traveler's needs, not just scheduling" for an annual OKR and "Delight our customers by offering alternative flights and hotels for last-minute changes," as a quarterly. Pick a direction, set an OKR around it, and start to get traction on it. You can always have a do-over next quarter with your learnings increasing your chance of success, or switch strategies if the first one doesn't pan out.

It doesn't have to be a perfect strategy, but in
you risk wasting time and resources. For start-ups'
fit[6], the OKR is always "get to product-market
that company grows, it's important to plan that growth.

Third, Practice Metrics Thinking

The OKR methodology requires the ability to measure critical metrics and then move them. Some companies I work
with have not instrumented their site or app and thus have
no baseline to work from. Many pay attention only to traffic
and clicks. But a few stop to ask themselves, "What does
this number actually tell me?" A wedding site gets a lot of
daily active users (DAU) but only for a few months. Is that
okay with you? Click through is nice, as it indicates good
conversation, but is it sustained? Was it gamed by a product
manager looking for a bonus or will it continue to be successful over time? What are the most commonly searched for
items? Are you monitoring your search logs, or just digging
them up as you need them?

Alistair Croll and Benjamin Yoskovitz say, in their
excellent book *Lean Analytics*:

> "A good metric is comparative. Being able to compare a
> metric to other time periods, groups of users, or compet-
> itors helps you understand which way things are moving.
> Increased conversion from last week" is more meaningful
> than "2% conversion."

---

6   Product-market fit is the degree to which a product satisfies a
strong market demand. Product-market fit is the first step to building
a successful venture in which the company meets early adopters, gathers
feedback, and gauges interest in its product(s).

A good metric is understandable. If people can't remember it and discuss it, it's much harder to turn a change in the data into a change in the culture.

A good metric is a ratio or a rate. Accountants and financial analysts have several ratios they look at to understand, at a glance, the fundamental health of a company. ou need some, too....

A good metric changes the way you behave. This is by far the most important criterion for a metric: what will you do differently based on changes in the metric?"

When I was working at Yahoo! search, I learned a lot about metrics thinking. We knew how to get people to click on an ad and how to point them at the search results. We used that knowledge to balance customer satisfaction and revenue. We knew that when people performed a unsuccessful search, they were more likely to change search engines than look at the second page. We knew that people often clicked on the first two results and the last one and moved to ten results per page so people would get more relevant results. Knowledge is power.

Everyone on the product and services side of the company should know what the most important metrics are. If your company or parts of the company are bad at thinking about what numbers matter, you might want to spend a quarter instrumenting[7] your products and creating a baseline before trying OKRs.

---

7   Instrumentation is when you add trackers to key elements of your products and services so you can track your numbers over time.

Finally, Make a Safe Place for Learning

"There's no team without trust," says Paul Santagata, head of industry at Google.[8]

We've all worked in a place where no one felt safe enough to speak up. In that context, very little learning happens, and none of it can be social. To have an effective team, you *must* have psychological safety.

I wrote *The Team that Managed Itself* because this is a complex topic deserving of hundreds of pages, not hundreds of characters. Here's the short version: Bringing a group of people into a room isn't enough to make them a team. An effective team requires personal connections and psychological safety.

People don't feel safe unless they feel connected.

Unfortunately, Americans are weird about showing their human side in the workplace. Work is treated like another world, where we are machines instead of people with histories and feelings. A leader's job is to unite the team; one tactic is to create social opportunities where team members can talk about their kids, their life, and their family. Building opportunities to see "that engineer" as "Joe, who loves to knit with his daughters," leads to better team dynamics. This doesn't have to be a company picnic or enforced happy hours. It can be as simple as starting meetings with "share something awesome that you saw this week in one sentence," or starting a new team with an "introduce each other" exercise. The details shared are an

---

8   "High-Performing Teams Need Psychological Safety. Here's How to Create It," by Laura Delizonna https://hbr.org/2017/08/high-performing-teams-need-psychological-safety-heres-how-to-create-it

excuse for conversation, and conversation leads to friendships. A leader models and encourages an atmosphere where humans genuinely care about each other and can give caring feedback with a helpful attitude. That group of humans then grows as individuals and as a team. You're going to need that mutual empathy when time comes to discuss why numbers are going down when they should go up.

If you want to build psychological safety in your team, another approach is to create formal expectations of how to work together. When working with clients, I lead teams in creating a lightweight team charter that everyone agrees to adhere to. The charter can and should evolve as the team reflects on the quarter's work during the larger OKR reflection meeting. It's critical that it's built by the team themselves, not handed down from management. The act of making one reveals possible conflicts in expectations and teaches a team to understand each other's points of view.

CREATING A TEAM CHARTER

Once you've brought everyone together, ask them to talk about the best teams they've ever been on. What worked? What didn't? Then ask about the worst teams they've ever been on. From those starting points, you build rules of engagement. How do we want to work as a team? Are we going to talk through Slack? At stand-up meetings? Do we take notes or have agendas? What happens when someone does something out of line? The point of this exercise is not just the final product—the point is to allow people to speak up, to be uncomfortable, to debate, to have a conversation. By making agreements together out of those hard conversations, the whole dynamic at work changes. Instead of people walking around with resentment after something goes wrong, we build an opportunity to make it go right together. We also agree on what will happen when it doesn't. This reduces uncertainty and increases safety.

Inevitably, situations will arise when there's a mismatch between the needs of an individual and a team. For example, if you are a conflict avoider, you still may need to work with a team that believes in arguing everything. That will be hard regardless of the expectations you've set, because your natural mode of behaving is different than the culture. A good team charter lets you know what you're in for in advance. Then you can adapt or choose to leave, without feeling resentful because your expectations weren't met.

Take the time to set ground rules and build personal relationships. It will make your OKR meetings more honest and effective. And that will accelerate every other result you have.

Why a Project Completion Can't Be a KR

All those lovely ideas you have for projects get moved into your pipeline. Pipelines are more suited to OKRs than Roadmaps.

To avoid semantic arguments, I'll define Roadmaps as a plan for our desired future and Pipelines as a collection of ideas of projects that might get us to our desired future. Roadmaps have dates. Pipelines use impact/effort/confidence to prioritize the best ideas. By saying Pipelines are preferable to Roadmaps, I simply mean that Pipelines give you flexibility as you try to reach your Objective. If you call it a Roadmap but treat it like a Pipeline, that's fine. The critical idea is that you have a long list of potential solutions to try out.

If you have a Roadmap, you'll want to dismantle it and put it in a Pipeline format. Then you want to brainstorm more potential solutions. You don't want just one idea to make your OKRs; you want a breadth of choices. See if you can get at least five potential projects that will move a given Key Result. Then evaluate them.

Project	OKR/Health Effected	Impact	Effort	Confidence/ Evidence
Sign-up redesign	Acquisition	Low	Low	Usability studies show sign-up is confusing.
Social media registration	Acquisition	High	Medium	Comparative research shows this is common.
Enhanced privacy settings	Satisfaction	Unknown	High	There has been a spate of negative press around privacy.
Internal Wiki	Team health	Medium	High	90% of the teams are upset because they spend too much time chasing assets and research.

As this table shows, a Pipeline lets a leader quickly assess which efforts are more effective and which aren't. At this point, the leader can make a go/no-go call or ask for more research. For example, perhaps the registration team could try to get other companies' numbers on social media registration. Or they could do a small test to get more data.[9]

---

9   *Testing Business Ideas: A Field Guide for Rapid Experimentation*, by David J. Bland and Alexander Osterwalder, is a great resource to learn how to run effective tests. https://amzn.to/3047520

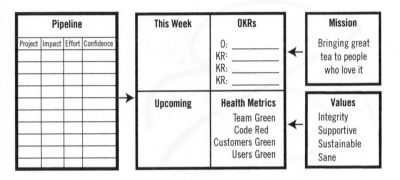

OKRs are all about setting the goal in order to have more flexibility in accomplishing your goals. Pipelines support flexibility. Roadmaps are guesses on what might work, stuck frozen into a Gantt chart like a bug in amber.

What About Everything Else We Have to Do?

OKRs are part of your management approach, but they are not all of it.

There are things you have to do as a business to stay in business that don't make you money. Contracts, taxes, accounting, payroll, and more. You need to do these things to a certain level of quality, or the company will be in trouble.

A lot of service departments evolve rather than innovate. Engineering, design, marketing... most of the time they are working fine. Every so often you may wish to push them to improve, but in a healthy company they are in a gentle rhythm of doing good work.

Let's call all of these efforts "operations." They don't need OKRs, as they are not regularly looking for radical improvement. A manager needs to be able to monitor the

OKRs while tracking a few other key indicators that need to stay consistent. The metrics you track in order to spot when things are changing are called "Health Metrics" in the OKR framework.

Health Metrics act as the canary in the coal mine. If working toward overambitious OKRs is burning out the team, you need to know. If the team is so caught up in a new shiny project they neglect existing customers or systems, you need to know. The Health Metrics protect what you've already accomplished while you try to grow new metrics via your OKRs.

Some examples of potential Health Metrics

- New customer sign-ups
- Customer satisfaction
- Code health (ignore this and expect to see your technology start crashing)
- Team health (ignore this and expect burnout followed by mass departures)

Once in a while a Health Metric can be promoted to an OKR. Let's say customer satisfaction has been slowly declining. The CEO might say, time to turn this ship around! And set an Objective around delighting the customers and some good Key Results to know when it's gotten better. If customer satisfaction reaches its desired goal, they can make it a Health Metric again.

What Makes OKRs Work? The Cadence.

Many companies who try OKRs fail, and they blame the system. But no system works if you don't keep to it. It's not enough to set OKRs. You have to track progress toward them regularly. The OKR cadence is actually what makes OKRs work, and is more important than setting an inspiring Objective, and even more than setting your Key Results as outcomes. When people ask me what the difference is between OKRs and SMART goals, KPIs, or other goal-setting approaches, I tell them it is the cadence of check-ins. The cadence is what makes the difference between goal setting and goal achieving.

When I first started helping start-ups with OKRs, I had to modify the OKR tracking approach from what I did at Zynga. Young start-ups have an extremely low tolerance for any meetings, much less daily, deep analysis of tactics and metrics. I trimmed the meetings down to two key meetings a week: one to set intentions and one to celebrate progress. This bookended the week with clear reminders of what the company was trying to accomplish. As my old boss Jeff Weiner used to say, "When you are tired of saying it, they are starting to hear it." The cadence of setting efforts toward the OKRs and celebrating progress toward OKRs means you are repeating yourself a lot. In a good way.

Monday Commitments and the Four Square

Each Monday, the team should meet to check in on progress against OKRs and commit to the tasks that will help the company meet its Objective. I recommend a format with four key quadrants:

Intention for the week: What are the three or four most important things you must get done this week toward the Objective? Discuss if these priorities will get you closer to the OKRs.

Forecast for the month: What should your team know is coming up that they can help with or prepare for?

Status toward OKRs: If you set a confidence of five out of ten, has that moved up or down? Have a discussion about why.

Health Metrics: Pick two to five things you want to protect as you strive toward greatness. What can you not afford to eff-up? Key relationships with customers? Code stability? Team well-being? Now mark when things start to go sideways, and discuss it.

The reason to provide this overview is so you can see the efforts and the Objectives at the same time.

PRIORITIES THIS WEEK	
P1	Close Deal with TLM Foods
P1	New Order Flow
P1	3 Solid Sales Canidates in for Interview

OKR CONFIDENCE

Objective: Establish Clear Value to Distributers as a Quality Tea Provider

KR: Reorders ar 85%

KR: 5 WoM Referrrals

KR: Revenue of 250K

UPCOMING BIG PROJECTS

Passive Reorder Notifications

New Self-serve Flow for Distributors

Metrics for Distributers on Tea Sales

Hire Customer Service Lead

HEALTH METRICS	
Yellow	Team: Struggling with direction change
Green	Distributor Satisfaction
Red	Conversion to Subscriber

This document is first and last a conversation tool. You want to talk about issues like:

- Do the priorities lead to our hitting our OKRs?
- Why is confidence dropping in our ability to make our OKRs? Can anyone help?
- Are we prepared for major new efforts? Does marketing know what product is up to?
- Are we burning out our people, or letting hacks become part of the code bases?

Make time for the conversations. If only a fourth of the time allotted for the Monday meeting is presentations and the rest is discussing next steps, you are doing it right. If you end early, it's a good sign. Just because you've set aside an hour doesn't mean you have to use it.

Keep the review of the four-square short. Do not read them out loud to each other. Use color coding and skimable sentences so you can dive into any problem areas. Focus on problems and complications. Feel free to say, "Everything is on track, no need to discuss." Time spent talking in meetings is not a success metric.

When you meet, you can discuss only the four-square, or you can use it as a status overview, then supplement with other detailed documents covering metrics, a pipeline of projects, or related updates. Each company has a higher or lower tolerance for meetings.

Trust your team makes good choices in their everyday work. Set the tone of the meeting to be about team members helping each other to meet the shared goals they all have committed to. As the leader, you can model this by saying something like, "It looks like our second Key Result is in trouble. Can we brainstorm some ways to get it back on track?" Asking for ideas and being visibly grateful for your team's insights will go a long way to empowering them.

Over time your team will learn that you don't have all the answers, and that they matter to the company.

BALANCING HEALTH METRICS AND OKRS

I typically mark the Health Metrics simply as green/yellow/red. Green means all fine, yellow means keep a watch out. But red means something critical to the health of our company is in freefall.

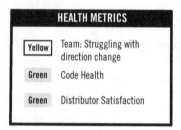

At any time (not just Monday), anyone can call a "Code Red" for a Health Metric in the red zone and prioritize a fix (or prioritize finding a path to a fix) over OKR efforts.

Calling a Code Red both provides formal notification to the management team that work on OKRs has been halted and creates a record of a problem. When the teams do their end-of-quarter retrospective, they can look at the Code Reds to learn what keeps the company from living up to its potential. For many companies in 2020, the entire year was one giant Code Red. But if those companies survive, they will want to learn from the crises and reinvest in strategic efforts that make them crises-proof. Track everything and commit time to learn from your experience.

Fridays Are for Winners

When teams are aiming high, they fail a lot. While it's good to aim high, missing your goals without also seeing how far you've come is often depressing. That's why the Friday wins session is so critical.

In the Friday wins session, teams all demo their work in progress. Engineers show bits of code they've got working and designers show mock-ups and maps. But beyond that, every team should share something. Sales can talk about who they've closed, customer service can talk about customers they've rescued, business development can share deals. This has several benefits. One, you start to feel like you are part of a pretty special winning team. Two, the team starts looking forward to having something to share. They seek wins. And last, the company starts to appreciate what each discipline is going through and understand what everyone does all day.

Providing beer, wine, cake, or whatever is appropriate to your team on a Friday is also important to making the team feel cared for. If the team is really small and can't afford anything, the CEO should at least buy a pizza or a case of beer. Do what you can to show your appreciation. As the team gets bigger, the company should pay for the celebration nibbles as a signal of support. Consider this: The humans who work on the project are the biggest asset. Shouldn't you invest in them?

Do not require attendance. Do not hold it at 6 p.m. when people just want to go home. I've seen companies try to do this to eke out a couple more hours of work on a Friday. If your team is working hard all week to make serious progress, by 4 p.m. they are worn out. Making them stay two more hours just means they'll play video games on their PC while resenting you. Hold the win session at 3 or 4 p.m.

I often get questions about remote teams, and I've seen a lot of smart approaches. If you are within a couple time zones of each other, you can do it over video conferencing. There will be no sharing food (you can still have it delivered), but at least people can see each other's faces. Some teams have a bragging channel on an internal chat tool such as Slack. Some teams have the CEO or general manager read off the top wins in a video conference or send out an email. This is not as satisfying as breaking bread together, but it still shows genuine appreciation and makes progress visible.

The rituals that make OKRs work can be adapted to the company culture. As long as you have a commitment ritual and a celebration ritual, you can do it in a way that fits the company's organization and culture. You can experiment with different approaches as well. A CEO I work with writes, "As soon as you start doing something week after week, it runs the risk of getting stale." It may be useful to change up how you celebrate occasionally so it's still fun to gather. If you have multiple groups, you could have a different one present each week. Be sure to timebox them; i.e., say, "You've got fifteen minutes and after that I will stop you from continuing." Or you could run a science fair style demo, where people go around to talk to representatives set up at stations.

Be sure to do a quick check after with a short, three-question, anonymous survey on how it worked. I love these exit tickets that ask, "What should we keep doing? What should we change? What should the management team know?" I use them in my classes as well to make sure people are learning and the class is improving.

You've hired smart people; let them h[...]
a better company!

Keep the Cadence and Make It You[...]

I get many questions about implementing OKRs in atypical circumstances, such as with remote teams, companies that have multi-business lines or companies balancing R&D while supporting the current profit makers. Large companies can't get everyone into a room (Google eventually moved their all-company meeting outdoors as they grew). Or time zones make it hard. Or the agile planning session clashes. You can adjust and move the Monday/Friday cadence to be Friday/Tuesday. You can hold the celebrations over video. You can brag in the status email or in a Slack channel. The how is flexible, as long as you set and celebrate.

OKRs are great for setting goals, but without a system to achieve them, they are as likely to fail as any other process that is in fashion. Commit to your team, commit to each other, and commit to your shared future. And renew those vows every week.

Improve Weekly Status Emails with OKRs

I remember the first time I had to write a status email. I had just been promoted to manager at Yahoo! back in 2000 and was running a small team. I was told to "write a status email covering what your team has done that week, due Friday." Well, you can easily imagine how I felt. I had to prove my team was getting things done! Not only to justify our existence, but to prove we needed more people. Because, you know, more people, amiright?

So I did what everyone does: I listed every single thing my reports did, and made a truly unreadable report. Then I started managing managers, and had them send me the same, which I collated into an even longer, more horrible report. This I sent to my design manager, Irene Au, and my GM, Jeff Weiner (who sensibly requested I put a summary at the top).

And so it went, as I moved from job to job, writing long, tedious reports that, at best, got skimmed. At one job, I stopped authoring them. I had my managers send them to my project manager, who collated them, then sent it to me for review. After checking for anything embarrassing, I forwarded it on to my boss. One week I forgot to read it, and didn't hear anything about it. It was a waste of everybody's time.

Then I got to Zynga in 2010. Now, say what you want about Zynga, but they were really good at some critical things that make an organization run well. One was the status report. All reports were sent to the entire management team, and I enjoyed reading them. Yes, you heard me right: *I enjoyed reading them*, even if there were twenty of them. Why? Because they had important information laid out in a digestible format. I used them to understand what I needed to do, and learn from what was going right. Please note that Zynga, in the early days, grew faster than any company I've seen. I suspect the efficiency of communication was a big part of that.

When I left Zynga, I started to consult. I adapted the status email to suit the various companies I worked with, throwing in some tricks from Agile. Now I have a simple, solid format that works across any org, big or small.

1. **Lead with your team's OKRs, and how much confidence you have that you are going to hit them this quarter.**

You list OKRs to remind everyone (and sometimes yourself) *why* you are doing the things you do.

Your confidence is your guess of how likely you feel you will meet your Key Results, on a scale from one to ten. A one is never going to happen and ten is in the bag. Mark your confidence red when it falls below three, green as it passes seven. Color makes it scannable, making your boss and teammates happy. Listing confidence helps you and your teammates track progress and correct early if needed.

2. **List last week's prioritized tasks and if they were achieved.**

If they were not, a few words to explain why. The goal here is to learn what keeps the organization from accomplishing what it needs to accomplish. See below for format.

3. **Next, list next week's priorities.**

Only list three P1s, and make them meaty accomplishments that encompass multiple steps. "Finalize spec for project xeno" is a good P1. It probably encompasses writing, reviews with multiple groups, and sign off. It also gives a heads up to other teams and your boss that you'll be coming by.

"Talk to legal" is a bad P1. This priority takes about half an hour, has no clear outcome, feels like a subtask and, not only that, you didn't even tell us what you were talking about!

You can add a couple P2s, but they should also be meaty, worthy of being next week's P2s. You want fewer, bigger items.

4.   List any risks or blockers.

Just as in an Agile stand-up, note anything you could use help on that you can't solve yourself. Do *not* play the blame game. Your manager does not want to play mom, listening to you and a fellow executive say, "It's his fault."

As well, list anything you know of that could keep you from accomplishing what you set out to do—a business partner playing hard-to-schedule or a tricky bit of technology that might take longer than planned to sort out. Bosses do not like to be surprised. Don't surprise them.

5.   Notes.

Finally, if you have anything that doesn't fit in these categories, but that you absolutely want to include, add a note. "Hired that fantastic guy from Amazon that Jim sent over. Thanks, Jim!" is a decent note, as is, "Reminder: team out Friday for offsite to Giants game." Make them short, timely and useful. Do not use notes for excuses, therapy, or novel-writing practice.

This format also fixes another key challenge that large organizations face: coordination.

When I was a general manager at a midsized organization, in order to write a status report the old way, I had to have team status in by Thursday night in order to collate, fact check, and edit. But with this system, I know what my priorities are, and I use my reports' statuses only to make sure their priorities were the same as mine. I send out my report Friday, the same time as I receive my reports'. They don't need to wait for me, or I for them. We stay committed to each other, honest and focused.

```
Week of 10/15/2016

exec-team@teabee.com

Week of 10/15/2016

Objective: Establish clear value to restaurant suppliers as a quality tea provider,
KR: Reorders at 85%                    6/10
KR: 20% of reorders self-serve         5/10
KR: Revenue of 250 K                   4/1

LAST WEEK
P1 Close new deal with TLM Foods  NOT DONE - extra surprise level of approvals
P1 New Order flow spec'd and approved
P1 3 solid sales candidates in for interview NOT DONE one flaked, need better pipeline. Discuss?
P2 Customer Service Job Description to recruiter DONE

NEXT WEEK
P1 Close deal with TLM
P1 Offer out to Dave Kimton
P1 Usability tests: discover and prioritize key issues with self-serve.

NOTES
Anyone know the procurement VP at Johnson Supplies?
Also, lmk if you want to sit in on usability! It's good for your soul, y'know...
```

Work should not be a chore list, but a collective push forward toward shared goals. The status email reminds everyone of this fact and helps us avoid slipping into checkbox thinking.

Coordinating organizational efforts is critical to a company's ability to compete and innovate. Giving up on the status email is a strategic error. It can be a task that wastes key resources, or it can be a way that teams connect and support each other.

On Radical Focus

I called this book *Radical Focus* and not "A Guide to OKRs" for a reason. I believe the one thing that makes the difference between excelling and flailing about in mediocrity is focus. Focus is hard, but it's necessary. Doing the hard work to decide on *one* company Objective is key.

One, not four, or ten "critical objectives." One Objective to rule them all.

OKRs are a framework for creating and ensuring focus on what really matters, but they don't work if you stuff them full of every single business-as-usual initiative you have going. OKRs are not a way to control the way your employees spend their time; they are a way to share your vision so your employees can make their own judgment calls about what's most important.

Why only one Objective? The problem with multiple OKR sets is that complexity increases exponentially. Let's say the company has five OKR sets. That means the company is asking everyone to keep in mind twenty pieces of data (five Objectives and fifteen Key Results). Next let's imagine each product team has, say, three OKR sets of their own. Three times four is twelve, so now each employee has thirty-two things they have theoretically memorized and live each day. What if your department has OKRs? Add in another four to twelve. If you're doing individual OKR sets, add in four more, minimum. Hopefully the OKRs are all aligned to the company OKR set, but even so ... how could anyone know what to work on with such a large group of priorities?

Companies should adopt OKRs because they seek focus and the acceleration that accompanies it. That only happens if every single person in the company knows what the company OKRs are and can make decisions based on them. Which means they have to remember them. Having only *one* Objective for the organization helps immensely.

There is one exception: if the company is very big and has multiple business models that have very little to do with each other. Consider Alphabet: It's hard to imagine what objective could unite self-driving cars and search advertising in their efforts (beyond "let's make lots of money). So if you use top level OKRs in a very large corporation, such as a Pepsico or a General Electric, you need to know what the top is. My rule of thumb is one OKR set per business model per quarter. If you are not that big, it's time to focus so that someday you might be.

Now that you've admitted to yourself you aren't Facebook yet, it's time to focus. Here's some advice based on what I've seen work:

1. Don't try to jam years of work into a single quarter.

Yes, we want it all and we want it now. But if we try to change everything at once, we spend a tiny fraction of our time on each thing and progress is infinitesimal—the too little peanut butter over too much toast[10]. There is a very real cost involved in task switching that adds up over time. Trying to do everything at once means nothing really gets done. Instead, choose one Objective at a time, and prioritize and sequence your effort for maximum impact.

Do less, better.

2. Don't make a company OKR set for every department.

I've seen companies who have a marketing OKR, an engineering OKR, and a product OKR as their "company

---

10 Yahoo! Memo: The 'Peanut Butter Manifesto,' *Wall Street Journal*, Nov. 18, 2006

OKRs." A company OKR should unite the company toward a single goal. Not every department needs an OKR, but every strategic effort does.

To get to that "one Objective to rule them all," I first ask why is that marketing/engineering/product OKR important to the company? How will the company be changed if they succeed? What do these goals have in common?

I'm looking for a unifying theme. In the previous example, everything was about getting ready for a B-round of funding. Maybe instead the company's year has goals about moving into a new market, or establishing dominance, securing your lead, etc., etc. ... If you find an OKR set that really is about the company's success, other teams will find ways to make it happen as well, from customer service to legal.

Here is an example of an OKR for a company that makes a mobile app. See if you can spot the problems before reading on.

Lapsed customers become habitual customers.	Customers find our newsletter fun and inviting.	User-to-user messages and gifts are compelling, and users love to get them.
• 23% customers return every day (DAU) • 40% return once a month (MAU) • Revenue for in-app purchases is >$5K a week	• 15% open rate • 20% higher click-through • Get to 2% bounce rate[11]	• Reduce customer service complaints about "too many notifications" 75% • Click-through up 50% • Personalize option used 25% of interactions

The first OKR is pretty good. It unites the company and focuses everyone on a key problem; retention. The second is

---

11   Learn more about bounce rate: https://www.campaignmonitor.com/blog/email-marketing/2019/05/making-sense-email-bounce-rates

a bad company OKR. It only really applies to marketing and engineering (and maybe product). Plus it's redundant. I recommend making this a sub-goal for marketing.

The third is probably a good OKR for the team that does notifications and in-app messaging, but it's not a company OKR.

3. Not everyone will lead; some will support.

There are always situations where the most important thing to the company doesn't need everyone's full attention. For example, a huge product launch. While engineering might be working day and night, your legal team will only be needed for a few days to craft a TOS or broker a deal. The company OKR doesn't tell them how to do their day-to-day business, but it does let them know they should drop everything when they are needed. You do not need an OKR for every department. Maybe legal will decide to set a departmental OKR, perhaps something about contract turnaround time. But when the big launch needs someone to update that TOS, they'll know it trumps any efficiency effort they are making.

We can't all be the hero of the story; some of us are support. Frodo wouldn't have gotten very far without his Samwise. Give respect to the supporting folks, and invite them to the Friday celebrations. Everyone deserves bragging rights.

4. Don't let politics distract you from clear, concise OKR sets.

When I review OKR sets for clients, often I see people trying to stuff more items into the company goals. Sometimes company execs are as bad as politicians, tacking their personal projects onto the OKRs. I then have to tear apart the OKR set to find out what the core goal really is.

For example, sometimes I ask, "What is the difference between these two OKR sets?" and people point at the Key Results. Apparently, they had five metrics they wanted to measure. At which point I wave my magic wand and give them permission to have five Key Results and one Objective. The rule of three Key Results is not a rule. It's more of a guideline. For reasons stated earlier, you really don't want too many elements to a goal if you want it to be remembered and lived. But if you only have one OKR set and people only have to remember the Objective and the particular Key Results they can affect, it's not a problem.

Other times, when asked about the difference between two Objectives, people will shrug and say, "I don't know." At that point it makes sense to combine them or vote for the one you like best. Just don't turn your indecisiveness about who wordsmithed the best Objective into confusing marching orders for your team.

Sometimes (especially in face-to-face workshops) people try to put everyone's ideas into the OKR sets. Perhaps they are trying to be respectful of a high-powered exec's ideas; or maybe it's a team that has troubles with conflict and they try to keep everyone's favorite phrasing. You might think, "What's the harm?" but if you aren't prioritizing and simplifying, you are shirking your duty to the company.

When I was at Yahoo! working in Larry Tesler's group, I learned that every application has a certain amount of complexity that cannot be reduced. Larry Tesler argues that, in most cases, an engineer should spend an extra week reducing the complexity of an application versus making millions of users spend an extra minute using the program because of the extra complexity. This is the same situation with creating OKR sets. It's better if you spend an extra hour getting OKRs right than losing your employees' focus by burying them with unnecessary language, dozens of priorities, and watered-down goals.

Be clear.
Be simple.
Be memorable.
Achieve your Objectives.

OKR COACHING EXAMPLE

Quantifying Engineering's Contribution to Sales

By Ben Lamorte, principal at OKRs.com

Ben Lamorte coaches business leaders to define and make measurable progress on their most important goals. He's coached hundreds of managers at dozens of organizations. For more about Ben, see www.OKRs.com. In this short essay, he shows how to coach someone into setting good OKRs.

Let's look at an excerpt from a real OKRs coaching session to illustrate how coaching leaders, through creating their own OKRs—rather than a CEO dictating their OKRs—can dramatically improve the quality and effectiveness of OKRs. Here's an excerpt from a coaching session for the engineering team at a large software company.

Engineering VP: My key objective is to help our sales team achieve their targets.

OKRs Coach: At the end of the quarter, how would we know if engineering helped sales achieve their targets?

Engineering VP: Hmm, that's a good question. (Pause.)

OKRs Coach: Okay, can you name a particular customer who purchased within the last year where engineering clearly contributed to the sales process?

Engineering VP: Actually, no. But that would be very good data to have. It's not so much that we help sales close deals, it's more like we keep the prospect in the mix.

The Engineering VP went on to propose the following Key Results:

"Provide sales support for five major prospects in Q2"

"Develop training for sales team by end of Q2"

While these two statements are directional, they are not measurable. Let's look at how the OKRs coach helped the VP translate these two statements into measurable KRs.

Statement 1: "Provide sales support for five major prospects in Q2"

OKRs Coach: Is there a distinction between a major prospect and a minor prospect? (Makes this *clear* by addressing ambiguity.)

Engineering VP: Not really.

OKRs Coach: Do you and the VP of sales agree on the definition of a "major prospect?" (Ensures *alignment* across departments is jointly defined.)

Engineering VP: Let's replace "major prospect" with "prospect with $100K+ year-one revenue potential." Then we can run this definition by the VP of sales.

OKRs Coach: Have you measured the number of these sales support events in the past? (To confirm metric history so we know the KR is *measurable*.)

Engineering VP: No.

OKRs Coach: What is the intended outcome of engineering providing sales support? (Probes intended outcome of achieving the goal to focus on *results not tasks*.)

Engineering VP: It results in either a continuing sales process or kills the deal.

OKRs Coach: What if all five sales support calls result in dead deals? Will we have achieved this goal? (Boundary condition question to ensure *alignment*.)

Engineering VP: No. The meeting is really not considered a success when we lose the deal for technical reasons. Maybe we should define this as, "Provide sales support with no more than three $100K+ prospects deciding to not evaluate our product for technical reasons."

OKRs Coach: While this is heading in the right direction, the Key Result is now framed negatively. I recommend the following positively framed version of this goal: Obtain a baseline on "technical pass rate." For example, if we have meetings with ten $100K+ prospects and eight of them advance without technical objection, the technical pass rate is 80 percent. (Ensures KR is *positive*.)

The engineering VP liked the idea of tracking technical pass rate. As a result of this OKRs coaching session, the engineering VP agreed to confirm with the VP of sales that technical pass rate is a useful metric to quantify the extent to which engineering contributes to sales. ■

PART TWO:
Objectives and Key Results in Practice

IMPLEMENTING OKRs FOR THE FIRST TIME

I f you are ready to put OKRs into place, you'll want to plan out implementation. Assuming you've done a training (or done your research), and everyone understands and *is on board for OKRs*, choose your approach to the first OKR cycle very carefully.

The first time you try an OKRs cycle, you are likely to fail. This is a dangerous situation, as your team may become disillusioned with the approach and be unwilling to try them again. You don't want to lose a powerful tool just because it takes a little time to master.

There are three approaches you can use to reduce this risk.

1. Have *one* team adopt OKRs before the entire company does. Choose an independent team that has all the skills to achieve their goals. Don't choose a broken

147

team; choose a healthy, high-performing team that loves continuous improvement. Wait a cycle or two until they perfect their approach and then trumpet their success. Teams will be eager to experience that same sort of success and acclaim and will be more willing to adopt OKRs. Over the years, this has been proven to be the most successful approach to adopting OKRs.

2. Start with only one OKR for the entire company. By setting a simple goal for the company, your team sees the executive team holding themselves to a high standard. It won't be surprising when next quarter they are asked to do the same. And by not cascading it, you both simplify implementation *and* see which group will align their work to the OKR and who will need coaching. This is a good approach if you are a relatively small company that needs focus.

3. Start out by applying OKRs to projects, in order to train people on the Objective-Result mindset. Every time you have a project proposal, ask, "What is the Objective for this project?" and "How will we know if we've succeeded?" This approach works well with companies that are not used to being data-driven. Once people learn to evaluate their daily activities by measuring the impact they have, you can then introduce OKRs as a way to drive strategy across the company.

By starting small and focusing on learning how OKRs will work in your organization, you increase your chances of your company adopting a results-based approach and reduce the danger of a disillusioned team.

DON'T TRY TO IMPLEMENT OKRS ACROSS THE ENTIRE COMPANY ALL AT ONCE.

Over the last half-dozen years helping companies adopt OKRs, I keep getting the same story. I pick up the phone and hear, "We tried out OKRs and it went badly. The teams no longer want to use them." I've said before, OKRs are simple and hard. Running a marathon is also simple and hard. You don't try to do it in one go. You build up to it.

Jojo Alexandroff of Format.com emailed me, "When we first rolled it out, we made the cardinal mistake of rolling it out to the whole team. So we had company-level OKRs, team-level OKRs, *and* individual level OKRs. Wow, was that chaos!"

I ran a survey of my readers and had two hundred fifty replies. What people told me they struggled with were the same things I see when I consult: Companies try to jump into the deep end of the pool with OKRs. Then it slows down productivity and frustrates the entire company. It's better to start with a small pilot, and avoid some of these issues:

- Support teams have a hard time aligning to company OKRs. This makes sense, since finance, HR, and customer support are much more concerned with keeping the lights on. In the early months of moving to OKRs, it's better to leave support teams focused on Health Metrics and not worry about OKRs.
- OKR software is often mismatched with company cadence. I recommend not investing in software until OKRs are running smoothly. Then you can find software that supports your process instead of trying to jam yourself into someone else's idea of how the world should work.

- It's hard to figure out what Key Results are good indicators of success. Many companies want to use OKRs to become more data-informed, but this is backwards. You have to learn what metrics matter before you decide which ones you want to grow and which ones you want to protect.
- "OKRs became so much work, that setting them, talking about them, negotiating them, closing them, etc., became too much. Having to work on the OKRs took away from doing the actual work required for the business." Jojo puts her finger on the biggest danger of any new methodology: process bloat.

KEEP IT SIMPLE.

How did Format get themselves out of this mess? By simplifying. "So now, we have a simple high-level goals spreadsheet and each team has their own goals spreadsheet. We try to make sure that all teams' goals align to the company high-level goals."

There is an old Italian proverb, "Il meglio è l'inimico del bene," which translates to, "The best is the enemy of the good." Many companies who adopt OKRs want to do them perfectly. But perfection is an illusion that keeps you from getting to a simple starting place from which you can grow. Ask yourself, "What is the smallest possible starting point to begin my journey to success?" Then do that, learn from the experience, and try the next step. It will be slower but it also will be better and more robust, and have greater returns.

If only culture change was as easy as buying software! But if buying software was the secret to success, we'd all be great novelists as soon as we opened Microsoft Word.

Change is a marathon. Warm up by practicing outcome thinking and measuring your company impact. Then steadily set harder and more audacious goals and trust your team to figure out how to make them happen.

OKRS
FOR PRODUCTS

By Angus Edwardson,
product director at GatherContent

We use OKRs in a few different ways at GatherContent and have done various experiments with them over the past few years.

We've used OKRs as a company-wide tool to align everyone's focus, we've had them for each department to allow autonomy, and we've also used them on an employee level, to encourage personal development.

The most consistently effective application of OKRs, however, is using them for the product team's projects. At GatherContent, it's a requirement for anyone initiating a new feature to outline a clear Objective and a set of Key Results to better understand why we are doing this work, and how we hope it will succeed.

AT THE CENTRE OF THE PRODUCT LIFECYCLE

At GatherContent, we try to reduce the complexity of new features until we have a minimum viable product (MVP) we think is worth launching. Our product team works using Kanban, an Agile Development approach for scheduling. With Kanban, all potential projects are put on a wall and then "picked up" as developers move them from "To Do" to "Doing" to "Done."

When my team is ready to start a new project, we pull that MVP off the Pipeline and put it into development.

All the MVPs on the Roadmap are displayed on Kanban cards which have required fields, including the standardised description, requirements, and any additional notes and sketches.

This structure makes it easy to communicate to the rest of the business what's coming next, and ensures work can be smoothly passed into development. We also include the Objective for the project and the Key Results we hope to see if it succeeds.

Including OKRs on the Kanban cards forces the team to answer two important questions before anything is built:

1. What are we trying to achieve with this feature?
2. How do we measure success or failure?

Here's how our cards are structured:

You'll notice that we switched from using "Objective" to using the ever-so-slightly-semantically-different "Hypothesis." This is to encourage more of an experimental approach to product development. Instead of saying, this will happen, we say, "We think this will happen." Then our hypothesis is proved or disproved. It makes us feel like scientists.

LOGIC UPFRONT:

As well as the value we get upfront from having all features scoped out with clearly communicated rationale, using OKRs in this context also brings a massive amount of value to other parts of our process.

PRIORITIZING WORK:

An obvious use of these OKRs is that they allow us to prioritize work on the Roadmap based on its expected impact. Meaning we can prioritize work based on the goals of the business.

CONNECTING PRODUCT AND BUSINESS OBJECTIVES:

If the business has an Objective to increase the activation rate of new customers, we can prioritize features that we think will have the biggest impact on that area. It's a lovely example of mapping business and departmental OKRs and keeping everyone pleasantly aligned.

COLLABORATING WITH 'OTHERS':

People love to talk about what's coming next. While discussions around the Roadmap with different people in the business are great, without structure they are prone to stalemating because everyone has a bias toward the areas of the business they are closest to. Being able to quickly recite the business logic behind a feature and its position in the queue can make these conversations much more efficient (and less emotional!).

If someone has something they think is more valuable, you can simply discuss why they think it's valuable (hypothesis) and how valuable it might really be (Key Results). This encourages constructive collaboration.

MEASUREMENT AND LEARNING:

The greatest impact of measuring quantifiable targets is in helping us evaluate results, and more important, learn from those results.

We track the Key Results of all of our released MVPs in a simple spreadsheet, and review it regularly to see what we can learn. We've struggled in the past with the question of when we should measure the results, so we've started setting deadlines for each OKR measurement.

Once the deadline hits and we gather the results, we all get together to discuss any inconsistencies, unexpected outcomes, or other learnings.

Adding OKRs to our Kanban cards has allowed us to prioritize better, learn faster, and communicate more effectively. It's also a great way to develop the habit of communicating why we are doing what we are doing. ■

How to Hold a Meeting to Set OKRs for the Quarter

Setting OKRs is hard. It involves taking a close look at your company, and it involves having difficult conversations about the choices that shape the direction the company should go. Be sure to structure the meeting thoughtfully to get the best results. You will be living these OKRs for the next quarter.

Keep the meeting small—ten or fewer people if possible. It should be run by the CEO, and must include the senior executive team. Take away phones and computers. It will encourage people to move quickly and pay attention.

A few days before the meeting, solicit all the employees to submit the Objective they think the company should focus on. Remind them of the company mission, any strategy that is in place, and the annual OKR (if you have one). Be sure to give them a very small window to do it in; twenty-four hours is plenty. You don't want to slow down your process and, in a busy company, later means never.

Have someone (a consultant, the department heads, an intern) collect all the suggestions and bring forward the best and most popular ones.

Set aside four and a half hours to meet: two, two-hour sessions, with a thirty-minute break.

Your goal: cancel the second session. Be focused.

Each exec head should have an Objective or two in mind to bring to the meeting. Have the best employee-generated Objectives written out on sticky notes, and have your execs add theirs. I recommend having a variety of sizes available and using the large ones for the Objectives. Cramped writing is hard to read.

Now have the team place the stickys up on the wall. Combine duplicates and look for patterns that suggest people are worried about a particular goal. Combine similar Objectives. Stack rank them. Finally, narrow them down to three.

Discuss. Debate. Fight. Stack rank. Pick.

Depending on the team you have, you have either hit the break, or you have another hour left.

Next, have all the members of the exec team freelist[12] as many metrics as they can think of to measure the Objective.

It is a far more effective way to brainstorm, and results in better and more diverse ideas. Give the team slightly more time than is comfortable, perhaps ten minutes. You want to get as many interesting ideas as possible.

Next, you will affinity map them. This is another design thinking technique. All it means is you group stickys with like stickys. If two people both write DAU (Daily Active Users), you can put those on top of each other. It's two votes for that metric. DAU, MAU, WAU[13] are all engagement metrics, and you can put them next to each other.

---

12 In case you forgot, it means to simply write down as many ideas on a topic as you can, one idea per sticky note. You put one idea on each sticky note so you can rearrange, discard, and otherwise manipulate the data generated.

13 Daily active users, monthly active users, and weekly active users.

Finally, you can stack rank and pick your three types of metrics. Write the KRs as an X first, i.e., "X revenue" or "X acquisitions" or "X DAU." It's easier to first discuss what to measure, then what the value should be and if it's really a "shoot for the moon" goal. One fight at a time.

As a rule of thumb, I recommend having a usage metric, a revenue metric, and a satisfaction metric for the KRs, but obviously that won't always be the right choice for your Objective. The goal is to find different ways to measure success, in order to have sustained success across quarters. For example, two revenue metrics means you might have an unbalanced approach to success. Focusing only on revenue can lead to employees gaming the system and developing short-term approaches that can damage retention.

Next, set the values for the KRs. Make sure they really are "shoot for the moon" goals. You should have only 50 percent confidence you can make them. Challenge each other. Is someone sandbagging? Is someone playing it safe? Is someone foolhardy? Now is the time for debate, not halfway through the quarter.

Finally, take five minutes to discuss the final OKR set. Is the Objective aspirational and inspirational? Do the KRs make sense? Are they hard? Can you live with this for a full quarter?

Tweak until they feel right. Then go live them.

You'll find a worksheet to help you out at: http://elegan-thack.com/an-okr-worksheet

The Timing of OKRs

If you are ready to put into place OKRs, you'll want to plan out the timing for implementation. After you've had a successful pilot or two and you are ready to roll out OKRs to the entire company, this will be your rhythm.

1. All employees submit the Objective they think the company should pursue next quarter. This increases buy-in for the OKRs and provides interesting insight into the health of the company culture. Give employees a short time to submit these ideas. Twenty-four hours should do it.
2. Exec team, in a half-day session, discusses the Objectives proposed. They choose one. This requires debate and compromise and deserves plenty of time. Then the team sets the KRs, as outlined previously.

I have seen teams set OKRs in as little as a ninety-minute meeting. Things that make OKR setting slow include putting off the meeting, skipping the homework, and refusing to make decisions. These are HR issues and should be addressed by management. Your company goal is your company's life. Commit.

3. Executives' homework: introduce the OKR for the quarter to their direct reports and have them develop team OKRs. This also can be done in a two-hour meeting with the department head and her team, run in essentially the same way: freelisting, grouping, stack ranking, selecting.
4. CEO approval. About one hour, plus follow-up discussions if any department heads are way off base. Set aside an entire day for focusing on just this.
5. Department head gives the company and department OKRs to any sub-teams, and these teams develop their own.

6. All hands meeting in which CEO discusses why the OKR is what it is for that quarter, and calls out a few exemplary ones set by directs. As well, covers last quarter's OKRs, and points out a few key wins from the quarter. Keeps tone positive and determined.

This is the standard rhythm you will keep from quarter to quarter going forward. If you cannot set OKRs in less than two weeks, you will want to examine your priorities. Nothing is more critical than setting a goal for the company to rally behind.

Two Weeks before the Quarter Ends

If you have been running a regular commitment and celebration cadence, then you should be able to determine if you have made or whiffed your OKRs two weeks before the end of the quarter. Don't lie to yourself that you might pull a rabbit out of a hat in those last two weeks. Only the occasional miracle can help you hit a truly hard goal in such a short time. No reason to put off the inevitable.

Admit you have missed a KR, or admit you set a KR too low and hit it too easily. Celebrate getting 80 percent of the way and celebrate all the good things that you learned as you worked. Get that learning and roll it into your next goal-setting exercise.

OKRs are about continuous improvement and learning cycles. They are not about making check marks in a list. So you didn't hit any of your KRs. Ask yourself why and fix it. So, you hit them all? Set harder goals and move on. Focus on learning, getting smarter, and having better things to celebrate every Friday.

OKRs FOR PRODUCT TEAMS

*By Marty Cagan, founder of
the Silicon Valley Product Group*

*During the course of the past thirty years, Marty Cagan has
served as an executive responsible for defining and building products for some of the most successful companies in the
world, including Hewlett-Packard, Netscape Communications,
America Online, and eBay.*

OKRs are a very general tool that can be used by anyone in
the organization, in any role, or even for your use in your
personal life. However, as with any tool, there are consid-
erations as to the best ways to apply. OKRs have enjoyed
considerable success especially inside technology product
organizations, from large to small, and there have been some
important lessons learned as teams and organizations work
to improve their ability to execute.

The central organizational concept in a product organization is a *product team* (a.k.a. durable product team, dedicated product team, agile product team, or squad). A product team is a *cross-functional* set of professionals, typically
comprised of a product manager, a product designer, and a
small number of engineers. Sometimes there are additional
people with specialized skills included on the team, such as a
data scientist, a user researcher or a test automation engineer.
Each product team typically is responsible for some significant part of the company's product offering or technology.

For example, one product team might be responsible for the mobile apps, another might be responsible for security technology, and another might be responsible for search technology, and so on.

The key is that these people with their different skill sets usually come from different functional departments in the company, but they sit and work all day, every day, with their cross-functional team to solve hard business and technology problems. It's not unusual in larger organizations to have on the order of twenty to fifty of these cross-functional product teams, each responsible for different areas, and each product team with its own objectives. The problems these teams are asked to tackle are, as you might expect, communicated and tracked through the product team's OKRs. The OKRs also help to ensure that each team is aligned with the objectives of the company. Moreover, as an organization scales, the OKRs become an increasingly necessary tool to ensure that each product team understands how they are contributing to the greater whole, for coordinating work across teams, and in avoiding duplicate work.

The reason this is all important to explain is that when organizations first start with OKRs, there's a common tendency to have each *functional department* create their own OKRs for their own organization. For example, the design department might have Objectives related to moving to a responsive design; the engineering department might have Objectives related to improving the scalability and performance of the architecture; and the quality department might have Objectives relating to the test-and-release automation.

The problem is that the *individual members* of each of these functional departments are the actual members of a cross-functional product team. The product team has business-related Objectives (for example, to reduce the customer acquisition cost, or to increase the number of daily active users, or to reduce the time to onboard a new customer), but each person on the team may have their own set of Objectives that are cascading down through their functional manager.

Imagine if the engineers were told to spend their time on re-platforming, and the designers on moving to a responsive design, and QA on re-tooling, and so on. While each of these may be worthy activities, the chances of actually solving the business problems that the cross-functional teams were created to solve are not high. What all too often happens in this case is that the actual people on the product teams are conflicted as to where they should be spending their time, resulting in confusion, frustration, and disappointing results from leadership and individual contributors alike.

But this is easily avoided.

If you are deploying OKRs for your product organization, the key is to focus your OKRs at the *product team* level. Focus the attention of the individuals on their product team Objectives. If different functional organizations (like design, engineering, or quality assurance) have larger Objectives (like responsive design, technical debt, and test automation) they should be discussed and prioritized at the leadership team level along with the other business Objectives, and incorporated into the relevant *product teams'* Objectives.

Note that it's not a problem for *managers* of the functional areas to have individual Objectives relating to their organization, because these people aren't conflicted, as they're not normally serving on a product team. For example, the head of UX design might be responsible for a strategy for migrating to a responsive design; the head of engineering might be responsible for delivering a strategy around managing technical debt; the head of product management might be responsible for delivering a product vision; or the head of QA might be responsible for selecting a test automation tool.

It's also not normally a big problem if individual contributors (such as a particular engineer or designer or product manager) were to have a small number of personal growth related Objectives (such as improving their knowledge of a particular technology), just as long as the individual isn't committing to a burden that will interfere with their ability to contribute their part to their product team, which of course is their primary responsibility.

The key is that the cascading of OKRs in a product organization needs to be up from the cross-functional product teams to the company or business unit level. ■

Cascading OKRs at scale

How do you avoid the slow waterfall of goals? Move from cascading OKRs to aligning OKRs.

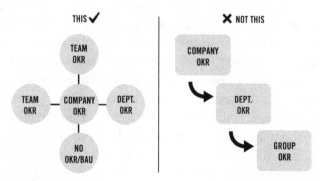

CASCADING OCRs

Because I initially experienced and worked with OKRs with start-ups, I advocated in the first version of *Radical Focus* that you cascade the OKRs. When you have a team of twenty, cascading OKRs is simple. But if you are a big company, cascading doesn't scale *at all*. And just as Lean Start-up had to adapt to enterprises wanting some of that speedy iterative goodness, OKRs need to adapt also if they are to work for large organizations.

When the organization has only one or maybe two levels of hierarchy, a straight cascade might make sense. The executive team sets the company OKRs, then product teams can set theirs. Engineering and design can skip having OKRs for their departments, because 99 percent of their work is with the other teams.

But when a company grows, it changes. I heard a story about a (real but I won't name) new CEO who came into a very large company that was on the skids and tried to use OKRs to straighten it out. Sadly, she was a micromanager, and it took a month to get her to approve all the department head OKSs.

Let me say this clearly and loudly: OKRs are *not* for command and control. Do not use OKRs if you want to control people's activities. Only use OKRs if you want to direct your people toward desired outcomes and trust them enough to figure out how. OKRs *only* work for empowered teams, otherwise they are a travesty (a travesty reminiscent of how Agile is implemented in most companies, so not that shocking, but still upsetting).

So what should you do?

Assuming you have run your pilot with a high-performing, self-sufficient team; assuming you have adjusted the setting, check-in, and evaluation process to your culture; and assuming you know what you are doing and are ready to scale, then this is what has been proven to work: Trust your teams.

Trust your teams to set their own OKRs based on company strategy. Trust your teams to know how to make them happen. Trust your teams.

Enter the Cone of Uncertainty

- ✓ You have a mission. Check.
- ✓ You have a strategy you wish to pursue. Check.
- ✓ You have an annual OKR set or have decided not to have one. Check.

Now the exec team sets four Objectives and three Key Results: the first quarter Objective with its accompanying Key Results and then three more *candidate* Objectives for the other three quarters, but no Key Results for them. I recommend this approach for two reasons: one, setting Key Results takes quite a bit of time, and two, it's hard to predict future organizational needs. In 1958, J.M. Gorey used the term the cone of uncertainty. The cone of uncertainty states that the farther we predict into the future, the less accurate our predictions become. However, without a long-term goal, it's hard to make long-term plans and move from reactive to strategic. We solve this by having specific goals for the near future, and lightweight drafts for the less knowable far future.

Half-Built Strategy

In 2010, Constitución, Chile had a massive earthquake. It left more than five hundred people dead and about 80 percent of Constitución's buildings ruined.

An architecture firm called Elemental was hired to create a master plan for the city, which included new housing for people displaced in the disaster. Elemental decided to give people half of a house.

The houses are simple, two-story homes, each with a wall that runs down the middle, splitting the house in two. One side of the house is ready to be moved into. The other side is just a frame around empty space, waiting to be built out by the occupant.

What do half-built houses have to do with OKRs? They are an inspiration for what I call a "Half-Built Strategy."

A Half-Built Strategy follows the cone of uncertainty's warning about predictions. You create a complete OKR set for the next quarter. Let's call that Q1, as it often is. You have the Objectives and three or so Key Results pinned down. You feel confident entering this quarter that your OKR set is difficult but not impossible.

But can we create an OKR set for Q2–4? Probably not, as we need to see how Q1 goes first. But rather than just hand wave at plans for the future, we can put in three draft Objectives for the next three quarters.

Why don't we have Key Results? As I've taught people the OKR methodology, I find that Key Results are often harder to set than the Objective. They take a fair bit of time as you discuss which metrics matter and if you can access them. The longer you work on something, the more precious it is to you. (This is called the Ikea Effect, if you want to look it up!) So by making the Half-Built Strategy four Os and three KRs (all for Q1), we still have a North Star to work toward, but it was made quickly, so the team doesn't feel they wasted time making an unusable plan. They'll be more willing to evolve the plan as more data is collected each quarter.

> *Deliberate building in of strategy absence*
> *may promote flexibility in an organization....*
> *Organizations with tight controls, high reliance*
> *on formalized procedures, and a passion for*
> *consistency may lose the ability to experiment and*
> *innovate.*
> *— Andrew Inkpen and Nandan Choudhury, "The*
> *seeking of strategy where it is not: Towards a the-*
> *ory of strategy absence"*

Let's look at how this plays out in real life. Let's say that there is a start-up that is going to have to start raising their B-round in Q1 2018 and it is now the end of Q4 2016. I'll name this company TinkWorks, for convenience.

First you choose an annual OKR set. TinkWorks' annual Objective is something about being ready to raise that B-round of investment. TinkWorks' CEO will then choose an Objective each quarter that leads to the desired end state: showing traction in order to raise money.

We all know you don't pour whiskey through a leaky funnel into a flask and hope to get drunk; you don't want a dozen Objectives for the same reason. So TinkWorks' clever CEO decides to theme each quarter. Q1 is all about retention, Q2 is all about conversion, and Q3 is about acquisition, and by Q4 she'll be able to settle into pitch and roadshow prep.

Now that she has a loose Roadmap for the year, she settles in to wordsmith her Q1 Objective and pick the right Key Results with her executive team. She goes ahead and picks those with her team, and she's done.

Choosing Key Results after the EOQ retrospective means that the next quarter's OKRs will take the learning of the previous quarter into account. If there is a better metric to watch, for example, or something about the retention that will affect the conversion strategy, the KRs can reflect that correctly. Picking the right metric and calculating the right amount of growth is a lot of work. It's best done just-in-time.

You want just enough planning to know what to do and what to watch for, but not so much you are locked into a bad game plan.

Appropriately sequenced Objectives also create institutional learning. Imagine a team spends a quarter thinking day and night about retention. The next quarter they are profoundly focused on conversion. Do you think their memory was wiped clean? No! Retention is now part of the company DNA. You can make retention a Health Metric if it needs continued monitoring.

WHAT DOES THIS LOOK LIKE FOR TEABEE?

Mission: Connect the best tea growers with the customers who love quirky and delicious tea.

Annual Objective: America looks forward to discovering new tea after a fine meal, thanks to TeaBee.

KR: Revenue of $20 million in more than five geolocations

KR: Aided brand awareness is up 10%

KR: 500 or more requests for TeaBee teas for home use[14]

Q1: The west coast loves TeaBee

KR: $1 million revenue booked in L.A., Portland, and Seattle

KR: Five restaurants have "TeaBee served here" stickers in windows

KR: At least one early adopter has booked TeaBee deliveries through the year

Q2: New York loves TeaBee

Q3: Austin loves TeaBee

Q4: D.C. loves TeaBee

TeaBee now has the flexibility to change the Q2–4 OKRs as they learn from Q1, yet the idea that they are expanding via locations is clear to the company.

Next all self-sufficient teams can set their OKRs. These are autonomous, empowered teams that have all the resources they need to proceed. It's often product teams that have dedicated design and engineering resources (and more, depending on your company type). These candidate OKRs can be reviewed and discussed with the direct manager of

---

14   These numbers are completely made up.

the teams. This "review" is more for the manager to share any intel they have from being able to see what's happening in other groups rather than to "approve" them.

This can be a peer review instead. Teams can share their OKR sets with other teams to get feedback and raise awareness of what the teams will be focusing on. This encourages greater autonomy and a less hierarchical workplace.

HAVE A SHORT AND ITERATIVE REVIEW PROCESS

Within forty-eight hours of the company OKRs being set, the rest of the company should be able to publish their OKRs. I'll say it again: THE BEST IS THE ENEMY OF THE GOOD. A short review process—twenty-four hours if possible—allows teams to look at what other people are doing and adjust their own OKRs or critique others. Anyone can critique anyone else's OKRs: this should be a process in which the entire company is helping everyone in the entire company get better. We succeed together, or not at all. After this window closes, you live with it until next quarter when you get a chance to get better at this. Analysis paralysis is a real thing, and it's critical to plan to avoid it. Get OKRs into play so you can learn how to do them better next time.

Of course when you review, you may find someone is working on the same problem your team is. IT'S OKAY. I recall chatting with Google Ventures partner Ken Norton about when he first started at Google. Google was already huge at that point and they had an unintuitive approach to duplication of effort: they believe that there is no way to know what team will succeed and how they will succeed, so don't worry about duplication until you have multiple successful options. I think this is the right way to look at innovation: It's more important to be effective than efficient. Efficiency kills innovation.

There is a schedule that looks a bit like this (some steps will be familiar by now):

- Grade OKRs two weeks before quarter ends (there are very few hail Mary's possible in the last two weeks, unless you're in sales). Determine if you should move to the next expected Objective, change it, or have a do-over.
- Annual OKRs are set by execs, typically at an offsite (for focus reasons).
- Two weeks or so before EOQ, the execs set company OKRs. This will be a two-hour meeting once you've got the hang of OKRs, but at the beginning of your process, reserve more time. I recommend scheduling three, two-hour meetings, and think how nice it will be to cancel them if you don't need them!
- Publish company OKRs a week before the quarter ends. Teams and departments set OKRs.
- Publish team and department OKRs (if departments have them).
- Short review period
- Short revision period
- Hit the ground running on day one of the new quarter.

This is the only way to scale OKRs without dragging your company to a halt every quarter. It requires you to do several brave things:

1. Hire well
2. Set clear outcome-based goals
3. Give up control of tactics to achieve company goals
4. Trust your teams

But if you don't have trust, OKRs aren't going to help much anyhow.

OKRs and the Product Portfolio

In larger companies, you will need to figure out who needs to use OKRs and who doesn't. There are groups that will really struggle if you give them OKRs and others that will flourish. The three groups I see struggle the most are service teams, bread and butter teams, and individuals.

Let's start with a company's product portfolio. Boston Consulting Group had a nifty 2×2 box that I find myself returning to again and again.[15]

15 The BCG Product Portfolio: Cow by Laymik from the Noun Project / Dog by Luis Prado from the Noun Project /Star by Three Six Five from the Noun Project / Question mark by Icon Lauk from the Noun Project

All your products should fit into one of these quadrants. Should all of these quadrants have OKRs? What should you do in each quadrant?

I've created the 4Es Product Portfolio diagram[16] to help you think about who needs OKRs and who can get by with just KPIs.

The question mark is a market where you don't have many (or any) products, but it is growing like crazy. Think of the baby boomer market or China a few years back. For this quadrant, you can use Exploratory and Hypothesis OKRs (see the chapter "Beyond the Usual OKR approach").

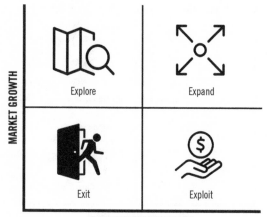

The star is the Expand market. You've got success AND products and services already in the market. Time to see how high the ceiling is! You'll want to use traditional OKRs here.

---

16   Explore by The Icon Z from the Noun Project / Expand by sevgenjory from the Noun Project / Exit by Adrien Coquet from the Noun Project / Money by Max Hancock from the Noun Project

Cash cows are those businesses where you have saturated the market and you haven't found any way to grow but it's still making money. If there really isn't any way to grow this market, then don't subject them to OKRs. It will merely be frustrating.

And if it's a dog—a market fading with your product success—then it's time to exit. Do not ask this team to use OKRs. Instead, look at trying to automate as much as possible and defund it.

So why can't we use OKRs on the shrinking market products? If you ask people to do the impossible and you tie their compensation to it, you will get bad results. First, it's depressing to be asked to do the completely impossible. Second, if people have their compensation tied to it, they will cheat and try to game the system.

What do these two companies have in common?

- Wells Fargo
- VW

Both had executives who set impossible goals and didn't take no for an answer. They both tied compensation (and even continued employment) to meeting the impossible goals. And that led to profit ... until someone found out.

In the early 2000s, Wells Fargo created a cross-selling campaign called "Going for Gr-Eight" (giving impossible initiatives cute names does not help, btw). Incentive schemes were created for everybody from tellers to district managers. At some branches, employees couldn't even go home until they met their target!

In 2013 though, reports started to come out that the Gr-Eight campaign was leading to employees engaging in shady practices, like signing customers up for accounts or credit cards without their permission. And as news of the scandal was coming out, Wells Fargo fired about five hundred people for ethics violations, did ethics training, and told employees not to create fake accounts ... but they didn't change the "Going for Gr-Eight" targets. So, the cheating kept on going. Finally, when the regulators audited Wells Fargo, they discovered two million fake accounts and credit cards and sold services to customers under false pretenses.

> *Cheating and covering up are natural by-products of a top-down culture that does not accept "no" or "it can't be done" for an answer. But combining this culture with a belief that a brilliant strategy formulated in the past will hold indefinitely into the future becomes a certain recipe for failure.*
> —Amy C. Edmondson, *The Fearless Organization: Creating Psychological Safety in the Workplace for Learning, Innovation, and Growth*

VW had a culture of fear and impossible goals in their quest for clean diesel. Engineers there decided to come up with code that detected when the vehicle was being tested ... and reduced the emissions. When it was back on the road, though, the car spewed forty times the level of air pollution regulations permitted.

It's better for managers to work with their teams to come up with a stretch goal that makes sense for the group. Short-term profit is nice, but long-term profit created by employees who are working at their best is better.

Service Departments Will Struggle

A service department is a group that supports product teams. Service departments can include but are not limited to:

- Engineering (including ops)
- Design
- Legal
- Customer service
- Marketing
- Finance

The service departments decide if they wish to set OKRs for areas they wish to improve at with the expected time remaining after they have supported the product teams. Typically, they have only 5 to20 percent of time during the week they can commit to their own projects. When the group is big enough to require internal resources (project management, etc.) the team can set OKRs when they feel they need them. I recommend NOT attempting to do OKRs in service groups unless you have both control of your own resources allocation and enough people to make something happen.

Let's say we are talking about service groups in larger companies that are well resourced. These service teams do NOT have to wait for the self-sufficient product teams to set their OKRs. If these service teams do NOT know how much time they can control each week, the team should use a time tracker to measure its workload for a quarter before setting any OKRs.

Some groups, such as legal or finance, have more predictable schedules than product teams. They do not always need OKRs and can use Health Metrics to keep quality at a steady state.

Let's Talk about Individual OKRs

Just say no.

After years of companies struggling with individual OKRs, I think it's time to retire them. It's just too hard to keep them from being anything other than demotivating tools of micromanaging productivity in order to squeeze every last ounce of work out of an individual until they are discarded, burned out. People are not cogs in a machine that can be replaced easily when they wear out. People gain value over time as they learn and grow. The have a rich social network that the company can benefit from, they have experience and insight in the field in which they work, and they become the next generation of leaders. You want to help people live up to their potential and not exhaust them into quitting.

Many leaders ask me, "But if I don't use OKRs for performance reviews, how do I do performance reviews?"

In *The Team that Managed Itself*, I provided a simple canvas to use for hiring, managing, and reviewing an individual's work. Below is an abbreviated excerpt. If you are a new manager or wish to grow your people-management skills, you may find *The Team that Managed Itself* useful.

STEP 1: DEFINE THE ROLE

In order to hire effectively (internally or externally) for a role, you need to understand the role first. Every role has four parts.

First, you describe the things the role does—goals and responsibilities—and the things the role knows—skills and market knowledge.

Responsibilities are the steady-state activities any job has; e.g., a people manager has to create and manage budgets, coach direct reports, and keep upper management apprised of progress.

A role also has goals it is asked to achieve, aligned to company OKRs. Since goals change as companies do, you won't know all the goals the role will be trying to achieve forever. But you should have a sense of what the goals are for the short term. Grow a new team? Build new efficiencies? Develop innovation strategy? Make sure that your goals—whether they use jargon or not—are concrete enough you'll know when your new employee has hit them. If you say, "Develop innovation strategy," ask yourself, what would that look like? What is the exit criteria? How will I know how successful it is? Vague goals are the enemy of progress.

In order to fulfill these responsibilities and achieve the desired goals, the employee must have market knowledge and the right skills for the role. *Market knowledge* is how well a prospect knows the space your company operates in: commerce, health care, education. *Skills* refers to the hard and soft skills it takes to accomplish the job, from Python to collaboration. I put skills and responsibilities next to each other as they often are interdependent. A candidate may have to use Excel in order to do financial analysis in your company. Or the company may not care what software you use, as long as you deliver results. Placing them together will help you decide what you want to emphasize in the job description: what they do or how they do it.

I recommend freelisting the role's skills, stack ranking them, and then drawing a line between must have and nice to have.

HOW TO USE THE ROLE CANVAS

A *canvas* is a visual worksheet that helps you think through an understood problem. I've designed the Role Canvas to be simple, so you can easily refer to it throughout the role lifecycle. I've included the four attributes mentioned above: goals, responsibilities, skills, and knowledge, plus an area for questions.

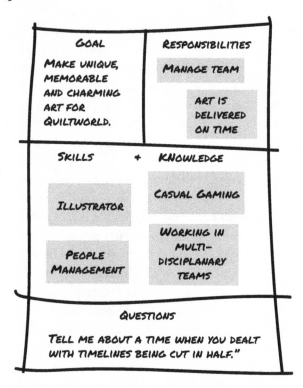

Take your giant wish list of qualities you'd like in the role that you carefully stack ranked. We're going to prioritize further.

In the goal area, only put one to three goals. One big goal, clearly articulated, is best to give you focus on your hire. I know you have a hundred wishes for the magical unicorn you hope to hire, but it's more important to get someone who will accomplish the most important thing you need to get done.

Example goals:
- Build out an internal design team
- Transform engineering to Agile process
- Create a new product category for our portfolio

If the potential employee can contribute to the company or product team OKRs, you may wish to put that there instead. Then you can track contributions to the OKR.

Knowledge refers to what market attributes they should they be familiar with. Healthcare? E-commerce? Pick one to three areas of knowledge.

Example knowledge:
- Familiar with best practices for e-commerce flows
- Understands social network dynamics
- Five years or more experience in online banking

When describing responsibilities, don't make a full laundry list. Try to get the list down to the five most crucial. There are only forty hours in a week, and most people like to sleep and see their families. Put in the most critical responsibilities, and let the job grow into more if it can. If it can't, at least the most important things get done.

Example responsibilities:
- Hiring, coaching, and firing direct reports
- Tracking and improving metrics
- Maintaining code base health

As you list responsibilities, you may find yourself thinking of the skills that are critical for fulfilling the responsibilities. It's useful to make these explicit in order to interview effectively and later, inform what training you'll want to fund.

Example skills:
- Photoshop
- Django
- Excel
- Usability practices
- Working with pattern libraries
- Multitasking

As you can see, skills are a bit of a catchall for everything from software to soft skills.

Now you have a description that covers the most critical elements of the role, but is not so exhaustive that there is no space for surprising and interesting orthogonal skills to show up. You may get a marketer who knows how to edit video. You may get a programmer who has a great instinct for usability. Humans are complex and delightful. It's useful to make space for the unexpected candidate.

As well, you'll get more diverse candidates. Studies[17] show that women will not apply for a job unless they are one-hundred-percent qualified, while men will apply when they are sixty-percent qualified. If you only list what you absolutely need in a candidate, you will get a bigger pool of prospects.

STEP 2. INTERVIEW AND HIRE

Before you interview, look over your role canvas and ask yourself, "How would I know?" How would you know if they had this skill? How would you know they could

---

17　Mohr, Tara Sophia. "Why Women Don't Apply for Jobs Unless They're 100% Qualified." *Harvard Business Review.* March 2, 2018. Accessed November 30, 2018. https://hbr.org/2014/08/why-women-dont-apply-for-jobs-unless-theyre-100-qualified

accomplish this goal? How do you know if they can fulfill this responsibility?

The answer is usually: Tell me a story ...

Sure, you could ask people, "Are you good at dealing with conflict?" They might say "No," if they are honest, but they are more likely to say, "Yes," since it *is* a job interview.

Instead try asking, "Tell me about a time when you and your team were experiencing conflict." This avoids speculation and gives you something to reference check as well. Enter your questions in the bottom of the Role Canvas, and use them as a guide to evaluating your candidates.

STEP 3: MANAGE USING THE ROLE CANVAS

Before your weekly one-on-one, review the Role Canvas. Are they making progress toward the goal that contributes to the company OKRs? Are they fulfilling their responsibilities? Do they have the needed knowledge and skills to do their job?

Now pick the most important topic to discuss. It might be how they are contributing to a team making its OKRs. But it might very well be feedback you've heard about them from another team member or a skill you believe they need to learn. Make a note to yourself on what the topic is and any salient details. Don't trust memory. Emotion can disrupt it.

Try not to have more than one to three things on your list. Just one is best. Remember, you meet every week. Discuss fewer things, better. And make sure you reserve 50 percent of the time or more for issues your reports bring to you.

Consider going for a walk rather than sitting in a conference room. It will be easier to talk and more relaxing, and it will get you out of the building. Start the conversation by asking an easy personal question about an interest you and the person share, such as sports or entertainment. If you don't know what they care about, ask! The best work is done when we all know each other as human beings.

When you return to your desk, take five minutes to write up the most important points of the conversation. If you like paper, you can put Post-it notes over the bottom of the Role Canvas creating layers. If you prefer digital, keep a running document with dates so you can quickly review it for the quarterly conversation. Start a new Canvas/reflection document each quarter, so they don't get too huge to be readable.

SET 4: EVALUATE AND GIVE FEEDBACK USING THE ROLE CANVAS

To this day, the words "performance review" make me feel a bit ill. When I was at Yahoo!, I had to add extra time to any project that occurred around the performance review time, because the team would be so depressed after the evaluations that work would grind to a standstill. I also recall other workplaces where managers would spring all my faults on me once a year and I'd be left shaken and contemplating job hunting. You can rename it the quarterly "conversation" or the quarterly "reflection" but the name isn't the problem; the problem is you if you are delivering performance reviews in the traditional way. If you manage people, you have got to learn how to give feedback well.

Be sure to give feedback quarterly, even if you still do annual performance reviews. This gives both you and your direct reports an opportunity to grow throughout the year by addressing issues and reinforcing positive behaviors swiftly. Do not use the company's schedule as an excuse not to have difficult but necessary conversations.

The quarterly performance review has two parts: prep and delivery. You absolutely cannot skip prep. Memory is untrustworthy. You have to do your homework in order to give fair feedback.

Review the weekly status reports and your notes from the weekly one-on-one meetings. Note how many times positive and negative behaviors come up. Look for patterns. Determine what is important and what is trivial.

Imagine a design agency. There is a team that likes to play music in the afternoon while they work. One member has a tendency to start it, so he can play his music. This annoys some of the more introverted folks, who aren't willing to confront him. This same designer has a bad habit of interrupting clients in presentation meetings. One problem is critical to address formally in the evaluation. The other is important to the health of the team, but can probably be addressed some other way, like rotating music choices on a chart.

Each problem should be addressed, but not all rate being discussed in the evaluation. If you give someone a lot of feedback, they'll become overwhelmed and tune out. Select the top two or three issues you wish to address. Or one. Then decide how you want to address the rest of the issues (if there are any). Some things can be discussed in a one-on-one. Some things can be addressed as a team. And some things just aren't worth addressing. None of us are perfect, and it's not a manager's job to try to make us so. As a manager, you are seeking problems that interfere with the team health and ability to perform.

As well, make sure you find opportunities to praise. While the famous "sh*t sandwich" of two compliments and one criticism has been proven not to work (look it up), you want to make sure people know they are appreciated. They may not be able to hear you in the meeting, especially if they are affected emotionally by your feedback, so make sure you write down your key points and give it to them.

Some quarters there may be nothing to critique. That's a good thing. Don't look for something. However, if there is nothing to praise, that is a bad thing. Consider if you really want to keep barely adequate people around. They tend to set the bar low. Use the quarterly evaluation to ask them to step up.

DAY OF REVIEW

Schedule at least fifteen minutes beforehand to go through your notes and get yourself in the right frame of mind.

What is the right frame of mind? You are here to help. You work for the team. In service to the team, you are going to help this person be the best teammate they can be. You're going to celebrate their strengths! You're going to coach their weaknesses. You're going to be there for them.

You are not punishing them. You are not giving them bad news. You are just like a golf or tennis coach. Bad form is something to be corrected. Bad behavior doesn't mean someone is a bad person. They just need help to see it and correct it.

But most of all, you are there to listen. Don't get so caught up in what you have to say that you don't listen to the other person.

You need to listen so you can react authentically *and* appropriately to the other person. Your goal is not to tell them what's wrong or right, but to point out problems in their contributions to the team, understand how they see the situation, and invite them to come up with solutions to fix the issue. Understanding takes listening.

The first time you hold a coaching-style performance review, you may need to say explicitly that you are there to help. I know every time I've walked into a review, I've been afraid. So many managers see this as a time they need to get tough, even if that is not their natural style. By explicitly saying you are there to help a report reach their potential, you can begin to build trust. And with time, that trust will go both ways.

At the end of the conversation, ask your report if they have any advice for you, either about your feedback style or leadership. The first evaluation, they probably won't have anything to say. Ask them to think about it and let you know in your one-on-one. Over time, it will become a habit to exchange coaching. You'll get better at your job and help build psychological safety as well.

Finally, document everything. Memory is fallible.

OKRs AND THE ANNUAL REVIEW

By Deidre Paknad, CEO of Workboard

Workboard enables and sustains OKRs, brings goals into people's day-to-day work focus, and provides continuous and cross-organization transparency.

Somewhere over the past decade, business goals were hijacked and lost their magic powers. In our personal lives they are aspirations, drivers of important decisions and provide purpose. Yet at work and especially in large enterprises, two-thirds of people think they've become largely irrelevant to all but the compensation process. One of the most potent motivators and sources of satisfaction has been neutered in many large organizations—removed from the tool set that individuals and leaders have to grow themselves, their teams, and their business.

When performance assessments drive goals instead of goals driving business performance, goals are created for annual reviews. When they're written to ensure compensation outcomes twelve months in the future, goals are necessarily vague and the achievement bar is low. As the velocity of business increases, annual goals get more disconnected from business reality and more watered down. While this is particularly true in large businesses, it should be said that in many younger organizations, goals are something the CEO shares with the board instead of the team. Either way, they don't help people make good day-to-day decisions about their time and effort or build up to great outcomes.

How Do We Restore the Magic Power of Goals?

It starts with reframing goals from a device to assess performance to one that inspires and amplifies it. That means transforming the model, cadence, and presence of goals within your organization. Combine aspirational near-term goals with aggressive quantitative metrics and a weekly execution and accountability cadence to achieve fast, great results rather than lower, slower outcomes. These are not old-school, back-office goals—these are dynamic, tangible, and genuinely inspiring to people every day. They tap into our free-will interest in reaching for great outcomes and their shorter cadence produces both more results and more satisfaction. The magic is five steps away:

Use Goals to Define and Drive Success

Goals work when they're inspiring and capture our natural intention for greatness. They should describe what great victory is for every team, and be a real-time rather than one-time rally point for people. When they're tangible, they provide purpose which improves everyone's contribution and provides a focal point for day-to-day execution. By defining clear short-term goals and metrics, you've defined priorities and given people permission to focus on the most valuable activities. (Leaders often overestimate how well people understand their goals—just 7 percent of people really do!)

Dump the Old-School Goal Model for One that Amplifies Results

Techniques like Objectives and Key Results (OKRs) help companies achieve the best *possible* rather than the most *probable* results. This method combines bold, aspirational statements with metrics for Key Results that reflect awesome outcomes. OKRs provide *radical clarity* for everyone in the organization on what they're trying to achieve and where to spend their time—they are the tie breaker. Where traditional approaches encourage people to set the results ceiling low, OKRs amplify results by removing the ceiling and focusing on the best possible outcome. When you're maximizing the possibilities with OKRs, disconnect OKRs from performance reviews.

Manage Achievement in Real Time

Goals and OKRs are only as good as their execution and with short-range goals (as with sales), every week in a twelve-week quarter matters. As business velocity accelerates, leaders can't wait for monthly and quarterly reviews to find out the team got distracted, can't overcome roadblocks, or lost its way. With real-time goals and continuous execution transparency, you can help people stay goal-focused, easily predict results, and drive accountability.

Make Goals as Present as Email

Your team should be able to find their goals and yours and see progress against them in three seconds. That's about how long it takes to focus on the last message in their inbox—which is your goal's competition for their time and focus.

Our research shows that high performers start their day by looking at their goals and then consciously aligning their time with their aspirations. If you want to be a goal-focused organization, make it easy for *everyone* to focus on them every day.

Goals Should Flow Top Down and Bottom Up

Pure hierarchies rarely work today; organizations that focus on teaming and leading across each level are more agile and successful. When goals only flow top down in large organizations, opportunities—maybe even markets—are lost. Talented people and great ideas are everywhere in an organization; let their aspirations flow and you'll be unstoppable. Rather than an over-rigid down line cascade that assumes the chief knows all, converge on goals so innovation isn't stifled *and* broader strategies progress smoothly.

So How Do You Assess Performance and Decide Who Gets Pay and Promotions?

Instead of a one-time performance review event, use continuous conversations to coach and calibrate. Have one-on-ones at least twice a month and calibrate on three things: engagement, performance, and alignment. We use five levels for each and recommend both manager and employee share their view so perception gaps can be addressed quickly. End of year, your employees had twenty-four conversations with opportunities to improve and recognition—it's more authentic, builds skill, and improves performance. Reviews are simple because the facts are shared, there are no surprises, and it is just another in a series of performance conversations.

Tracking and Evaluating OKRs

Two weeks before the end of the quarter, it's time to grade your OKRs, and plan for the next cycle. After all, you want to hit the ground running on day one of Q2, right?

There are two common systems for managing OKRs: confidence ratings and grading. Each has its benefits and downsides. We'll start with confidence ratings, which is my preferred approachConfidence ratings are a simple system best used by start-ups and smaller teams, or teams at the beginning of OKR adoption. When you decide on your objective and three KRs, you set a difficult number you have a 50 percent confidence in achieving. This is typically noted by a 5/10 rating on the status four square.

In your Monday commitment meeting everyone reports on if and how their confidence levels have changed. This is not a science; it's an art. You do not want your folks wasting time trying to track down every bit of data to give a perfect answer; you just want to make sure efforts are directionally correct. The first few weeks of OKRs, it's hard to know if you are making progress or not on achieving your Key Results. But somewhere in week three or four, it becomes very clear if you are getting closer or slipping. Each team leader (or team member, if a small company) will start to adjust the confidence rating as they begin to feel confident.

Then the confidence rating will start to swing wildly up and down as progress or setbacks show up. Eventually around two months the confidence levels settle into the likely outcome. By two weeks from the end of the quarter you can usually call the OKRs. If they were truly hard goals, the kind you only have a fifty-fifty chance of making, there is no miracle that can occur in the last two weeks to change the results. The sooner you can call the results, the sooner you can make plans for the next quarter and start your next cycle.

The advantage of this approach is two-fold. First, the team doesn't forget about OKRs because they have to be constantly updating the confidence level. Because the confidence level is a gut check, it's quick and painless, key for getting a young company in the habit of tracking success. The second advantage is this approach prompts key conversations. If confidence drops, other leads can question why it is happening and brainstorm ways to correct the drop. OKRs are set and shared by the team; any team member's struggle is a danger to the entire company. A leader should feel comfortable bringing a loss of confidence to the leadership team and know that he'll have help.

At two weeks before the end of the quarter, you mark your confidence as ten or zero. Success is making two of the three Key Results. This style of grading leads to doubling down on the possible goals and abandoning effort on goals that are clearly out of range. The benefit of this is to stop people spinning their wheels on the impossible and focus on what can be done. However, the downside is some people will sandbag by setting one impossible goal, one hard goal, and one easy goal. It's the job of the manager to keep an eye out for this.

The second approach to OKRs ratings is the grading approach. Google is the most famous for using the grading approach. At the end of the quarter, the team and individual grade their results with data collected. A grade of 0.0 means the result was a failure, and 1.0 means the result was a complete success. Most results should land in 0.6 to 0.7. From the Google official site on using OKRs, ReWork:

The sweet spot for OKRs is somewhere in the 60–70% range. Scoring lower may mean the organization is not achieving enough of what it could be. Scoring higher may mean the aspirational goals are not being set high enough. With Google's 0.0–1.0 scale, the expectation is to get an average of 0.6 to 0.7 across all OKRs. For organizations who are new to OKRs, this tolerance for "failure" to hit the uncomfortable goals is itself uncomfortable.

Ben Lamorte is a coach who helps large organizations get started and sustain their OKR projects. He regularly uses a grading rather than confidence approach. In his article, "A Brief History of Scoring Objectives and Key Results" (https://www.linkedin.com/pulse/brief-history-scoring-objectives-key-results-okrs-ben-lamorte), he writes:

As an OKRs coach, I find most organizations that implement a scoring system either score the Key Results at the end of the quarter only or at several intervals during the quarter. However, they generally do not define scoring criteria as part of the definition of the Key Result. If you want to use a standardized scoring system, the scoring criteria for each Key Result MUST be defined as part of the creation of the Key Result. In these cases, I would argue that a Key Result is not finalized until the team agrees on the scoring criteria. The conversation about what makes a ".3" or a ".7" is also not very interesting unless we translate the ".3" and the ".7" into English.

I've arrived on the following guidelines that my clients are finding very useful: Here's an example showing the power of defining scoring criteria upfront for a Key Result.

Key Result: Launch new product ABC with 10 active users by end of Q3
Grade 0.3 = Prototype tested by 3 internal users
Grade 0.7 = Prototype tested and approved with launch date in Q4
Grade 1.0 = Product launched with 10 active users

This forces a conversation about what is aspirational versus realistic. The Engineering team may come back and say that even the 0.3 score is going to be difficult. Having these conversations before finalizing the Key Result ensures everyone's on the same page from the start.

As well as precision, Google sets high value on transparency. As well as all OKRs, individual and team, being posted on the intranet, team progress is shared throughout. Again, from ReWork:

Publicly grade organizational OKRs. At Google, organizational OKRs are typically shared and graded annually and quarterly. At the start of the year, there is a company-wide meeting where the grades for the prior OKRs are shared and the new OKRs are shared both for the year and for the upcoming quarter. Then the company meets quarterly to review grades and set new OKRs. At these company meetings, the owner for each OKR (usually the leader from the relevant team) explains the grade and any adjustments for the upcoming quarter.

And ReWork warns against the danger of set and forget:

Check in throughout the quarter. Prior to assigning a final grade, it can be helpful to have a mid-quarter check-in for all levels of OKRs to give both individuals and teams a sense of where they are. An end of quarter check-in can be used to prepare ahead of the final grading.

This is also done differently across teams—some do a mid-point check, like a midterm grade. Others check in monthly. Google has always had an approach of, hire smart people, give them a goal, and leave them alone to accomplish it. As they've grown, OKRs are implemented unevenly, but OKRs continue to allow that philosophy to live on.

Ben Lamorte also shares a simple technique to keep OKR progress visible: progress posters. Several of his clients have set up posters in the hallway that are updated regularly with progress. Not only does this make OKRs more transparent and visible across teams, it can be effective for communicating scores on Key Results and really creating more accountability. It just doesn't look good when your team hasn't updated any scores and when you're already a month into the quarter. Most of these posters include a placeholder to update scores at four to eight planned check-ins throughout the quarter. Certainly OKR posters are not for all organizations, but they can be quite effective in some cases.

No matter if you use confidence check-ins or formal grading (or a combination of both), there is one last piece of advice from ReWork that is important to keep in mind:

OKRs are not synonymous with performance evaluation. This means OKRs are not a comprehensive means to evaluate an individual (or an organization). Rather, they can be used as a summary of what an individual has worked on in the last period of time and can show contributions and impact to the larger organizational OKRs.

Use the accomplishments of each person to determine bonuses and raises. If you use the status report system described in this book, it should be easy for each person to review their work and write up a short summary of their accomplishments. This report can guide your performance review conversations. Some things shouldn't be automated, and the most important part of being a manager is having real conversations about what an employee has contributed. And what he hasn't.

If you rely on OKRs results to guide your decisions, you will encourage sandbagging and punish your biggest dreamers. Reward what people do, not how good they are at working the system.

Beyond the Usual OKR Approach

As I've worked with companies over the years, I've noticed certain patterns in the challenges they faced that required a different approach to OKR setting. With my clients, I co-created new "flavors" of OKRs to support those efforts while making sure that the OKRs are still outcome oriented.

Some organizations struggled with setting goals when you have no idea what you are doing. Others wondered, when do we stop exploring and start doubling down on a strategic direction? Many struggled with long time horizons for development, such as those seen by finance companies or biotech.

Below are three common types of OKRs I have developed to help companies in the early stage of development, at the middle stage when you are validating a strategic direction, and finally, before committing to major efforts.

Exploratory OKRs

Disruption efforts, be it entrepreneurs or intrepreneurs, often struggle with adopting OKRs. OKRs were originally designed for exploiting—driving performance in previously identified, high-potential initiatives—and not for exploring unknown possibilities. Exploratory OKRs work well for very early stage start-ups or for R&D/innovation teams.

Exploratory OKRs were one of my earliest uses for OKRs in my personal life. If you've watched my talk, "The Executioners Tale," you've seen this OKR set.

> **Objective**: Be financially stable, preserve health, do work I like.
> **KR**: Earn $30K over three months doing work I'd do even if I wasn't paid.
> **KR**: Have a manageable budget to predict expenses
> **KR**: Zero acid reflux, zero back pain

In the above OKR set, I am envisioning an end state I want to see, defining it quantitatively, and then running a lot of experiments to try to achieve that state of happy and healthy.

I tried consulting at start-ups, paid speaking, Clarity (advice over the phone), and teaching a night class at General Assembly. I learned what I like, what kept me healthy, and what made enough money to live the life I wanted. I emailed my efforts and the results to my coach, who helped me make sense of it all. I can trace my current life at Stanford directly back to this OKR set.

In the early days of TeaBee, Hanna is trying to convince Jack to explore restaurant suppliers as a potential market. Exploratory OKRs could have made that run more smoothly.

In a business setting, Exploratory OKRs are a solid approach if you've got a bit of cool new technology and need to find a market for it (probably the hardest way to start a start-up, IMO). For example, let's say you are a researcher and came up with a way to quickly draw pictures in emails for when words fail. You invented it to scratch your own itch: Often you are frustrated trying to explain your ideas just with words and you wish you could just do a quick "back of the napkin" drawing to explain yourself. But who else has this problem? You love your product, and you are trying to figure out who else might use it.

Here is an example OKR set for that entrepreneur. (As ever, I use "X" as a stand-in for the actual amount. To get to that amount requires a lot of discussions and market research.)

> **Objective**: Market can't live without our tool for drawing pictures in email.
> **KR**: Preorders at X
> **KR**: 3 B2B deals signed
> **KR**: X beta users

It's okay to get this wrong. The numbers don't have to be right, since you barely can guess what you have to make to achieve these goals. This kind of OKR acts more as a North Star. It reminds you what you are trying to do and reminds you to try to measure your success every week. The early stages of development are gooey, and it's too easy to wander off after the next shiny object.

In game development we call this "wandering in the wilderness." Often the only goal for a game is the ever elusive "fun." The struggle is how to get fun to happen for enough people to make the game worth developing.

> **Objective**: Target market finds our game fun.
> **KR**: Play testers eagerly recommend three friends to playtest
> **KR**: In play tests, 80% of players complete the game
> **KR**: 30% of players buy the game at the "pre-release price"

Setting an Exploratory OKR set makes sure you focus on your goals when it's so easy to get excited by a new lighting approach, or a great idea for sound design. OKRs remind you that you are doing this for your audience and for your business—not just for giggles.

As TeaBee grows, and raises their series B-round, Hanna and Jack discuss how they will expand. Jack is still in love with retail shops. Hanna resists because retail is very expensive. She pushes back, and suggests subscription service. Raphael overhears them arguing, and asks Jack and Hanna why each makes sense.

Jack says, "We can create an experience for our drinkers, like Starbucks or Philz! We can build a strong brand and increase retention and revenue!"

Hanna says, "Retail is hard and expensive. Subscriptions is much easier. We can still grow awareness and loyalty with a great unboxing experience followed by great tea!"

Raphael says, "It sounds to me like you share a goal: Have a direct relationship with our tea drinkers. We've been B2C for a while. Are you certain?"

Hanna responds, "Absolutely. We're at the mercy of the suppliers now. A second revenue stream, especially providing a direct relationship with our tea drinkers, will create more resilience in the company."

Jack nods. The three then come up with their exploratory OKRs.

> **Objective**: Find a way to have a direct relationship with tea drinkers.
> **KR**: Aided brand recognition of TeaBee at 7/10
> **KR**: Preorders at $5K
> **KR**: Open rate of emails at 12%

Now they can brainstorm other ways to get to the goal and stop arguing about their pet theories. For the rest of the quarter they'll have small, multidisciplinary, team-run experiments around the various tactics to getting the numbers they want. They may do a small pop-up tea house, they may set up a sign-up for people to join a subscription service, they may hand-deliver some tea to see if tea delivery might work. This is the Lean Start-up approach: Go small to reduce risk. This approach to OKRs can help any early-stage start-up or internal innovation effort.

What if one of their ideas did work? What's next?

Hypothesis OKRs

Exploratory OKRs are good for finding that first hint of product-market fit. Using them may lead to a strong hypothesis of how to execute against that lofty strategic goal. But don't dive in right away. Now that we've picked a good candidate for the next big thing, we want to test if it really will be big.

Hypothesis OKRs are useful for getting the data you need to prove you are on the right track or that you need to pivot. In a Hypothesis OKR, the Objective is a hypothesis about a success state, and the Key Results are the metrics that prove if it's true. If you achieve your Key Results, you can prove you have product-market fit to yourself and to your investors.

Here's how it works: The Objective is your value proposition. It should include the target market. For example:

- Bookkeepers are delighted by our auto-categorization system.
- Designers can't imagine designing interfaces without our usability error detection algorithm.
- Product managers love meetings when using our agendaware.

The KRs are the way the market would react if the value proposition was true. This can include:

- Sales/revenue
- Conversions from competitors
- Willingness to recommend your software to peers
- Prepayment for vaporware

Beware of "weak indicators" like NPS or email signups. People don't lie with their wallets.

Without trying to fit all of "how to make a start-up succeed," I'll say that if you have done your market research and you have a guess about how big your SOM is, you should be able to put together a credible guess at what your KRs should be. Even if you can't, the sooner you start benchmarking, the sooner you'll understand the metrics that affect you. Practicing prediction develops intuition about your market.

Example: Brand X has pivoted into B2C from B2B.
O: Customers embrace our product.
KR: X units sold (a high number)
KR: X returns (a low number)
KR: X number of 4–5 star reviews on sales website Y

At the end of a quarter, "failing" to make your OKRs is a good thing. It tells you the market isn't going to be viable or the promise of your product was overhyped. You analyze the results and make a decision to try again with a different strategy or kill the product.

Last quarter at TeaBee the little innovation team tried several approaches. Counterintuitively, the subscription service had very little interest. Hanna argues it will take more time to get the word out. But the numbers for the teahouse were surprisingly good. The execs and the innovation team gather to discuss what would be a strong signal that they could commit further to this idea.

TEABEE'S HYPOTHESIS OKRs

Objective: Create a compelling independent teashop experience.
KR: Capacity at 100% during rush times
KR: $40k in takeout sales
KR: Yelp review 4

The teashop pop-up was a great success. But brick and mortar businesses are pricey. What if we only open one? With a short lease? Then we take however long it takes to prove this could be profitable or discover it isn't. Deciding to kill a project (or company) is a really difficult choice. It crushes morale and leads to angry emails from customers. Let's not even talk about all the money that went down the drain! But if you go a little slowly and reduce risk along the way, you might be the next Starbucks.

Milestone OKRs: Outcome-Based Milestones

When you have a big initiative, you need to set Milestone OKRs: outcomes you want to hit to know if your current efforts are pointed in the right direction. This will reduce risk for projects that take multiple quarters. By iterating, you can shift your strategy if something isn't working.

Companies in slow-moving industries often struggle with the quarterly cadence of OKRs. So I invented Milestone OKRs for efforts that last more than a couple quarters. I came up with them when I was working with a Mexican restaurant owner who was expanding from England into Switzerland. He said he had things he "just had to do" like finding a location and getting permits and hiring. How could OKRs help?

I asked, "Will any location do?"

He said, "No, it has to have the right zoning, enough foot traffic, parking, public transit access ..." etc., etc.

We came up with the Milestone OKR for Q2 of, "Be prepared to have a successful pre-opening test run." The KRs were about quality of location, quality of hires, etc.... that way he could still try different things to get to a successful Milestone. The new Milestone was about measurable opening success and the third was about the next branch of the chain.

Since then, it has worked well for R&D, biotech, finance, and other companies that have longer development cycles. A year is too long to go without checking in, so the Milestones are to create clarity about what research is being done to what end, and what success looks like. These Milestone OKRs are never around what we'll do, but always about where we'll be. The Objective will probably not change much. It is usually, "Get to shipping this new thing."

The Key Results are the metrics you want to hit or you may need to kill this effort.

Here is a list of traditional Milestones followed by Milestone Key Results.

Milestone: Get new CPAP lightweight mask prototype built.
Milestone KR: New CPAP lightweight mask prototype produces better sleep for 8 of 10 testers

Milestone: Strategy for 2021 draft finished.
Milestone KR: Strategy for 2021 draft approved by C-suite (trust me, it's a stretch goal)

Milestone: New quality assurance tracker database finished (task Milestone for a new quality assurance tracker tool)
Milestone KR: New quality assurance tracker database approved by stakeholders and SME's (subject matter experts)

In order to get people to think about these as outcomes, not output, I give you permission to call them MORKS. It should liven up some meetings.

Here is TeaBee's. We are using the "4Os and4KR" format.

Annual Objective: Wow TeaBee fans with in-store tea consumption experience.
Q1 OKR: Research indicates strong market position.
KR: Market size of 20 million/annual identified
KR: 3% of our restaurant customers preorder discounted gift certificates for when we are open
KR: Margins of servings are viable, at least 2%

Pipeline

- ✔ Get numbers from local Starbucks
- ✔ Survey for free samples?
- ✔ Cost analysis?
- ✔ More pop-ups

Q2 Objective: Pilot "Pop-up" is loved.

(Obviously, this can be changed if Q1's OKRs aren't met sufficiently)

Q3 Objective: Store is set up for a successful opening.
Q4 Objective: First store opened.

It's the difference between doing something and doing something effectively. To figure out what your Key Results should be, ask yourself: What would happen if we did this Milestone to the best of our ability? What external signs would indicate we'd done well?

Nothing is more intoxicating than a team that's making real measurable impact in the world.

OKRs Are Always About Outcomes

No matter what you are trying to do and how you are trying to do it, OKRs are there to help you do it well. You can be just beginning an effort with a vague idea, like, "I wonder if it's worth creating a cooperative publishing company for books about weird ideas with small markets?" You can be a little further on, like, "I know a bunch of folks with these book ideas and they all have a good following, but is there enough to actually make a living?" Or you can be ready to commit to something huge, but it's scary to risk a year or more on a (validated) hunch: "I want to launch a publishing group that is sustainable and influential."

You want your work to have impact. Don't make a to-do list. Don't build a kanban board full of tasks ... yet. Decide what impact you want to have and then work toward that, measuring the entire way. Only then will you know when it's time to pivot, when it's time to quit, and when it's time to double down. Use feedback from the real world to make a real difference.

Don't just make stuff. Make an impact.

Using OKRs to Increase Organizational Learning

OKRs, when done with the *Radical Focus* approach, are designed to create faster organizational learning. To explain why, let me give you just a smidgen of learning theory from John Dewey. I promise it won't hurt.

There are at least three ways to learn: what I'll call instruction, action, and reflection. All three are important, but the most important is the least practiced: reflection.

Instruction

Instruction is what we think of when we think of teaching. Organizational leaders hire some outside person to give a talk or a series of talks about a topic. Udacity delivers online lectures. Or you buy a book on the topic! Instruction is when someone stands in front of you and talks at you, and while that has its uses, instruction is the weakest approach to education by far.

Action

The second educational approach is action—learning by doing. You may be familiar with this style from school when teachers gave us projects and essays. Action is inherently powerful, as it allows you to create a personal relationship with knowledge and learn practical skills. Heart surgeons and pilots both put in hundreds of hours under supervision before we consider them qualified for just this reason—book knowledge often isn't enough. The skills you get from learning by action go deeper, and remain with you longer, than the knowledge you get from instruction.

Reflection

Almost everyone neglects the last part of learning: reflection. To learn from experience, you need to reflect on what has happened and what it means. In education, this takes the form of writing essays, Q&A, and discussion (and more, if you have a good teacher).

In the Lean Start-up methodology, learning is also built in. You build hypotheses that you can then test, and reflect again, to learn in an accelerated way. If you run your OKRs in a quarterly cadence with the weekly check-ins and quarterly grading, you harness the same kind of reflection. Your OKRs set a goal, and the priorities—or task list, or Roadmap—you set to get to that goal are just hypotheses. You test those hypotheses every week. Then, at Friday check-ins, you reflect on what your actions have taught you and course correct for the upcoming week. The reflection focuses and guides practical learning through action. Your hypotheses get better, and you make more goals.

You also make time for reflection at the end of the quarter. You stop in order to codify the learning from your OKRs the last three months, and you grade the effort you've made. The grading is not about passing or failing. Rather, the value of grading is holding honest conversations you have while you're grading. "Why did we not make this? Why did we make it? What did we learn? Where are we sandbagging? Where are we growing?"

Those who do not slow down to learn from their mistakes are doomed to repeat them.

Social Learning on the Scale of an Organization

When we talk about teams, we often talk about them as if they were isolated entities, and assume that learnings they create exist only within the team. The truth is, in organizations, no one is on only one team. Raphael, head of engineering, belongs to the executive team, the engineering team, and a project team planning to re-architect the company's major database. In a large company there might be dozens or hundreds of overlapping teams: executive teams, design teams, sales teams, and teams that pop up for a single project. Hanna and Jack's tea company is a team made up of designers, sales, management, and so on…. Even a small start-up is a team of teams. As they grow bigger, so does the team network.

When someone has social connections to other teams, that person will talk about their experiences. Raphael sees the OKRs process for several teams, and he'll learn from the reflection for each. He will then argue for a good idea from the project team to be applied to engineering as a whole, or for an executive idea to be demo'd in the small scale in a sample team in his department. Every fast-learning, fast-growing team I've ever seen shares what they're learning. In a healthy organization, everyone evangelizes.

When your company gets too big for everyone to attend Friday bragging sessions, you may wish to add some formal cross-team learning events. Fast-learning companies often have lunch-and-learns where various teams present to anyone who shows up (and with free food, people do show up). Someone can share how they nailed a tricky Key Result. Another can rave about a new market insight. Others can share tips for sequencing a Pipeline based on effort, impact, and confidence. Eventually, everyone becomes very good at watching for learning, and talking about what worked with others. Cross-team learning becomes built into the cadence of your week.

The Friday status email also builds cross-team learning in two key ways. First, very short emails sent to everyone (or available in a public place like a Slack channel) will be read. Wonder what the acquisitions team is up to? Read their status email. It takes thirty seconds, and lets you know if it's time to pay them a visit. Second, the one person who has to read it—the boss—knows who has tripped over a useful insight and can nudge that person to share in the Friday bragging session or a lunch-and-learn.

Everyone circulates what works and learns from the things that don't. Failures become something you talk about, and learn from, with other people.

Learning becomes something the company does together.

OKRs Are Built for Organizational Learning

Let's go through another example based on the *Radical Focus* team. Perhaps Jack notices two restaurant suppliers who look the same to him except that one signed up with TeaBee and one didn't. At the OKRs reflection team meeting, he might ask the team to discuss why they're different. "If we can solve this mystery, it could help the company target the people who will buy," Jack says.

The team brainstorms possibilities. After twenty minutes of discussion, Hanna notices one distributor only sells to low-end restaurants. She suggests that they might want tea bags, not loose-leaf tea. Everyone loves the insight, and suddenly the whole company is off in a new direction, studying how to attract the loose-leaf customers and pass on the ones who want tea bags. Or maybe they create a new line of products. How do they test the hypothesis? Then what does it mean for marketing? For packaging? For website design? Suddenly from one discussion, a whole range of hypotheses to test becomes available.

Each observation results in a hypothesis that must then be validated as true or false. When those insights are validated, they are shared. This becomes company lore. Then each department and team must create a hypothesis for how to apply that insight to their own team. For example, what else do the more affordable restaurants want, and how does that affect suppliers? Should TeaBee tailor their marketing materials to each? Maybe create a second brand? Every learning we get from reflection is a clue that helps solve the bigger mystery of how to make the business successful.

Not all learning is about customers and products. Sometimes you learn how to learn. Sometimes teams test out ways to work together, and learn what does and doesn't help the company move forward.

The OKR cadence manifests new insights through awareness, experimentation, conversation, and reflection.

When we live that cadence, we learn, and apply that learning. We slow down and think, and act out that thinking to learn at an even deeper level. Through action and reflection, we build meaningful, practical, deep knowledge of the market.

OKRs are built for learning.

Adapting to Change in a Changing Market

As I've said, the most important advantage (and asset) a company can have is its speed of learning. The rate of change in the market is only growing. Everyone, from customer service to technical writers to the person who makes your banner art, needs to be learning at an individual and a company level to succeed at the pace we're talking about. In the 21st century, being cogs in a wheel isn't going to cut it anymore. We must learn, and learn to adapt.

Living your OKRs in the cadence I've described will build in learning. Sure, OKRs help set good goals, but the methodology does more than that. With Radical Focus, you make the social commitment to the Objectives and Key Results. You move toward them intentionally, sharing what you've tried and reflecting on how it works as a group, and course correct as a result of that reflection. Learning compounds through the process. It turbocharges your learning, and therefore, turbocharges your growth as a company.

Just setting metric-defined goals—even if you call them OKRs—isn't enough. OKRs without focus and a cadence of learning become an exercise in making your numbers. That might sound fine, but it has unfortunate consequences. When you judge people's success by raw numbers without conversations and context, you end up with all sorts of "hacks"—people cheating to hit the numbers because the stakes are high and failure isn't acceptable. In those circumstances, no one's getting smarter; they're all just inflating a balloon that will pop at some point. When you emphasize learning, you'll fail more, and fail more publicly. That's the point! By being willing to fail, and then have a conversation about that failure, you'll learn. You'll be delivering real value to your market, and growing fast, while your competition is sitting around worried about how they're going to cheat to make their numbers.

OKRs help you adapt. No one ever truly understands what's coming tomorrow; OKRs let you navigate the changing world with confidence as you go. This process harnesses one of the most powerful forces in history: humans' ability to learn. It builds knowledge, keeps you nimble, and allows you to adapt to nearly anything.

SCORE YOUR OKRS; IT IS WORTH IT.

A guest essay by Magdalena Pire Schmidt,
management coach and OKR trainer

I have seen teams enthusiastically craft their first set of OKRs (Objectives and Key Results). But when it is time to score them, it is like pulling teeth. More on this later. Let's start by looking at why you should score your OKRs and how to do it.

Scoring OKRs has two steps:

1. Score each Key Result from 0 to 1.
2. Obtain the Objective score from the average of the Key Results.

Easy.
Scored OKR example:

Objective: Get rid of our customer service backlogs. [0.22][18]

- KR: Decrease average response time from 7 to 3 days [0.5] Note: The average is 5 days.

---

18 Key Results were weighted the same in the average. There are always going to be some Key Results that are harder than others so the team may be tempted to assign them more weight. Weighted Key Results add unnecessary complexity. The goal is not a weighted "grade." The goal is to know exactly where you are to decide what to do next.

- KR: Maintain weekly CSAT at 85% [0.17] Note: CSAT was maintained 2 weeks out of 12. The weekly average CSAT was 69%.[19]
- KR: Reduce cost per request from $3 to $2.70 [0] Note: Cost increased to $3.10.

It is important to score with numbers.

Providing numerical scores for OKRs is critical for the process. It helps:

1. Improve the quality of your Key Results. High-quality Key Results are measurable and unambiguous. If you find yourself mid-quarter having to provide a lengthy explanation for the scores, chances are that the Key Result was not the measurable outcome it was supposed to be. Even for experienced practitioners, writing measurable and meaningful Key Results takes several drafts. Asking ourselves, "Are we able to measure this at the end of the quarter?" helps in that process.

2. Face reality. Numbers have a way of bringing reality to the forefront. This is not to say that a low score is always bad news. There are many reasons for low scores (the Key Result was deprioritized, we realized we were tracking the wrong metric, the initiatives simply did not work but gave us valuable learnings, and so on). Once we reckon with reality, we can decide

---

19   I scored "Maintain weekly CSAT at 85%" based on the number of weeks (2/12). There is also the option of scoring it as 0.81 based on the weekly CSAT (69/85). This is too generous and it could lead the team to "achieve" the OKR while having a very low CSAT. When there is ambiguity, choose the scoring that better reflects success.

how to proceed: What needs to change to make more progress? Was this not accomplished because it was not that important? Does it need more attention? These are questions you don't want to be asking at the end of the quarter. I strongly recommend scoring OKRs numerically mid-quarter. Have a moment of reckoning, then identify what to focus on and what to drop for the coming six weeks. Score again at the end of the quarter.

Score actual results

As much as possible, stick to scoring *results*. OKRs are a powerful methodology precisely because execution is driven by outcomes, not by plans or initiatives. How many of us have celebrated the launch of a new project only to realize later that it did not work? I certainly have. Being anchored on actual results helps teams become more innovative, pivot, and experiment.

That said, there are different scoring practices out there:

Practices	Scoring Confidence	Scoring Milestones	Scoring Results (recommended)
What	Assesses if the project(s) are on track or not to deliver on the result.	Provides an update of how much of the needed initiative(s) has been completed.	Provides an update of the results seen so far.
Pros	Visually represents the progress made even when results may not be seen yet. It can be motivating especially for initiatives that won't show results until the very end of the quarter.		Clear and transparent state of affairs. Incentivizes metric-driven KRs. Incentivizes the team to see results before EOQ.
Cons	Risk that the team may deliver on the initiative(s) without seeing the expected results. Risk of becoming a project management process.		Can be demoralizing as the score does not reflect the amount of effort invested.

The interpretation of the score changes depending on the scoring practice. Take a Key Result from our example: *Decrease average response time from 7 days to 3 days.* [0.5]

Scoring Confidence: 0.5 indicates that we have 50% chances of meeting the 3- day target. Note that it doesn't say anything about the current average response time.
Scoring Milestones: 0.5 indicates that half of the work needed to lower the response time has been done. Maybe a new team was hired and trained but they haven't worked through the backlog yet.
Scoring Results: A 0.5 indicates that the average is 5 days.

Now let's talk about our feelings

Why the hesitation to actually score OKRs throughout the quarter? We avoid it because it requires effort and we are afraid of bad news. According to researcher Heidi Grant-Halvorson, lack of self-monitoring is one of the top goal saboteurs. The team may be especially concerned about low scores if they believe that the low score will have repercussions on their performance assessment. It is critical for management to divorce OKRs from performance assessment (a topic of another article). If a team comes from a tradition of using objective completion to assess performance, it may take a couple of cycles of OKRs for folks to be more at ease with low OKR scores.

The good news is that once teams get in the habit of scoring OKRs, they learn to appreciate the clarity and agency that comes with knowing where they stand.

How to assess the score at the end of the quarter

Scoring throughout the quarter is more important than obtaining the final score. If you are doing it right, by the last month of the quarter the team will have an idea of where they stand. They will be able to start drafting the following quarter's OKRs before the month is over.

That said, I find it critical to do a final score. This is a good opportunity to reflect, gather learnings, and incorporate learnings into the next cycle.

Once you have scored each Key Result and obtained the Objective score, here is a guide on how to interpret the final score:

Score 0.7–1.0: Achieved / Green
Score 0.31–0.69: Partially achieved / Yellow
Score 0–0.3: Not achieved / Red

This scoring interpretation incentivizes ambitious OKRs by considering anything above 0.7 as achieved and anything above 0.3 as progress.

On that note, when interpreting the final score, it is useful to distinguish between stretch and committed OKRs. Committed OKRs are those that the team agrees are feasible and are a priority. For committed OKRs, only a score of 1.0 represents achievement.[20]

In general, when I see a team that is consistently scoring above 0.7, it raises a red flag. The team may be sandbagging: only working on OKRs that are feasible. In this case, I push teams to be more ambitious.

---

20 Christina's note: As I have said, I don't think two kinds of OKRs are a good idea. It both complicates what people have to hold in working memory and makes it possible for your team to deliver "as usual." As long as there are no financial incentives involved in masking your OKRs, it should be fine to do OKRs correctly: all stretch goals. Gentle stretches, but stretches.

After the numbers come the narrative

Scoring your OKRs is a critical step to stop, think, and assess if what you are doing is working or not. But the numbers are just a guide, they are not the final assessment.

First, there is much subjectivity in this process. A score of 1.0 will mean little on a superficial Key Result and a score of 0.1 may represent a significant impact on an ambitious Key Result. Let's go back to the example above. The objective has a score of 0.22. But when we look at it, I would say that the team had a good impact. They reduced their response time significantly, barely increasing the cost. The quality has suffered but, overall, they are on the right track, and they know what to focus on next.

Second, there are many things going on in a team that are not represented in the OKRs (all the business-as-usual team events with members coming or leaving, challenges that came our way, etc.).

At the end of the quarter, reflect on the whole: the OKRs scores, the business-as-usual and KPIs, team events, new challenges, and opportunities of the past quarter. At Google, I kept a running document where once a quarter I wrote few bullet points for each of the following sections:

Highlights: great results on projects and business-as-usual

Groundwork: areas where we made progress, put in a lot of effort, but have not seen results yet

Lowlights*: areas where we didn't make progress or new challenges that emerged

Nowhere in this document did I mention the OKR score. The team can see the OKR score. It informs the narrative and our understanding but no one remembers scores. The useful conversation was: what was our impact, and where are we going next? ■

A Note on OKR Software

When you set a resolution, what is the first thing you do? Want to lose weight? You buy an expensive treadmill. Want to start running? You buy fancy shoes. And when you plan to diet, you go out and get the best scale on the market. Or maybe you just buy fifteen diet books. Sadly, adopting OKRs is treated the same way. People buy software, and hope it'll do the hard work of setting and managing your goals.

There are a ton of tools for OKRs out there, and many are quite good. But buying a tool is the last step you want to take, not the first. The right way to adopt OKRs is to adopt them in a lightweight fashion, then experiment with different approaches until you find the system that gets you results.

Start with these tools first:

- A whiteboard, to write ideas of what your Objectives will be.
- Sticky notes, to brainstorm good KRs.
- PowerPoint, to track confidence and efforts against the Objectives.
- Email, to send statuses out.
- Excel, if you decide you wish to do formal grading. (Google offers a tool for grading on their Rework website. https://rework.withgoogle.com/)

The first quarter you feel you have truly mastered OKRs, then go shopping.

Simple but Hard

When I describe OKRs to people, I say they are simple but hard. It's a bit like the advice, "Eat less and exercise." Sure it works, but who can do that? People who really want to succeed at losing weight. It's the same if you want your business to succeed.

To be successful, you have to focus on what matters. You have to say no a lot. You have to check in with your team and hold people accountable to their promises. You have to argue about whether or not your tactics are working and admit when they aren't.

There isn't much complexity to OKRs, but they take quite a bit of discipline to do well. OKRs might not be right for your company ... yet. Yet is an important word.

Carol Dweck said, in her TedX talk[21] on growth mindsets:

> I heard about a high school in Chicago where students had to pass a certain number of courses to graduate, and if they didn't pass a course, they got the grade "Not Yet." And I thought that was fantastic, because if you get a failing grade, you think, I'm nothing, I'm nowhere. But if you get the grade "Not Yet" you understand that you're on a learning curve. It gives you a path into the future.

As you struggle to work with OKRs (or dieting), you'll have to experiment, come up with new ways to do the rituals, learn what you are good at and what you are bad at. It's okay if you didn't write a very inspiring Objective one quarter, or

---

21 http://www.ted.com/talks/carol_dweck_the_power_of_believing_that_you_can_improve/transcript?language=en

one of your Key Results was a task. Stay with it. You will get better.

And when you are tired and frustrated just tell yourself, "Not Yet." Followed by, "But soon."

CREDIT WHERE CREDIT IS DUE

In the course of my research, I've spent time talking to Rick Klau, the OKR proponent from Google Ventures. The Google implementation of OKRs is quite different from the one I recommend here, and it's worth exploring the video and materials he shares. In my personal experience, the approach I lay out here is effective for start-ups to larger enterprises. But every team is different, and you should feel free to iterate.

A few years after I wrote *Radical Focus Measure What Matters* came out. If you read it, you will find some tactics I recommend are contradicted. I'm not the boss of you, and you can do what makes sense for you. But if you struggle, consider scaling back to the *Radical Focus* approach.

I want to especially thank Cathy Yardley, who helped me write like a fiction author. As well, these fine folks were beta readers, and gave me a *ton* of advice and insight on how to make this book better:

Magdalena Pire Schmidt, James Cham, David Shen, Laura Klein, Richard Dalton, Abby Covert, Dan Klyn, Scott Baldwin, Angus Edwardson, Irene Au, Scott Berkun, Jorge Arango, Francis Rowland, Sandra.Kogan, A.J. Kandy, Jeff Atwood, Adam Connor, Charles Brewer, Samantha Soma, Austin Govella, Allison Cooper, Ed Lewis, Brad Dickason, Pamela Drouin, David Holl, Stacy-Marie Ishmael, Kim Forthofer, Derek Featherston, Jason Alderman, Ammneh Azeim, Adam Polansky, Joe Sohkol, Brandy Porter, Bethany Stole, Susan Mercer, Kevin Hoffman, Francis Storr, Leonard Burton, Elizabeth Buie, Dave Malouf, Josh Porter, Klaus Kaasgaard, Evan Litvak, Katy Law, Erin Malone, Justin Ponczek, Erin Hoffman, Elizabeth Ibarra, Harry Max, Tanya Siadneva, Casey Kawahara, Jack Kolokus, Maria Leticia Saramentos-Santos, Hannah Kim, Brittany Metz, Laura Deel, Kelly Fadem, Francis Nakagawa, An Nguyen, the three hundred people who replied to my email asking for stories about OKR implementation, and you, the person I forgot to list, you were the most helpful of all and you can yell at me next time we see each other.

Dearest readers, please write me and let me know what you learn! And help me to make the next version of this book even better.

Visit cwodtke.com to get updates and learn more.

ABOUT THE AUTHOR

An established thought leader in Silicon Valley, Christina is a "curious human" with a serious resume. Her past work includes re-designs and initial product offerings with LinkedIn, MySpace, Zynga, Yahoo! and others, as well as founding three startups, an online design magazine called *Boxes and Arrows*, and co-founding the Information Architecture Institute. She is currently a Lecturer at Stanford in the HCI group in the Computer Science department.

Christina teaches worldwide on the intersection of human innovation and high-performing teams. She uses the power of story to connect with audiences and readers through speaking and her Amazon category-bestselling books. Christina's work is personable, insightful, knowledgeable, and engaging.

Her books include *Information Architecture: Blueprints for the Web*, *Pencil Me In*, and *The Team that Managed Itself.* Her bestselling book, now in its second edition, is a business fable called *Radical Focus*. It tackles the OKR movement through the powerful story of Hanna and Jack's struggling tea startup. When the two receive an ultimatum from their only investor, they must learn how to employ OKRs and radical focus to get the right things done.

To connect with Christina or to get more information on how to become a whole-mind, high performing team, visit cwodtke.com or eleganthack.com.

Other Books by Christina Wodtke

101 Thesis on Design
Information Architecture: Blueprints for the Web
Pencil Me In: The Business Drawing Book for People Who Can't Draw

Curious how to solve other problems faced by organizations using OKRs, or how to create empowered teams? Read on for an excerpt from Christina Wodtke's story of management, *The Team That Managed Itself*.

Get your copy today.

THE TEAM THAT MANAGED ITSELF

"Baby needs a new pair of shoes!" Allie screamed.

Rob laughed out loud at that. "Really?"

She threw the dice. "When in Vegas, roll like you're in Vegas! You got to live every damn movie cliché!"

Rob nodded. Her best friend might be sober and keeping his money off the table, but he was whooping and cheering with their team. Tonight, they were celebrating.

"Snake eyes!" the croupier announced.

The table groaned, and the dice passed to George.

"Let me show you how it's done, honey," purred the studio general manager.

Allie had a sudden sense of perfection, like a key snapping into a lock. She had her best friend on one side, and her dream boss on the other. Rob was a tall African American, and Allie was a tiny mestizo. George was something and Chinese, and even if they didn't look like the usual bro-co team, they had managed to snare the third quarter of top earnings at SOS. And they had done it all with a game that was basically Minecraft with quilting squares—a girly game. Allie wished the first-person shooter fanboys she went to high school with could see her now.

Allie placed her bet next to Rob's and George's. Why not? Her bet on QuiltWorld was winning, as it had been for months now.

Then her phone vibrated against her hip, where she had stuck it in the waistband of her skirt. She didn't dare leave it in her purse in the noisy casino. Weekend or not, she was always on call.

She pulled it out and looked. Midnight stats were in.

"Easy four!" called the croupier.

Yep, George had gotten her another win. Allie grabbed her chips and stepped back from the table to look at her game's numbers.

As lead product manager on top-earning mobile game QuiltWorld, it was her right to be here in Vegas with the team. They had blown away revenue expectations and her CEO Rick had rewarded the QuiltWorld team with a trip to Vegas. But as lead PM, she still needed to keep an eye on numbers, in case something went sideways. Her boss could chill out and get drunk, because he knew his team had his back.

Plus, she wanted to watch the numbers. She was excited. She had crafted a new bold beat—a special event designed for the game—under the tutelage of the lead game designer. She was dying to see how it performed. She didn't consider herself creative, not like the game designers or the art team, but she had correlated numbers across the various games in the studio and had seen a pattern that inspired a fresh idea.

In late summer, all the games at SOS got the doldrums. Their biggest competitor was a sunny day. Games that spoke to the desire to play in the sun could get a lift midafternoon in the workday. You can't sneak outside, but you can sneak a peek at a pretend outdoors on your computer. Allie had come up with an idea that was all about playing outside on a playground, with swings and slides and a baseball field. They packaged it up as a "sewing kit"—QuiltWorld's name for mini-expansions to the game— and offered it to players so they could make their own playground.

QuiltWorld was a strange beast inside of SOS. SOS had started out as just another game company trying to ride the popularity wave of mobile games. They began with a combination of gambling and pulp-fiction inspired games. Vampires, cops and robbers, gangsters. But then a tiny mythical group—George, Pete, and Christie—had a new idea. They took the popularity of a sandbox game, where you take modular units and build things with them, and rethemed it with quilts. It was Minecraft, but with quilts. Rick, had thought it was the stupidest idea he'd ever seen, but because it was George, and George had a track record at another company of taking stupid ideas and making a lot of money from them, he'd funded it—given them their time, plus an engineer and a game artist to make the images. They launched an alpha and the numbers were beyond any anyone had seen. Players went insane for it. Rick still couldn't understand it, but it didn't stop him from taking credit for it.

QuiltWorld was now the biggest studio in SOS, dwarfing even Baccarat. SOS had cloned the core concept to great success. ClayTown, another sandbox game but themed on claymation, was the second biggest, and Sketchworld was the up-and-comer. Rick was overjoyed. A serial entrepreneur, he always told them at company meetings that SOS was what his entire life had led up to, and they would be reinventing the very nature of fun. He was so proud he was able to be profitable and respectable at the same time.

The Vegas trip tradition came from the time when all the games at SOS were on the sleazy end of respectability. You made the most money, you got to go to Vegas. No matter how many times at the company meetings Rick talked about "forever games" and "innovation" and "high quality production," what got you to Vegas was revenue. At SOS, a good game was a game that made money.

George lost the dice and peeled back from the table. "Waitress hasn't been by in a while. Want to get a drink?"

The two of them wove through the crowded casino. When they had claimed the craps table, the casino was sparsely populated by a handful of dedicated gamblers. Now every square inch of floor space had a human on it. The bar itself was also lined with humanity—drinking, laughing, flirting. An unrepentantly cheesy piano man swore to play any song for the right tip.

Allie wedged her way in near a tall middle-aged man and leaned in to get the bartender's attention. In her outstretched hand she held a twenty, in case money was a better bartender lure than cleavage. The man next to her caught notice.

"Hey, where you from?" Vegas's standard opening line, from hawkers on the sidewalks to men at bars.

Allie was used to a bit too much attention. Her hard-to-place ethnic features and hip-length black hair were a magnet for certain kinds of men.

"She's with me," George said, placing an arm on her shoulder. The man turned away with the complacency of the unsober.

"Ew!" Allie laughed, shrugging George's arm off her. "What will your wife say?"

"She'll say I'm watching out for you."

The bartender finally swung by and got their order. Allie ordered two shots of Patron.

"So, we're toasting?" asked George.

"Toasting what?" grinned back Allie. She gestured at the Patron.

"You got the midnight numbers. I can look at them on my phone, or you can tell me."

"SummerQuest is doing quite well. Even in the evening, we're up 8 percent!"

George offered a hand for a high five, and Allie smacked it. They turned to their shots and downed them.

"Good work, half-pint! You've got a knack for this!"

"Ah, the numbers just like me. They tell me their secrets."

"The number whisperer." George ordered a margarita. "Never mix, never worry."

Allie ordered a soda water. She believed drinking was like a game: It was all about pacing. She looked back at the table where her team played on. They screamed as one and went into an impromptu wave.

"We're going to get kicked out," she said.

"No way," George replied. "It's Vegas, baby. To Quilt-World!"

They clicked glasses merrily.

Allie felt a tap on her shoulder. Where her admirer had stood now was a middle-aged woman. She was perhaps from the south, with very tall hair and a thick layer of makeup. "Excuse me, but did I hear you work on QuiltWorld?"

"Why, yes," Allie replied. George's smile faded from his eyes, though it remained on his lips.

"Oh, I love that game! My quilts are so beautiful. I work on them every day when the kids are at school!"

"Have you tried Original Martha?"

"Oh my God!" she squealed. "Oh, gracious, didn't mean to curse! I love it so much! It was like traveling back in time."

Allie heard George mutter, "Not quite."

"I felt so patriotic, like I was part of history! And so good of you to donate to history education. My sister made her first in-app purchase to help out!"

Allie shot George a look. It was her idea to use a donation element to up in-app purchases. It had bumped revenue, got positive PR, and raised money for history books for public schools.

George returned her look with one that said, "Okay, okay," with a slight eyeroll.

"Would you like to see my quilt?"

"See it?" Allie responded.

"I have my iPad! I took screenshots!"

"I'd love to," Allie said quite sincerely.

George stepped back, then off toward the table. Pete, his CTO, greeted him with a fist bump and a bro-hug. Pete's mass almost knocked George over. Allie was glad to not participate in the ritual. She preferred spending time with her players. The woman showed her screenshots of her quilt structures, including the quilted White House that was part of the Fourth of July bold beat, and then showed off her QuiltWorld towns. She had two—one a miniature New York and one that looked like a small midwestern town. She must have spent a fortune over the years on these.

"I'm trying to make my hometown," she admitted shyly. "I know some people take apart the kits and make their own QTs," she said, pronouncing it "cuties," "and I thought I'd try to do it, too."

"It's darling! Is your house here?" Allie asked, fascinated. *Is this common?* She thought rolling-your-own was an advanced player trick, but if it was spreading, then maybe they should consider how to build that in for more players.

"It's right here." The woman smiled widely, yet Allie could see she was anxious about sharing her work.

"Wow, you did that!" Allie knew there was only one right response when a creator was brave enough to share.

Now the woman was beaming. "Sure did! I actually found our house's blueprints, you know, to get ideas for how to make it. You see here, I'm using some of the Valentine's Day kit to get the lattice work on the porch right!"

"That is beautiful." Allie sighed. She meant it. The house was fine, but what was beautiful was this woman finding her way to creativity and the pride of making something new. That's why she loved working on QuiltWorld. When she met the players and found they were unlocking their creativity, she felt proud. And perhaps a little jealous. But mostly proud.

Her phone vibrated. She ignored it for a second, but it vibrated again and again. A call. She smiled at the woman. "I have to take this," she said, and moved toward what she hoped was a quieter corner of the casino as she answered, "Jenova."

It was Noam, one of the engineering pod leaders. He had volunteered to stay behind to mind the shop because "I hate Vegas. It's a pit of despair."

He sounded tense. "The new bold beat is in freefall. We can't tell if it's a reporting problem or a bug in the back end. I just know everything's testing fine here. Can you grab Rob or Pete?"

Allie pivoted and headed toward the table. She tapped Rob, her lead dev, on the shoulder. He looked up as she said into the phone, "Okay, we'll poke around and get back to you."

Rob gave her a look that said, "Of course." He shook his head and walked away. He didn't gamble, but he believed deeply and completely in the importance of spending face time with his team and was sad to have to step away from the celebration. They walked to the elevators.

"I can't really tell much from my phone," Allie said. "But Noam is right, something isn't working. There is no way our numbers can be taking such a severe hit. I really hope it's a reporting error or I'll be having fun explaining this to Rick Monday."

Rob punched the number 32 on the console, and the elevator smoothly ascended. Allie's ears popped.

He sighed deeply. "Something always breaks. If George would give us time to work on code rot, instead of always chasing the next bold beat, we could elevate and maintain all of our numbers instead of this moronic roller coaster ride."

"You've made that argument."

"So I have."

George's counterargument was that a dead game with good code was not as valuable as a spaghetti code that made money.

They walked to Rob's room, and he sat at his laptop on the small desk. Allie eyed the two beds, one made neatly, and one covered with jeans and T-shirts celebrating game releases.

"You're sharing with Pete?"

"Why not? He doesn't sleep at night while he's in Vegas. It's a lot like no roommate at all. Plus, I think it comforts Marie to know I'm rooming with comic book guy."

"Fair. Can I help?"

"Not yet. Hold on."

Rob played his laptop like a jazz pianist. Allie sat on the edge of the clean bed and flipped through her emails on her phone. There were no clues. Her eyes wandered over to the T-shirts. Pete had been at SOS since the beginning and wore nothing but SOS release T-shirts as a badge of honor. She saw one on the bed from six years ago, before she'd joined, once a dark blue but now a faded sky blue. His first big hit. He must've worn it a lot to remind people what he'd accomplished. SOS had no memory, so it was probably a decent strategy. The blue shirt was the size of a small blanket, probably a triple X—as Pete liked to joke he was. He was a walking caricature of an old-school nerd. She sighed and thumbed back through the midnight numbers. Might as well bask in the one thing that was going right.

"Got it. API change. Give me a second ..." He typed, then snapped his lid shut. His lips pressed together hard, like he was struggling to hold back a string of obscenities.

"I can announce the fix then?" she asked.

"Yes. But it will break again. This," he waved his hands in frustration over his laptop, as if it held the entire code base of QuiltWorld, "is a frigging house of cards. One strong breeze ..." His voice trailed off as he contemplated the various ways it could break next.

Allie was taken aback. Rob never swore. Never showed anger. She knew he was unhappy about the state of Quilt-World's code and ached to fix it. There was nothing quite so alarming as when a quiet man was angry. She ducked back to her phone to forward his fix and add a few notes.

When she looked up, his anger had passed like a tropical storm.

"Sorry," he said. "I just don't think this is how one should run a technical team."

"No need to apologize," she replied. "Shall we head back?" She noticed Rob was absent-mindedly rubbing his left forearm, his fingers kneading into the muscles afflicted with carpal tunnel. She didn't know if he was in pain just now, or this was an anxiety reflex. She knew that even if his face was calm, his mind wasn't.

"Go ahead. I'd like to take a moment to look over the fix again." He looked at her blandly, but she wasn't fooled.

"Sure. Later!"

As Allie rode down the elevator, she wondered if they really deserved to be celebrating tonight. Her ears popped.

Sunday Afternoon

Allie got out of the shuttle van and waved at her teammates as they dispersed, some heading to the parking garage, some calling for rides. None of them had slept much; more than a few were still drunk. It had been an amazing weekend. She had spent the entire night at the craps table and left seventy-five bucks up. She didn't care about the win, but she loved craps. There was camaraderie in screaming at dice together.

She looked up at the SOS building and sighed. It'd feel good to go home, but she really wanted to run a couple of database queries before Derek picked her up after his softball game. She looked at her watch. 3:20. Yeah, she could sneak in an hour of work.

She paused indecisively for a moment and looked again at the concrete building. It was shaped a bit like an early game controller, two rounded towers connected by a lower flat building. It was mostly glass, a giant '80s style post-modernist monument. It had held Sega at one point, and then had been broken into smaller offices when they moved to cheaper property. Shiny Object Syndrome, or SOS as it was known to all, had started in a single office on the third floor, now owned the first through the third floor on the left hand of the controller, and was negotiating to own the entire building. She started to trudge toward the front door when she recognized the man standing outside of it.

"Derek!"

Her husband walked toward her, swift yet unhurried, and swept her up in his arms. "Darling, you smell like an ashtray!"

"Flatterer! You could have waited until I got home and showered." He looked fresh as a daisy. "Shouldn't you be at your game?"

"I didn't dare let you go upstairs. I knew if I didn't collect you, I'd be eating another pizza alone."

"Not after a weekend away!"

"Maybe." He put an arm around her. "Anyhow, here I am."

"Here you are." Her arm fit nicely around his waist, and she squeezed him. He was a solidly built blond, a blend of the British Isles and something that let him tan rather than burn in the sun. He didn't approve of the team trips to Vegas, either personally or professionally. SOS frowned on bringing spouses—said it interfered with team bonding, though Allie suspected it was cheapness. And while he trusted her to stay out of trouble, he found it questionable that they'd go on a business trip to a place committed to a variety of sins. He'd put on his HR hat to complain that it was unfair to addicts or put on his husband hat to complain it was yet more time he didn't get to spend with her.

"You know, I'd like to go lie by the pool with a daiquiri and catch a show." His husband hat was jealous in a variety of ways.

Allie decided to defuse the issue. "Why don't we just go sometime? It's a short flight."

"My birthday is next month." He looked down at her and fluttered his eyelashes.

"Be a good boy until then and we'll see."

"Hmmp."

Thirty minutes into the drive, they'd finished catching up and he started fiddling around with his phone to get music playing.

"Stop that, it's dangerous."

"Not as dangerous as your taste."

"No, dearest, it isn't. Drive." She grabbed the device away from him and put on one of his playlists.

After a few moments, he spoke up again. "I really don't like it, you know."

Allie turned the music down. "I know. You know it's good for team morale."

"Abusive spouses always separate their victims from friends and family."

"It's one weekend a month when we are the top-earning team! Hardly a plot."

"Maybe. But when you have your own company, you won't take them to Vegas, will you?"

"No. I'll take them to Disneyland."

"And you'll take me?"

"Every time." She gave his knee a light squeeze. *When* she had her own company. *If* was more like it. She grew up in East Palo Alto, on the wrong side of this very highway they were driving on. On her left, her family. On the right, Stanford and all the startups it fathered. Instead of attending Stanford, she had taken over her half-brother's Nintendo when he'd grown bored with it, and his computer when he moved to New York, and then used the Internet to teach herself what she needed to get a customer service job at Hurricane, the best game company in the country (in her opinion).

Then she just worked harder than everyone else and look at her now. No degree, but hey, enough stock options to be a millionaire if the IPO went well. She just needed to keep hustling and eventually, she'd get promoted to general manager. Then she'd know enough to finally found her own start-up. She was living the Silicon Valley dream.

Rob Leaving QuiltWorld

At 7 a.m., SOS felt deserted to Allie. The parking lot held a half-dozen cars, so she knew someone was here, which made the office even more eerie. The front door was locked, so she swiped in with her keycard. There was no receptionist at the front desk. The grand staircase could hold more than a hundred people at a time and did when they took their annual year-end photo. She hopped up the stairs, eschewing the elevator, eking out what exercise she could from the office since who knew when she'd get to the gym. Her mind chattered at her, avoiding the question of how to explain the latest numbers dip to her CEO. The kindest thing one could say about Rick was that he was mercurial. She'd seen him go from delighted to incensed in seconds. He was determined, ambitious, and driven by inner demons without names, and had built up SOS from zero to six hundred people in under three years.

He had an unerring instinct for trends and drove everyone faster and faster trying to stay on top of each opportunity as it appeared, generally succeeding. She had learned more in her two years there than her entire career before and had paid in blood. It was clear that the payments were not stopping anytime soon.

Allie walked into the studio. A glance around the open space showed only one person in the cavernous room. SOS eschewed cubes in favor of tables in rows with computers on each table. It had a sweatshop for nerds quality. Rob called it the panopticon—a prison where you were always watched. And Rob was the room's sole occupant. Most of the engineering crew stayed until 2 a.m. most nights and wandered in around ten. Rob preferred silence to program, so he'd become a lark rather than a night owl. On a launch night, she'd still be there when he came in at 5 a.m. She'd learned that just because he came in that early didn't mean he wanted to talk to people at that hour. She looked at him as she entered, and he gave her a slight nod, suggesting perhaps he'd had enough coffee to be social. That made one of them.

She dropped her coat at her desk and headed to the break room to pour a second cup. She heard Rob come up behind her.

"What's brought you in before ten? I thought you resolved the dB error?" Rob's face showed only the slightest trace of concern.

"Metrics meeting."

Rob winced. "I thought that was on Thursday."

"Rick moved it."

"Again? Typical." Rob looked into his milky coffee. "Heya, so, I wanted to ask you something."

**Buy *The Team That Managed Itself*
to keep reading.**

https://amzn.to/357q6rr